P9-DDD-126

Also by Catherine Cookson

CATHERINE COOKSON

THE RAG NYMPH

A NOVEL

SIMON & SCHUSTER
NEW YORK   LONDON   TORONTO   SYDNEY   TOKYO   SINGAPORE

SIMON & SCHUSTER
Simon & Schuster Building
Rockefeller Center
1230 Avenue of the Americas
New York, New York 10020

This book is a work of fiction. Names, characters, places
and incidents are either products of the author's
imagination or are used fictitiously. Any resemblance
to actual events or locales or persons, living or dead,
is entirely coincidental.

Copyright © 1991 by Catherine Cookson
Originally published in Great Britain in 1991 by Bantam Press,
a division of Transworld Publishers Ltd.

All rights reserved
including the right of reproduction
in whole or in part in any form.

SIMON & SCHUSTER and colophon are registered trademarks
of Simon & Schuster Inc.

Manufactured in the United States of America
ISBN   0-671-86477-7

PART ONE

The Child

1

The road was narrow. It could be measured by the width of a coach with a man walking at each side, but even so it was wider than the streets and alleys leading off from both sides of it.

It was the last Wednesday in June, 1854. The day had been hot; in fact, the previous week had been very hot and so the roads and streets were paved with ridged flags of mud, hardbaked, but not so hard as to prevent their surfaces being skimmed off into dust which, in some streets of the town, seemed to be floating waist high like a mist rising from water.

But Felix Road wasn't in the main town, nor yet on the outskirts; it was situated to the north of the city and gave its name to the acres of housing that was home to the poor, the destitute, and the dregs of humanity. It also housed countless bars and gin shops, as well as a number of churches, chapels, and temperance halls, the latter set up, as it were, in opposition to as many brothels.

The members of the various denominations fought hard against the evils and wickedness of drink and immorality, and in this they were aided by the Constabulary. However,

11

the law, it would seem, was not so much concerned with those who drank as with those who sold their bodies for gain.

It was five-thirty in the evening, and there were still very few people to be seen on Felix Road. It would be different at six o'clock when the surrounding mills spewed out their weary and gin-thirsty humanity. But now, along the middle of it came an old woman pushing a hand-cart on which was a pile of rags. She and the cart were half-covered by the shadow of the buildings on her left; but further back up the road, walking deep in the shadow, was a young woman holding a child by the hand. Yet so striking was the colour of the child's hair and of that which showed beneath the flat straw hat of the woman as to appear like distorted jogging lights in the dimness.

Then an odd thing happened. At the sight of a man approaching from a distance the woman seemed about to thrust the child against the wall but, changing her mind, she walked forward again, and she spoke to the man.

From the way he gesticulated the man was apparently upbraiding her, and when he lifted his arm and signalled to someone behind her she gripped the child by the hand and ran.

The rag woman was turning her hand-cart into a narrow alley when the child was almost flung against it, the young woman crying, 'Go home! Go home!' even as she continued to run.

Agnes Winkowski turned from the frightened child clinging on to the side of her hand-cart and looked back to watch two men of the law speeding after the woman. The sight was not an unusual one. Hardly a day went by but she saw some lass or other picked up by them snots. However, what she couldn't understand was why any lass on the make would be lugging a child around with her.

She now looked at the child, saying, 'Was that your ma?'

12

The little girl made a movement with her head but did not speak.

'D'you know your way home?'

Again the same movement, but now the voice came out in squeaks, saying, 'But Mama has the key.'

Mama, she called her mother. Not Ma, but Mama . . .
'Where d'you live?'

'Nelson Close . . . the bottom.'

Nelson Close? Well, there were worse places than Nelson Close. But still, it was on the fringe of The Courts, with only the railway line separating it from Salford.

She took up the handles of the hand-cart and began to push it, and now there was room only for the child to walk by the side of it. And this she did, holding on for support to the iron rail that rimmed the wooden edge of the cart and which helped to keep the rags in place.

The alley opened out into a large square courtyard from which, on all sides, reared five-storey buildings, all in a state of dilapidation, and outside of each was a mound of filth and rubbish, some giving off a stench which left nothing to the imagination as from what it was derived.

As the old woman pushed the hand-cart across the yard a number of children scampered from various heaps to gather around her, gabbling. But the gabble was such that the child couldn't distinguish what it was they wanted, until the old woman cried, 'No candy rock today! 'Tis all gone, all gone,' at which, one after the other, the children, as if at a signal, stopped gabbling and took up the chant: 'Raggie Aggie! Raggie Aggie! Baggie Aggie! Baggie Aggie! Lousy Loppy Aggie! Narrow old bugger Aggie!'

The old woman seemed not to hear the children, yet on leaving The Courts to pass through another narrow alleyway, she bitterly emitted one word: 'Scum!' Then as they emerged into a street she looked down at the child, and nodding backwards, she said, 'It saves ten minutes of pushing that way.'

She now pulled the hand-cart to a halt and, looking at the child, said, 'Well, what you gonna do, love?'

'I don't know.' The child's voice had a tremor in it.

'Got any neighbours . . . I mean, that you could go to?'

'No. Mama doesn't have neighbours, not there. It . . . it was in the cellar.'

'What was in the cellar?'

'Where . . . where we lived. It's . . . it's down the steps.'

Aggie looked closely at the child. Her hair was hanging almost to her small waist and it was of a colour she had never seen before, not around these quarters anyway. Fair-headed little 'uns, but none like this one. Then there were the child's eyes, grey, clear, large and at this moment expressing fear, if she had ever seen it. The rest of the face matched the eyes and the cream blush-tinted skin. She was a bonny young 'un, right enough, and from a bonny mother, from what she had glimpsed of that lass as she skidded down the road with the polis after her. She must be on the game, all right. But why take the child with her? That would put any bloke off, surely. Or did she use her an' all? Oh, no, no; she wouldn't want to think that. And yet, look at all the old buggers that would sell their souls for a little bit of humanity like this one. Kit's brothel down there was noted for it; and the dirty old customers, and not so old, some of them, came in their carriages, but after dark, of course. Why didn't the bloody polis get on to him and clear his place out? They had cleared Paper Meg's out last week. But then, that was nothing; they all knew she would start up some place else. But the churchmen had to be satisfied; hoodwinked would be a better word . . .

'Please . . .'

'Yes, love?'

14

'Can I come with you?'

'Come with me?' Aggie looked from the child to the heap of rags, then down at the mountain of clothes covering her own body. She smelt; the contents of the cart smelt; the cart itself was impregnated with stench; and here was this gleaming child, yes, aye, that was a word to describe her, she gleamed, and she was asking to come along with her. Well, if she said no, what would happen to her? Oh, she had a pretty good idea: she only needed to go back to Felix Road or even Nelson Close, where she said she lived, to find out. Poor little bugger.

'Don't you know anybody else you can go to? Haven't you any relations?'

'No.' The head was shaking again.

'Nobody?'

Aggie watched the child thinking, and then she said, 'Well, there are the uncles.'

'Uncles? You've got uncles?'

'I called them uncle. They came to the house two or three times, but . . . but that was last week. I don't know where they live.'

'Jesus in heaven!' Abruptly Aggie picked up the handles of the flat-cart, then almost growling 'Come on!' she pushed it along the road, the child trotting beside her now.

It was a good ten minutes later when they seemed to come to the last of The Courts, for the houses dropped down to two-storey, then one-storey; and then they were confronted by an iron open-work gate set in a brick wall all of seven feet high. Aggie did not rest the hand-cart and open the gate but, giving it a hard thrust, she pushed it against the iron work and the gate swung open and into a large yard all of forty feet square, the further half of which was surprisingly paved with flags. And where the flags ended there rose three large stone arches, forming a sort of veranda to the front of a

15

house, a real house with six windows visible, three above the flat roof of the stone veranda and three above that again.

As they entered the yard a figure rose from the side of a pile of tins lying on the unpaved part of the ground, in his hand what looked like a piece of iron guttering. This he threw with a flicking movement on to a pile of scrap iron before making his way towards them, kicking out of his path and on to yet another pile the remnants of what had been a pair of trousers.

His eyes were fast on the child and hers wide on him and his odd shape as he said, 'What's this then? What's this?'

'Wait and you'll find out.' Aggie answered sharply. 'Get this lot sorted.' She thumbed towards the rags on the cart.

'Aye, I will. Will I sort her out an' all?'

'There'll be somebody else sorted out if you're not careful . . . Sold anything?'

'Aye, three bob's-worth out of the basket. And Arthur Keeley popped in. He'll take the scrap tomorrow, but I think he wanted to have a word with you. His wife's scarpered. D'you know where she is?'

'No. D'you?' She had turned and was holding her hand out towards the child.

'The kettle's boilin'.'

'I'd have somethin' to say if it wasn't.'

The child followed Aggie through the middle arch and towards a heavy, paintless oak door, then into a room dimly lit by a window that looked on to the covered way. The room was filled with an assortment of clothes, some in wash-baskets, some hanging over clothes-lines, others attached to nails driven into a wooden frame fixed to the walls like a chairback panel. The smell wasn't as strong as that which permeated the yard, but nevertheless it was heavy with the odour of ageless sweat.

16

Now they were going through another door and into a different kind of room, and this room caused the child to stop and slowly look about her. A fire was burning in a black grate which had an oven to the side of it; a large black kettle was sizzling on the hob. And at the foot of the iron structure was a high steel fender, suggesting from its dull surface that it had never seen emery paper since the day it left the foundry.

Set at right angles to one side of the fireplace was a two-seat wooden settle, and at the other side a much larger leather couch. In the middle of the room was a round table covered with oilcloth, and four high-backed carved chairs set around it. Along one wall stood a plain sideboard. It was black, as if once it had been varnished; and this gave it a sheen of its own.

The room was evidently a kitchen, but holding dining- and sitting-room furniture. Along each side of the long window hung a heavy brocade curtain, the colour having long since disappeared, but which still retained an air of quality. The curtains were not drawn half across the window and so closing out the light as most curtains were wont to do, but were wide apart showing, of all things, a piece of grassland parched by the sun but, nevertheless, still giving evidence that it was grass by the strip in the shadow of the house.

The child stared towards it as if in recognition of something held in memory; then she turned and looked at the old woman, who was sitting on the couch unlacing her boots, and she said, 'You have a garden.'

'Huh!' Aggie turned and looked towards the window and she repeated, 'Garden? A piece of grass. But I've seen the time it was. Oh aye, I've seen the time it was. Take your hat and coat off. Are you hungry?'

The child considered for a moment, then said, 'No. No, thank you. But . . . but I'd like a drink, please.'

17

'Well, you'll have that in a minute once I've eased me feet an' got some of these togs off.'

The child watched her now stand up in her stockinged feet on what had once been a fine Persian rug but was now worn in parts to its back, and unpin her hat. After her coat was thrown down on to the couch, to be followed by the long mud-fringed skirt and tattered voluminous blouse, there appeared before the child a fat woman, a very fat woman, in what seemed to be a clean blue-striped blouse and a long grey skirt with a fringe.

'Ah! that's better. One of these days I'll go out like this and scare the whole population, 'cos they'll think I'm in me bare pelt.' She now turned and, gathering up the coat, the blouse and the skirt, and the black hat, she threw them behind the couch, saying, 'See you tomorrow, my dears;' then looking at the child, she said, 'Well now, you're dry, you said,' and, taking her hand, led her across the room and into the original large, stone-floored kitchen, and from there into an equally large pantry. Here, taking a milk measure from a marble slab, she bent over a big brown earthenware jar, took off the wooden lid, dipped in the measure and scooped up some clean water, which she handed to the child, saying, 'Drink that.'

The handle of the can pushed up by her right ear, the child drank, and then, her mouth dripping, she smiled at Aggie, saying, 'It's lovely, cold.'

'Aye, and it's clean. You can bet on that, it's clean; the well sees to that.' After taking the measure from the child, Aggie refilled it and then she herself drained it, after which she put the lid on the brown jar and hung the can on a nail. Then, from a shelf in the pantry, she took down a large covered dish, sniffed at the contents, and, smiling now on the child, said, 'Nothing much goes rotten in here. Good as an ice box, this.' Then taking a smaller dish from the shelf she turned

18

to the child, saying, 'You carry that in; 'tis butter. Now all we want is some bread and some onions an' we're set. Go on,' saying which, she lifted her knee and pressed the child gently forward.

And so they returned to the kitchen again; and after the meal was put on the table Aggie went through the other room and from the door yelled, 'Ben!' just the once before returning to the kitchen.

As she sat down at the table she said to the child, 'Sit up now.'

When the boy, as she had thought of the youth but who was actually seventeen, came into the room he needed no urging to sit at the table; then grinning at the child, he said, 'What's your name?'

'Millie. What's yours?'

The question was innocent but it brought a great guffaw from the youth and he answered, 'Ben Smith, Jones, or Robinson.' Then turning quickly to Aggie, he added, 'Long time since I said that, isn't it?'

'You should know.'

'And you an' all.' He nodded at her. 'It was to your dad in the yard out there.' He thumbed behind his shoulder. 'Seven, comin' eight I was; just like yesterday. I'd heard that Billy Steele had died that mornin' from the fever and there I was after his job. "What's your name?" your da said. "Ben," I said. "Ben what?" he said. "Well, take your choice," I said: "Smith, Jones, or Robinson." And he cuffed me ear, an' not gently at that. But he took me on. Aye.' He looked down now on to the plate on which lay a pig's foot and two pieces of streaky pork; and picking up the pig's foot in his two hands, he gnawed at it for a moment before looking at the child again and asking her, 'Well, what's your other name?'

'Your hands are very dirty.'

19

There was the sound of a smothered chuckle from Aggie. And now the child watched Ben slowly lay down the half-eaten trotter and hold up both hands before his large face. Looking first at one, then at the other, he said, 'Aye, you're right, they are dirty. But a speck of dirt never hurt anybody, as far as I've learnt. And if you're goin' to stay here you'll get your hands dirty an' all before long.'

There was a slight clatter as Aggie dropped her trotter on to the plate, demanding, 'Who says she's goin' to stay here? She'll be home tomorrow; her mother'll be out.'

'Out of where?'

Aggie drew in a long breath and glanced at the child before answering Ben. 'Out of where she'll be spendin' the night,' she said. 'Now, no more questions. And your hands *are* dirty, mucky's the word I'd say.'

'What about your own?'

'I can have dirty hands if I like. You're here to take orders, an' don't forget it. You're gettin' too big for your boots.'

'No! Am I? Well, that's good to hear after ten years, Aggie. Well, now that I'm too big for me boots, d'you think me legs'll sprout?'

Aggie turned her head slightly away, took up the knife that was lying to the side of her plate, cut a piece of meat in two, then picked it up with her fingers and ate it; then she turned to the child and said, 'What's your second name?'

'Forester. It's spelt, F-o-r-e-s-t-e-r.'

'My! my! we've got a learned one here.' Ben was nodding his head towards Aggie now. 'And by the look of her she hasn't seen six yet.'

'I'm seven.'

They both stared at the child.

'Seven, are you, me love? Well, as he says, you don't look it.'

'Can I have a fork, please?'

20

Aggie again looked to the side as if to help check the escape of some quick retort from her lips. Then, without looking at Ben, she said, 'Get her a fork out of the top drawer.'

When Ben came back to the table he placed the fork with great ceremony to the side of Millie's plate, saying, 'There you are, madam. Is there *hanything helse* you would desire?' He was bowing over her, and he was nonplussed when, smiling up into his face, she said, 'You are teasing me now, aren't you? But I always have a fork, a knife and fork; it's . . . it's bad manners to eat with your fingers.' Then looking quickly from one to the other, she added, 'At least for . . . for children.'

Ben now straightened his back and returned to his seat and, looking at Aggie, said, 'Besides which, there is what is called a diplomat in our midst, Mrs Winkowski.'

When Aggie sat back in her chair and her great fat body began to wobble, slowly from her open mouth there issued deep bellows of laughter. Ben, too, joined in, and Millie, looking from one to the other, smiled widely at them.

Of a sudden Aggie rose from the table and left the room, and the smile slid slowly from Millie's face and she looked at the funny young man, as she thought of him, and said, 'Is she vexed?'

'No. No, she's not vexed. But you've done something tonight, you know. It's the first time I've heard her laugh in years . . . years and years. Chuckle, aye, smile now'n again, but never laugh like that . . . Have you got a dad?'

She shook her head. 'No, not now. I had.'

'Is he' – he paused – 'is he dead, then?'

'I . . . I think so. Mama said he was dead.'

'You don't seem sure. Is he dead or is he not?'

'He . . . he went away.'

'Just recently . . . like?'

21

She paused before answering him, her eyes blinking as if she were thinking; and then she said, 'It was last year . . . or sometime longer, when . . . when we lived in Durham.'

'Oh! You lived in Durham, did you? All the way up there? Durham's near Scotland, isn't it?'

She thought for a moment, then said, 'Not really. It's . . . it's near Newcastle. That's the city.'

'Oh aye, Newcastle. And your dad . . . did he work in Durham?'

'Yes; sometimes I think, and Newcastle.'

'What was he?'

'Oh, he was a tall man.' Then she shook her head and laughed. 'I thought you meant, what was Dada like. I . . . I don't rightly know but only that he worked in a shop, a big shop, and he always wore a nice suit. It was black and he had a big shiny hat. And sometimes—' She looked away from Ben towards the corner of the room where a picture was hanging at a slight angle, and her head moved to one side as if to see it better. Then looking at him again she said, 'He sometimes had a walking stick, and . . . and on that day he bought me a parasol.' Again her eyes were blinking as if her memory were groping to recall the special occasion when her father had a walking stick and she had a parasol.

'How long have you been down here in Manchester?'

Neither of them now took notice of Aggie's returning to the room and seating herself down on the leather couch. And when Millie answered him, 'It . . . it was before Easter, in March. Yes, in March,' she was nodding her head.

Ben now sat back in his chair, then glanced towards Aggie. Following this, he took the last piece of pork from his plate, chewed on it, then swallowed it before asking the next question. 'Does your mother go to work?' he said.

'Well, she went to the factory to make buttons, but they didn't give her enough money. Then she hired a machine to do shirts, but they wanted too many shirts done. I liked the hat room.' She looked from one to the other. 'It was right upstairs above the shop and all the women were nice. And there were lots of pretty colours, but—' She now looked down towards her hands, her fingers flicking against each other, and after a moment she said, 'I fidgeted. It was a long time to stay quiet all day until eight o'clock at night. And one day at dinner time I tripped and spilt a can on the table. It . . . it was full of beer and it flowed over the ribbons and spoilt a hat and the mistress of the room was very angry and told Mama I hadn't to be brought back again, so Mama left.'

Aggie, sitting looking into the fire, nodded as she thought: And aye, Mama took the only step left to her, and look where it's got her.

She now turned towards the table when Ben said, 'You finished?' and the child replied, 'Yes, thank you. Can I help to wash up?'

'Who said I was goin' to wash up? We just blow on the plates here.'

Millie smiled widely at him now, and once again she said, 'You are teasing me.'

'You seem to know a lot about teasing, young lady. Well, take your plate into the kitchen and put it into the sink. And oh, don't forget . . . your fork, and your knife an' all.'

As she went out of the room carrying her plate and the cutlery, he stepped towards Aggie, saying softly, 'What d'you make of her? She's canny, isn't she? And did you ever see such a bonny piece? She must have been decently brought up.'

'Aye, maybe. But I can't see her with a very decent future with the mother she's got.'

'Bad type, was she?'

'No; no, a young lass really, very like her.' She nodded towards the far door. 'But by the sound of what she has just said her mother wasn't cut out for work, not the kind

23

you'll find in this quarter, except her last job. And then she's made a hash of that an' all. They must have been on to her or somebody's given her away, one or t'other, 'cos it must have been a set-up cop. I'd passed that fella on the road an' when I looked back she was talking to him; then when I turned the cart into the alley the next minute, she was flying past, almost throwing the child at me. Well, not at me, she yelled at her to go home. But as the bairn said, she hadn't a key, it was on her mother. So there you have it, that's how it happened. And from what she's been prattling on about she's had a number of uncles.'

'It sounds as if the old man scarpered. She doesn't seem to know if he is dead or not. She said he wore a black suit and worked in a shop.'

'Oh aye. Sounds like a shop-walker.'

'Could be. Shush! Here she is.'

'I couldn't find any water but I've rubbed my plate with a cloth, and my knife and fork.'

'Well, that's a clever lass for you.' Ben was laughing down at her again. 'D'you want the job as in-between maid, one pound, one 'an wompence a week?'

'That's what my mama was; she was a maid to a lady.' She now turned quickly towards Aggie, adding, 'She will come for me in the morning, won't she? She . . . won't go away, will she? I mean . . . not like' – she now lowered her head – 'I want her. I want my mama. She always put me to bed . . . and read me a story.'

They both remained silent, looking at her; then Aggie said, 'She'll come for you in the mornin'. Would you like to go to bed now? There's . . . there's a nice bed upstairs. Well, it's a big one with a feather tick. It's a snuggler.' She smiled.

'I'm . . . I'm afraid to be in the dark.'

'Well, it won't be dark for a long time yet. By that time I'll be upstairs.'

'Will . . . will you be sleeping with me?'

'Well!' Aggie glanced at Ben; then her head drooped and wobbled from one side to the other before she said, 'Well, if you don't mind, miss.'

'Oh no. I . . . I think I would like you to.'

'That's very kind of you.'

They now looked towards the door through which the young fellow was making a hurried exit, and, somewhat impatiently, Aggie said, 'Come along with you, come along,' and led the way through yet another door and into a passage-way, and so into a square hall from which a stairway rose.

The stairs were bare, and before mounting them Millie looked down at Aggie's stockinged feet and said, 'Aren't you afraid of getting splinters?'

It was on a sigh that Aggie replied, 'No, love, I'm not afraid of getting splinters. I crawled down these stairs forty-eight years ago and I've walked up and down them ever since, mostly in me bare feet, and I've never got splinters.'

On the landing Millie stopped and, looking about her, she said, 'This is a big house.'

'Aye; I suppose it is.'

'There are lots of doors.'

'Aye, there are lots of doors, and through this one' – Aggie pushed a door wide – 'is me bedroom. Now come on and no more lip, an' get your clothes off and into that bed, 'cos there's things I've got to do before I sleep tonight.'

'Are you vexed with me?'

Again Aggie sighed and she half closed her eyes before answering, 'No, child, I'm not vexed with you, but, as I said, I've got things to see to. Now, off with your clothes and no more chatter. D'you hear me?' Her voice had risen and the child now sat down on a low chair and quickly took

25

off her shoes, then pulled her grey stockings down over her knees before, standing up, she asked, 'Will you unhook me, please?' And Aggie, bending down, undid four buttons on the back of her dress.

After the dress, the child took off two white petticoats, and Aggie noticed that the material was quite good; and when it seemed that the shift was about to be taken off too, she said, 'I would keep that on, if I were you; you haven't got a nightgown.'

'Oh yes. Yes, I forgot. I haven't got a nightgown.'

'Well, up you get!'

'I must say my prayers.'

'Oh. Oh aye. Well, get on with it.'

When Millie knelt by the bed and the mattress seemed out of reach, she had to raise her clasped hands head high to rest them against it. Then she began: 'God bless Mama and Dada, and please take care of them. And thank you for this day and make me grateful for what I've got. And God bless Mrs Melburn and this big woman . . . lady who has been kind to me today. And please bring my mama back early in the morning. Amen.'

As she rose from her knees Aggie said, 'Who's Mrs Melburn?'

'She was a lady in Durham who was kind to us, the parson's wife. She let us stay with her for a week after Dada—' She paused, and again her hesitation appeared as if her mind were groping for an answer or a revelation to something she couldn't understand; then she said, 'After Dada . . . died. And . . . and she set us to the station, and . . . and Mama promised to write.'

'Did she? I mean, did your mother write?'

'Yes, and so did Mrs Melburn.'

'Well, get up into bed.'

'Do you have bed bugs?'

26

'No! I do not have *bed bugs*. A flea now, here and there, but no *bed bugs*. *Get in!*'

When the child shrank back against the edge of the bed and made no attempt to climb up on to the mattress, Aggie put a hand to her head before muttering, 'I'm sorry. I'm sorry. Don't look so scared. But I'm particular about me bed. All right, you might find everything that crawls in the yard an' they might get as far as downstairs here and there, but not up here. And not on me clothes either, not if I know anything about it. If I do find them, they get short shrift. So come on, love.' And she leaned down towards the child, her thick arms going out and around her, and she lifted her into the bed, saying softly, 'There now. Isn't that nice and comfy?'

Still shaking somewhat with fright, Millie swallowed twice before she brought out in a small voice, 'It's very nice, thank you.'

'Well then, go to sleep now. But I'll leave the door open, and it won't be dark for a long time. I'll be popping up and down to see how you are, an' when it gets dark I'll light the lamp. But I'll be up long before that. Now the pot's under the bed if you want to do a number one. You'll be able to get out on your own, won't you?'

'Oh, yes, yes, thank you.'

'Well then, snuggle down.'

Aggie took two or three steps backwards, smiled, and turned and went out of the room, leaving the door wide open. At the head of the stairs she paused and gripped the broad banister; then slowly descending the stairs, she muttered to herself, 'A little of that one will go a long way.'

Back in the sitting-room she found Ben packing the fire with tins filled with coal dust mixed with dried mud, and he turned to her, saying, 'One of these days you'll go daft and buy some real coal.'

27

'Why should I? What'll we do with all the tins?'

'You could always get a few coppers for them.'

'Coppers, aye, but it takes more than coppers to cart them there; they won't come and pick 'em up.'

He straightened his back and while dusting his hands he said, 'You got her off, then?'

'Aye, I got her off, and thankfully. By! she's got a tongue.'

As she sat down on the couch, Ben sat opposite her on the settle, his big body and large head topping the back of it while his short legs hardly touched the floor.

'She's been well brought up,' he said.

'Aye, she has, finicky, I would say. And you can imagine it, if her mother has been a lady's maid or some such. I wonder what happened to the father? I bet you a shillin' he's not dead. Done off, more like it. By what I can gather they must have lived in Durham for a time, 'cos when she was saying her prayers she brought in a Mrs Melburn, a parson's wife, who was kind to them after the father died or whatever, an' from what I made out of her jabbering the woman and the mother have written to each other. Now' – she leant towards him, her finger wagging – 'first thing in the mornin' you get down to the station and have a word with Constable Fenwick; he'll know what's goin' to happen to that lass. Don't say anything about the bairn being here. Just make out you're interested in her, the woman called Forester.'

'Oh, Aggie, that's a laugh for the wrong side of me face. Now, I ask you, me bein' interested in somebody, a woman who looks like that bairn upstairs . . . Have a heart.'

'Well, all right. If your feelings are so tender about your damned legs, tell him that Aggie was enquirin' about her. Make up some tale that I've spoken to her on me rounds. D'you hear what I'm sayin' to you?'

Ben's voice was solemn as he said, 'Aye, I hear you, Aggie. Sometimes I wish I didn't; you don't half rub it in.'

'I don't rub it into you more than you rub it into yourself. You're not above mentioning your height, even bragging about it at times, saying you're as good as any two men twice your size. Aye well, you might be, the upper half of you, but you've got to reach them and you do it with your tongue. So I'm not speakin' about any part of you you don't bring to the fore yourself.'

A silence fell on the room, and its increasing heaviness made her heave herself up from the couch and take the three steps to throw herself on to the seat beside him; and to put an arm around his shoulder and say, 'Come on, lad, come on. You know me. There's nobody in this world more sorry for you at times than I am, for you could have been a real good-lookin', strappin' fella. You're still good-lookin'; and after all, you've got Annie.'

'Aye, I've got Annie.' He turned towards her now, adding, 'And you don't think much of Annie, do you? And you've made that plain enough.'

'Well, lad, it's only because I think you're worth somebody better than her. And it isn't the first time I've said that, is it? You undervalue yourself. There's plenty of men that haven't half your appearance and are five feet or so who have married decent lasses and brought up a family.'

'Aye, well, Aggie, there's a lot in the "or so" bit. "Or so" could be two, four, or six inches. But I'm five feet dead and it wouldn't look so bad if I was narrow from the legs up. But to have an upper bulk like mine and a head like a bull, well, I can't see all the good, kind lasses falling over themselves and saying, "Aw, Ben, come on to bed with me." ' His voice had changed during the last few words and she pushed him hard against the end of the settle as she said, 'No, they won't come running, but have you ever thought of you doin' the askin'? Anyway, what I'm askin' you to do now is to get on your feet and go and get me a drop of gin and a couple of pints of beer.'

'Is it a party?'

'Well, it could be; but then, you might want to get away.'

'No, I don't want to get away. They can all wait, all those stupid bitches beggin' me to strip 'em. You get tired of doin' it.'

Aggie pushed him and he got to his feet, saying, 'Will I take the money from the box?'

'Aye, where else?' she said as she, too, rose from the settle and returned to the couch, from where she watched him go to the box that was standing on the end of the sideboard, and from it take a piece of silver, then button his coat across his broad chest, take his cap from his pocket and, having put it on at an angle, salute her, saying, 'Your servant, madam.' Then, clicking his heels together, he turned on his short legs and marched from the room.

After the door shut behind him, she sat looking at it, wondering what she would have done over the years without him. She, too, remembered the day he had come into the yard and cheeked her father, telling him he could choose his name from Smith, Jones, or Robinson. He had said he thought he must have been eight but that he didn't really know. At that time he would have been like many thousand of other youngsters, the sweepings of the hungry 'forties.

He must have been born in the middle 'thirties, when hunger was already rampant. The corn laws had seen to that. He had been with them for some time; two or three years before, he had told her that he didn't know where he had been born, or who his parents were. He only knew of the life he had led in the baby-farming house, one of seventeen young children. He had made his escape on the day he later confronted her father in the yard. She had taken to him from

30

the first, and he to her, perhaps, on his part, because she had given him some hot mutton broth and let him eat as much bread as he could manage, which had been half a loaf; and then she had rigged him out in odd things.

Her father would joke about him to her when he'd had a drink over much: 'Ready-made son you've got now then, daughter, is it?' he'd say. 'Why didn't you have a shot when the goin' was good? It's too late now.' And many were the times when she had wanted to bawl at him, 'And who was to blame for that? You were, and me mam.' Lazy bitch, she was: lying on this couch day after day feeling too bad to move; but she could go upstairs and carry out the duties of a wife whenever the fancy took her. More likely in case he should go along the road to ease himself on Alice Mulcahy. Yet he was the kindest man you would wish to meet when the drink wasn't on him. It was she who had cared for him, and looked after him, too, until he died, and in the bed upstairs in which he had been born, and his father before him, in the days when this house had really been a farmhouse and the land about had been glowing with crops in their rotation. There had been cows in that yard outside and horses stabled around.

Her great-grandparents had lived in this house; it was her great-grandfather who had bought the farm; but from where had come the money for a Polish immigrant to buy a farm in those far-off days remained a mystery to both her grandfather and, of course, her father. All her father remembered about his grandfather was that he was a dour man and that the only relaxation he ever gave himself was at the races.

Therein, she thought, lay the source of the money as well as its eventual loss, because, when her grandfather inherited the place, the farm was already in debt. By the time he died there were no animals left in the yard, nor land to call his own, for it had been sold to the building men, who were throwing up The Courts in order to house the rabble from starving Ireland

31

and those flooding in from all the villages from miles around, all in the hope of being set on in the great new factories that made linen and lawn and blankets and shawls, everything that would go to cover a human being.

It had been from this influx that the rag business had started. Before that they had sold coal from the yard. She remembered when the coal had finished. It was the time when her mother took to the couch because she couldn't stand the sight and sound of the hordes of women and children with their buckets, and the arranged fights among the urchins so that one or two of their gang could get away with some lumps of coal, which would make all the difference between having a fried meal or freezing both inside and out.

She could never remember just how the rag business started, but she recollected that she no longer went three times a week to the paid school. Her education from then on was the Sunday afternoon spent in the basement underneath the church in Halton Street, chanting the catechism.

It was scrap iron that came into the yard first, and bits and pieces of lead. What prompted her father to go out with the hand-cart she didn't know, because underneath it all he was a proud man. She only remembered that right from the beginning he took her with him, and it was she who was sent to the doors to ask politely if they had anything to sell. At first they never went round The Courts; the route was always to the outskirts and to where houses had gardens, small or large. But there again, he never sent her to the really big houses because, as he said, if there was anything going, the servants would have had the first pick. Later, he was to learn that the terraces were really the best area, for here a woman would take pride in being seen to hand over some cast-offs, because, in a way, this indicated that she was well able to replace them.

The Saturday morning market in the yard was taken from the pattern of the street market, where the clothes were laid out in heaps on the ground with a decent garment on the top of each pile to tempt the passer-by to look further. So, what they had managed to gather during the week, her father would arrange on makeshift trestles in the yard. Should it rain, he would bring the stuff under the arches. But if a woman should ask for a particular garment, he would take her into what had been the front room of the house and there, in comparative privacy, she could make her choice and try on the clothes. Yet with all his hard work and, definitely, hers, too, he seemed hardly to make a living.

It wasn't until almost his last breath that he told her of the board beneath his bed and what was under it, assuring her he had saved it for her. And after raising the board and finding six washleather bags of sovereigns she had really believed him, and for only the second time she could remember in her life, she had cried. That was until the day of his funeral, when his fancy woman, Alice Mulcahy, through gin-inspired sorrow, told her that they had been making plans to go to America. She had known her father to be a kindly man: he would do anything to keep the peace and keep people happy. But then, a week later, she had a visit from a strange man enquiring for her father, and who, after being told of his demise, informed her he had been asked to sell the property for which he had felt able to assure her father he would get a good price, seeing that land around was scarce. And he had ended by saying, 'He'll never get to America now.'

She remembered, following the man's visit, that she had sat dumb with rage, and had then rushed upstairs to his room, and every article belonging to him, even to his razor strop, she had brought down and thrown into the yard for the Saturday morning onslaught. And that morning's takings had trebled and brought her new custom, for he

33

had always seen to it that he was shod well and had good small clothes and shirts.

It was now ten years since he had died, and during the first year she had herself pushed the hand cart out almost every day for, except for young Ben, she was on her own. With the years, it had seemed to get heavier, so that now she made only two excursions a week, mostly to the outskirts, making a point never to visit the same house more than twice a year. And there was also another point she made: she would discard her black coat, black skirt, and black hat once she left the environs of The Courts. Early on, she had learned one thing: if the poor saw you prospering they didn't deal with you if they could help it, their idea being they weren't going to give you a hand. So, for The Courts she would wear the old black coat with the large pockets at the side holding the narrow strips of candy rock in one and the coppers in the other. However, it wasn't often she had to fork out the coppers when pushing the hand cart through The Courts. A caring parent would pay a penny or tuppence for some old coat or skirt that could be cut up to meet the needs of some child.

She had discovered, too, one good source of decent clothing: periodically, churches and chapels would hold a sale of garments given them by their better-off parishioners. To those ladies who were responsible for dealing with this charitable effort, she would offer as much as five shillings for a bundle of what appeared to them as less attractive articles, especially if they were food-stained, as some old gentlemen's coats often were. But she knew that Chinese Charlie would clean and press a garment to make it look almost new and she could get as much as two shillings for a good overcoat or a suit.

So, over the years there had been a number of leather bags added to those under the loose floorboards beneath

34

the bed in which she now spent her nights and, in her time, expected to die . . .

Ben came in, saying, 'Billy the welder is roaring in The Crown. That'll mean he'll flail the lot of them tonight, an' there won't be a penny of his pay left for her. He was screaming his head off about the war and the Russians. He was all for sending Gladstone over to the "bloody" Russians.' He grinned now. 'It was really funny to listen to him. They just stopped him from choking the life out of Bobby Carter because he had said everybody was for the war: if we didn't show them Russians what was what, who would? By! I thought Bobby Carter was a brave man to stand up to Billy, and him twice his size.'

As he put the bottle and the can on the table, he said, 'Have a drop of gin first, eh?'

'Aye,' she said. 'An' don't leave the glass dry. But about Billy Middleton. Something should be done in that quarter. He's practically crippled that oldest lad of his, and him not ten yet, and she won't have a word said against him. Stupid bitch! The next thing'll be, he'll do for one of them, then she'll find out where she stands.'

'Odd, when you come to think of it' – he handed her a full wine glass of gin – 'but they say he's like he is because his father and mother were religious. When he was a lad they used to tie him up in the cellar, starve him for days and read the Bible to him as food for his soul. So since his old fella died and he couldn't take it out on him, he's taken it out on his young missis and the young 'uns.'

He again sat down on the settle opposite her, and sipped a glass of beer before saying thoughtfully, 'Funny, when you come to think about it, but it's what happens when you're a bairn that sets the pattern for a man or woman, in most cases anyway.' Then looking up towards the ceiling, he added, 'I wonder what she'll turn out to be like, that young 'un?'

35

'Well, there's one thing that seems sure to me: she's not goin' to have it as easy as she's had it up till now, by the sound of her.'

'What d'you think'll happen to her if her mother goes along the line?'

'It'll be the workhouse, where else? But then, from what I hear, that's overrun with bairns; they've stopped gathering them in from the streets. So, likely, they'll farm her out to somebody and she'll be put to work, probably as a runner in one of the mills.'

'That'll be a pity. I wouldn't like to see that happen to her.' He looked down into his glass and in a much lower voice now he said, 'Annie was put into the mill when she was seven, the same age as that young 'un.' Again his head jerked towards the ceiling. 'She did a twelve-hour day, sometimes fourteen. They say things are better for the bairns now since they brought the hours down to ten, but some of the pigs get over that. Before, they used to count their breaks in the twelve hours, now their breaks are in their own time. It's against the law, but they get off with it. Annie never knew what it was to have a pair of boots on her feet until she was ten.'

'Oh, my God! D'you want me to cry over her? Anyway, she's had almost twenty years since that to get her feet warm.'

'There's two sides to you, you know, Aggie, and one's unfair and as bitter as gall.'

As he rose from the settle and put his glass down none too gently on the table, she said, 'Aye. Well, now go on and tell me me good side.'

'I doubt if you've got one.'

For a moment, she said nothing, but sat watching him pour out a mug of beer; then she said bitterly, 'You're an ungrateful devil. You know that?'

36

He put the can back on the table, placing his free hand across the top of it for a moment; then he took the mug over to the couch and, handing it to her, said, 'You know that isn't true. The fact that I'm here at this minute proves it.'

She sipped at the froth, then sat looking towards the fire. But when he went to take his seat again on the settle, she said, 'There's no need for you to hang about; get yourself away. But lock the gate and take the key with you, and don't make a rattle when you come back. And tomorrow, you could put a drop of oil on that loft door, and the stable one an' all; they screech like barn owls.'

He grinned at her. 'Barn owls?' he said; 'well, they might be an' all as we only close them at night. Barn owls . . . You'll be all right?'

'Have you ever known me to be anything else?'

'Aw!' He shook his head with impatience. 'Nobody can be kind to you, can they, Aggie? You won't take kindness, will you? You get worse, you know that? more sour.' He turned now and went hastily from the room, and she repeated to herself, 'You get worse, you know that? more sour.' . . .

The twilight was fading fast when she entered the bedroom but she could see that the child was still sitting bolt upright in the bed.

'You should be asleep.'

'I . . . I was waiting for you. It . . . it was getting dark.'

'It's a long time off dark. Lie down now.'

The child lay down; then she watched the big fat woman undress herself, noticing particularly that she did not wear corsets like her mama, but that she wore a habit shirt, and one bodice petticoat and two waist petticoats. Her shift, too, was white, but it was sticking to her body here and there with sweat. She watched Aggie ease it off her flesh, then take a nightdress from a drawer and pull it over her head, and lastly, sit on the side of the bed and draw off her stockings.

37

When Aggie climbed into bed, such was her weight that the child rolled towards her, and her head seemed to fall naturally between her breasts, and when the small face peered up at her and the small whisper said, 'You're very big,' Aggie said, 'Aye, I'm very big. An' you're very small; an' you have too much to say, so go to sleep.'

As the head snuggled into her and the thin arm came round her waist, Aggie drew in a long tight breath; then when her own arm automatically went around the child, she closed her eyes tightly, because for the first time in her life she was feeling flesh close to her own.

2

It was eight o'clock the following morning when Ben came back from the town. Aggie was dressed for the day: her hands and face looked clean, her hair had been combed; she was wearing a clean blue-striped blouse. She had just finished her breakfast of dripping and bread and a piece of cold bacon when Ben came into the room. She said immediately, 'Well?'

'She'll be up at ten o'clock before the Justice.'

'Did you find out anything more? Who did you talk to?'

'Well, would I talk to anybody else but your dear Constable Fenwick.'

'Well, what did my dear Constable Fenwick say?'

'He said, she's among the others. There's nine of 'em. But he has no details of her because he didn't bring her in, he said . . . which was kind of him.' He now pulled a face at Aggie and went on, 'He said he thought she was new to the job.'

'Is that all?'

'Aye, except he pointed out that if she was new to the job and she tried to muzzle in around that quarter, the others would soon make short shrift of her. Remember the other month, it was in the papers, wasn't it? about them tearing the clothes off that one who tried to queer their pitch? If I remember, that was on a Saturday night when the gents came down for their pickings. Anyway, I've been thinkin' about her. She's not up to much, is she, if she takes a bairn like that 'un with her when she's on the make?'

'Well, likely it was the lesser of two evils. She would have had to leave her alone in the house, and Nelson Close isn't in the suburbs, is it?'

'Is she still asleep?'

'She was when I left her.'

He sat down at the table now, and she pushed the bread board and the dripping towards him, saying, 'Want a piece of bacon?'

'No; I don't feel like it this mornin'.'

'No, you wouldn't. You didn't get back into the loft until one o'clock, did you?'

'Timing me now, are you?'

'No, but I did wonder why you don't move your bed along there. Dear Annie'll make room for you.'

'Yes, I could. I've thought about it, an' all.' They stared at each other; then, his tone changing, he said, 'What's goin' to happen to the young 'un if the mother goes along the line?'

'Well, we went into this last night, didn't we? All I'm concerned with is handin' her over to her rightful parent or whoever's goin' to take responsibility for her.'

'You're goin' down there?'

'I'm goin' down there to the court? Aye, I am.'

'Well, well, well. You mean to get rid of her, don't you?'

She now placed her large square hands on the table and leant towards him, and her voice was low and hard as she said, 'Well, what's the choice? Can you see me keepin' her here? Look around you, look at the refinements I've got to offer.'

40

He didn't answer her for a moment; when he did, it was quietly. 'She could do worse, a hell of a lot worse. I can speak for that, can't I, Aggie?'

She straightened up now and bawled across at him, 'You were a lad; now you're a young man. She's just a chit, and a knowin' one at that, who's been brought up in a different atmosphere. It mightn't have been the class but there's been some schoolin' there an' some refinement. Can you see her fittin' into this? Aw!' She shrugged. 'You're soft in the head. You know that? It's them books you're readin'. Mr Dickens is gettin' at you. Help the poor. My God! What does he know about it? The only thing I feel about Mr Dickens is he's makin' his money out of exposing misery.'

'Aye; well' – he got on to his feet now – 'it takes somebody to expose it. God Almighty! there's plenty of it, and nobody's bothered much with it except here and there. They keep their distance; the smell of the poor's enough for them. Mr Dickens is doin' some good.'

'Well, he's certainly got a supporter in you. But while we're on, I'll tell you this; you'll go blind readin' that small print.'

'Oh Aggie, shut up!' He had turned and was starting to walk towards the door when he received a full blast from her as she yelled, 'Don't you tell me to shut up! you young prig, else you'll find the door locked on you. Aye, you will. I'm not as soft as all that. It's come to something, hasn't it, when I can't speak in me own house now.' She addressed the fire, saying, What's come over him anyway? He's never stood up to me before. All through that 'un.

She started as the voice of 'that 'un' said, 'Good morning. I found my own way down. There was no water to wash. There was a basin and a jug in the room but no water. And I've managed to do up two of the buttons at the back, but I can't reach the top two. Would you, please?' As the child

41

turned her back to her, Aggie bent down and buttoned the top of the dress; then she said, 'You hungry?'

'Not very; but I would like a drink, please. And may I get washed? I should have washed before I put my dress on, you know. But when I see Mama and I tell her, she won't mind.'

Aggie looked down on the child. She said she was seven. As Ben had pointed out last night, his Annie was scurrying between the looms when she was seven, and barefoot. This one had certainly had it soft. And God help her! Whichever way her life was goin' she would never have it soft again, not as she saw it at this present moment.

'There's a pump round the back of the house. Go on out there; Ben'll show you where it is. Ask him to put some water in a bowl, and you can bring it into the scullery. There's soap and a towel there.'

Millie looked at Aggie for a moment before saying quietly, 'Thank you.' Then, as if forced to say something polite, she said, 'I slept very well. It was a nice bed. Thank you,' and turning about, she went out, not running like a child but walking sedately.

A few minutes later she returned with Ben, who was carrying a tin bowl of water. The child was smiling and she looked up at Aggie, saying, 'The pump was funny. It talked the water out; it went gurgle, gurgle, gurgle.' And Ben raised his eyebrows as Aggie looked at him.

When he returned to the room, having left the child in the kitchen, Aggie was pouring some milk into a mug, and she said to him, 'Look at that! You can see through it. That churn's stood out in the rain for a long time. By! I'll see that bugger tomorrow mornin' if I have to get up at five, an' I'll tell him what I've meant to do for a long time; I'll take the can along to the authorities. By God! I will. That cow would have kicked the

42

pail out of the byre in shame if it had squirted anything out like that.'

'Oh! Aggie.' His smile was wide. Then changing the subject completely from milk and children to the necessity for a clean yard, he said, 'I know where I can get some broken slabs. I'll only have to pay him a dollar and the cartage, and there'll be enough to cover the rest of the yard. When it's wet it's a mire out there. How about it?'

'Oh, well, yes, if you're afraid to get your feet muddy. Yes, of course, sir. But a dollar, no more. How many loads would it be?'

'Oh' – he shrugged his broad shoulders – 'two, three. It's heavy stuff, even for a horse. It could be done in half a day; I mean, the cartage.'

'Well—' She went to the fire and ground the kettle on top of the glowing tins, then added, 'As you're takin' over, you'd better see to it.'

'That'll be the day when you allow anybody to take over. Anyway, Aggie—' He sidled close to her and looked into her face, saying, 'That little 'un's got under me skin. If her mother has to do the month, keep her here till she comes out. Will you?'

She jerked herself away from him. 'Not on your life, lad,' she said. 'Not on your life.' Then in a lowered voice, she added, 'What would I do with her in here all day? And when I'm out, take her with me? Her lookin' like that! Then, look at this place. What is it like? A hovel.'

'Well,' he hissed back at her, 'it needn't look like a hovel, if you'd get off your big fat arse at times and do a bit of scrubbin'.'

Her hand shot out and caught him fully on the side of the face, causing him to wince. Rubbing his cheek, he said, 'It's years since you did that. It struck home that, didn't it? 'cos it was the truth. You're always talking of speaking the

43

truth yourself, aren't you, Aggie? but you can never face up to hearin' it. We'll forget about this now but I'm warnin' you, Aggie, never raise your hand to me again. Never! 'Cos I would die of shame if I retaliated and hit back; and I would, because I've levelled men almost as big as you before today, and you know it.'

'Is this milk for me?'

They both turned to look at the child. She was pointing to the mug. But Aggie's anger rendering her unable to speak, Ben said, 'Aye, me dear. Drink it up.' And going to the table, he asked, 'Would you like some bread an' drippin'?'

'Yes, please.'

'And there's some bacon there.' He pointed to the plate on which were some slices of cold streaky bacon.

She reached over to look at the bacon before saying, 'No; thank you. I'm not very fond of fat.'

Making a sound in his throat, he turned his head away, then said, 'Funny thing, but neither am I; yet I've had to get used to it;' and on this he went out, leaving Millie looking at the big fat woman and feeling she must make conversation: 'It's a beautiful morning,' she said. 'You have a lot of clothes in the next room. And why are all those heaps of things in the yard? Is it a kind of shop?'

Oh no; she couldn't put up with that, not at this moment; and so, saying, 'Stop your jabber and get on with your breakfast. Then stay put until I come down,' Aggie walked to the door leading to the hall.

In the hall, she stopped and looked about her. 'It needn't look like a hovel,' he had said, 'if you'd get off your big fat arse at times and do a bit of scrubbin'.' She had worked like nobody else for years, right from when she was ten, and before that, hard manual labour. But during these last few years she had felt tired, weary. It was as much as she could do to push the hand-cart and to carry her body around with

44

her. It was too big, too cumbersome. If she could only stop eating. But why should she? Aye, why should she?

Not one of these questions had hit her before. It was since that child had come into the house last night. Was it only last night? My God! It seemed that she had been here years, and already she had driven a wedge between her and Ben. And Ben was all she had for companionship; those who would have been her so-called friends she wouldn't let over her step, and those she would have liked to call friends wouldn't come near her step. No; she had only Ben, and she had struck him.

She must get rid of that child.

She stood at the back of the dingy room, the child close by her side, and she listened to the clerk calling out the offences — soliciting was a common phrase, but once he said 'Procuring of men' — and she noticed that the Justice hardly raised his head: 'One pound or one month. One pound or one month. One pound or one month.' He had seen them all before. They mightn't have a pound between them but he knew it would be paid. Big Joe would see to that, or one of his cronies. But he raised his eyes and then his head when the last one stood before him. He hadn't seen her before.

'Soliciting . . . she was known to have men at her house and was seen to stop them in the street. Constables Walton and Makepeace apprehended her.' Et cetera, the et cetera going on to explain that she had been taken to the hospital and there examined by Doctor Bright in the presence of Constable Makepeace.

What Aggie didn't know about the ways of loose women, prostitutes, and pimps wasn't worth learning, but it was a business and she believed that everybody should mind their own business. Only one thing she drew the line at and that was when the prostitution took up bairns. She couldn't stand that.

Until now her knowledge had come from conversation and confidences and such; she had never before been in a morning court and listened to the proceedings.

From this distance, and her being among the other women, the child had not recognised her mother, but when the sentence was passed, 'One pound or one month', and the woman turned about and the child saw her face, a cry escaped her, and she was about to spring forward when Aggie pulled her tight against her leg and, bending down, hissed at her, 'Quiet! Be quiet!' only for the child to hiss back, 'That is Mama. What is going to happen to . . . ?'

'Shut up! *Shut up!*'

Gripping the child's arm, Aggie pulled her from the room and through into a hall and there she stood waiting, for she guessed that the women lined up like felons against the wall would now be led out to pay their fines at the desk in the corner, or be taken through the door back to the cells. She was not surprised that most of them were laughing and giggling.

Two men were standing near the main door. One was a big man with a bullet head and a short neck, with shoulders almost as broad as Ben's; but he had height with it, being all of six foot tall, which in itself made him different from most other men, for it was only here and there you would see his like. His companion was a head shorter and he was thin; but a reader of character would have stamped him the more evil of the two.

The women knew that their fines had already been paid, and so, after signing their forms, in most cases by making crosses, they joined the men the while throwing quips at the policemen standing by the door.

The last in the line was the fair woman. She wrote her name on the form; then, as the wardress motioned her forward, she

46

turned and looked at Aggie and the child, and with a quick gesture she thrust out her hands towards them. But as the child again made to run to her mother Aggie held her firmly and the wardress pushed the woman through a door; even so contriving to keep her head turned towards her child.

The crowd of women and the big man had gone out into the street, but the thin man remained; and he looked from the child towards the closed door before he, too, turned and went out.

'Don't cry. Don't cry.' They were out in the street now and Aggie, for once in her life, stood helpless, knowing not what to do.

'Is Mama wicked?'

'No, no.'

'Then why has she gone away? What has she done? She . . . she shouldn't have gone. She loves me. She said she did.'

'Be quiet. Here! dry your eyes.' Aggie took a surprisingly clean man's handkerchief from her pocket and handed it to Millie.

'Where am I going? Am I to stay with you?'

She couldn't answer.

They were turning the corner at the end of the road when they almost ran into Constable Fenwick, and he greeted them: 'Hello, Aggie.'

She didn't respond in like manner but said, 'She's got a month.'

'Well, it was to be expected. When they go into that business they know what they're doing.'

'Was she really in it?'

'Oh yes; using the house an' all.'

'But Nelson Close is quite a way from here. How did your lot find out?'

'Some Nosey Parker in the house. And then they were thinking of—' he indicated the child with a slight nod. 'But I

47

was surprised at her type; you would think she could have got a job, a decent one somewhere. But then,' he again indicated the child, 'they're a handicap where jobs are concerned, unless you farm them out for the day, or altogether. What you going to do with her?'

Perhaps it was the term 'farm out' that brought the retort: 'Hang on to her until she comes out, I suppose.'

'That's good of you, Aggie. God knows what would happen to her if she was let loose. Slim Boswell would soon do a bit of trade there.'

'He was there this morning with Big Joe.'

'Oh? Well they look after their own. I can stand Big Joe, but not Slim.'

'Then why don't you arrest him?' Her voice was harsh.

'Oh, we do, we do, Aggie. But when you keep the big names supplied with a particular kind of amusement you can always depend on it that the police are found to be in the wrong, or that they are framing an innocent man, or that the children in question are his nieces. And he will produce a sister, or a cousin, or an aunt. My God! I've seen it all. But things are changing, Aggie, things are changing. It'll take time. It'll take time. And it will be women that'll change it. Oh yes, women. There's one or two ladies already shouting their mouths off. And I can tell you something' – he bent towards her – 'their husbands have been warned to gag them, or else. But I know one in question who said, to hell, or words to the effect' – he grinned – 'that he couldn't gag her if he tried. Women have power, you know, Aggie, if they but knew how to use it. Look at yourself, for instance.'

'You trying' to be funny?'

'No,' he said, and seriously: 'no, I'm not. There's a good few people around this quarter afraid of you and of what you can do when you open your mouth. And you have once or twice, haven't you? Anyway, have you any news for me?'

48

'No, nothing of importance, except I think you want to keep an eye on Billy the welder. He'll go berserk one of these days and murder the lot of them. And the papers will get at you and ask why wasn't something done before. He was mortallious last night, so I bet hardly any of those bairns will be able to move this mornin'. She certainly won't. Oh, somethin' should be done with her. I'm not for the workhouse, you know that, but I think they'd all be better off in there.'

'I'll look into it, Aggie, and I'll have a word with the committee.'

'You might as well spit on it as go to them.'

'All right, all right, yes; but they do the best they can.'

'Maybe; but they're knocking their heads against brick walls when it comes to Billy Middleton.'

'He's not the only one that uses the belt, Aggie. You know that. And it's part of the Christian doctrine, you know, spare the rod and spoil the child.' And he added somewhat sneeringly, 'Jesus loves little children, they say. Well, He's the only one who seems to, yet He doesn't do much about it. Get a few ranters together and they give you broth if you let them save your soul. But there' – he sighed – 'that isn't altogether true. There's Parson Wheatley, you know, over in the Dyke district. He's got a school going. Free, that's something, free, not tuppence, fourpence, or sixpence. And it's true, you know, some of them do charge sixpence a week, I'm hearing. But with the parson, the youngsters do a half day in the mill and a half day at his school, an' you wouldn't believe the difference it's made to those little 'uns. And what's more, his wife has classes at night for women. And it's growing; you just wouldn't believe.'

'Well, that *is* something,' said Aggie. 'But different from what you hear about the convent; you know, Christ the Saviour's place. They don't take them under a shilling a week, and God knows what they charge when they live in. And of course they don't want any snotty-nosed ones, no. Holy nuns. My God! mean as muck, they are. I've found that out.'

'Now, Aggie.' He laughed at her. 'Don't stamp on the Catholics; else I'll have to run you in for kicking me mother in the face.'

'*You* a Catholic then, constable?'

'I am, for me sins.'

'I would never have believed it.'

'It's a dark secret, Aggie. An' you know, little pigs have got big ears and this little pig is looking up at me.' He now smiled down into the wet, tear-stained face, saying, 'You're going to be all right. Aggie'll look after you. In the meantime, if you would like to come to church with me next Sunday, it'll be my pleasure.'

'No, by God! She's goin' to no Catholic Mass as long as she's under my care. Good day to you.'

'Good day to you too, Aggie. You're a good woman in spite of the muck.'

Her step slowed and she was about to turn round to voice some rejoinder but continued on, gripping the child's hand hard now and stepping up her walk into almost a trot.

Well, she had saddled herself with something, hadn't she? Dear God! she had. How she was goin' to put up with the wee 'un's fancy talk and fancy ways, she didn't know. And a month was a long time . . .

Ben said, 'I knew you would keep her.'

'Well, you knew more than me. It was the last intention in me life to saddle meself with her. But I'll tell you this much: she'll have to spend most of her time with you 'cos I couldn't put up with her round me feet all day.'

'Oh, I'll see to her. Don't worry about that. So she got a month? Well, well.'

'Aye, well, well; but I'll tell you, there's one thing I'm sure of an' that's the child will take to the yard quicker than the mother will take to the cells an' the life she'll be forced to live there. Good God in heaven! Aye.'

Five days later Aggie felt she could stand no more. The child never stopped talking, and in that refined voice too. And the questions she asked! She was causing a stir in the yard, too, upsetting some folks, while making others laugh. She would advise a customer not to have that: it looked too old, or it smelt. One good thing she had done was to point out two women pushing articles up under their coats without paying. Obviously very pleased with herself over this and Aggie's reaction, she then brought it up so many times that Aggie was eventually forced to yell her into silence.

Aggie was now in the market-room, as they called it, talking in a low voice to Ben. 'I can't stand her and her jabber any more, Ben,' she was saying. 'I'm sorry. I'm sorry, lad. Look, take this sovereign and go down to the station. I should have done it at first; I could have paid it then. It never struck me at the time. If those pimps could pay, I could've paid. Oh aye, I could've paid the fine. Anyway, take it down. See the sergeant and ask him to let her out. Of course, it'll take a day to get it settled; but I can put up with that.'

Ben took the coin from her hand, then looked hard at her before he turned abruptly and went out. She stood looking after him for a moment; then she dropped on to an upturned box, and bending her head into the folds of flesh under her chin, she asked of herself why she had to do this. What was the matter with her? Was it that the child was too refined and showing up her own shortcomings? Was it that just the sound of her voice grated on her? Was it that her bright loveliness caused something like a pain in her chest every time she looked at her? Was it that she was getting old and past

51

bothering with children? What was it she was afraid of?

She stopped her questioning, then got up heavily from the box and went into the kitchen.

Well, it was done. This was the last day she'd have to put up with her. And there she was, washing the bottom panes of the window. She couldn't reach very far, but for as far as she could, the window was clean, bright. The sun was showing a different sheen as its beams passed over a stretch of the stone floor.

The child, now turning a smiling face towards Aggie, said, 'I'll stand on the chair and that'll take me half-way up, but you'll have to do the rest, as I can't reach. It must be a long time since they were cleaned; they are very dirty. I've been over this part twice, and look at the water.' She pointed to the tin dish. 'And I've scrubbed the table again.'

Aggie did not remark on the child's handiwork; instead, she said, 'Who taught you to do housework?'

'Mama, of course. We had to keep the house clean; Dada liked a clean house. He was always very well washed, and Mama, too. And from I was a little girl I went round with Mama cleaning the house.'

'And I suppose you're a big grown-up girl now?'

A gurgle issued from the small throat as Millie answered, 'Well, not really big, but I'll grow.'

'Did you ever live in a big house?'

'Not as big as this. But in Durham we had three rooms and a toilet outside and a little garden where you could sit in the summer. And then there was the river. The river was beautiful. And the cathedral. Have you ever been to Durham Cathedral?'

'No; I haven't been to Durham Cathedral.'

'Oh, it's very grand. It's the best one in the world, you know. It's built on the edge of the river. When you're in a boat you can look up to it. I've been in a boat.'

'You've been lucky.'

The smile slipped from Millie's face and it was a moment before she responded: 'Yes, yes I've been lucky.' But the words were not said as if from the mind of a child but from that of an adult who had experienced many things. It caused Aggie to say brightly, 'Well, I think you'll still be lucky, because you might be seeing your ma later today.'

'Oh! Oh! Mrs Aggie. Oh! will I?' The child was now standing before her, gripping her hands. 'Oh! thank you. Thank you. Oh! I'll tell Mama when I see her how good you have been to me. You'll like Mama. She's very pretty, you know. Well, you saw her, didn't you? But' – her voice dropped – 'she looked tired. She never used to be tired. She would dance with me and take me long walks. Oh, you'll like Mama.'

'Aye. Yes, yes, undoubtedly I'll like your mama.' And she forced herself to add, 'I'll tell her what a good girl you've been in cleanin' me place for me.'

'Oh, that is nothing.' Millie moved back to the window now. 'I like doing things. I like cooking. I have never cooked here, have I?'

'No. No, you haven't. We . . . we don't do much cookin' here.'

'But you have an oven?'

'Yes, yes, we have an oven.'

'What a pity! If I had been staying with you I . . . I would have shown you how I can make a scone . . . scones. People say sconnes when it should be scones, shouldn't it?'

'If you say so. Yes, if you say so, it should be scones.'

Aggie now walked heavily through the market-room and out into the yard. And she made herself look about her, at the odd heaps lying on the rough ground, and she said to herself, 'Yes, he was right, it'll be better if it's paved. And I wonder if he's put any oil on that door?'

53

She walked over to an outhouse which, in comparison with the rest of the place, looked extremely tidy in that on the shelves were arrayed different tools of all shapes and sizes; and on the walls, hanging from nails, was all the accoutrement that went to the dressing of a horse: collars, bridles, saddles, some stiffened with age, others looking usable. Taking up an oil-can she went out and towards the old outbuildings, to the door next to the one leading into the barn and, moving it, she found that it hadn't been oiled. The door led upstairs to what had once been the stableman's rooms, and which now housed Ben. After she had oiled the hinges, she paused a moment before lumbering up the stairs.

She stood looking about her; at his plank bed with the bedclothes neatly pulled over it; at the old easy chair with the stuffing sticking out of its seat. A hard kitchen-type chair was set near a table with three legs. An orange box was obviously being used as a replacement for the missing leg as well as serving as a miniature bookcase, for there were seven tattered books on the dividing shelf and a stack of old newspapers below it.

Whatever it was her mind had said to her, she answered with, Well, it's better than thousands of others in the town, and many a one would be glad of it. And anyway, you couldn't get a decent table up those stairs, they're too narrow.

She had just reached the foot of the stairs when she saw Ben entering the yard; and when she stepped from the doorway he called towards her, 'Been on a tour of inspection, then?'

'Aye, you could say that. I think you should try to get a table up there, or at least fix a leg on that one. And of all the single ticks that have come in, there's bound to have been a decent one among them. Why haven't you taken one up?'

'I prefer me hard pallet; it's a sort of penance for me sins.'

'Don't be too bright. What happened?'

He put his hand in his pocket, then handed her back the sovereign, saying, 'She's gone. She went the same day, they tell me. I couldn't get it out of them who had paid for her, but old Alex the cleaner told me on the side: Boswell, Slim Boswell.'

'Oh my God! No!'

'Oh my God! Yes! And he's only got to see her' – he thrust his head back – 'and it'll be mother and daughter. Oh aye, definitely daughter.'

'She needn't be with him; he could have paid for . . .'

'Don't talk soft, Aggie. If she hadn't been with him she'd have been here before now. You said she saw you with the child and there's not two Aggie Winkowskis kickin' around this quarter, or the town itself, and somebody would have told her where you lived.'

Her response was almost a plaintive mutter: 'What are we goin' to do?' she asked.

He noticed that he was being drawn into making the decision by the 'we'; and so he said, 'Well, speakin' for meself, it would sicken me if I thought the young 'un got into his hands.'

She started to walk across the yard, and he followed her; and they had reached the house door before her decision came: 'I'll take the cart down there later on; if he's put her to work she's likely pacing The Strand,' she said.

'Oh, I doubt not, not on The Strand, Aggie, for a beginner.'

She swung round to him, grinding out in a low voice, 'She mustn't have been any beginner, not goin' by the uncles the child's had. And what's strikin' me now, she took the child with her when she was on the game just as a draw.'

'That needn't have been, Aggie. We talked about that, didn't we? She couldn't have left her in the house. Anyway, as I see it now, if the authorities have got wind of her havin' a youngster, we'll have some of them officials and the do-gooders comin' round, and it'll be the work-house in the end.'

She said nothing directly in answer to this, but carried on into the house, saying, 'I'll have to tell her she's gone somewhere.'

In the sitting-room, Millie was standing on a chair and reaching up towards the upper panes of the window.

'Come down off that! Come down off that! You'll break your neck.'

'No, I won't; I'm very steady on my legs.'

Aggie closed her eyes for a moment; then slowly she ordered: 'Come . . . down . . . off . . . that . . . chair.'

The tone brought Millie on to the floor and standing before Aggie, saying, 'I . . . I just wanted to help.'

Aggie drew in a long breath, bowed her head slightly and said, 'Aye, I know you did, love; but come and sit down a minute.' And she took the child by the hand and walked her to the settle, and when they were seated she looked at the small figure by her side, at the hair, like a golden halo round the oval face, and the limpid grey eyes gazing so trustfully at her. And as she stared, there was interposed on the fair skin the face of a man, a thin man, and he was leering at her as if in triumph, as he would do if he were to get hold of this unusual-looking child, for he'd make a pretty penny out of her, no matter what channel he sent her along, his nursery, the street, or the boat. Any one of them would bring in a good profit.

As if the child were sensing her dilemma, she said, 'I am going to see Mama today, am I not, Mrs Aggie?'

For once the preciseness of the words did not irritate Aggie, and she answered gently, 'I'm sorry, love, but . . . but she's had to go away for a day or two.'

'Where to?'

56

Aggie was stumped for a moment, but then she thought of Durham, and so she answered, 'Durham.'

'But . . . but she can't. She said she would never go back there.'

Aggie pulled herself up from the seat, saying, tersely now, 'Well, love, she has.'

'But . . . but why didn't she come and take me with her? She never leaves me.'

'Well' – Aggie was walking towards the table, her back to the child – 'she . . . she was in a hurry. Something had come up.' She now rubbed her hand over the oilcloth as she waited for the next question. But when it did not come, she turned about and saw the child with her head bowed and the tears running down her cheeks. Returning to the settle, she seated herself again by the child and said kindly, 'Come on now, come on. You're quite a big girl. Grown-ups have things to do, you know, an' they can't always explain them . . . well—' She put her arm around the narrow shoulders and pulled the child into her side, and when again the arm came around her waist and the head was pressed between her breasts there arose in her that pain that was both an ache and a pleasure: a pleasure that had no future that she could see; a pleasure that she had been deprived of all during her womanhood. And now here was a pleasure that was also an irritant. It was a pleasure that she wanted to press into her body while at the same time throw it off as far away from her as possible.

The sound of the door being opened made her instinctively push the child aside from her. Ben, however, did not remark on the scene he had just witnessed, but said, 'There's a friend of yours in the yard who would like to have a word with you. He dropped in off his beat, sort of.'

'Oh aye.' She nodded at him; then as she passed him she said quietly. 'Stay with her, but keep your mouth shut, else you might contradict my story.'

57

In the yard Constable Fenwick was looking at the pile of tins; and, as she approached him, she said, 'Goin' cheap: a penny a score.'

'What on earth d'you use them for? Who buys them?' he asked, as though he couldn't believe anyone would do so.

'Oh, there's always a buyer for everything. They grind them down. But I use a lot meself. Best form of fuel and the cheapest: fill them with a mixture of coal dust and mud and you've got a fire goin' all day and night. The tins hold the heat.'

'Is that a fact?'

'That's a fact.'

'I've been away for a day or two; I lost me father.'

'Oh.' Her light tone changed. 'I'm sorry about that. Was he dear to you?'

'Aye, very dear, and a good man.'

'Did he live hereabouts?'

'No, in Newcastle.'

'Oh; Newcastle.'

'Aye, that's where I was born and reared. I would have been there the day but I had to go and marry a lass from down here, and she wouldn't leave her mother. Women are the limit, aren't they, Aggie?'

She did not respond to this, but stared at him, until he spoke again, saying, 'I'd have been along before now, but I heard about me father the very day when we last spoke, and so I had to go off straightaway to Newcastle. Before I went, though, I managed to have a word on the side with the lass. She was waiting to be moved to start her month. She begged me to take this.' He put his hand in his pocket and brought out a key. 'She asked me to give it to the lady who had been in court with her child, and to ask if you would take care of her till she could come for her.' As he handed her the key, he added,

58

'Apparently she wants you to take the personal things from her lodgings.'

Aggie stood holding the key in her hand. It was all of three inches long, and as she looked at it, she said, 'I shouldn't be landed with this. What life will it be for a child stuck in here?'

'There's many a worse place, Aggie, and many a worse person to take charge of a child. I can vouch for that. Anyway, if it becomes known the lass left a child behind, the authorities will be visitin' you, and then you'll be able to get rid of her.'

'Huh!' She bridled now. 'What if it should then happen I don't want to get rid of her, eh? What about it then?' . . . Why in the name of God! had she said that?

'Oh, well, that could be easily arranged. You'd have to sign some sort of form. And if they ever want a reference, I'll stand for that. And there are others an' all, I'm sure.'

'Where?' Her voice was scornful now. 'A rag woman in a hole like this! What! they would say. Taking charge of a child, and such a one? Aye, and such a one' – she was shaking her head – 'who'd talk a hind leg off a donkey, and with such politeness that it gets up your nose and under your skin and on your nerves.'

He was laughing now.

'Well, perhaps you'll learn something from her.'

'I've had all the education I need, thanks. But anyway' – her tone changed again – 'I'm grateful to you for your help.'

'Any time, Aggie, any time.' He again looked at the pile of tins. 'I'll have to tell me missis about that trick, and tell her to get going and save some money . . . Ooh! I'd better not, though, not if I want to live a little longer. Well, I'll look in again, Aggie; and mind you, see everything's above board' – he glanced around the yard – 'no dealing in stolen property; no organising of crime in any one of its many forms. But I think you'll stay clear until Thursday.'

He grinned at her, then went from the yard. And she stood looking down at the key in her hand, while she said to herself, 'Well, this seems to decide it, doesn't it?' and turning, she yelled, 'Ben!' And when he appeared in the yard, followed by the child, it was to her she spoke, saying, 'Go and put your hat and coat on; we're goin' for a walk.'

'A walk?'

'Yes, that's what I said, we're goin' for a walk.' Then with an impatient movement, she said loudly, 'Your ma has sent the key to your house. We're goin' there to pick up some of your clothes.'

'Oh, we are? Oh, that is so nice. And I need a clean petticoat on and . . .'

'Go on! Get your hat and coat on.'

After Millie had turned to run back into the house, Ben said, 'So that's what he wanted. How did he get hold of it?'

'Apparently he had a word with her while she was waiting to be taken along the line. It must have been just before Boswell picked her up. Get the hand-cart out of the barn; there'll likely be things to bring back.'

Without more to-do he hurried from her, and she herself went into the market-room.

From a cupboard, she took a large, brown, straw hat and a dark grey coat; and after first pinning the hat on to her hair she shrugged herself into the coat. But it wasn't large enough to button and showed her blouse and skirt, and so when she appeared in the yard again Ben, standing ready by the cart, grinned at her, saying, 'That's nice! Smartish.'

'Aye, smart . . . ish. Where is she?' She turned and looked towards the house door. 'Don't tell me she's washing her face again!'

'Here she is.' Ben waved to the child, and when she approached them she exclaimed loudly while looking at Aggie, 'Oh, you are dressed! You look different. That is a nice hat.'

'Thank you. Thank you.'

That was another thing that annoyed her about the child: she always had to find something nice to say.

'Well, come on, let's get away,' she said.

'Have a nice trip.'

Aggie turned a scornful glance on Ben, then pushed the cart through the gateway on to the road.

'Are you a real rag woman, Mrs Aggie?'

Here we go again. 'Yes, I'm a real rag woman. Now what are you goin' to make out of that?'

'Nothing. Mama says that honest work, no matter how lowly, is something to be proud of.'

God in heaven! That mama, that proven whore who was now in a brothel and was likely to stay there, that's if Slim didn't ship her out an' all, because she was a looker all right.

'Are you going to shout for rags?'

'No, I'm not. And keep your tongue quiet.'

Millie kept her tongue quiet for some time, until she felt forced to say, 'I would have never known this way home.'

Aggie made no reply to this, and the child remained quiet until it was evident that she recognized the entrance to the area, for she exclaimed, 'Oh! now I know where we are.'

'Whereabouts is your house then?'

'It wasn't a house, I think I've told you, it was outside. We go round the corner here.'

They went round the corner, and the child stopped in front of a flight of steps leading up to a dilapidated house, one of a number in the street. But to the right of the steps was a low iron gate, and leading from it more steps, but downwards;

61

and the child exclaimed, 'Down there! down here!'

Aggie looked up and down the narrow street; then, taking a chain with a lock attached to it from under a piece of sacking in the corner of the cart, she pushed the cart close to the gate, and tied a leg of it to the iron post.

'Why are you doing that?'

'Just in case somebody takes a fancy to it.'

'No-one would run off with a hand-cart.'

'Well, they've done it before.'

'Really?'

'Yes, rea-lly! Get yourself down those steps, and see if I can follow you.'

The stone steps were narrow, and she didn't like stone steps, they were greasy when wet, but she made the bottom of them and inserted the key in the lock. She followed the child into the room, but there she stood aghast. It was a cellar, stone-floored and stone-walled, and stone cold. It was obviously partitioned into two rooms by a rough wooden screen. In the part in which she was standing was a small table and two chairs and an iron contraption that looked as if it might be used for some form of heating. There was no chimney attached to it; so she guessed it was for paraffin oil.

She walked round the end of the partition. In this part, there was a narrow iron bed, covered by a patched quilt, and at its foot was a large suitcase. Near the wall was a bass hamper. Clothes, mostly small garments, were hanging from the rails that had been knocked in the partition.

The child had followed her, and as she started to finger the clothes, she said, 'It . . . it isn't a very nice place. It's always cold. But . . . but, as Mama said, as long as we kept it clean and it was only for a short time . . . But—' She turned and looked at Aggie as she ended slowly, 'But it wasn't like the house we had in Durham. That

62

'... that was so nice. I ... I miss that house. I miss Durham. I ... I ...'

'Now, now! there's no time for cryin'. Come on, come on. Stop that! I'll take these clothes down and you fold them on the bed there, nicely, then we'll put them on the cart. And the cases an' all.'

'Why? Why? Mama will be coming back.'

'Look! Do what you're told! Your mama sent word for me to do this. You understand? I told you. And you're to stay with me ... well, until she comes for you or other arrangements are made.'

'Where is Mama really?'

'I told you, she had to go to Durham.'

'I ... I don't believe you, Mrs Aggie.'

To put it in her own words, as she explained the scene later to Ben, she was flabbergasted. And she had to ask herself if this young 'un was seven or seventeen.

'You don't, eh? You don't believe me? Well then, all right, you can stay here by yourself, and see to yourself, until your mother comes for you.'

'I ... I cannot stay by ... by ... my ... self. I'm ... I'm afraid, and ... and I'm too little.'

'You're only little in stature, not in your tongue or your mind. So look, let's have no more of it. If you don't fold them up I'll just toss them on the cart like I do the rags. It's up to you.' She now stripped the partition of the clothes, threw them on the bed, and then went and lifted the lid off the case, only to find that it, too, was full of clothes, both the woman's and the child's. She groped under the clothes, thinking there might be anything else, probably a small box of some kind, and recognized the feel of leather.

When she took out the leather writing case, the child turned and cried, 'That's Mama's! She keeps her letters in there.'

63

'Oh aye!' Aggie retorted, while thinking, that should be interesting. And then she said, 'Look, there's no way I can get this case and that bass hamper up them steps, full as they are, I'll have to tie the stuff in bundles an' put them on the cart. I'll hand them up to you from the bottom of the steps, and you stay by the cart.'

During the next half hour they worked in this way, and when the empty cases and the bed covers were at last placed on the cart, Aggie locked the door, then hesitated for a moment, wondering what to do with the key. Her rent would have certainly been paid in advance and the rent man, whoever he was, would likely be the only one who would come down here, except of course the child's *uncles*, and they must have been hard put to it to resort to this hole. Aye, but, of course, there was the bed, and the woman. But what did this child do while it was going on? Likely what hundreds of others had to do: wonder, and think, and stick their fingers in their ears; some, on the other hand, might even ask themselves how long it would be before they could try it. But this child was so different, and so bonny. Oh, for God's sake! get on with it, woman. With a final gesture she put the key on the sill of the narrow window and pulled herself up the stone steps.

After unlocking the cart from the gatepost, they were off, the child now walking between Aggie's outstretched arms and adding her small strength to the pushing.

'What d'you make of it all?' Aggie looked at Ben, who shook his head, saying, 'Beats me. Those are all good clothes. Best quality; some of the woman's bits are real high-class stuff, I would say.'

'So would I. But about these letters. They tell you something, and yet they tell you nothing. This Mrs Melburn, the parson's wife . . . she seems a motherly figure, in a way, but

64

that bit' — she pointed to the page of a letter that was on the table — 'that bit tells you why they came this way.' She picked up the page and read aloud:

'I'm sorry at the disappointment you found that your friend had left the town without leaving a forwarding address. I can understand how upset you were after expecting to make your home with her. Human nature is very odd. Perhaps it was her husband's doing.'

Aggie lifted her head and looked at Ben, saying, 'Reading between the lines, the husband of this friend, whoever she was, wasn't going to allow his wife to get mixed up in something. What d'you think?'

'It reads like that.'

'Then this other one.' She picked up another letter, and again read aloud:

'I think of you often and of the happy times we had at The Hall, and they were happy times. We never thought then that there was such a thing as tragedy in life and such falseness.

'Then this last one. Just a few lines on this page:

'I am distressed for you, my dear. You must come back. Don't do anything silly or anything you would be ashamed of. It isn't like you. Do come back. People forget. They have short memories. John is with me in this.
   My love to you in friendship. Yours Jessie.

'Again I ask, what d'you make of that? I think it must be as I said: either she'd done something or her man had done something. That's as far as I can think. Except that it's more likely the man, because, you know, the child talked about him dying, but in a funny way, as if dying was another name for something else. Well, I don't suppose we'll ever know the real ins and outs of it. But I've got a good idea about one thing: that little miss upstairs knows more than she lets on. That look that comes over her face when you start probing. Like this afternoon, when I said to her, "There's no letters from your father in here. Didn't he ever write to your mother at some time or other?" and she said, "I . . . I don't know." But there's something she does know and she's keepin' it to herself. She had another cryin' bout, too, when I took her upstairs.'

'If the authorities find out that her mother's walking the sidelines,' Ben said, 'there'll be no chance she'll get her back. Would you then sign a paper for her?'

Aggie gathered up the letters from the table, returned them to the writing case, then rose heavily, saying, 'Time enough to think about that. See what happens in the meantime. But I think I'll write to that parson's wife and see what she has to say about it.'

The meantime came to an end three days later.

The weather had changed. It had been pouring with rain all day, and half the yard was a quagmire. The lanes, courts, streets, and roads were the same.

It was Aggie's day to visit the outskirts, but as she looked out of the window on to the patch of grass that was welcoming the steady downpour, she said, half to herself, 'It's a good job I'm not forced to go out,' and a voice in her mind added, 'You need never go again if you don't want to.' And she answered it: 'Then what would I do with meself? Sit and listen to Madam Correctness for the rest of me days? Oh no!'

She turned and looked towards the child, who was sitting hugging a doll. It had a china head, a stuffed cloth body, and wooden legs. But the legs were cleverly jointed at the knees and the ankles, and the whole was prettily dressed. They had found the doll in the bass hamper where, Millie had informed her, it slept when they were out of the house. She had been foolish enough to ask if it had a name. And when told it was Victoria after the Queen and that the Queen was a wonderful lady, and her Prince was wonderful, too, she'd had to bite her tongue to prevent herself from saying, 'Aye, she's a wonderful lady all right, she's still for bairns your size working twelve hours a day. And she with a squad of her own. Don't talk to me about the wonderful Victoria.'

As she looked at Millie rocking herself slightly like a little old woman getting a child to sleep, she thought, If I were to tell her her mother has died, she would likely think it was the same way as her father had, whichever way that was, which wasn't real dead. So what am I to do?

Her answer came at seven o'clock that evening.

She heard Ben come into the market-room, but when the kitchen door did not immediately open, she went over to it and saw him throwing off a wet sack that he had been wearing over his head and shoulders like a cape. And when he bent to take off his boots, she said, 'You're wringin'.'

'What d'you expect?' he said, without looking at her. 'D'you think I walk between the drops?'

'Take off your pants.'

'Me pants can stay where they are . . . Is she upstairs?'

'No. Come right in and close the door.'

Inside the room he wiped his face and neck with a piece of old towelling. Then he said, 'The decision's been made for you.'

'What d'you mean?'

'She hung herself.'

He straightened up, and they stood looking at each other. Then Aggie turned and looked around her before making her

67

way to an upturned box, saying, 'Oh, dear God! No!'

'It's the best way, I think.'

'Oh, shut up! How did it happen?'

'By puttin' a rope round her neck.'

'By God! If you joke about this I'll put a rope round your neck.'

'I wasn't meanin' to joke, Aggie. It just comes out with me. You know it does. I'm sorry . . . I'm sorry for the lass: she's past feeling anything now. And it wasn't the rope, it was a pair of fancy stockin's that they dish out, so I was told.'

'When did it happen?'

'Last night. And I'll tell you something more: it would have been hidden up, as many another's been, an' she would have been dumped somewhere, or found in the canal, but one of the lasses that found her had a screaming fit and ran out into the street, went barmy, they said, yelling, "She's hung herself! She's hung herself!" Well, the polis was brought, naturally, and they took the body away to the workhouse mortuary. And you know what happens from there, she'll be dumped in a common grave: there'll be no pious words said over her, her being a suicide. But the other thing. Apparently, when the polis went back this morning he found the house empty, bare, absolutely stripped, and Slim Boswell and the lasses gone, and every stick of furniture just vanished, the lot. It's happened before, the midnight flits. But that was a biggish house, ten rooms or more, so I heard. Slim'll surface again, though, never fear. You see, he knew if they had taken him in and it was proved he had been using her, or, as a little bird told me, he had got her ready for shipment, they would have surely sent him along the line this time, and stripped the house of all his fine pieces. And that's another thing I heard: it wasn't only bairns and young lasses he collected, but furniture and foreign crockery, mostly from China, they say. Oh, he had taste in his own way. But my God! When

68

I think what that lass must have gone through before doin' that, I could spew.' And then he added, 'I was talking to one of Big Joe's bouncers and it was his opinion that she got wind of what was to happen, before they had time to give her a dose, likely. He seemed pleased that Slim had disappeared from the district 'cos Big Joe was never for tradin' in bairns. Huh!' He tossed his head. 'You wouldn't believe it, Aggie, but he talked as if Big Joe, being above that kind of thing, could be classed as a caring, honest man. People are funny, aren't they?'

She looked up at him, saying, 'That's enough for now. You talk as much as she does.' Then added, with a little concern, 'Go inside and get yourself warmed.'

'I'm not cold, not now. Anyway, you'll keep her if you can, won't you?'

She paused and allowed her gaze to wander round the room before she said, 'I hate the authorities and their bits of paper.'

'Well, far better that. And do it now rather than them pounce on you later and accuse you of hidin' her. I'm sure your friend will put a good word in for you,' which brought from her the sharp retort: 'Yes, he will! There's good and bad in every quarter, and he's a good bobby. He's been kind to me.'

'Oh, you've repaid him: you've opened his eyes to things that've been under his nose, and he couldn't see the wood for the trees. Oh, you've repaid him.'

'Huh,' she said, and then smiled faintly as she said, 'Odd, you know: you tell me that Annie's a good woman, and I suppose she is, but I can't stand the sight of her; then I tell you the constable's a good man, and you know he is, and you can't stand the sight of him. Funny, isn't it?'

'Aye, Aggie, it's funny.' And he was about to add, 'But you know as well as I do there's a reason in both cases,' but instead, he said, 'Well! well! Now I'll go and join the new permanent member of the family. I suppose I can look upon her as a younger sister?'

'That you can't, because I'm mother to neither of you.'

He had been about to open the door into the kitchen, but now he turned and looked at her, and his next words cut her to the bone as they were apt to do when they spat the truth at her. 'And for that you're to be pitied, Aggie.'

PART TWO

The Nursemaid

1

Millie stood by the pony's head, stroking its muzzle while she talked to it, saying, 'Don't worry, you'll soon be home, laddie, then you'll have your tea. I could do with my tea an' all.'

Two years ago she would not have said 'an' all', but, 'too'. However, many things had happened during the two years since she had been told that her mother had died of the fever and that, prior to this, she had not been allowed to see her in case she should catch it and spread it further. And it wasn't until she had knelt by the heap of earth that signified her mother's unconsecrated grave that she had stopped crying. It was as if she had accepted the fact that her mother had gone out of her life and that her future lay with this big fat woman, who alternately yelled and cajoled, and the nice man called Ben.

She had been content to stay in the house all day and to try to clean it; but Mrs Aggie had told her she must go to school, at least for part of the day. They both told her that. And so she went out to school every morning, not to the threepenny one run by the Council, nor to the Church of England, but to the penny school run by the Methodists.

At first she had complained to Aggie, saying they were stupid because they taught nothing but the abc and counting, and that most of the time was spent singing hymns and listening to stories from the Bible. She remembered, too, how surprised she had been when Ben had said, 'Well, you can go to the Ragged School and see if you like it there. There's one thing sure, you won't have much time to grumble because you'll be taken up with scratchin' yourself. And that beautiful hair of yours will walk off your scalp with dickies.'

Yes indeed, she knew now if she had ever gone to the Ragged School that's what would have happened. She always felt sorry for the children at the Ragged School and there seemed to be hundreds and hundreds of them. Another funny thing she had had to have explained to her was why some grown-ups would go to the Ragged School at night time.

Oh, she knew she had learned a great deal during the last two years; she also knew that a good part of herself was happy, mostly, she thought, because she had come to like Mrs Aggie and living in her house. Of course, she still shouted at her and still grumbled. But she, too, seemed to be learning. She had heard Ben tell her it was about time, too, but almost too late; that was when she had stopped pushing the hand-cart and bought Laddie and the flat-cart.

What was more, she'd also got a cover for the couch and some rugs for the hall and a stair-carpet. As for the yard, it had become almost clean over the last two years; it was all paved now. And Ben had painted the front of the house, and the barn doors and such; and the market-room had been moved into the barn itself, and that room had been painted, and papered, and odd pieces of furniture put in. She smiled as she recalled that Mrs Aggie had sworn a lot whilst that was being done. But that, too, was the time when Mrs Aggie struck her so hard that she had fallen on her back, and all

74

because she had called Mrs Nelson 'a bloody cow'. Well, that was Mrs Aggie's other name for Mrs Nelson. Anyway, Mrs Aggie had been very sorry she had struck her and she had taken her into the town and bought her a real new bonnet, although she would allow her to wear it only on a Sunday. During the week, whenever they were out, she insisted that she roll her hair up and put it under the cap. She liked wearing the cap; it made her feel different, as did the long grey coat that went down to the top of her boots, because then she did not feel like Millie Forester, whose mother and father were dead and had no-one belonging to her, except the fat woman and the man with short legs, but more like a princess who, every now and again, donned strange clothes and went out among the common people, and was kind to them, and yet always remained a princess under the disguise.

It was during the night that she would conjure up this picture of herself; in the daytime she was practical. That Mrs Aggie no longer went ragging in The Courts, but, instead, encouraged the children to bring what rags they had to the yard, there to receive their candy rock, and also the women to come on a Saturday morning to the barn and buy what they wanted, she knew was very wise. She also felt somewhat pleased, feeling that it was better for Mrs Aggie to concentrate her collecting efforts in the nicer part of the town. Ben called it breaking new ground; she herself would have put it 'widening her scope'.

She had read the words, widen your scope, in a phrase book. She liked it. But she recalled it was to do with God. All the books that people read were to do with God. Everybody seemed to be praying; except, of course, the children who went to the Ragged School and those who flooded The Courts at the back of the house and round about . . . But there; she was wrong when she thought that everybody prayed, because Mrs Aggie didn't pray, nor did Ben, nor his Annie. She liked his Annie, but Mrs Aggie didn't. She wondered why. Perhaps it was because Annie was thin and not very pretty. But, then, she was nice to talk to, and she was jolly. The last time Ben had taken her there – on the quiet; it was to be a secret – Annie had done the clog dance to Ben's playing his tin whistle.

That was another thing that gave her pleasure; to listen to Ben playing his whistle. He could make it sad or gay, or even funny. Ben liked Annie, and Annie liked Ben. But she was older than him. In fact, she was very old; she was twenty-four years old and she worked in the mill and earned eight shillings a week.

She herself earned a wage. Mrs Aggie gave her a shilling a week, because, as she said, she was her assistant; for there must be someone to hold the horse and look after the cart and see that the children didn't nick . . . steal the clothes off it.

Mrs Aggie was now paying a visit to one of her good houses. She called it a good house, because the maid always kept things for her. Mrs Aggie would give her anything up to a shilling for them. Generally, they were the cast-offs of two children in the house who happened to be about her own age, and this could mean a pretty frock coming her way, but only if, Mrs Aggie said, she kept her nose clean. That was a funny saying, wasn't it? because her nose was always clean.

She now turned from the pony and looked towards the side gate separated from the front gate by a hedge of trees. All the houses along this road had two gates. From where she was standing she couldn't see the house, but she knew it was big, red-bricked and square. They were all big, red-bricked and square along this road.

It would be very nice, she told herself, to have a house red-bricked and square with two entrances. Perhaps one day she might live in a house like this. Perhaps, in the years to come, she would get Mrs Aggie to move, but

76

that would only be when she was too old to take the cart out.

A snort from the pony interrupted her day-dreaming; and immediately her slight body stiffened: walking quickly down the road towards her was a man, and even over the distance she knew he was smiling at her.

She almost jumped forward and darted towards the side entrance, dashed through the gate, up the shrub-bordered path and into the yard where, at a far door, Aggie was standing in the act of handing something to the maid. And they both turned startled faces and looked at her, as she cried, 'The man! Mrs Aggie. The man! He's . . . he's in the road.'

Bending and whipping up the wicker basket full of odd garments, Aggie nodded hastily towards the girl, saying, 'Ta, lass. Ta.' Then as fast as her legs would carry her, she shambled down the path towards the gate. Outside, she looked up and down the road; then turning to Millie, she said, 'There's nobody here now.'

'He was, Mrs Aggie, he was. And . . . and it was the same man who . . . who took off my cap that day when he was with the lady, and before that, asking if . . . if I'd like to see the fair on the green.'

'Get up.' Aggie pointed to the seat at the front of the cart, and immediately Millie had done so, she gripped the iron frame of the seat, heaved herself on to the first step, then, almost with a lunge, on to the seat; but this time she didn't say, as she usually did, 'I'm past this; I'll sit on the back in future and you'll take him,' but she jerked the reins and put the pony into a trot.

Twenty minutes later, she was driving into the yard. Neither she nor Millie exchanged a word during the journey, evidence of the seriousness of the situation felt by them both.

Ben was there to help her down, and once on the ground, she said, 'I want to see you inside.'

'Oh?' He turned an enquiring gaze upon her as she marched towards the house, but before following her he held out his hands to Millie as she went to jump off the last step, saying now in a low tone, 'It looks a good enough day' – he pointed to the back of the cart – 'what's up?'

She had her head down as she said, 'That man, the one who frightened me. He was on the road. He was smiling, and I ran to the house and told Mrs Aggie.'

Even before she was finished speaking he was walking quickly from her towards the house.

Aggie had taken her hat and coat off and had dropped on to the settle, and as he entered the room she said immediately, 'Somethin' will have to be . . . ' but paused as Millie came in on Ben's heels, and she nodded towards her saying, 'Go and take your things off and set the tray.'

Millie was about to speak, but Aggie barked, 'Go on! Do as you're told for once, without opening your mouth.'

After Millie had flounced away to do her bidding, Aggie said, 'She came in that yard as white as a sheet. She senses what he's after: she can't exactly explain it, but she knows that he could take her away. Something's got to be done. I can't keep a stronger tag on her than I do now, almost night and day. I hadn't left the cart more than five minutes. Oh! no, not that.' She shook her head. 'The lass had apparently got the bundle ready for me. A nice lot of stuff: a whole man's outfit an' all, the grand-dad had died; an' there was bairns' clothes. I gave her half a dollar this time. She was pleased an' all. But before she could say a word that 'un came rushin' in.' She sighed deeply before ending, 'What's to be done, Ben?'

He was standing before her, one arm extended, the hand gripping the mantelpiece, and he said, 'You can't keep her here much longer. I've told you that before. He or one of

78

his bloody cronies will pick her up. I don't know how he found out that she belonged to that lass, but find out he has. God help her! She seems to be suitable material for what he wants: her father a murderer and her mother a prostitute.'

'The parson's wife's letter didn't actually say he was a murderer. A man had died through him, that's what she said.'

'Well, you don't get twelve years for a busted jaw or a black eye. I thought it odd when you wrote and asked her how it had come about an' you got no answer. And d'you remember what else you put in the letter? You asked her if she would like to have the bairn, her being a minister's wife. But no; their Christianity wasn't goin' to go that far.'

'Blast her to hell's flames!' And with this interjection Aggie now beat her closed fist against the end of the settle as she added angrily, 'If she had acted like the friend that she was supposed to be to the mother I wouldn't be faced with this lot tonight.'

'You could send her away to a school.'

'How could you be sure that he wouldn't pick her up from there? He could dress up one of his ladies to look respectable an' make a call.'

'He wouldn't know where you put her. Anyway, if it was some place like where those sisters are.'

Aggie was on her feet now. 'Nuns? No. I'm surprised at your suggestin' them.'

'I thought it would have appealed to you, bein' as your friend Fenwick's one of their ilk.'

'He's not one of their ilk, not in that way; he's respectable, an' there are respectable ones.'

'He's a Catholic, nevertheless. And it surprises me that they took him into the Force, 'cos he's made no secret of it an' you know yourself how they're thought about.'

79

'Aye, I do, by the Protestants, the Baptists, the Methodists, the Temperance-ites, an' every other bloody one of the ranters. But I didn't think you were among them.'

'Oh, me? You know me, I run with the hare an' hunt with the hounds: I'd suck up to the devil himself for a penny.'

'Oh, shut your mouth an' talk serious about what we're goin' to do.'

'Well, I'll talk serious. You've got to get her away from here if you don't want her to end up where her mother was; an' the best place, as I see it, is a closed school, an' there's not a closer one, I should imagine, than the one under them sisters. Now don't let your hair rise. You asked me advice an' I'm givin' it to you. I get around, as you know; I've seen all the schools, right from the ragged one, the penny, the tuppence, the threepence, right up to the fourpence a week one. I've seen the type of bairns that go in and out of them. And I'll tell you something else. I've heard mothers enquiring why their little daughter hasn't come home. Even little boys have gone missing. There's a racket goin' on, Aggie; but you know as well as me it's been goin' on for years. Probably always has done. But the middle class an' the upper lot don't seem to recognise it goes on, not until lately anyway, when one or two ladies seem to be trying to get somethin' done about it. As far as I understand from the gossip there's nothing'll come out of it by goin' to the polis; it's got to come from Parliament. They've got to make a law, like, an' them that break it . . . well' – he drew in his breath noisily – 'I would like to see them swing.' He turned abruptly away now, saying, 'Take my advice, Aggie, get her into a closed school.'

'What closed school?'

Millie had come into the room carrying a tin tray, and as she put it down on the table, she looked from one to the other and said, 'What are you talkin' about, closed schools? Is the school going to close?'

80

In answer, Aggie did not bawl at her but said quietly, 'Come here, love. Sit down there.' She pointed to the couch, and when Millie was seated she lowered herself down beside her and, taking her hand, said, 'You're frightened of that man, aren't you?'

Millie bowed her head and said, 'Yes. Yes, I am.'

'Why?'

'Why?' She was looking up into Aggie's face now. 'Well—' She thought for a moment. 'I . . . I didn't like his face and . . . and the way he got hold of my arm that first time,' she said. 'And then, when he brought the lady . . . no, she wasn't a lady, she was just a woman, and her voice was common and she called me duckie and . . . and I said to them, "I'm going to scream." And when there were two men passing he let go of me and I ran. I . . . I—' She turned to Ben now, saying, 'I don't know why I was afraid, they just made me afraid. They weren't like . . . well, ordinary people. I don't know.' She shook her head. 'I just didn't like them, nor him. His face was nasty, and he kept smiling.'

'Well, love, you're nine years old, coming on ten quick, an' you've got a head on your shoulders, so, I'm goin' to talk to you straight. He's a bad man. A very bad man. And I'll tell you somethin' else: your mother wouldn't have died if it hadn't been for that man.'

'But . . . but Mama died of a fever, you said she did.'

'Yes, it was caused by that man.'

'How? How can a man cause a fever?'

'It's hard to explain. But . . . but when you're a bit older I'll . . . I'll tell you how. In the meantime, tell me, has . . . has he ever said anything to you except askin' you if you would like to go to the fair?'

'No; but the woman said she would show me some pretty dresses, new ones, not—' She looked downwards now before she said, 'Smelly stuff off the cart.'

81

There was silence for a moment, and then Millie lifted her head as she said, 'He . . . he called me a funny name. I . . . I didn't tell you before because it was about the rags.'

'What did he call you then to do with the rags?'

'Rag Niff. That's what I thought it was at first but when he said it the next time it sounded different, it was nymph, rag nymph, that's what he called me. "Hello, Rag Nymph," he said.'

'Nymph?' Aggie was looking at Ben, and he looked questioningly at Millie as she said, 'A nymph is a kind of fairy, I think. I've read about them in one of my stories. They live in woods and dance round toadstools.'

The almost simultaneous intaking of breath by both Ben and Aggie was audible; then, again taking Millie's hand, Aggie said, 'Listen carefully, child. That man is bent on takin' you away from us. He is an evil man, bad, very bad. Now neither Ben there, nor me, can watch you every moment of the day. You go to school. Ben takes you there and he brings you back, but there are the in-between times, and evil men are clever. And then there's the time with the cart when you stand, like this mornin', lookin' after it and the pony. Well, you know, if you hadn't been quick and run into me he could have caught up with you. And what then? Now, I want the best for you, the best that I can give you, because in a way you belong to me now, and Ben there.' She put her hand out towards him. 'And we both . . . well—' She could not bring herself to say 'love you', but instead said, 'care what happens to you. So, we think for a little while ahead you should go to a school where you'll be looked after; I mean, where you can sleep, and where he won't get at you.'

'I . . . Oh! Mrs Aggie, I don't want to go to a school where I won't be able to get out and come home. Why can't you tell the police about him?'

82

Aggie looked helplessly at Ben and he, moving forward and dropping on to his hunkers, brought his face level with Millie's as he said, 'He . . . he hasn't done anything yet. He hasn't run off with you. There's what you call no case against him, not at present, anyway. Aggie's friend knows about him, but, as he said, they can't pin anything on to him; they've been tryin' for a long time. But he's got to be caught in the act. You understand?'

'Yes' – she nodded at him – 'I understand. Oh . . . oh, Ben, I . . . I don't want to leave, I mean' – there was a break in her voice now – 'I don't want to go away. I . . . I love it here; and . . . and I keep everything clean, don't I?' She turned towards Aggie, who had to turn away and look towards the fireplace.

It was Ben who answered for her, saying, 'Aggie knows that. You've got the place like a little palace, or a big palace.' He grinned now. 'It's never been so clean in its life. You're a marvellous worker; and what's more, you make the best currant buns I've ever tasted. Oh, love.' He now put out a hand and stroked her cheek. 'I'll miss you; we'll all miss you. But you see, you'll come home for the holidays, Easter and Christmas; and they have holidays in the summer an' all, don't they, Aggie?'

Aggie mumbled something in her throat; then, hastily pulling herself up from the couch, she said, 'Well, now we all know where we stand, so let's eat. I've never had a bite since mornin',' which made Ben exclaim on a laugh, 'I can't believe that. Never! Can you?' He looked down on the bent head, but there was no response from Millie. And now he put his hand on her hair and stroked it, saying, 'It'll be all right. You'll see, it'll be all right. And you'll be what they call educated. Oh aye, and you'll come home and you'll cock a snoot at us.'

'*I never will. I never will.*' The tear-stained face was turned up towards him now. 'I'll never turn my nose up at *you*, and *never* at Mrs Aggie. *Never!*'

'No, I know you won't, me dear. That's one thing I'm sure of. But come on, set the table. Here's another one that's as hungry as a hunter. We'll leave the tea till after, to wash the chitterlings down. I love chitterlings, don't you?'

'Not very much.'

'Go on with you! Go on! the dish is in the pantry. Go and bring it.'

He let her leave the room before going across to Aggie, who was standing now looking down into the fire, and he patted the back of her shoulder, saying, 'You're doin' the best thing, Aggie, the only thing. That kind of education will take her back likely to what she was; I mean, what she could have been. 'Cos you know somethin'?' He bent his head forward and whispered now, 'She hasn't got past the "bloody old cow stage" completely. The other day I heard her come out with a bloody. When Laddie kicked over a bucket of mash, she said, "You bloody silly donkey." '

Aggie turned quickly towards him now, saying, '*She didn't!*'

'She did.'

'Well' – she straightened her broad shoulders – 'perhaps everything's turning out for the best then. Let's pray to God it is, anyway.'

'Oh Aggie, that's a daft thing to say. As if He'd have any time for us with the mob of Holy Joes He's got to see to. You might as well hope to get manure from a rockin' horse's backside as help from Him.'

Her hand came out and she thrust him backwards on to the settle.

And that's how Millie saw them when she entered the kitchen again, carrying the plate of chitterlings: the two people she cared for most, and who were about to lose her, laughing their heads off.

The queer feeling came over her, that choking feeling in her throat which she experienced in the night, when she was lying awake trying to recall and piece together dim, fleeting memories of another time in which she had lived, when things had been both happy and sad, when angry broken sentences would not meet and so explain the odd pictures that formed in her mind. It was then that the lump in her throat would break and spill the tears from her eyes and cause her to make choking sounds which she did not try to prevent, knowing they would not penetrate Mrs Aggie's deep snoring.

But the sound she now made in her throat brought both Aggie and Ben's eyes on her, and as she turned and fled from the room and Ben made to go after her, Aggie's voice halted him, saying firmly, 'Leave her be! She'll cry over more than that before she's finished.'

2

The House of Christ the Saviour was situated in the better-class district of Benton Fields. Aggie had passed the grounds many times and noticed that the stone wall was topped with broken glass and that there was a double wooden gate with an iron-bell pull attached to its side. She'd had no idea what the house looked like, until she was going through that wooden gate when, holding Millie by the hand, she espied it in the distance.

The nun who admitted them appeared to be covered from head to foot apart from her eyes, nose, and mouth, for after she had bolted the gate behind them she tucked her bare hands into her sleeves, then led the way up a gravel path, on either side of which a lawn extended as far as a further high, stone wall, its top also embedded with glass. Judging by the front of it, the house was quite large, for it showed three windows each side of the front door, the same above them, and a row of small windows jutting out from the roof.

Without a word, the nun ushered them through the broad, thick oak door and into a tiled hall, there to be confronted by a statue of the Virgin Mary with the Child in her arms, and above her, on the wall, a large crucifix hanging at such an angle it appeared that Christ's bent head was viewing Himself as a child in His mother's arms.

There were numerous doors leading from the hall, and the nun approached one, knocked, and when bidden to enter, she thrust open the door, stood aside and proclaimed in a low voice scarcely above a whisper, 'Mrs Winkowski, Reverend Mother.'

It was so seldom that Aggie heard herself addressed by her surname that she turned and looked at the nun, but the woman's eyelids were lowered as if in shame; then she inclined her head towards the woman sitting behind the desk before turning and closing the door quietly behind her.

'Sit down, Mrs Winkowski.'

Aggie recalled that Constable Fenwick had said that the Mother Superior, as she was called, was a bit of a foreigner, half French, he imagined, but a nice woman for all that, and very holy.

Aggie sat down on the wooden chair and drew Millie close to her side as the woman at the far side of the desk smiled gently at her, saying, 'I am very pleased to meet you, Mrs Winkowski. I understand you wish to put your ward in the care of the house.' She did not say, in my care, but added, 'Which will be in God's care, too. How old is she?' She looked down at the sheet of paper on her desk. 'Ah yes; you are ten years old, Millie, aren't you?'

'Yes; I am ten years old, but only lately.'

The tone of the voice seemed to surprise the Mother Superior just the slightest, and she said, 'You have a clear speaking voice, child. That is good; you will be open to education. Which school did you attend? Was it the Church of England Sunday School?'

'Yes, partly.' Millie nodded towards the woman. 'But that was only on a Sunday. Mrs Aggie' – she turned and glanced at Aggie – 'paid for me to go to the penny school.'

'Oh, was that the Wesleyan or Methodist? It wasn't a Catholic school, was it?'

'No, ma'am; it wasn't a Catholic school, it was the Methodist.'

'Oh, yes, yes.' The Mother Superior was now addressing Aggie. 'So she knows nothing whatever about religion?'

'Well, I wouldn't say that, ma'am. The Methodists preach religion and so does the Church of England.'

'Yes. Yes, of course; but I mean the Catholic religion.'

'No, nothing. Why should she? I mean, how could she? She wasn't brought up a Catholic to my knowledge.'

'You, I understand, have been her guardian for two years?'

'Yes, that's right.'

'And I'm sure you found her a very biddable little girl?' She now turned her smile on Millie, but she received no answering smile, only a stare from what she thought were those very odd grey eyes. A very odd-looking child altogether. Too beautiful for her own good. Oh, yes, from what Father Dolan had said and through information he had got from Constable Fenwick, much too beautiful for her own good. Well, she would have protection here. No sin would reach her in this house. And her next words went on to express this when she said to Aggie, 'Well, you can rest easy, Mrs Winkowski, your ward will be well looked after. You need have no fear that she will come in contact with any intruders. And I think you will agree it will be to the best advantage of all if the holidays were curtailed. You yourself may come and visit her for an hour once a month. Don't you think this is a wise plan?'

She was talking now as if the child were not present, but the child was present, and she spoke up: 'An hour a month? Oh, that's awful. And you promised there would be holidays.' She was looking at Aggie now, and Aggie said, 'Well, there will be holidays, dear, there will be holidays;' then turning

88

to the Mother Superior, added firmly, 'She'll have to come on a holiday three times a year, otherwise it's no go.'

'Oh well, it's your responsibility, Mrs Winkowski, when she's out of our care. The only thing is, I want to reassure you that she will be perfectly safe here. And of course she will be mixing with a very good class of pupil.'

'I understand that all right.' Aggie's tone was aggressive now. 'But understand, from my side, that I'd like to see her once a fortnight, if it's just for an hour, and that whatever holidays the other bairns have, she's got to have the same. Is that understood?'

There was a long pause before the Mother Superior said, 'Yes, if that's how you wish it, Mrs Winkowski.'

'Yes, ma'am, that's how I wish it, because it'll be me that'll be payin' the fees, won't it? Ten and six a week is a deal of money, indeed it is, don't you think?'

Mother Francis stared at the enormously fat and none too clean woman. This is what came of dealing with the common herd. It was hard to remember that God had made them, too, and that He begged for leniency for them. Inwardly praying that she might be able to show her piety and understanding, she said, 'Yes, I'm sure it must mean a lot to you. But, you know, real education never comes cheaply. And then the child has to be fostered, fed, and provided with a school habit and hood, besides night attire. Did you ever go to school, Mrs Winkowski?' God hadn't fully maintained His help to keep condescension from her tone or to prepare her for the answer when it came: 'Yes, I went to school, ma'am. I started at the early age of five, and I was taught until I was ten, and all day at that. And from then on I read. I could repeat the catechism for you from beginnin' to end, and chunks of the Bible. But perhaps I've been misinformed, like, for I understand you don't read the Bible.'

'Yes, I'm afraid you *have* been misinformed, at least in some parts, Mrs Winkowski.' The tone was stiff now. 'Those who can understand the Bible are allowed to read it, but there are passages that could be misinterpreted by the unintelligent or those of simple understanding.'

'Oh, aye; it's not good to let people know about human nature, is it? And that the so-called Holy men were not above ... '

The Mother Superior didn't need to check Aggie's flow, she did it herself, saying, 'Well, this one here' – she now thumbed towards Millie – 'I'd like to bet she's read the Bible from beginnin' to end, an' many other books besides. We get all kinds thrown into our yard, you know.' Then she couldn't help but add, 'It's amazing how educated some of the ignorant people are. Surprising. Surprising.'

The Mother Superior knew it was time to end this interview, so now she stood up, saying, 'Well, Mrs Winkowski, I'm sure you can leave your charge with us with an easy mind. And I shall look forward to giving you a good report when you next visit us in a' – she paused – 'fortnight's time. Say three o'clock in the afternoon a fortnight today. Will that suit you?'

Aggie, too, was on her feet and her voice was much lower now as she said, 'Aye, it'll suit me.' Then turning to Millie, whose expression almost broke her down and gave her the urge to take her by the hand and run from this place, only her good sense stopped her; and bending down, she put her arms around the child and when she felt the tightness of the embrace and the pressure of the thin body against her belly, it was only with an effort she stopped the tears from flowing. But they were in her voice as she whispered down to her, 'It'll be all right. It'll be all right. And ... and if you don't like it, we'll think of something else. You've just got to tell me. D'you hear? You've just got to tell me.'

When the arms reached up and her head bent to the face, for the first time she kissed and was kissed. It was too much. Almost thrusting the child away, she turned and stamped from the room, banging the door behind her; and, had not the Mother Superior moved quickly round the table and caught Millie's hand, the child would have followed her.

'Come, my dear, it will be all right. Sit down. She's upset; and I suppose naturally, she seems very fond of you. Were you fond of her?'

'Fond?' Millie's lids were blinking, and her lips were licking up the salt tears as she brought out, 'I ... I love her. And Ben.'

'Ben? Who is Ben?'

'He is the man who works there, lives with her. She ... she took him in when he was a little boy.'

'Oh, she's a good soul.'

'She's lovely.'

Lovely? That half-washed, great hulk of a woman? Maybe she was quite intelligent; but she was no more so than were quite a number of the poor she already knew. Yet, what was she thinking, poor? when she could apparently afford to pay the fees for this child. Obviously there was money in rags. But she had to admit that this child was of a different type altogether: her voice, her manner suggested a refined type of background. She'd have to find out more about her. The only thing Father Dolan had been able to tell her was that her mother had died of a fever soon after arriving in the town; he himself had learned this from the constable. Apparently there were no relatives, the father, too, being dead.

Again she rang the bell, impatiently this time, and the nun who appeared was contrite, saying, 'I'm sorry, Reverend Mother; I ... I had to show her out. She was agitated; she was walking across the lawn instead of to the gate.'

91

'It's all right. It's all right, Sister Aloysius. What is your class doing?'

'I left them sewing, Reverend Mother.'

'Well, we have a new member of our family. Her name is Millie Forester. Isn't that right?' She was looking down on Millie now, and Millie answered, 'Yes, that is my name . . . Millie Forester.' And the tone of the voice seemed to surprise Sister Aloysius as much as it had done the Mother Superior. And the sister was further surprised when, holding out a hand to Millie, it was not taken, but, instead, the child began to walk out before her, only to be brought to a stop by the nun saying, 'You must always ask Mother Superior if you may leave her presence. You say, "May I go now, Mother Superior?"'

'Why? She . . . she knew I was leaving the room.'

The nun and her superior exchanged glances; then Mother Francis, with a small inclination of her head, gave the nun leave to take this very awkward child away.

If the Mother Superior and the nun were thinking the child was odd, it was nothing to what Millie was thinking about them and her introduction to the school and its inmates.

3

Everything that happened to Millie during that first week in the House of Christ the Saviour she objected to. She discovered there were seventeen pupils, ranging in age from six to twelve, and that they were housed in two so-called dormitories, which were divided by panels into cubicles, each being about twice the area of its narrow iron bed, just enough to hold a chest of drawers and leaving standing space in which to undress. There was no chair. And that first night she experienced how one undressed for bed and how one was expected to lie. Sister Mary saw to that. Having been told to strip off her clothes, even her shift, without looking at her body, and don a long, unbleached, calico nightdress, she was then told how she must lie in bed, straight down, her hands by her sides. And when she protested she never lay like that and had proceeded to demonstrate how she did lie, crossing her legs and pulling her knees up, she had let out a high squeal when the side of Sister Mary's hard hand came across her knees in a whacking thump. For a moment she had lain stunned, then had vowed to herself she would be out and away by the next morning. It didn't matter about that evil man with the smiling face;

she would go to the police herself and tell them what he meant to do.

She knew she wouldn't sleep; moreover, she was hungry. That had been an awful tea they'd had at five o'clock; two slices of bread and fat, a slab of hard cake and a bowl of milk; then nothing else, only a drink of water, if they wanted one, before they came to bed, and it only half-past seven. And then there was that chapel and the kneeling. No, she couldn't stand it; and she wouldn't sleep. No, she wouldn't sleep . . .

She was startled out of her wits by the clanging of a loud bell being rung over her head, and then somebody shouting in the dormitory: 'Up! Up! Up!'

She was sitting in a daze on the edge of the bed when a head came round the partition, saying, 'You had better put a move on else you'll get scalped.'

'What?'

'Hurry up! Get into your clothes, all except your dress. Put on the cloak.' The hand came round now and thumbed to a hook on the wall. 'You've got to wash.'

She didn't hurry getting into her clothes, although she felt cold, and so she was last in the line of children to scramble down the stone stairs and into a room with a linoleum-covered floor. Along the length of one side there were also cubicles; along the opposite side were narrow benches, on each of which was a basin of cold water, also a piece of blue-mottled soap, with a rough towel hanging from a nail in the wall above the basin.

Very intimate sounds were coming from the cubicles, but it wasn't until the girl who had beckoned her earlier on came out of one of them and pointed to another where the door was open, and whispered harshly, 'Don't you want to go?' that she realised, Yes; yes, she did want to go. But dear! dear! In front of all these girls? Yet each cubicle had a door, although she noticed there was no bolt on the inside.

94

When she came out to the sound of splashing and spluttering, she made her way to the end bowl, and there she washed her face and hands; but again she was last in the line to run up the stairs and finish her dressing.

When there came, in the distance, the sound of another bell ringing, the girl from the next cubicle actually came in and tugged her out into the room, whispering, 'You've got to line up!' Having got her into the line the girl glanced at her and whispered, 'What's your name?'

'Millie.'

'Mine's Annabel, Annabel Kirkley. Stick with me; but watch out for Mabel Nostil, that's her at the end with the black hair. She sucks up. How old are you?' This question came out of the side of her mouth and Millie, quick to catch on, muttered, 'Ten.'

'I'm nearly eleven.'

'Quiet!'

The command was bellowed. 'Get moving!' The voice was thick Irish. Millie remembered it from the previous evening. This nun had read passages of some sort to them but Millie had been unable to make out half of what she had said.

The children marched down the stairs, the nun coming behind, and in the hall they met up with the older girls and, now forming two files, they walked, hands joined as if in prayer, slowly along a corridor, and into the chapel.

The chapel was a large household room. At one end was an altar; and to the side a group of statuary of the Holy Family, on the other stood a plaster saint arrayed in a brown habit. He could have been anybody, one of the hundreds of saints; but, later, Annabel informed her that he was known among the girls as Mr Billy Brown.

Millie thought that they would never cease praying. She didn't know what they were praying about. She was tired of kneeling, listening to their voices droning on: 'Our Father who art in heaven, hallowed be Thy name', and 'Hail Mary, full of grace', which was all she could make out of the second bit, because what followed was just a mumble.

She was ready to be lulled asleep by the monotonous chant when they all stood up and repeated, 'God the Father, God the Son, and God the Holy Ghost.' She'd often wondered about the Holy Ghost, and now wondered further if Mr Dickens's stories had any connections with Him. She liked Mr Dickens's stories.

She was surprised still further when more prayers had to be said before they could start their breakfast: 'Bless us, O Lord, and these Thy gifts which we are about to receive from Thy bounty. Through Christ our Lord. Amen.'

Ben knew a number of Grace before meals, and they were all funny. This one certainly wasn't.

A large dollop of thick porridge was placed before her, and a nun came round and poured a minute amount of milk over it. There was no sugar on it, but it tasted of salt. Then followed a slice of bread with half a sausage lying across it. She rather enjoyed that. The hot drink was supposed to be tea but tasted awful. Then more prayers: 'Thank You, O Lord, for this Thy gift of precious food. May we be worthy of it this day. Amen.'

Following breakfast, she stuck tight to Annabel. It was upstairs again, and now twenty-past eight, and she was informed by her apparent new friend that they had to join a small team to clean the toilets, which meant bringing the buckets downstairs, emptying them in the larger buckets arrayed along the wall by a side door; then wash out each utensil under a pump and return it to its particular cubicle.

Following this ritual, she was separated from Annabel while waiting for it to be decided which class she would attend first.

So it was a short time later she found herself under the hard eyes of Sister Mary, the large nun she remembered from last night, and her very hard hand. She it was who took the reading, writing, and arithmetic, but, of course, not until after more prayers.

Millie was two hours under Sister Mary, and during this time she learned that the nun did not always bother to use her hand, she also used a ruler that seemed as flexible as rubber, for when it hit knuckles it bounced back from them.

When the ruler first came in contact with Millie's knuckles she actually cried back at the startled sister, 'Don't do that! I have done nothing wrong. My sums are correct.'

The nun's eyes seemed to be popping out of her head as she again wielded the ruler. This time it caught Millie across the wrist, and when she reacted by rising from her seat in an effort to leave the room, she found herself thrust back with such force that her head bobbed on her shoulders. Then the big face was brought down to hers and the words came between small misshapen teeth: 'Do we understand each other now? Eh, miss?' she demanded. 'No, your sum wasn't wrong, but you are writing instead of printing. Do you understand me? I want your work printed. There's plenty of time to show off your handwriting when you've doubled your age. You understand?'

She didn't quite, but what she did understand was that she hated this woman, and the thought momentarily came to her that that man wouldn't surely have been as bad as this mean-faced nun.

At ten-thirty, Sister Mary left the class and Sister Monica took her place. And now there was a new form of prayer. It was called Scripture and Bible stories.

Millie did not care much for Sister Monica either. She was sarcastic: when she herself was first asked a question, and she answered it, the woman made game of how she spoke. But she did not retaliate: she was too upset, almost confused at her previous treatment to even pay attention.

Sister Monica stayed with them for half an hour. Sister Aloysius followed. She was small. She, too, was Irish, but she had a soft voice and a kind face: her job was to teach sewing and singing. This was to be a singing lesson, and she wrote the words of a hymn, in print of course, on a blackboard. Then, taking a funny little instrument, she struck her desk with it. It went 'Ping!' and then the children began to sing.

Millie found this half hour soothing. When a bell rang the singing immediately stopped; and there were more prayers. At twelve o'clock the class was dismissed, and there followed a rush for the toilets and ablutions. Ten minutes were allowed for this.

Dinner consisted of pea soup, which Millie found quite nice – she could taste there had been some kind of pork boiled in the liquid – followed by a meat pudding. There was quite a good helping of pudding but only a tiny piece of meat. However, with the two medium-sized potatoes and a spoonful of carrots, she found this also quite to her liking.

After dinner, they were all marched out to the back garden, which was similar to the front, where they could walk about or play catch ball, but were not allowed to stand and talk to each other.

School restarted at one'clock, with more prayers. These went on for fifteen minutes, again under the hard gaze of Sister Mary. But at a quarter past one Sister Benedicta took over. She taught geography, but it seemed that there was only one country in the world and that was Ireland. Nevertheless, she had a quiet voice, and Millie could put up with her. She was later informed by Annabel that she was known as Body Smell because she had to empty the slops into the cesspit. They did that for their sins, she said, a kind of penance. But it seemed that Sister

Benedicta must sin a lot because she always seemed to get the dirty jobs.

It should transpire that twice a week those who cared could learn to cook; but apparently Millie herself was to be given no choice; she was sent, with other five girls, to the kitchen at three o'clock and, there, came under the influence of Sister Cecilia, to whom God had given a nice nature and a light pair of hands with pastry. It was the time spent with this woman that became instrumental in deterring Millie from making her escape from this prayer-ridden, ignorant set of women, from which Mother Francis must be excluded. As Sister Cecilia was to say to her, one could live without reading, writing, or arithmetic, sewing, singing or geography; and yes – there would be a twinkle in her eye – with some, even without the good God; but one couldn't live without food and without those who knew how to make it appetising to the tongue.

After her first visit to Millie, Aggie returned home somewhat perplexed, and she said to Ben, 'I don't know quite what to make of her. She hates the place. As far as I can understand she's made only one friend; but that would be enough if it's a good 'un. But there's a sister there called Mary she would like to strangle. She said so. And you know something? She showed me the marks on the back of her knuckles and her wrist where that bitch had walloped her with a rod of some sort, right from the first day.'

'Well, why don't you bring her home? You'll find some place different from that. That was your friend's recommendation, wasn't it?'

'Don't forget it was yours an' all. Now don't forget that.'

'Aye. Yes, you're right. But it shouldn't be allowed, the hammerin'.'

'Oh, but I had to laugh, or nearly so, for you daren't laugh in there. There was a sister watching us all the time, and when we went to walk out into the garden she said it wasn't allowed. "Well, whoever told you it isn't allowed, tell them to come and tell me," I said, and I took the child outside. It was there she told me about this sister and showed me her hand. "Don't worry, Mrs Aggie," she said; "I'll get me own back on her before I leave this place, you'll see, if it's only kicking her shins." And she will an' all, she'll do it.'

Ben started to laugh now. 'You know, you can't believe she's the same child that was so polite a couple of years ago. She got on your nerves then, didn't she? Remember when she used to stand there and madden you with her politeness and that voice of hers. She's still got the voice but the politeness has slipped away a bit.' . . .

. . . Almost at that very moment Millie was standing before the Mother Superior, who was voicing that very word, politeness. 'You have been impolite to Sister Mary because she chastised you for taking your visitor out into the garden. She also tells me that you are unruly. What you must learn, child, is obedience. We must all learn obedience, obedience to God's will. And it should happen that it's God's will that you have been sent to us for protection and education. So, don't let me, ever again, hear that you have been impolite to any of the sisters. And, don't, don't' – she held up her hand, her voice holding a note of authority now – 'give me your opinion of the matter. And that's another thing you must learn: you should speak only when you're spoken to, unless you wish to make a serious request. You may go.'

Millie's visit to the sanctum was the first of many during the weeks and months that were to follow, and all resulting from Sister Mary's reports. There was an open war going on between the child and the nun, and the class was aware of it and daily seemed to await events. In the main, it was a time of misery which unknowingly strengthened her character and

100

at the same time introduced her to a friendship which resulted in her opening her eyes to another way of life, a life that she recognised and knew she could fit into; for it was during the first summer holiday that she was invited to spend a day with Annabel at her home.

Annabel had talked so much to her parents about the beautiful girl with the long golden hair, and how she had openly stood up to Sister Mary, that it was decided to invite this child to have tea with the family. Annabel's father was the manager of Crane-Boulder's Cotton Mill. It was considered one of the advanced mills, advanced in that their employees worked only the ten-hour day and finished work at one o'clock on a Saturday. So it should happen that Mr Kirkley was at home when the guests arrived and was able to add to his surprise and not a little amazement when his daughter's friend was delivered at his door by Raggie Aggie, for Aggie had long been a known character, she and her hand-cart, and now the pony-driven flat-cart; and of course the fact that she was almost as broad as it was. He recalled tales about her, that she had at one time belonged to a respectable family of farmers; unbelievable now, for she could certainly no longer be placed in that category.

Something would have to be done about this. He had imagined the nuns to be very particular whom they took into their house as pupils. However, before the visit ended the husband and wife both admitted to being charmed with Annabel's friend, and that they could understand their daughter's feelings towards her, for the girl was not only as beautiful as Annabel had described her, but also she had the most pleasing and cultured voice. They had understood from their daughter that her parents were dead. But why, they asked of each other, should a child like that be under the care of the rag woman? Kirkley thought it was something worth looking into.

He did, and when he eventually learned that the child's mother had committed suicide and that out of compassion the rag woman had taken her into her house to save her being put in the workhouse or farmed out, again they both agreed that the rag woman had worthy motives. And so, during the holiday, Millie was again invited to tea, and on this visit she amused them, together with their other children, a twelve-year old son, and a five-year old daughter, when she gave them an imitation of the nuns, excelling herself when she touched on Sister Mary.

It was Annabel's friendship and her acceptance by the Kirkley family that really kept her in the House of Christ the Saviour, where there was no laughter except in the kitchen with Sister Cecilia and sometimes a covert smile from Sister Aloysius.

Her stay, however, ended dramatically on the last Friday of January, 1858.

It was a biting cold morning. The water in the basins had a layer of ice on them, which had to be broken before the children could wash; then, in the dining room they sat shivering, for the fire at the end of the room did not take even the chill away.

In the classroom, Sister Mary's indiscriminate wielding of the ruler caused a great deal of wincing and tears. The children had been told to write answers to what happened to Jesus in the temple: What did He do there? and what did His parents say to Him when they found Him?

For Millie, the lesson needed no thinking, for the sister had practically told them what to say, but she wove a story round it as if the incident were happening in Benton Fields at the present time. Unfortunately she made a mistake of naming the church where Jesus was found as St George's, which happened to be a Church of England edifice.

After the monitor had gathered up the papers and placed them on the small, square, wooden table that acted as the sister's desk, the class sat quiet, waiting anxiously for the verdict, a tick or a large cross, the while automatically mumbling Hail Marys. At no time in the day must there be an idle moment or a silent one; any spare time must be filled with prayer.

The sharp sound of Sister Mary's hand banging down on the square of writing paper stopped the chanting. She was yelling now, 'Stupid! Stupid! A waste of good paper. Come out here, you!'

If the finger had not been pointed, all the class would have known who was being called to face the fearsome sister, and when Millie stood by the side of the nun's desk, the sheet of paper was immediately thrust into her face with the demand, 'What do you mean by that? A waste of paper! A waste of good paper. Rubbish! Rubbish! Trying to be clever. Rubbish! And that hair.' The woman flicked her hand and knocked one of the long plaits from Millie's shoulder as she continued her tirade: 'I've told you, haven't I? I told you yesterday, one plait and at the back, and tight. Stand still, girl! Turn round!' And without giving Millie time to obey, she yelled again, 'Turn round! Turn round! girl,' and swung her round by the shoulders, and while holding her with one hand she ripped the pieces of tape from the end of each plait, before she tore at the hair until it hung in uneven strands; then she almost lifted Millie from the floor as, using both hands now, she drew the strands together and began forming them into a tight rope-like plait.

This done, she whipped up a piece of tape, which she tied some inches from the bottom; then, while still holding on to the hair with one hand, her other hand shot out and pulled open a drawer from which she grabbed a pair of large scissors.

103

There was a gasp from the children and a high scream from Millie as the scissors went snip, snip, snip. Flinging herself round and seeing at least three inches of her hair lying on the wooden floor, she yelled, *'How dare you! How dare you!'* And now she did what she had promised herself she would do, and lifted her foot and aimed it at the nun's shin. That it had made contact was evident, for Sister Mary let out a cry, a weird sound that was rather a yell not a scream. Then again she was grabbing the plait, screeching now, 'I'll cut it off. Right to the scalp. Right to the scalp. *You're wicked! Bad.'*

Some of the children were screaming as they watched the tussle going on between the nun and the girl whom they secretly admired and envied because she wasn't afraid of the dreaded Sister Mary.

'You're evil. Evil. You want shriving.' The nun had hold of the plait again, while endeavouring amid her screaming to bring her other hand, holding the scissors, down to finish its work. But Millie, her body twisted, her two arms extended, was gripping the woman's wrists while being tossed to and fro in the struggle, and she, too, was screaming, *'You won't! You won't!'*

Whether it was Millie's infuriated strength that caused the woman's grasp on the scissors to slacken, or that she changed her tactics and meant to direct the scissors towards the child's face, couldn't be known, but Millie grabbed at the open blades and, managing to twist them round, consciously or by accident drove one of the blades into the nun's arm.

As the scream rent the room the door was thrust open and Sister Monica and Sister Aloysius rushed in, just in time to stop the nun's hands going round Millie's throat.

The room was in an uproar, the children huddled together and all screaming. The big nun's arms were flailing while the other two attempted to hold her. It was Sister Aloysius who turned her head and cried to one of the bigger girls, *'Go and fetch Reverend Mother!* Take the children. Take them with you. Out! Out!'

All the children, except Millie, scrambled from the room: she had staggered over to a side wall and was leaning against it, her hands hanging by her side, her mouth wide open to let her gasping breath free.

'I'll kill her! I will. I will. She should be dead. She's wicked! Wicked.' The nun was screaming now at the top of her voice; then for a moment she became still and silent as she looked at a trickle of blood flowing down over her fingers; and she now screeched again. 'Look! Blood! Blood! She's evil.'

'Quiet. Quiet, dear.' Sister Aloysius was wiping the hand now with a piece of rough linen she had taken from a pocket in her habit. 'It's all right. Mother will soon be here. Be quiet now. Be quiet.'

'Never! Never! She must be locked up. She's bad, wicked. And her hair shorn. I'm going to shear her hair. I am; I am. She was born evil. Father Dolan told Reverend Mother all about her, all about her. She's from the dregs. Her mother was on the streets. I heard him. She took her life . . . evil. I spoke to God. Two inches at a time, He said, until she is cropped; the vanity is in her hair. Pride, all in her hair. It's got to come off.' And as her voice ended on another high scream the door opened and the Mother Superior came in. Her voice was calm as she said to Sisters Monica and Aloysius. 'Leave go of her.'

'But, Mother.'

She turned her cold stare on Sister Monica, saying, 'Do as I bid.'

They did as they were ordered, and when the arms began to flail again Mother Francis brought her hand in a resounding blow across Sister Mary's face, sending her backwards against the wall, where she stood, quiet now, her mouth agape and froth around her lips. Stepping back

105

and looking at the other two nuns, the Mother Superior said, 'Take her to her cell.'

Almost as if leading a child, they took the woman from the room, and the Mother Superior, herself on the point of leaving, turned and looked towards where Millie was still standing riveted to the spot. It was as if she hadn't been aware of the girl's presence, but she said, 'Stay where you are, child. Don't move,' and then went out.

How long Millie stood alone, she didn't know. There was a continuous whirling of thoughts in her head: Was she evil? Had her mother been evil? What did she mean, her mother had been on the streets? She had heard that term before. It was in some way connected with bad things. But had her mother been evil? And so, was she evil? She wanted Mrs Aggie. *Oh, Mrs Aggie, Mrs Aggie.*

When the door opened and Sister Cecilia came in, still wearing her kitchen apron, the whirling thoughts ceased and she said, 'Oh, Sister.'

Sister Cecilia held out a hand towards her, saying, 'Come child, come,' then led her out of the room, through the corridor, upstairs, and into her cubicle. She did not immediately help her to get her things together, but sat on the side of the bed and drew Millie towards her, saying, 'It's a sorry day, child. It's a sorry day;' then leaning towards her, she said very quietly now, 'I'm not blaming you, my dear. I'm not blaming you. It is a strange thing, and you will find it more so in our way of life, that some people cannot stand the sight of beauty. It is a joy they're missing, but it is never revealed to them. Poor dear Sister Mary has never known joy. You must forgive her.'

The nun looked away from Millie now and towards the partition as she said in a voice little above a mutter, 'He bids us come, and if at first we don't obey Him, His voice is insistent. "Come. Come, my child. You owe me your life,"

106

He says. "Let Me show you how to live it," but then once you have given Him your life He becomes distant; you have to struggle to touch Him. Yet He said to me, "Cecilia, you have two blessings, you love beauty and cooking. What more could you desire?" '

Turning to look at Millie again, she ended, 'But one always wants more: just to see His face in the night, not in plaster, in the flesh. But I tell myself it will come. God's will be done.'

She put out a hand and touched Millie's cheek now, saying softly, 'I ramble on, child. You don't understand what I'm saying, yet some of my words might remain with you, for I think you are old enough to understand what I am about to say to you now. Resist evil, my dear, the evil that men do. Do you understand me? Resist the evil that men do.'

Millie didn't really understand. Her mind still wanted to whirl, but she would remember the words, 'Resist the evil that men do.' And on the thought there came into her mind the picture of the thin-faced man.

'Well now, child; let us pack up your things and let us be ready when your guardian comes. She is being sent for.'

'I . . . I to go home?' She slipped off the edge of the bed as if she had been injected with new life.

'Yes. Yes, my dear, you have to go. And I am very sorry, because you have the makings of a splendid cook. You won't forget what I have taught you, will you?'

'No, Sister; because I love cooking. No, I won't forget, ever. Nor you.'

As she went to put her arms around the nun a gentle hand pressed her back, and the voice, so gentle, said, 'I . . . I understand your feelings, child; and I, too, feel . . . but . . . but,' and the voice became rather thick as she ended, 'we will not demonstrate them.'

After the bass hamper that had held her belongings was refilled and strapped, Sister Cecilia said, 'Sit there quiet, my

107

child, until they send for you.' She paused, and her fingers lightly touched Millie's cheek, as she said, 'My prayers will go with you and I shall remember you always.'

'Oh, Sister, I'm sorry, I'm sorry. I . . . I mean . . . well, I mean, I'm not sorry to leave the school, leave here, but I'm sorry to leave you, and I wish I could see you again. I . . . I won't be able to, will I?'

'No, my child, you won't; but you will always remain in my memory. And you will remember my words, won't you? Beware of the evil that men do.'

'Yes. Yes, Sister.'

'Goodbye, my child; and God be with you always.'

Millie sat again on the edge of the bed, her head bowed deep on her chest, the tears running unheeded down her face. Beware of the evil that men do. Beware of the evil that men do. Yes, she would remember those words, and always remember Sister Cecilia.

4

Millie had been home for nearly three months when she received a letter from Annabel. It was the first communication she'd had with her since the day she left the convent ignominiously and in dire disgrace. And during that time the house had become brighter in all ways, not only through her cleaning and her presence but also through her cooking.

She had become expert in at least three dishes while under the tuition of Sister Cecilia: the meat pudding, a lamb stew thickened with lentils, barley, and vegetables and topped with dumplings, and, a real piece of expertise: the making of light pastry with either pig's fat or beef dripping.

From the time she returned to the house, both Aggie and Ben ate better, lived more comfortably and were happier. Yet, their frame of mind was always streaked with anxiety that caused them both to be forever on the watch. They made it a rule that she was never to be alone. If she went out of the yard, which was rarely, one or other would go with her, and they never both left the yard together.

Although their protection wasn't evident Millie was conscious of it, and there were times when she felt as hemmed in as she had done during that tortured year or more when guarded by the sisters.

Then came the letter; and she read it aloud to them:

'Dear Millie,

My mama asks if you would care to come to tea on Saturday afternoon at four o'clock. Also Mama would like to speak with your guardian about something that may be of benefit to you.

I miss you very much. I am no longer with the nuns but am to attend a day school. I have such a lot to tell you, and I'm looking forward to our meeting.

Your friend, Annabel.'

She looked from Aggie to Ben, and it was Aggie who said, 'Something that may be of benefit to you. What does she mean by that?'

Ben was grinning now as he looked at Millie, saying, 'Perhaps they're goin' to adopt you.'

'I don't want to be adopted, Ben; I've been adopted.' She smiled at Aggie; although Aggie gave her no answering smile, but just said, 'Well, the day's Thursday. We'll have to wait an' see what the benefit's goin' to be . . . Would you like to go to school again?'

Millie did not answer straightaway; then, thoughtfully, she said, 'I thought I might like to go to the day school. I mean, like I did before. Yes' – she nodded now – 'yes, I think I'd like more schooling.'

'Why?'

She turned towards Ben as she answered him, 'Well, because I know there's a lot to learn.'

'Can't see that. You can read a newspaper from beginning to end and you can write better than those fellas who keep the thing goin'. As for talkin', I would say there are few who

110

could talk better. That's when' – he poked his head forward, a mischievous grin on his face now – 'you don't let drop one of those naughty words; you know, like you did yesterday.'

'I didn't. I didn't swear. Well . . . I mean—' She shook her head, then looked at Aggie, saying now, 'If you didn't say it so often, I wouldn't either.'

'What's this I say so often?'

'Damn and blast your eyes.'

'I don't say that very often.'

Both Ben and Millie now began to laugh, and, getting to his feet, Ben said, 'Know thyself, woman. Know thyself. Anyway, if you're goin' to tea with the toffs you'd better get scrubbed down and pick out some decent clothes.'

'There was nothing mentioned in that letter about me havin' tea.'

'Well, if you're not invited *I* won't stay either. But as Ben says, put on some nice things. There's . . . there's the print frock I let out that fits you. It's nice. And there's that nice cape you got last week.'

'Shut up! both of you.' Aggie pulled herself up from the chair. 'Why don't you strip me down and go over me with a scrubbin' brush?'

'That's an idea.' Ben's expression was serious as he nodded towards Millie, and she answered him, 'Yes; yes, it is. But we'll have to do it with cold water and the yard broom.'

'That's enough! D'you hear? That's enough.' When Aggie swung round with a lightness that always denied her heavy bulk and made hastily for the door, Millie flew after her and, jumping in front of her, threw her arms around her waist as far as they would go, crying, 'I'm sorry. It wasn't nice. I was just trying to be funny, like Ben. You're . . . you're so clean underneath, and nobody knows except me. I'm sorry. I'm sorry. And I love you. Oh, I do love you.'

'Shut up and be quiet. Stop your jabber. And leave go of me.'

111

As Aggie pulled the arms from around her waist she glanced to the side, for Ben was no longer in the room. 'Come here,' she said as she walked back to the fireplace. And when again Millie stood close by her side she looked down on her and said, 'Never try to be funny at other people's expense. Ben can do it because . . . well, he's a man, and one expects it from a man. But with a woman or girl, no, unless it's against yourself. You can be funny against yourself . . . you know what I mean, belittlin' yourself like, but don't be funny belittlin' anybody else. You understand?'

Millie's voice was breaking as she said, 'Oh, yes, yes, Mrs Aggie, I understand. Oh, yes, I understand, and I'll never do it again.'

'Oh' – Aggie now wagged her head – 'be as funny as you like, but don't level it against anybody to hurt them. That's unless they've deserved it, or done something bad. Oh, what am I yammerin' on about? Go on, get on with your work. You were goin' to make a tart, weren't you? I'll tell you what else you can do; you can make half a dozen or so of those currant buns of yours and take them with you on Saturday as a kind of present for the lady.'

It was as much as Millie could do to check herself from saying, 'Oh, I don't think I should do that. I mean, they've got a cook.' She had already hurt this dear, kind, woman. And to point out to her now that she didn't know the right thing to do when visiting people like the Kirkleys would be, in a way, against the advice she had just given her, although it wasn't to do with talking; more like behaviour and deportment or some such. Well, whatever it was, she knew she'd have to bake her little cakes and present them to Mrs Kirkley on Saturday.

The maid who opened the door to them could not take her eyes off the great fat woman in the biscuit straw hat with big cloth roses on its brim, and the cape that just covered her shoulders and showed an expanse of blue cotton bosom, the like she had never seen before. As she was about to say, 'I'll tell the mistress you've come,' there was a scampering of feet on the stairs, and Annabel almost threw herself on Millie, crying, 'Oh! how lovely! How lovely to see you!'

Millie was smiling widely at her friend as she proffered the coloured plate, saying, 'I . . . I baked some currant buns for you.'

'They're for your mother, love.' Aggie was smiling brightly at Annabel.

'Oh, then Mama will love them. Oh! here she is. Mama, Millie has brought you a present; they're currant buns. She makes lovely cakes. I told you.'

It says much for the calibre of Mrs Kirkley that, after greeting Aggie with an inclination of her head and a smile, she looked at Millie, who was handing her the present, and said, 'Oh, thank you very much, Millie; I'm sure they'll be delightful. We must have them for tea. Jessie—' She turned towards the maid, who was standing apart and, handing her the plate, she said, 'Have these put on the table for tea, please.'

The maid took the plate from her mistress as if it were hot. Then Mrs Kirkley led the way into her drawing-room and there, after indicating that they should all be seated, she looked at Millie, saying, 'Well, isn't this nice! I'm so pleased to see you again. And how are you?'

'Very well, ma'am, very well.'

'Have you been attending school at all?'

'No; not yet; but we' – she glanced towards Aggie – 'we are thinking about it, considering it.'

'Oh, well then, that in a way will be a pity, at least for us, because the proposition that Annabel indicated in her letter is to do with a post for you.' She inclined her head deeply now; then, after a moment she turned her attention to Aggie,

113

saying, 'You see, my cousin is looking for a nursemaid to help with her six children. It would be a very good position for any young girl, and a happy one. My cousin is married to the bailiff on Mr Crane-Boulder's estate. They are the mill owners, you know.' As if by way of explanation that a cousin of hers should be married to a bailiff, she now added, 'My cousin was very young when she married. Her husband is from a good family; in fact he is distantly connected with the Crane-Boulder's family, but . . . but he was the youngest son, and you know what positions go to the younger sons.'

She held out her hand, palm upwards now, and moved her head slowly as she looked at Aggie as if she were talking to a friend who would understand that a cousin of hers had not married beneath her. And then she went on, 'They live in the grounds. Not in the lodge; it is a very nice, large house. It would have to be' – her smile widened – 'with six children, wouldn't it? Well, there it is. I'm sure that you would want to talk this over, but if you do feel you can consider it' – she was still addressing Aggie – 'I could ask my cousin to keep the position open for a week or two. In the meantime, I am sure if Millie here would like to go and see my cousin and discuss the whole situation, my husband would be delighted to provide escort.'

She did not add, He would jump at the chance of someone filling that post, so that he wouldn't be asked to take the children off Rose's hands until she is once more fixed up with someone who could manage her unruly crowd, as well as herself and the house. By the end of last year, when they had three of the children, he had been almost driven to distraction. He blamed Rose, and wouldn't have a word said against William.

Oh yes, he would take Millie there. And she, too, felt the girl would fit in. She was certainly still young enough to play

114

with children, but, in a way, she seemed to have an old head on those shoulders.

And so she smiled now as she said, 'There it is. You must, as I said, have time to think about it.'

'I would have thought there's plenty of lasses ready to jump into such jobs, ma'am, jobs of all kinds bein' scarce.'

'Yes. Yes, there are plenty of . . . girls, Mrs Winkowski, but they are not the type my cousin would appreciate. She has already experienced some. As I'm sure you know, the majority of girls seeking such posts can neither read nor write and are of such low intelligence that they have no control over the children; in fact, the children soon take advantage of them. Children are very wily, you know. So, thinking it needed someone superior who might fit the requirements of the position, I thought of Millie as a most suitable person, and decided to put the proposition to you, Mrs Winkowski. Of course, that is if you don't intend to allow her to continue with her schooling. Yet, I'm sure she will learn a lot from being in contact with my cousin and her husband, not to mention with the Crane-Boulders themselves, you know, the owners of the estate, because they socialise liberally. Ah' – she looked towards the door – 'there is the signal for tea. Would you like to come along?' . . .

They had tea, just the four of them. Mrs Kirkley ate one of Millie's buns and praised it highly; and after Annabel had eaten one, and then asked if she might have another, her mother exclaimed in mock sternness, 'Oh! Annabel. Your manners!'

It was when tea was over that Mrs Kirkley said to her daughter, 'Would you like to take Millie round the garden, dear?' And when Annabel exclaimed, 'Oh, yes, Mama,' the two girls turned towards each other before hurrying from the room. Aggie, of course, knew she was in for, what was termed, a bit of confidential chat; and she wasn't mistaken,

115

because Mrs Kirkley, without any preamble, began by saying, 'There is more than one reason why I have suggested this position for Millie. You know, Mrs Winkowski, girls will talk, and I suppose it was during one of Millie's lonely periods while under the sisters that she confided in Annabel why she had been sent to the school. It was because of her fear and your concern regarding a certain man who seemed bent on . . . well, how can one put it, except by plainly saying, abducting her. And for what purpose we won't go into. She is aware, as you yourself only too well know, that her looks are bound to attract attention, and that beautiful hair; its colour is so unusual that that alone will draw eyes to it. Well, need I point out?'

'No, you needn't, ma'am. As for the abduction business, I think we can say that's over. We've never seen hilt nor hair of that man for well over a year now. He could be gone from the town.'

'Oh yes.' The delicate eyebrows were raised. 'On the other hand, there is the possibility he couldn't. But there, you are the best judge of that. I only put it to you. By the way, do you know much about her mother?'

'No, ma'am, only that she died before her time and had been a lady's maid.'

'Oh, indeed; a lady's maid? Ah yes; likely it is from the mother that the child gets that air she possesses . . . Or was it from the father, do you think? Do you know anything about him?'

'Only that he seemed to be in a decent position, and that he died.'

'Oh. Oh.' Mrs Kirkley sat back in her chair. 'I'm so glad we've had this little talk; and it's so nice to think that she and Annabel are friends. Annabel thinks the world of her.' She did not go on to express the next thought in her mind: thank goodness Annabel was going away to school, and very soon

116

the association would be closed, for its continuance would create an impossible situation.

It was Aggie who now rose first from her chair and so bringing the conversation to an end by saying, 'Well, ma'am, I thank you for your hospitality, and also for your kindness to the child. I'll think over what you've said, and also put it to Ben. He's a sort of help and partner, and he's had part of the rearing of her from the time I took her, and his advice is always sensible. So now we must be off.'

'Of course. Of course. I'll call the girls.'

The goodbyes were said; Annabel and Millie clasped hands, but Mrs Kirkley gently prevented her daughter from seeing their guests to the gate. And perhaps it was just as well because there, on the seat of the rag cart and sitting as patiently as the pony was standing, was Ben. And from the pavement he looked a big, decently dressed young man, for his head and shoulders were well above the back of the seat.

On sight of them, he jumped down and first helped Aggie, then Millie up, and lastly squeezed himself corner-wise into the seat, took up the reins, and shouted, 'Gee up! there.' And so they made for home.

A short time later they were sitting round the table. Aggie had explained to Ben what had turned out to be the reason for their invitation to tea; and now she broke into his silence by saying, 'Well! Can't you say something?'

What he said was, 'It's not for me to say, Aggie, it's for her. Let her go and see if she fancies staying there. Ten miles out, you say, and there's a squad of kids to look after?' He turned to Millie, saying, 'How does that appeal to you: six kids, the eldest ten?'

'Oh, I wouldn't mind that, not for a time anyway. Perhaps I wouldn't like to stay there very long, because, as I said, I might want to go to school again. But,' she now smiled

117

from one to the other, 'it would be an experience; and, as Annabel told me, I'd get one and six a week and a half day off, besides a full day every month.' She made a face now as she added, 'Annabel seemed to think that was generous.'

'Well, compared to the leave they get in the big houses I suppose it is; half a day a month for some of them, and then no leave at all if they're known to come from the workhouse, or one of the settlements. Well, it seems that you'd like to go and take a look at the place and the people before you make your mind up; and I suppose that's only right. But have you thought what I'm goin' to do here, left on me own? This place'll turn into a hovel again. And what about our fancy meals, eh?'

'Oh, Mrs Aggie' – she put her hand across the table towards the plump elbow resting there – 'I won't go. As I said before, I could go to half-day school here. Yes; why not? It's a silly idea, and I'm big enough to take care of myself now . . . ' Her voice trailed off as the two pairs of eyes fixed on her and her head drooped as she said, 'That was a silly thing to say. But you could always take me and fetch me back as you did before.' She had addressed herself to Ben, and he said, 'Aye, I could. But you know something? For your own good, at least for the next year or so, I think you'd be best out of the way. And at the bottom of this one's heart' – he thumbed towards Aggie – 'I'm sure she thinks the same. And I promise you something: I won't let the house get into a hovel; I'll do a bit of cleanin' up meself. And if she would only let me have Annie round' – his thumb was wagging again – 'the place would be spotless.'

The look that Aggie fixed on him silenced his tongue but left his face in a wide grin.

Aggie rose from the chair and went into the scullery, and Ben, reaching along the table, covered Millie's hand with his own, and she turned and gazed at him.

118

There was always something comforting about Ben: she felt that she loved him as much as she did Mrs Aggie. And on the thought, she lifted the hand, the squat unusually clean hand, and held it against her cheek.

'Oh, Millie love. Millie.'

There was something in his voice that made her want to throw herself into his arms; but then she knew that Aggie wouldn't like that. Mrs Aggie wasn't for shows of affection, which, she felt, was a pity, for love should have an expression.

5

Up to the previous evening there had been questions
bandied back and forth between Aggie and Ben as to
whether, after all, it would be necessary for Millie to
take the post she had been offered. But at half-past
seven the next morning they knew they had made the
right decision. In fact, for a moment, the situation facing
Millie seemed to be God-directed when, at seven o'clock,
as soon as Ben had opened the gates, a Mrs Walton came
hurrying in.

'You haven't seen anything of our Betty, have you, Ben?'
she asked.

'Betty? No. No, Mrs Walton. Why? Is she lost?'

The woman looked around the yard as if she expected
to see her daughter emerge from one of the doors or from
behind a pile of rubbish. Then she repeated, 'Lost? Oh, aye,
she's lost. But himself said this would happen, because I
was always washin' her bloody hair and keepin' her face
scab-free, unlicing her an' the rest, instead of gettin' meself
out to work. He said it's my fault; but I did it for the
best.' And now, her hand outstretched, and with a break
in her voice, she appealed to Ben: 'Don't tell me she's

been picked up. It's been the fear of me life, because she's so wayward. Scamperin' round the market whenever I let her out of my sight. And she was bonny. You know she was bonny.'

'Aye.' Ben nodded at her. 'Aye, she was bonny, Mrs Walton. How long has she been gone?'

'Since last night. Since last night. She wasn't outside the bar waitin' for him. He always' – again the hand was expressive – 'he always goes in on his way from the mill. He gets dry, you know . . . the flax. Feels choked at times. And anyway, if he knows she's there it brings him home. And now he's in a rage. He never went in this mornin', and he's knocked on every door in Foley Street. But if they had her there, d'you think they would let him know? Now he keeps blamin' me for keepin' her clean. Being the first of the lasses, she was always his favourite; the lads didn't seem to matter. What am I gona do?'

'Have you been to the polis?'

'Oh, aye. Aye, I went to the polis. But what'll they do? Himself is right: half of them must be in the pay of the Foley Street mob. Well, it's funny, isn't it, that they never manage to find any missin' youngsters. And it's funny an' all that the dirty buggers don't go for the ragged-arsed lot that's swarmin' the place. No, they take their pick. Oh, my God! Ben, if she's gone it'll kill him. I tell you, it'll kill him. And then he'll go for one of those buggers, an' he'll do for 'em. Then what'll it be? Swingin', or Australia. And we were just gettin' on our feet, three of the lads workin' and himself bringin' it in, at least what's left after his Friday night do's. But, nevertheless, we managed. An' you know yourself, I've come every week here and set them up in different bits and pieces.'

121

She turned from him now and looked towards the house door where Millie was standing. And she stared at the girl for a full minute, before turning to Ben again and with a helpless gesture saying, 'My God! It's a wonder that one's escaped.' Then she added, with a plea in her voice again, 'You get around, Ben. And your Annie, if all tales are true, she's got a relative that's no better than she should be an' livin' nicely on it. Perhaps you could find out somethin' through her . . . would you, Ben?'

'Yes, certainly, Mrs Walton. I've got to go on an errand this mornin', but as soon as I get back, I'll . . . well, I'll do the rounds and I'll come along an' tell you. You're in Booth Court, aren't you?'

'Aye, number fifty-six. Three floors up. Ta. Thank you.' She turned now and glanced towards Millie again before hurrying from the yard. Instinctively, Millie made her way across to Ben, saying, 'Is she in trouble?' And he looked straight into her face as he answered, 'Aye, she's in trouble. Her little girl has gone missin'. You know her, Betty, the lively one; she was into everythin' in the yard here.'

Without saying anything further, Millie turned and went back into the house; and Ben followed her, there to see Aggie shambling into the room, and although her eyes looked full of sleep, their powers of discernment were indeed wide awake. 'What's up now?' she demanded.

'Little Betty Walton has gone missing,' Ben answered. He didn't say, 'He's at it again and he's getting nearer.' But after a moment's silence he said, as if casually, 'She's a scamper, that one; into every hole and corner, if I remember rightly, so she's likely stayed out late and is frightened to go home – if old man Walton had a load on she'd be introduced to the buckle end of his belt. He could be paralytic and she could bring him home, but . . . '

122

'Aye. Aye,' put in Aggie. 'But it's about time there was some breakfast on the table. And you've got a journey before you, you two, so let's get down to the business of the day. And you, Ben Smith, Jones, or Robinson, spruce yourself up, because it's among the gentry you'll be goin'.'

They had left The Courts, passed the countless rows of back-to-back houses, no cleaner, no more sanitary than the half-mile of buildings behind them. They had crossed the market, the shopping centre, passed the churches, chapels, religious meeting rooms, fighting to outdo each other and against the countless bars; even hoping through the wave of religious revival, and the example set by the Queen herself, that they would eventually withdraw sinners from the flames of hell-fire and place them in the arms of the Lord.

And then there were the mills. Everywhere you looked there were the mills: cotton mills, textile mills, grim forbidding buildings, all of them, many cheek by jowl with the slums they had created.

Then, as if a dividing line had been drawn across the outskirts of the town, the scene changed: Ben was now driving the cart past terraced houses with lace curtains at the windows, and the bath-bricked steps leading to painted front doors, with here and there a little maid scrubbing the steps, or sluicing the pavement outside the small railed gardens.

These were the homes of the upper working class, the artisans, clerical workers, shopwalkers.

They now reached what appeared to be open country, but which soon became large areas of garden, each surrounding a single house approached from the roadway through magnificent iron gates.

'Be prepared to bend your knee, and keep your mouth shut. And yes, bite your tongue.' He grinned at her.

'Well, I just might have to, mightn't I? But would you ever do it?'

'Me?' He pushed out his chest. 'Never! What you call a free soul, that's me; free as the wind.'

'Except for Mrs Aggie and the yard.'

'Don't be pert with me, miss. But aye, you're right, except for Mrs Aggie and the yard. We must never forget, mind, either you or me, if it hadn't been for Mrs Aggie and her yard, God knows where we would have been at this minute. She could easily have given me the push after her dad died, and taken on somebody . . . well, more presentable, like.'

'You're very presentable, Ben, very.' She looked him up and down now, and yes, he was very presentable. She had never seen him dressed as he was this morning. He was wearing the suit belonging to that old man who had died. Chinese Charlie had altered the lot to fit him, and he had pressed it, too, and it had made such a difference to Ben. He looked . . . well, she couldn't put a name to how he looked. She discarded handsome, yet he had such a nice face and plenty of brown hair and his upper body was so fine. It was only his legs. What a pity about his legs. If they'd only been a few inches longer; or perhaps if his upper body wasn't so big then his legs wouldn't be so noticeable. And he had a nice voice. He didn't always speak correctly, but still he had a nice voice. Everything about him was nice. She liked Ben. Yes, she liked Ben. Impulsively now, she put her hand out and laid it on his, saying quietly, 'I'm going to miss you all over again, Ben, that's if I take this place.'

He drew the pony to a stop, looked down at her hand still lying on his and said, 'You're not the only one, Millie. That place is like a dead house when you're out of it. But no matter' – his voice rose now – 'you've got to go there for a time, anyway. And you understand, don't you?'

124

'Yes. Yes, Ben, I understand. But at the same time I keep asking, Why? Why?'

'You know as well as I do.'

He had almost bawled at her; in fact, so loud was his voice that he turned instinctively, feeling he must have been overheard, and looked towards the two gates which had 'The Grange' easily discernible as part of the wrought iron. And just as instinctively lowering his voice, he said again, 'You know as well as I do. There's no need to go into it.'

'But there is.' She was hissing at him now.

He stared at her while drawing in a deep breath, which expanded his broad chest further; then he said, 'Well, if you want to know, you shouldn't look as you do; you attract the wrong kind. That's the answer, and I'm sayin' no more. So come, get down. This is the place.' He pointed to the gate.

When, a minute later, he pulled on the handle of the iron bell and it clanged loudly, the door of a small house just beyond the gates opened and a man appeared and stood looking at them for a moment before speaking. 'Well, what's your business?' he asked quietly.

'She . . . Miss Forester here is expected. She's to meet a Mrs Quinton.'

'Oh.' The man now moved his head slightly and looked at Millie; then, pointing with his forefinger, he said, 'Further along the road there's another gate. You'll come across the house half-way up the drive.' He looked beyond them to the pony and cart, then added not unkindly, 'You could get that up the drive.'

'Ta,' said Ben. 'Thanks,' said Millie. They had spoken together, then turned away, smiling.

Ben now said, 'You walk along; you might have to open the gates . . . He was quite a civil bloke, wasn't he?'

'Yes, a nice man.'

'Well, as it says in the books, it could augur good.'

Millie burst out laughing, and as Ben pulled himself up on to the cart, she said, 'You know, you are funny, the things you say.'

He looked down at her. 'Well, you're not the only one who reads books, you know. I could beat you along that line if I liked. And I will an' all; we'll have a competition some day when you start readin' the grown-up stuff.' And he slapped the reins along the pony's back.

She was walking at its head when she turned and said, 'Why don't you go to school, Ben?'

'What! What you sayin'? Go to school? Me? a man!'

'Lots of grown-up people go to school at night, some of them after work. I know Father Dolan has a night class.'

'What! Join the Catholics? Are you askin' for him an' all to be stabbed with a pair of scissors? . . . Oh, I'm sorry, lass. I'm sorry.'

'Oh, you needn't be.' She pulled the pony to a stop opposite this second set of gates. There were open, and, nodding up to Ben, she said, 'I've never felt any guilt or regret over that. She was a horrible woman, cruel. And not only to me. But there are other people taking night classes, Ben; like Parson King. He's Protestant.'

'They're all holy Joes. But get out of the way and let *me* turn him in if you're not goin' to lead him.'

They were now proceeding up a driveway bordered on each side by shrubs: and then quite suddenly they emerged into an open area. It was like a small field, only the grass had been cut; and there to the side stood a house. In comparison with those they had passed along the way, it could be considered small. It looked as if it had only two storeys, but suggested an attic under the fanlight in the roof.

Ben had hardly put his feet on the ground when, from the side of the house, there emerged what appeared to be a mob of children coming at them in a rush and then skidding to a halt about three yards distant. There were five of them: the biggest, a girl, looking not much younger than Millie herself. There were three girls and two boys. And it was the taller of the two boys who looked at the others before explaining, 'He's got little legs.' Then they scattered, yelling, as Ben gave a jump towards them, shouting on a laugh, 'Yes! but they can run.'

There now appeared at the door of the house a young woman, and she called in a high voice, 'Children! Betty! Paddy! you, Daisy, come. Come this minute.' As if the children hadn't heard her or were not aware of her presence, they all ran back towards the side of the house, and there they stood as a group, staring at the man with the short legs and the girl with hair that looked almost white, walking towards their mother.

'Oh, you're here. Good morning. Well, you had better come in.'

Millie took in at once that Mrs Quinton was a nervous lady and that she wasn't very old; in fact, she looked young. And her hair was untidy and she was wearing an apron. She didn't appear to be at all like the kind of lady who would be engaging a maid. Not a bit like Annabel's mother.

'Come into the kitchen,' she said, and led the way across a small hall and into quite a large kitchen, dominated, Millie noticed, by an oblong table under which were a number of stools. And she also noticed straightaway that the open fire feeding an oven to one side and a water boiler to the other was very like the one Sister Cecilia had introduced her to.

'Sit down. Oh, dear me, dear me.' Mrs Rose Quinton now pulled out two stools from under the table and indicated that both Millie and Ben should be seated, and when they were, she stood before them looking slightly helpless but smiling now as she said, 'You have, unfortunately, already been introduced to my family; at least, all except the baby.

127

They are, what you would term, a handful, but they are not really naughty children, only impetuous, you know.'

Millie smiled at her, and she smiled back, saying, 'I . . . I must be frank with you. They . . . need a firm hand. Well, I mean they need to be managed. And again I must be frank in telling you, because if I don't tell you this, one of the maids of the house will likely inform you very shortly, that I've had two helpers already this year. You see, I don't want you to come on the . . . well, shall we say' – her smile widened – 'on false pretences. You understand?'

'Yes. Yes, ma'am, I understand; and I have worked with children before . . . well, when I was at the nuns' school, it was part of the older pupils' duty to be in charge of two or three of the younger ones to see they washed properly and . . . well, things like that, and just before I left I was doing this.'

'You were at the nuns' school? Oh, yes. Oh yes.' Mrs Quinton closed her eyes for a moment as if recalling her cousin relating this girl's history, which had not included the scissors' business with Sister Mary as being the reason for her leaving because that might have put any caring mother off from engaging such a virago.

'My cousin did tell you the terms?'

Millie paused a moment, then said, 'Yes.'

'And they're suitable?'

'Yes. Yes, thank you.'

'Well now, when can you start your duties?'

Millie now turned to Ben, and he shrugged his shoulders, saying, 'It's up to you; but I could bring you back tomorrow, if you would like that?'

'Yes. Yes, I would like that,' she said, and looked straight back at Mrs Quinton, saying, 'I will start tomorrow.'

'Would . . . would you like to meet the children now? Well, I know you have seen them already, but if I could call them and . . .'

128

Millie rose from the stool and, looking at her prospective and harassed mistress, she said, 'Oh, it's all right. We'll get to know each other tomorrow, I'm sure, and very quickly.'

'Yes. Yes, perhaps that'll be best. But oh, by the way, you do know there are other duties? I . . . I have a person who comes in for two hours every morning, but . . . but she does just the very rough work. I sometimes need help in the kitchen and . . . '

'Oh, I'd be pleased to help wherever I can.'

'She's a splendid cook,' Ben said.

Rose Quinton looked at the extraordinary man and thought as many another had: what a pity! He could have been a handsome man. She said, 'She is?' And he nodded his head firmly, saying, 'She is. You take it from me, ma'am. I like my food, and she's the best I've come across.'

Mrs Quinton was again smiling down on Millie. 'Oh, that would be a great asset. Well, you will come in the morning about . . . at about the same time?'

'Yes, ma'am.'

Millie's new mistress paused as if uncertain what to do next; then turning quickly about, she led them from the kitchen into the hall and to the open front door again, and looked to where her children were all standing round the pony and cart. In fact, her son Patrick was actually in the cart.

'Oh, dear me! Dear me! That boy! I'm sorry,' she muttered.

'Nothing to be sorry for, missis, I mean, ma'am. It's a good sign when children like animals and are playful with them. Good day to you.'

'Good day.'

Standing before her future mistress, Millie did not know whether or not to dip her knee. She decided against it, and so set a pattern which was soon to become questionable. What she said now was, 'Good morning, ma'am,' and Rose

129

Quinton answered in a similar tone, 'Good morning;' then added hastily, 'Your name is?'

'Millie, ma'am.'

'Oh. Millie? Well, good morning, Millie.'

Again Millie said, 'Good morning, ma'am,' then turned and followed Ben to the cart, from which there was now a great scattering away of children, before once more they formed a group as if into a combined force. But when Millie, from her seat, lifted her arm and waved to them, they looked at each other, giggled, then all waved back, which Millie took as a good omen and Rose Quinton took as a sign of comparative peace. 'It was as if,' she said later to her husband, William, when in bed that night, 'I felt as if the house had suddenly been blessed. Strange, wasn't it?' to which he answered, 'Yes, indeed. Well, I'm looking forward to seeing this blessing. Indeed; indeed I am.'

6

Millie had been living with the Quintons, in what was called Little Manor, for six months now, and she couldn't recall a happier period in her life. She still looked forward to her half-day with Aggie and Ben, as she did her whole day once a month; but she was always glad to get back into the Quinton household, where she felt so at home she could never imagine ever wanting to leave them. But looking back, she always recalled her first week as a very testing time.

Mr and Mrs Quinton had their meals served in the little dining-room, whereas she had to take hers with the children at the kitchen table. And when nine-year old Daisy took a spoonful of hot soup and threw it in her face, and there was a giggle from the others, Millie, rising and going to a side table and deliberately choosing a larger spoon, returned to her seat, filled the spoon with the soup, and levelled it at her opponent, causing a scream from Daisy but silent gasps from her supporters. And when the astonished child screamed, 'I'll tell Mama!' Millie said, 'Go on then, tell her.' But when the child went to scramble from her stool, she was checked by Paddy, her younger brother, with the advice, 'Don't; Papa's in. You'll get your own back: just wait.'

The 'own back' took the form of locking Millie in her attic bedroom, which was reached by a ladder attached to the end of the landing. The hatch had two bolts on the outside. Why they had been placed there and not on the inside, no one knew.

The children had shot the bolts after Millie had retired to bed. But when, at half-past six the next morning, she found her way barred, she didn't, as they expected, bang on the trap door yelling her head off in frenzy; no, what she did was to return to her pallet on the floor, pull the clothes around her and lie there waiting. And she hadn't all that long to wait, for when Mr Quinton came downstairs for his seven o'clock breakfast and found a bare table, he hurried upstairs and informed his wife. Mrs Quinton's first remark was, 'Oh, she must have gone. And I thought she was different. I thought she would handle them. Or perhaps she has just slept in. Go and see, William.'

When William climbed the ladder and found the bolts shot he pulled them back, pushed open the hatch and in the dim light of an almost guttering candle he saw the maid sitting fully dressed on the side of her pallet, her feet stretched out before her, and she was smiling at him. He smiled back as he said, 'The little devils!'

What she said to him was, 'You won't have had any breakfast, sir, but I'll get it in a jiffy.'

She prepared his breakfast the while he visited the two rooms in which five of his children slept, but in which three of them were now wide awake, waiting for the screams and the thumps that so far hadn't been heard. And after clipping his sons's ears and shaking his daughters, telling them they should know better, he awakened his six-year old son, Robert, and his four-year old daughter, Florrie, with hard smacks on their buttocks. Then pointing from Betty to Daisy, and then to Paddy, he said, 'I warned you

132

what would happen, didn't I, if we lost another maid? No more school; and you, Betty, would go up in the big house kitchen; you, too, Daisy. There's a young girl up there who has to scurry around with muck buckets most of the day. As for you, Paddy, it will be the stables. Now, I mean that.' He lifted his hand. 'I'm not just saying it this time. This girl is a good, intelligent girl. She'll likely be able to teach you as much as you would be able to learn at school, because she's been to school, too. So that's the last warning I'm going to give you. You understand?' And he now bawled at his son, 'Paddy! do you understand?'

'Yes, Father, yes.'

'Do you want to go into the stableyard?'

'N . . . n . . . no, Father. I . . . I like engines. I mean, I can draw engines. You know I can.'

'All right, all right. But there you have it, the three of you. As for you, Robert,' he looked at his younger son, 'you had better follow their lead or you will end up in a stableyard, too. There's as young as you had to muck out horses before today.' On this he turned abruptly and left them.

His warning had stuck, but resentfully; at least, for the next few days and until Millie was able to break through it because she was a story-teller, and, moreover, because she could play with them. Probably, too, because she told Patrick she liked to hear him play his tin whistle, whereas, apparently, nobody else did. And she broke down the final barrier when, in a clearing in the woodland on an afternoon when the sun was shining and there wasn't a breath of wind, she danced for them, doing the Irish jig Ben had taught her and which he himself had learnt from Annie when he was a lad.

Blessed with a quick ear, Patrick was soon able to play the tune that she hummed to him. And then she had them all attempting to jig, the while filling the wood with their laughter, so much so as to attract the attention of two

133

young horsemen riding up the bridle path. Dismounting, they peered through the trees and in amazement watched the young Quintons' mob doing a weird dance round a girl they had never seen before. She had golden hair tied with a ribbon at the back, but the rest of it bounced from her shoulders with every step of the dance. They weren't to know it had escaped from its bun with the exertion . . .

Millie came to know these young men; or rather, became aware of them as being the sons of Raymond Crane-Boulder, just as she was to come to know many of the people in The Grange through the gossip of Jane Fathers, she being the lowest in the servants' hierarchy at The Grange because she was merely the slopper-out.

This term was very appropriate, for Jane took over from the housemaids the chamber pots and china slop buckets and emptied them into iron buckets; then, with the help of Ken Atkins, the boot boy, she carried them all of a hundred yards to the end of the kitchen garden, where lay the cesspits.

The beginning of the wood lying only a few yards distant from the cesspits, Jane would sometimes slip into the shelter of the trees and flop down and dream of the day when she might become a scullery maid if she kept on the right side of Mrs Potter, the cook, who would put a word in for her with Mrs Roper, the housekeeper.

It was during one of these appropriated short siestas that she first saw Millie and found a recipient for her knowledge of the members of the household. There was the old master who owned two mills in the town, but who never visited them because he was fat and had gout and hardly ever left his room. It was Mr Raymond, his son, who saw to the businesses, and Jane assured Millie that she would recognise him right away if ever she came across him, because he was tall, thin, and handsome. But the mistress now, Jane pointed out: she was another kettle of fish, different altogether, because – and the

134

information had been imparted in a whisper – she had a failing: she liked the bottle, and at times there would be the devil to pay going on upstairs. Flo Yarrow, she was the second housemaid, her and Jessie Kitson, she was the in-between one, they could tell some tales, and they did about the goings on upstairs: just like Ridley's pub on a Saturday night, they said it was sometimes. Then there were the two sons, Mr David, he was fifteen, and Mr Randolph, he was fourteen. They were real rips; they played tricks on the servants. Once they kicked a bucket of slops around her feet. Eeh! she had been in a mess, she said.

Millie learned that some of the servants were all right, that they would speak to you, but not Mr Winters the valet, nor the lady's maid Miss McNeil. The butler neither; he was uppish. But Mr Boswell the first footman, he was all right; well, he would laugh at you at times; but not John Tester, the second one; he was as snotty as a polis. There were four maids attached to the kitchen and three others on the first floor; and there were four men in the yard, and four gardeners.

At first Millie was confused with all their names, but through time, and at least twice a week listening to Jane's chatter, she felt she had come to know the members of the household and their particular jobs. But what she didn't know, because Jane herself didn't know, was the layout of the rooms in the house, for although the girl had been in service since she was eight and was now eleven, she had never got past the servants' hall, and certainly not past the green-baize door that led from the passage into the main hall, not even to receive her yearly pay of fifty-two shillings; for she received this, as the rest of the kitchen staff received theirs, from the butler, across a table in the servants' dining-room.

But Jane had high hopes that this year would be different, for, later on, the mistress's brother, or her half-brother, she explained, was going to have his coming-of-age party, and it would be a big do. And there was a whisper that there would be a special party for the servants, too. Wouldn't that be wonderful?

Millie felt sorry for Jane, and she told Aggie so on one of her half-days. 'She's from the workhouse,' she said, 'and so is the boot-boy, and they are treated as though they have the plague, by what I can gather. But she's so grateful for a kind word, and she keeps on about this party that's going to be held for the mistress's half-brother. But as far as I can gather, he won't be of age until next year. Sad, really. I'm so sorry for her.'

She was sitting on the couch by Aggie's side, and as she leant her head against the broad forearm, saying, 'She wasn't lucky like I was.' Aggie put her arm around her, and in an unusual show of her feelings said, 'And I was lucky in my turn to get you, my dear.' Then she pressed her away and, looking into her face, she asked quietly, 'D'you know what Ben's up to?'

'No. What?'

'That's what I'm askin' you, lass, 'cos he talks to you on the journey backwards and forwards. So, has he said anything?'

'What about?'

'Well, where he goes twice a week in that good suit of his. Now when he drops you off he doesn't wear it. He's decently put on, I'll grant you that; he always has been, even when he's goin' down to Annie's he's spruced himself up a bit, but this is something different. The night he puts on that suit he doesn't turn down the road that would lead to her place, but goes on towards the town. So where does he go? And he hasn't said anything to you?'

'No, Mrs Aggie. No; but it must be somewhere special he goes to, if he puts on that suit.'

136

'Well, that's what I think an' all, lass. I said to him, jokin', like, "Have you given your life-long friend the push and taken up with a fancy piece?" And you know what he said to me?'

Millie shook her head.

' "I shouldn't be a bit surprised." That's what he said: "I shouldn't be a bit surprised. Stranger things have happened." And then d'you know what he said? and he put one of those fancy voices on. "For the first time, Mrs Winkowski," he said, "you've given the right term to the association I have with Miss Annie Blackett." Eeh! I nearly threw the pan of stew over him, I did.'

But Millie too was curious as to where Ben would go in his good suit twice a week, and on the journey back to the Quintons' she asked him bluntly, 'What are you doing, Ben, going into town twice a week in your new suit?'

'Oh, she's been at you, has she? I've been waiting for it. Well, miss, if I told you, you'd know as much as me, wouldn't you? Then come Sunday you would tell her on the quiet.'

'Oh no I wouldn't, not if you didn't want me to. You know that, Ben.'

He glanced at her, then said quietly, 'Well, if I tell you, you'll laugh; at least you'll do that.'

'I mightn't laugh unless it's funny. Is it something funny?'

'No; I don't think it's funny. It's what I've wanted to do for a long time but hadn't the nerve. But then, I got to thinkin': there's you, a bit of a lass, and your head's full of all kinds of things; and there's me, ten years older than you, a fully-fledged man, and I know practically nowt. Well, what I mean is, me mind's workin' all the time, but it's goin' round in circles, like, and the circles are not gettin' any wider, if you know what I mean. So, I thought: well, there's many a better man than me started to learn when he was well on in age.

137

And so that's what I'm doing. I joined the night class.'

'*Oh Ben. Oh! I am glad.* What made you think I would laugh at you? And as for me having more in my head than you have, that's silly. I've always found you wise.'

'Me, wise?'

'Oh yes. Yes, the things that you say in your summing up of things . . . and people. But I'm so glad you're going to night classes. What are you learning?'

'Well—' He flapped the reins, calling, 'Gee up! there, Laddie,' and he seemed to ponder a moment before he answered her question: 'It seemed daft, the first time I went, just listenin' to the fella readin' bits from this and that, then askin' what you thought about it. Well, I wasn't the only one there that couldn't tell him what they thought about the Poor Law unions before the Board of Guardians came into bein'. I ask you. But as one bright spark said, the less he knew about the workhouses the happier he would be; he had just come to the class in order to help him get a better job to keep him out of the workhouse. We all laughed at that, and the teacher fella did, too. It sort of broke the ice. Mind, I nearly did say something when he got on about the Public Health Act that had come in in '48. Eeh! I wanted to say they must have overlooked the mile warren of Courts, where the rats have more space than those livin' there. But it all makes you think. Well, it's opened my eyes. But mind, I felt a bit rattled when he said there were good workin' class houses goin' up and people wouldn't go into them because they were used to herding together in lice-ridden hovels. One fella did stand up and go for him, but he told him to go to Boston Lane and there he would see what he had said was true. And you know, Millie, it was, 'cos I went along there meself an' had a look. They were smallish houses, but neat like, brick built, yet half of them were empty. I wouldn't have believed it until I saw it.'

138

'It all sounds interesting, Ben; makes me wish I was there with you.'

'Oh, you are better off where you are, far better off lookin' after those rips of bairns, as Aggie's police friend calls them. And one of the lessons was about children, bairns, and the New Act of 1842. According to that, apparently, children shouldn't be sent to work until they are ten years old. But half the country were up in arms against it: farmers, even parents. I mean the young 'uns' parents, because they were breadwinners. Of course, they were cheap labour for the factories and the farmers. Well, I've always known that. But when you hear it read out to you, an' you hear of the laws that were passed against it and weren't carried out, it makes you think. So, there you are, Millie Forester, that's what I'm doin' in me good suit twice a week: learnin'. And reading more – when I get the chance.'

'Oh, I am proud of you, Ben. I really am.' And when he muttered, 'You must be the only one then,' she shook his arm, saying, 'Don't be silly. I'm not. Mrs Aggie loves you.'

She waited for the denial, but it wasn't forthcoming, not even the cocky one that would have come easily to him, 'Aye, I can't help it, she can't help it.' Instead, he just shouted to the horse, 'Gee up! there.'

Thinking of Ben going to school, even if it was only a two-hour night class twice a week, set her mind working again on the thought that she, too, would like to go to school. Yet, she knew she couldn't have it all ways; and she loved working with the Quinton children, as she did helping Mrs Quinton. In fact, she did most of the cooking now, and she knew that they appreciated her and thought of her in a way as perhaps being different from a servant. Even so, on the three Sundays in the month when the children had their mid-day meal in the dining-room with their parents, she was never asked to sit down with them. And yet they made her feel as if she was one of the family, whereas Nellie Fuller, the coachman's daughter, who came for two hours every morning, was given no privileges at all. Mrs Quinton was kind to her in that she never shouted at her – but she was never offered a drink or a bun before she left, and her wage was always given directly to her father.

She was another one Millie was sorry for, and she sometimes sneaked her a currant bun that she had kept over from her own middle morning break, and which Nellie always accepted and ate without saying a word.

But it was one morning when she was escorting the children on their mile walk to the church school in the village that she got an idea, and that evening she put it to Mrs Quinton in a very diplomatic way.

It was Mrs Quinton herself who gave her the opening, saying, 'I bless that school. They get on so well there, and your reading to them at night has helped considerably, Millie. You know, you yourself could be a teacher.'

'Well, I have high hopes of being one, ma'am . . . ' The idea had never entered her head. 'Before I came to look after the children I was going to return to school, and I would like to do that again.'

Before she got any further, Rose Quinton cried, 'Oh, no! Millie. No! You couldn't possibly leave the children, not now. And they love you, they really do, they really love you. You have been able to manage them like no other; in fact, they obey you more than they do me. Oh, Millie, Millie, you're not thinking of leaving us, are you?'

'Well, I really would like to go to school again, if it was only for half a day.'

'Oh, Millie, Millie. I thought you would be settled here until the children grew up, I really did. You are such a help to me. And we do appreciate you, both Mr Quinton and I. He will be so disappointed.'

140

'But I am not going right away.'

'No; but you've got it in your mind, haven't you?'

'Well, yes. Yes, I have, but . . . but there is a way out if . . . if you really feel that the children would want me to stay.'

'Yes? Yes? What is it; I mean, the way out?'

'Well, if it were possible for me to attend school with the children two or three mornings a week just for half the day, I'd make that do for a time.'

Rose Quinton seemed to think for a moment, and then she said brightly, 'Yes. Yes, indeed, Millie, that is an idea. I must speak to Mr Quinton, and he will talk to Mrs Wilkins. She is the teacher, you know, and I'm sure, in a way, you could likely be of help to her with the younger ones. Yes. Yes, I will speak to Mr Quinton as soon as he comes in. That is a way out. And the children would love it and they wouldn't take advantage of you. Well, you don't let them, do you?' She nodded knowingly at Millie before rising and leaving the kitchen, sighing deeply as if with relief.

So Millie went to school again and life went on very smoothly, and such was the feeling of the family for her, she was given tea in the dining-room on her thirteenth birthday.

And it could be said that life took on a rosy glow for Millie during the months ahead, until the celebrations at The Grange for the coming of age of the mistress's half-brother Bernard Thompson, and the staff party that followed it, changed things entirely.

7

During the week before the great event, the growing activity
and excitement it was engendering in The Grange itself was
also seeping into The Little Manor, and especially was it
felt by Millie, who had been given to understand from Mrs
Quinton that she would be invited to the staff party, which
was to take place the day following the main party, and which
Jane had told her was to be held in the big games room.

During one of her collections, Aggie had been given a lady's
taffeta dress with a blue silk lining. The outside of the dress
was marked in various places, but the inside of the material
looked as good as new, as did the lining. She had taken it to
Chinese Charlie and asked him if his wife could turn it into a
dress for her Millie. Mrs Charlie was very good at remaking
clothes and it was she who suggested that the material would
be suitable for a Chinese style of garment. And so that was
what was being made for Millie to wear on the great day.

Millie was as excited about the dress as she was about
the party itself; but she was anxious, above all, to see the
inhabitants of the house; except for the coachman and Ken
Atkins, the boot-boy, who sometimes slipped into the wood
with Jane, for what purpose she hadn't yet discovered, nor

would allow her mind to guess at, because she liked them both; yes, except for these and, now and again, a gardener, she had seen no other members of the household, for The Little Manor was as separate from The Grange as if it were set in another part of the town. The staff never used the drive that led past The Little Manor, having been ordered not to pass the bailiff's residence. The party was due on the coming Tuesday evening; but this was Saturday, and there was no school on Saturday; and Saturday afternoon was a time for play, inside or outside the house. On this afternoon it was to take place outside the house.

It was a bright but cold day, and Millie had had the children running around in the wood to keep themselves warm, and the game they all liked was to skip behind her the while following Patrick as he played on his whistle.

In and out of the trees they went, and always in this game Millie herself became a child again, dancing and experiencing a particular kind of joy through the exuberance.

It was in this state that Millie emerged from the wood behind the whistle player, followed by the four children, to come to a staggered halt when confronted by the tall lady and the gentleman.

Not having seen the master and mistress of the house, Millie had not imagined what they were like. But she was immediately given their identity by Betty, stumbling over the grass verge and on to the road and dipping her knee and looking from one to the other as she said, 'Master . . . Mistress, we were playing.'

Berenice Crane-Boulder stared down on the girl and, her voice belying the slightness of her frame, she said, 'I should have thought you were beyond the playing stage, child. And this girl—' She flicked her fingers towards Millie; then stared hard at her for a good moment before she said, 'Who is she?'

Before Betty could answer, Millie said, 'I am nursemaid to the children and helper to Mrs Quinton, ma'am.'

Both the voice and the manner seemed, for a moment, to deprive the mistress of speech; but only for a moment: assuming furt'ier authority, she rose her tone to a bawl and cried at Millie, 'Speak when you're spoken to, girl! Apparently your training has been neglected.' Then looking at Betty again, she said, 'Tell your mother I wish to see her at ten o'clock tomorrow morning in my office.'

'Berenice.' It was the master speaking now; but his wife, seeming not to hear, looked at Patrick, saying, 'Boy! go to the stables and tell the men a wheel of the carriage needs attention. Away with you!'

Millie watched the lady now walk away, the rustle of her voluminous skirts making a swishing sound, as if she were walking through dried leaves; and she imagined her to be a bird about to fly, for the feathers in her hat protruded from the back like wings.

The tall man was now patting Betty's head and saying, 'It is nice to play. One's never too old to play,' and the child, wide-eyed and smiling, said, 'Thank you, master. Thank you, master,' dipping her knee with each statement. Then he turned and looked at Millie before taking two steps towards her and saying, 'You like to dance?'

'Yes, sir.'

'How old are you?'

'Thirteen, sir.'

'Thirteen. It is a very nice age. Your . . . your dancing was so energetic, it has caused your cap to go awry.' And he put out his hand and pulled the small starched cap from where it had slipped almost to the back of her head and behind her ear, and bringing it into place again, he said, 'You have beautiful hair.'

144

As his hand touched her cheek her head moved back just the slightest, and she looked up into his face. It was a thin face, but with a kindly expression. She remembered Jane telling her he was thin. His eyes were brown, the nose pointed; his top lip, too, was thin, but the lower pouted a little in its fulness. And when he smiled as he did now widely, he showed a mouthful of gleaming teeth.

There then came a diversion, for Florrie's plump legs had seemingly given way beneath her and she sat down with a plop on the grass verge, saying, 'Oh, dear me,' which caused the children to titter, and the master to turn to Millie again and say, 'You have worn her out.'

Without answering the man, Millie picked up Florrie, slightly inclined her head in acknowledgement towards the man, and turned away to go into the wood again, and one after the other the children dipped a knee to the master and then ran after her.

Chattering among themselves they entered the house, and Daisy, quickly preceding the rest, ran into the sitting-room to her mother and father. Rose was sitting on the couch, William Quinton was at a table to the side, writing a report, and she cried at them, 'We saw the master and mistress! and the master straightened Millie's cap.'

Her father stopped his writing to say, 'What are you talking about, child?'

The rest of the family were now trotting into the room, and he looked from one to the other and Betty repeated Daisy's statement: 'We saw the master and mistress, Dada. The mistress was in a tear. She wants to see you in the morning, Mama, at ten o'clock in her office.'

The husband and wife exchanged glances; then William said, 'Where did you see them?'

'Just along the road.'

'On our drive?' He was on his feet now.

145

'Yes; the carriage had broken down. It must have been outside the gates at the bottom. She went for Millie, but the master was nice. He straightened her cap and patted her face.'

Rose was quickly on her feet, saying, 'He straightened Millie's cap? Why?'

'Well, we had been dancing through the wood and the jigging must have loosened the hair pins and it had fallen to the side and he straightened it and patted her cheek. And he talked to her.'

William again exchanged a quick glance with his wife; then looking down on his family, he said, 'You're all getting too big for jigging and dancing through the wood, especially you, Betty, and you, Daisy. And Paddy, I'm going to burn that whistle of yours. And what's more, Millie should have more sense.'

Patrick now said, 'If you did, Dada, I'd just make another. Taggard showed me how to whittle one.'

William spread his arms now, saying dramatically, 'What kind of a family am I rearing?' Then looking at his wife, he said, 'What kind of a family are you bringing up, woman, when my son defies me and my daughters act like abandoned females, dancing in a woodland? . . . Robert! you take that grin off your face before it is wiped off.'

When Robert rubbed his hand all over his face, leaving his expression tight-lipped, the children all burst out laughing, bringing the immediate command from their father, 'Get yourselves away, everyone of you! Out of my sight!' And they scampered from the room, leaving their parents looking at each other. And then William said a strange thing: 'I don't want to believe it,' he said, and his wife answered just as enigmatically, 'Perhaps it's because she's a dreadful woman.'

*

146

Aggie and Ben stood back and looked silently at the slim young creature standing before them in a blue brocade dress with its tiny stand-up collar and a sash waist, and at the skirt flowing down to the top of her black leather shoes. The sleeves were wide, and when Millie lifted her arms and swung round, it was evident that right down to the cuffs they were attached to the dress itself.

'Did you ever see anything so lovely as that frock in all your days?'

'Well, all I can say is, Charlie's wife's made a good job of it.'

'My! she has that. I knew it was a piece of good stuff when I first got the dress, but I never thought it would make up like that.'

'But look who's wearin' it, Aggie. Look who's wearin' it.'

'Oh' – Aggie tossed her head – 'that kind of frock would make anybody look good.' But her words were accompanied by a grin; and then she added, 'But you'll have to do something with your hair, lass. You can't leave it loose like that.'

'Oh, Mrs Quinton said she will gather it for me into a special kind of bun at the back.'

'She seems a nice woman, that Mrs Quinton.'

'She is nice, Mrs Aggie. Oh, yes, she is nice. And she's young . . . well, I mean she's had six children but she's still young somehow, in spite of being twenty-nine.'

'Twenty-nine?' Aggie and Ben looked at each other, and Ben repeated solemnly, 'Twenty-nine. She's practically ready for the grave.'

'Oh, you! Ben. You know what I mean. But isn't it lovely?' She stroked her hands down the skirt. 'I've never seen anything so beautiful in my life. Oh, thank you, Mrs Aggie. Thank you.'

When she threw herself on Aggie, Aggie pushed her away, crying, 'Look! It's . . . it's been steamed and pressed and cost me a pretty penny, I can tell you; half a dollar from beginning to end. So don't muck it up.'

'Oh.' Millie now gently caught at the two hands that were half extended towards her as she said, 'Oh, thank you. Thank you, thank you. You know, you're wonderful, and you can't stop me saying thank you. And you know what? I told the children a story about you the other day. I keep them quiet at night telling them stories. Anyway, I was in the middle of this one and there wasn't a sound, and I think that's why Mrs Quinton came upstairs. She sat on the side of Betty's bed and listened, and afterwards, when we had gone downstairs, she said to me, ' "That was a lovely story. It was about Mrs Winkowski, wasn't it?" '

'Oh, God in heaven!' Aggie went into her flouncing attitude, and as she turned away she glanced at Ben, saying, 'Did you ever! What'll we hear next? She'll be in one of those ranters' chapels telling the tale, and praisin' God while she bangs the bairns' heads together.'

As Aggie disappeared through the doorway and Ben, his body shaking with controlled laughter, was about to say something, Millie put in sadly, 'You can't thank her, can you? She won't take thanks.'

'Aw, me dear.' Ben went over to her and put his arm around her shoulder, only to withdraw it quickly, saying, 'Eeh my! I mustn't touch you, not with that on. But that's her way. If she had stayed a minute longer she would have been blubbing her eyes out. Don't you realise, me dear, that for her you're the sun that rises an' the moon that sets an' all that goes on in between.'

Millie was smiling at him now: 'That was nice,' she said. 'Who's it by? Did you read it somewhere?'

'No! No! I didn't. It came out of me own thinkin'.'

148

'Really? The sun that rises and the moon that sets and all that goes on in between . . . That says it all, Ben.' And now she added, 'You're still liking the night classes?'

'Aye. Yes, I'm still liking them and still havin' me say. Most of them are scared to death to open their mouths in case they'll be stopped coming to the classes. I've told them that wouldn't happen. And anyway there are other teaching places round about now. It's catchin' on. In my mind, though, they're going wrong in one direction: they're not making us write enough. They read to us and get us to read bits back; but it's all snatches, if you know what I mean. This week he's gone back to '47, dealing with the Corn Laws, you know, and how some of the big blokes were scuppered when the corn dropped from a hundred and twenty-four shillings a quarter to forty-nine and six within a few months. Poor people benefited, but sympathy seemed to go to the corn dealers and the bill brokers because they were ruined. And not afore time, I said. From then, apparently, the trade began to boom. But here we are at the end of the fifties, and are we much better off? There were all those who scarpered to the gold diggin's in California and Australia. Have we heard of any of them making their fortunes? A lot of them died, that's known. Bill Watson's brother, for instance. And, you know, Bill didn't even know until nine months later. All this talk of prosperity gets up my bloody nose, 'cos while there's a lot gettin' on in the world there's a lot more dying of poverty and muck. And a sevenpenny loaf! That's certainly not saving them in Ireland dropping dead by the hundred. Eeh! there's a place for you.

'One teacher said a golden era has dawned on all the Northern Counties, and right up to Scotland, and even into Wales. You know, Millie' – he sat down heavily on the settle – 'I'm in another world when I'm in that room listening to that fella. Sometimes there's a woman teacher. Oh aye, there're

149

women teachers an' all. But they get me a bit mesmerised, and I think, yes, things are gettin' better, aye, they must be; and then I walk half a mile back here to The Courts and I say to meself, what's up with you, Ben Smith, Jones, or Robinson? They haven't skimmed the skin off the top of the watery milk yet. And you know what I think, Millie, I mean, who's the cause of most of this muck and filth in The Courts? It's the Irish. The teacher said their poverty over there was caused by religion and ignorance and she said we might think there were some bad slums here, but they were nothing compared to those in Belfast and such places. Well, I said to her after, you want to come down to Belling Court, not five minutes down the road from where I live. That's what I said to her. They've brought over their pigs and muck; the place's full of 'em. There's fourteen living in one of the cellars there and they've got pigs in with them an' all, I believe. And of course, what d'they do? They work for practically nowt, and if the bosses can get cheap labour like that they're not going to pay an Englishman a decent wage, are they? Oh, Millie' – he shook his head from side to side now – 'I wish I was learned.'

'Well' – she laughed at him – 'you're going the right way about it. And you're telling me things I never knew. I'd like to go to those classes.'

'Oh, you'd have to grow up first.'

'I am grown up.' She was indignant. 'I'm coming on fourteen.'

'Aye, coming.' He rose from the seat, saying, 'Well, I'm off for a dander.'

'May I come with you?'

'No, you can't, not where I dander. And anyway, you'd better get out of that frock if you want it to be fresh for the party.'

'You always go for a dander on Sunday. Where do you go?'

'Oh, different places. Talk to different people. It's amazing how on a Sunday places change from their week-day look, and people an' all. They talk differently; they come out with things differently. Oh, you learn a lot on a dander on a Sunday.'

He now gave her a form of salute with his fingers to his forehead, then went out. But the door had hardly closed on him when Aggie came back into the room, saying, 'I would get out of that if you don't want it crushed to bits and the hem soiled. As you've likely noticed, miss, this floor isn't as clean as it used to be when you were here.'

'Well, I can clean it.'

'You'll do no such thing. It suits me. So, get out of that frock. And where's his lordship gone? Oh, need I ask? His Sunday dander. And he's gettin' too big for his boots by half.'

'He's a good man, Mrs Aggie, and you know that.'

'Look, am I to take that frock off you?'

Millie now hurried from the room and upstairs, where she changed into her Sunday dress; then she folded the beautiful garment and laid it in between two sheets of paper ready for its journey back to her happy place of work.

When she again returned to the kitchen Aggie said, 'Come and sit down a minute and tell me about the gentry you ran into yesterday. What's this I hear about the big master straightenin' your cap?'

'Ben told you?'

'Well, use that napper that's supposed to be bright; how otherwise would I be speaking about it now?'

'Well, if he told you word for word, and that's what he likely would do, there's nothing more I can say. That's what happened: he straightened my cap, patted my cheek and smiled.'

'What kind of a man was he?'

151

'He was tall and had a nice face and seemed kind. But his wife sounded a bit of a terror. I understand she drinks.'

'So do I, in moderation.'

'Well, I think she doesn't know about moderation. From what I can gather from Jane and from what she picks up with her big ears from the kitchen jabber, there's skull and hair flying in that house at times.'

'And that's where you're goin' on Tuesday night?'

'Yes, Mrs Winkowski, that's where I'm going on Tuesday night, and I'm looking forward to it.'

Aggie turned to gaze into the fire, saying softly, 'You'll move away from us and this quarter, like he's doin'.'

'What do you mean, move away? Look here.' She pulled at Aggie's arm. 'I'll never grow away from you. You know that. As for Ben, to say that about him, that's unfair.'

Aggie sighed, then said, 'I know the secret that's between you. I found out some time ago. I made it me business to find out, anyway. He's goin' to school, isn't he? At his age, goin' to school!'

'Well, I thought you would have been proud of him.'

'Education, lass, is all right in its place for them that needs it, if you're goin' to do something with it, if it means your livelihood or some such, but otherwise what does it do? It just stirs the mind and never brings pleasure, because the more you know the more you realise you don't know, an' so you go on probin'. Change doesn't do anybody any good. As I see it, God sets you in a space, and He gives you work to do, an' you do it the best you can. But you don't say to Him, I don't like this job You've given me, I'm made for better things, when deep in your mind it tells you that you couldn't do better things, any better than you are doin', if you follow what I mean.'

152

Millie followed what she meant, and it saddened her. She said, 'Then you don't like people getting on in the world, getting out of the rut?'

'Not if they're made for the rut, lass, not if they're made for the rut. Take Constable Fenwick. He was on this beat for years; then he goes and becomes a sergeant. I ask him how he feels about it and he answers truthfully, he doesn't know. He's missin' something 'cos his work now is different and he has to write a lot of things which keeps him indoors, whereas before, he knew almost all the people on his beat; and him bein' Irish and a Catholic, he helped those he could, especially the bairns. He's had a lot of them re-housed in his time. But now, with his rise, he's lost touch. There's hardly a day went by when he didn't pass that gate, and if he didn't look in he'd give me a nod, as he always did if I was on the road with the cart. And I know that he did things that no ordinary policeman would do. But now he's a sergeant he'll have to watch his p's and q's. And he told me he was doin' what you call studying. Studying what? I said to him. And when he said bits of the law, I remember I made him laugh when I said, if he carried the bits out he'd better not show his face in The Courts round about or they would pinch his bits, and more than his bits. No, I'm not for education, not really.'

'Then why have you pushed it into me? Why have you sent me to school? Why did you put me under the nuns? Why did you insist that I go to Mrs Quinton's?'

'Oh, that's a different kettle of fish. There was a reason behind that. It was a lesser of two evils. Oh aye, by God! the great lesser, and you know what I'm talkin' about.'

Millie sat back from her, laid her head against the end of the couch, surveyed the fat bulk for a moment, and then said, 'Mrs Agnes Winkowski, you are a complex creature.'

'Is that what I am?'

'Yes, and more, and I love you. Oh, oh, I know you will term that slaver, but I will say again, I love you, Mrs Agnes Winkowski.' And quickly now she leant forward and placed her lips against the sagging cheek, then ended, 'And if I didn't love you for anything else I would love you for giving me that beautiful dress.' She now struck a pose. 'By! it's going to startle the staff and their betters when I make my appearance in The Grange on Tuesday night.'

Aggie didn't smile, she didn't laugh, in fact, she said nothing, for if she had voiced her thoughts she would have startled and troubled Millie, for she would have said, 'I wish to God you weren't goin' to that party, love. I do. I do.'

8

William Quinton had taken her to the back door, smiled at her and said, 'Enjoy yourself.' Then he had pushed the door pen and said, 'Go on, or else they'll have started.'

She had passed through the boot-room, lit by two candle-lanterns hanging one each side of the door leading into the pan scullery, which was illuminated in the same way. She walked slowly, taking in, first, the enormity of the room, and then, the amazing number of iron pans arrayed along a bench and the tubs of water standing to the side. Now she was in the kitchen. And here she stopped to gaze about her in amazement. She had never imagined such a place. There were two ovens flanking a large fire and, over it, a spit from which was hanging a huge piece of meat; and turning it with a twist of the handle was Ken Atkins. He looked washed and scrubbed and, glancing over his shoulder, he said, 'I've just slipped out to turn it. They're all in the dining-room. Come on.' He held a hand out towards her; then stopped and looked at her. She was wearing the brown cloak over the dress, but it was open at the front; and glimpsing the material, he said, 'That looks pretty stuff. Look, you'd better leave your cloak in the hallway here.' He led her up the long kitchen and into a short passage that opened out into a small hall and, pointing, he said, 'Leave it on that chair there.'

After she had done so and stood before him, his mouth fell into a gape as he looked her up and down, then said, 'Eeh! My! Well!' and as if reluctant to take his eyes from her he stood gaping for seconds before he said, 'Come on.'

She followed him along another passage, from the far end of which came a high buzz of voices and laughter, which continued for a moment or so after they had entered the room; then one face after another was turned towards her.

Millie stared at these faces. She was shaking inside, for she knew she had made a mistake, or at least that the dress was a mistake. Nobody in the room was dressed in ordinary clothes; they were all in their household uniforms.

Someone started to laugh, but this was quickly squashed by a voice saying, 'Be quiet! Carter,' and the owner of the voice stood up and pointed towards the end of the room, to a plank table with a form alongside it on which Amy Carter the kitchen maid and Jane Fathers were already seated. Ken Atkins made his way quickly to the form and sat down; but when Millie did not follow him, Mrs Roper, the housekeeper, cleared her throat before saying, 'Take a seat.' Millie did not immediately obey the order, but in a clear voice she said, 'I'm very sorry. I understood it was a party.'

'Of course it's a party! But we know how to dress for a party. Take a seat!'

As she walked across the room to sit down next to Ken, her mind was crying at her: Mrs Quinton should have known, and she was given the answer. Perhaps she did, and she was going to tell me, but Mr Quinton stopped her, for it was he who had said: It's a party, Rose, and that dress is a picture. Let it be. And then he had said something that she couldn't understand: They want startling, that lot; and if it wasn't for one thing I'd be enjoying the effect.

156

Now she knew what he had meant, except for that one thing.

Slowly the conversation and the laughter rose again, and during it and between gulping her food, Jane Fathers gave Millie a running commentary on the hierarchy, from Miss McNeil, the lady's maid, and Mr Winters, the valet, and Mr Carlin, the butler, whose presence at the communal board appeared to her like visitors from heaven itself: if Queen Victoria and her Prince had been sitting here they could not have aroused greater admiration in the narrow breast.

The food was served in turn by the three housemaids, helped with great laughter from John Tester, the second footman, especially when, bowing to Millie, he exclaimed loudly, 'And what is your desire, madam, beef or turkey? I am here but to serve you,' only for the laughter to die down somewhat as the immediate company was brought to another silence when the chit who was dressed in brocade, like a Chinese lady, dared to say, and in no small voice, 'That I should be served with civility, if you please.'

When John Tester turned round and looked towards the housekeeper and the butler, this could have been the beginning of an awkward situation; in fact, could have put a damper on the whole party had not David Boswell, the first footman, chipped in with, 'Play acting at its best, if I've ever heard it. What d'you say, Mr Carlin?'

Feeling it was his duty to keep the party going merrily, the butler joined with his underling, crying, 'Well said! serf. Well said!' which brought guffaws and laughter, and once again the meal continued, except that Jane Fathers, her head down now, whispered, 'Eeh! you shouldn't have spoke like that, Millie. Nobody does. What's come over you?'

Millie didn't know what had come over her; she only knew she didn't care for the company and she wasn't going to enjoy herself, and that the whole thing had been a mistake. Her mind was again blaming Mrs Quinton. She should have put her wise; yes, she should. She shouldn't have let her make a fool of herself. Yet, she didn't feel a fool: at this moment she felt . . . well, she didn't like to put it even into a thought, but she felt superior. How many in this room, she wondered, had any learning at all, could even write their own name? Very few. How many would have the courage to go to night class as Ben was doing? None of them, she told herself. It would have been beneath them; it would have shown up their ignorance. Once this meal was over and she could get her cloak, she would slip out the way she had come in . . .

The meal was over, including the toast to Mr Thompson; and the exodus had started for the games room where, waiting for them, were two fiddlers and a flute player.

This, she thought, would be her chance to escape, but she was baulked by the man who had come to her aid before. Noticing that she had not risen from her seat with the others and sensing her feelings, Mr Carlin, too, stayed his departure and made his way towards her.

Taking her hand and bending down to her, he said, 'Never be ashamed of looking bonny, love. It might have been the wrong dress, but it had the right effect. Aye, it had that. Come on now and enjoy yourself.' And with this he led her through what seemed a maze of corridors to the two rooms that had been made into one by the pushing back of a partition.

By the time they entered the room, most were already seated along three of the walls; at the far end, in front of a step-high dais, sat the master and mistress, their two sons, sixteen-year old David, and fifteen-year old Randolph, together with Mr Bernard Thompson, in whose honour this function was being held. The musicians were already in place on the dais.

Although she was almost the last to enter the room her appearance certainly didn't go unnoticed by members of the family. The mistress herself had narrowed her eyes towards the girl, as if bringing her into focus, and had then turned to her half-brother, saying something which caused them both to laugh; her two sons apparently had the giggles, which was checked by their father; but he, too, was staring down the room at the young creature, whom he saw representing an exquisite piece of Chinese porcelain; and he could not keep the surprise from his voice when he muttered, 'My goodness!'

It was David, his elder son, who asked of no-one in particular, 'Why is that girl rigged out like that? Did she think it was a fancy dress ball?' As he spluttered, his mother pushed him gently on the shoulder, saying, 'I dare you to go and ask her to dance.'

'What! Me? Oh, Mama; don't be funny.'

She now turned to her half-brother, saying, 'You'd better get up and thank them for being here, and let them get on with it.'

'No; Raymond must do that,' he said quietly, but Raymond Crane-Boulder was quick to put in, 'Not me. It was your birthday, so get on your pins.'

Slowly the young man rose to his feet and, holding up a hand for silence, began hesitantly, 'Thank you. Thank you all very much for your kindness to me, and for your good wishes, and particularly for that very fine saddle you presented to me. Now, as you have already gathered, I'm no good at making speeches, so I suggest the musicians start up and we dance. Eh?' And on this he waved his hand back toward the three men on the dais, then sat down, to loud clapping.

The musicians struck up a lively polka; but no-one ventured on to the open floor until the valet took the lady's maid's hand and led her forward. From then, the rest soon followed, and the floor began to vibrate with the thumping of one, two, three, hop; one, two, three, hop.

When Berenice Crane-Boulder rose to her feet, her husband said, 'Where are you going?' And she, turning a disdainful

159

look on him, replied, 'Where do you think?' And turning to her son, she said, 'You coming, David?'

'Yes, Mama. Yes, Mama, I'm coming.' The boy was giggling and not too steady on his feet from the wine he had drunk at dinner, and he turned now and pulled his brother out with him.

As the three went out of a side door to the right of where they had been sitting, Bernard Thompson muttered under his breath, 'We can't all leave.'

'No, no, of course not,' the older man nodded assent. 'But that's her, that's her. You've seen for yourself, haven't you, these last few days? She's got worse, much worse. Never sober. And she's got those boys ruined. It's a good job they'll be going back to school next week.'

Bernard Thompson had been looking down the room to where, apart from three elderly couples, two young girls and a boy were sitting; and now, as if on impulse, he rose and, smiling, threaded his way between the dancers towards them.

Looking at Ken Atkins, he asked, 'Why aren't you dancing?' and the boy, who now stood up, answered, 'Don't know much about dancin', sir.'

'Well, you'll never learn sitting there. Look, take her.' He put out a hand and brought Jane Fathers to her feet and, pressing her towards Ken, he said, 'Just hop. Just hop.' And when they joined hands and both started to laugh, those who were dancing near-by laughed too. And this drew them into the throng.

Now he was left looking at the remarkable slip of a girl and, his voice changing, he said, 'Do you dance?'

'Yes, sir, I dance . . . in my own way.'

How odd: her manner was as strange as her dress. She wasn't like the rest of them. And why was she dressed like this anyway? 'What is your name?' he said.

160

'Millicent Forester, sir.'

'Well, Miss Forester, may I ask if you will give me the pleasure of joining me in this dance?'

Without hesitation and, as was said later in the staff room, brazenly, she stood up and put out a hand to him. As he took it, his other hand he placed on her slender waist, and without pause she put her free hand on his shoulder. Then they were dancing.

Their steps seemed to match, because he wasn't all that tall. She imagined, judging by Ben's height, which was a little over five feet, this man could be only six or seven inches taller. She had never done this dance before, but it was so simple, one, two, three, hop; one, two, three, hop.

When he looked down at her she laughed up into his face. But when he said, 'You're as light on your feet as a nymph,' her smile disappeared, for the words recalled the face of the man who had called her the rag nymph.

This man, however, was different: there was no evil in his eyes that she could see. He wasn't really handsome, but he was good-looking. And although he was the mistress's half-brother there was no resemblance between them; not in any way at least that she could see, especially not in his manner.

The dance came to an end amid great clapping. He led her back to her seat, and when she sat down he bowed to her, saying, 'Thank you very much, Miss Forester. I hope I may have the pleasure again during the evening.'

She did not answer him, just inclined her head towards him; and when Jane flopped down at her side, saying, 'Eeh! fancy. What was it like . . . I mean, dancin' with 'im?' she answered, 'Just like you dancing with Ken.'

Ken almost doubled up with laughter, and spluttered, 'But I stood on her toes; and I kicked McTaggart on the shins backwards.' Then he leant past Jane towards Millie,

161

and whispered, 'I've always wanted to do that,' which set them all off.

The music did not immediately restart and the room seemed full of chatter. Looking round, Millie realised that most of the staff were old ... well, in their thirties. In fact, some, she guessed, were in their fifties, as old as Mrs Aggie. Even the housemaids were fully fledged women. Jane, Ken, and herself, seemed to be the only young ones present.

When the butler stood up the chatter ceased, and he called out, 'Will you take your partners for the quadrille, ladies and gentlemen?'

There was more laughter now and bustle as some members of the company paired off and grouped into four couples, making a square. But when others seemed laughingly reluctant to get to their feet, the master and Mr Bernard Thompson rose together; and when Mr Bernard approached Sarah Cross, the first housemaid, the master continued down the room till he came to the three young people, and there, standing in front of Millie, he said, 'Will you do me the honour, my dear?'

Whereas she had accepted Mr Bernard Thompson's invitation without much hesitation, she now sat looking fixedly at the tall man, until he laughed down at her and, holding out his hand, commanded gently, 'Come;' then she allowed him to lead her to where there were only two couples standing. Having joined them, he turned round and looked towards his head gardener and cried, 'Come on, Benson. Don't tell me you're too old for a dance? And you, Mrs Benson, get him up.'

The feeling engendered by the master's picking that chit of a girl, that stranger, that odd-looking creature, to dance, was somewhat placated by his enticing of the gardener and his wife on to the floor.

162

As the fiddles and the flute struck up a lively tune, Millie now muttered, 'I don't know the steps;' and he, bending his head towards her, exclaimed loudly, 'What?'

'I don't know the steps.'

'Don't worry. Here we go!' And with this, he marched her briskly around in a circle; then turning her, he marched her back again. And so they progressed through the five figures of the dance.

Each of the other three men would take hold of Millie and swing her round, but Raymond Crane-Boulder always caught her under the arms and swung her off her feet.

By the time the dance was finished everybody was gasping for breath but seemingly happily.

On this occasion, she wasn't escorted back to her seat because her last partner in the dance was Fred Bateholm, and he turned from her to rejoin his wife, so leaving her to walk down the room to where Jane and Ken were sitting. When she flopped down beside them, Jane said, 'By! the master does dance, doesn't he? And he swung you off your feet. D'you know' – her voice sank – 'your dress came up and you could see your blue petticoat and your white stockings right up to your calves.'

Millie wasn't taking much heed of Jane's chattering because she was looking towards the doorway where the mistress stood. She had glimpsed her before watching the dancers, and now she knew she was looking at her. And when she turned away, she was struck by the thought that if she was in that woman's employ she wouldn't last long. But then she wouldn't be in her employ. She would never work for anyone like her.

It was when the butler was announcing yet another polka that Flo Yarrow, the second housemaid, who had been out of the room, came in and hesitated a moment before walking across the open floor towards them. Bending down

163

to Jane, she said, 'The mistress wants to see you in the study, and you've got to take her with you.' She nodded towards Millie.

'The mistress wants to see me? What for?'

'How should I know? That's all she said, she wanted to see you, an' . . . ' She nodded again towards Millie.

'But . . . but, Miss Yarrow, I . . . I don't know where the study is.'

'Come on out.'

Jane rose immediately, but Millie hesitated, and she, too, now said, 'Why does she want to see me?'

'You had better ask her, miss, when you see her.' There was sarcasm in the voice; but then her tone changed and she said, 'Oh, come along.'

Outside the room, she pointed to a wide corridor: 'It's the last door on the right side,' she said, 'and wait till you're told to enter.'

Flo Yarrow stood watching the two young girls walking away from her, and she bit on her lip and turned her head to the side as if pondering over something. Then she swung about and went back into the room where once again she saw Mr Winters, the master's valet; but he was dancing with Miss McNeil again, so she stood aside and waited.

In the meantime, the two girls had reached the end of the corridor, and before Jane tapped on the door she whispered to Millie, 'What d'you think she wants us for? She was watchin' you dance. Very likely it was because you showed your legs and your white stockin's.'

'Don't be silly,' Millie whispered back. 'Anyway, in that case, why should she want you an' all?'

Jane's hand was wavering in front of the door when they heard a gust of laughter coming from the room. They exchanged glances; and when Jane's hand dropped away from

164

the door Millie impulsively knocked twice, and then they waited. And in the waiting the laughter turned to giggling, then ceased, before the mistress's voice called, 'Come in.'

When Millie stepped into the room the first thing she noticed was that it was a kind of library. There were bookshelves round the walls, and where there weren't books there were silver cups and shields. In the fireplace a log fire was burning brightly. The chairs were all of brown leather.

The mistress was sitting in one to the side of the fireplace, her elder son in one to the other, with Randolph leaning against the back of it. Two decanters and three glasses were on a table to their hand; and it was obvious to Millie that the two young men were silly drunk.

'Come over here!'

The voice was imperious; and in answer to it Jane scurried forward, but Millie remained where she was within a few feet of the door. And strangely, in this moment, she wasn't seeing the mistress of the house, nor her drunken sons, but Sister Cecilia, who was saying to her, 'Beware the evil that men do.'

She heard her own voice, thin-sounding now, saying, 'What do you want with me, madam?'

'*Come here, girl!* and you'll find out.' The woman had pulled herself to her feet and, when Millie still did not move, she almost sprang across the distance to confront her.

Grabbing a handful of Millie's dress at the shoulder, she dragged her forward and thrust her towards her son, the while still holding her, and saying, 'You're made to tempt men and I'm going to see you're not disappointed.'

With a twist of her body, Millie freed herself and jumped backwards, and the woman only saved herself from toppling by falling against the long oak table in the middle of the room. And from there she now cried at her elder son, 'Go on! Davey boy. Make a start, and show your elders how it's done. Aye,

165

by God! show 'em. And you, Randy, take that clot there.'

'What! Her, Mama?' The boy threw his head back now and laughed. 'She's a midden mucker; she empties the mess pails. Not her, Mama.'

'Anything to start on, boy. Anything to start on.'

When there was a cry from the top of the room the woman turned and looked to where her son was warding off the girl's hands, and she cried at him, 'Strip her! boy. Strip her!'

Millie had her back against a row of books, and, putting her hand behind her head, she grabbed one. It was a thick leather-bound volume and, swinging it, she levelled it at the boy, and immediately the laughing, drunken timidity he had previously shown vanished: for now he yelled, 'You bitch! you,' and the next moment he had his fingers in the front of the collar of her dress, and the ripping of the brocade and the under petticoat filled her ears.

'You! You beasts! Leave me alone,' she screamed at him, and, flailing her arms, she brought her knee up, and when it caught him in the groin he yelled out in pain before actually screaming, 'You bloody she-cat!' Then he was on her, his fists thumping her, between tearing at her clothes.

When she fell with a thud to the floor, he on top of her, perhaps it was her screaming and the woman's laughter that covered the sound of the door bursting open.

Raymond Crane-Boulder, followed by Bernard Thompson, came to a momentary halt at the sight before them. It was as if they couldn't believe their eyes. And then with a bound and a sweep of his arm Raymond knocked his wife flying against the further wall, for her again only to be saved from falling to the floor by her younger son.

In a fury stronger than that which his elder son must have felt, the father whipped him off the prostrate figure of the girl and, holding him by his ruffled cravat, he took his doubled fist and levelled it against his face. His son's crying out seemed to enrage him further, for from the wall above a shelf of trophies he snatched a riding crop. He'd had to tug it from its hook, but once in his hand he brought it round his son's head, 'You young swine! You scum!'

After the third blow his arm was caught by Bernard who yelled at him, 'Enough! Enough!' and pulled him aside; and as he did so Berenice Boulder's voice screamed, 'Hypocrite! Hypocrite! Can't stand them being natural, eh? Hypocrite! Bloody hypocrite.'

The younger boy was crying and appealing to his mother: 'Be quiet! Be quiet! Please, please, Mama, be quiet!' which seemed to activate his father again: pulling himself away from Bernard's hold, he strode down the room and, grabbing the cringing boy, thrust him towards his brother, commanding them: 'Get out of here! And you, too.' He was now stabbing his finger at the petrified Jane. The door had no sooner closed on them than he advanced swiftly on his wife and, looking into her glaring, hate-filled face, he brought the crop across the side of it, crying, 'You filthy, evil, drunken slut! You're not fit to live. Do you hear me? Not fit to live. You would watch your son— ' He now closed his eyes tightly for a moment; then his arm dropped to his side as he stared at his wife who, after flinching from the blow, was standing straight, glaring back at him. She hadn't even put her hand up to her face. And what she said now was, as if she were solid and sober, 'I'll see the end of you yet, Raymond. And it'll be a slow end. I prophesy it will be a slow end, you unnatural swine.' And on this she turned from him as if she were feeling no pain and walked out of the room. And, as if defeated, he stood with his head bowed, before swinging round to where Bernard was kneeling on the floor holding Millie in his arms.

He hurried to him, saying, 'Is . . . is she all right?'

'I don't know.' The words were brief and curt sounding.

167

Bernard now rose from his knees; and bending, he lifted Millie and laid her in one of the leather armchairs, then pulled her torn garment over her bare chest before straightening and facing the man he thought of as his brother-in-law. 'But what I do know,' he said, 'is I no longer recognise Berenice as the half-sister I once knew. Nor can you be congratulated on your sons, Raymond, if you cannot control their drinking at their age.'

'You know nothing about it.' The words were ground out through Raymond's clenched teeth. 'Anyway, I don't need any criticism from you; this is my house.'

'It isn't your house yet, Raymond, it's your father's. And I wonder if, from his fastness up above, he knows what goes on down here. What would he say to this poor child being . . . ?' He paused: 'Well, I don't know if she's been raped or not, but your son had a damned good try at it, by the look of things.'

'Yes; but who drove him to it? Ask yourself that. Anyway, get out of my road. I'll take her down to the Quintons.'

'No. No, Raymond; you've caused enough speculative gossip already tonight back in that room, when you almost exposed the girl's limbs in your form of dancing when there was no need for it. You didn't act the same way with the other maids. And please' – he held up his hand – 'say nothing more, else more will be said, and we'll both be sorry for it. Just one thing: I won't avail myself of your hospitality any longer than tomorrow morning.'

Raymond Crane-Boulder stepped back from him, saying, 'That'll suit me.' Then he looked down at the dishevelled girl lying in the chair: her hair had become loose and part of it was hanging over one shoulder and lying across the bare nape of her neck; her small breasts were heaving, and in so doing were pushing aside her torn garment. And as he gazed at her his lower lip covered his upper one before being

168

drawn in between his teeth. Abruptly he swung about and went from the room; and Bernard, bending over the chair, said softly, 'You're all right. You're all right.'

Slowly, Millie opened her eyes. She had been aware of the men for some time, though at first their presence had been hazy. But the one thing she felt glad about now was that the master had gone. This one she didn't mind; he was different somehow. She looked at him, and as he said again, 'You're all right,' the tears slowly spilled over on to her flushed cheeks.

'Oh, my dear, my dear,' Bernard said. 'It's all right. You're going home. Here! let me dry your eyes.' He took out a handkerchief, and with it he wiped her face; and then he said, 'Sit quiet now. By the way, have you got a coat?'

Her mind said, 'A cloak,' but her lips refused to voice the words, and he said, 'Don't worry. Don't worry. I'll find someone. Just stay quiet.'

She was left alone. She did not move her head but her eyes took in the rows of books. And as they rested on them, she said to herself, 'Ben. Ben, I want to go home.' But that wasn't what she had meant, or meant to think; it was something to do with Ben and the books. He would love to be in this room with all the books. Why was she lying here? Her head was hurting. It was sore at the back. She had fallen, she had a bump. Had she danced too much? No. No, she hadn't danced too much. Why was she lying here?

As if a door had been wrenched open in her mind she suddenly knew why she was lying there, and she began to gasp, muttering now aloud, 'Oh, no! No! Please don't. Please don't.' But she was alone now; they had gone. He had torn her frock, her beautiful, beautiful frock; and Mrs Aggie had paid all that money to have it unpicked, re-made and pressed. She would never wear it again. Oh, no, no, no!

She could never wear it again. Not even if it was sewn up. She wanted to go home. If only somebody would come and take her home.

'It's all right. You're going home.'

She opened her eyes and there he was again, the nicer one of the two; in fact, the nicest one among them. There was another man with him and he was holding her cloak; and the nice man said to him, 'I'll have to carry her, Winters. I don't know if I can carry her all the way, so you'll have to give me a hand.'

'She wouldn't be able to walk, sir?'

'You heard: she was rambling. I think she's been slightly concussed. I'll lift her up, you put the cloak around her.'

She knew she was being lifted and that her head was lying against his shoulder. He was carrying her home. She was so glad. And tomorrow morning she would wake up and go down to the kitchen and set the breakfast for Mrs Aggie and Ben. Oh, that would be nice . . .

Bernard Thompson managed to carry her through the house and down the drive to the Quintons' with the help of George Winters, who walked by his side, holding her dangling legs. And when at last he placed her on the couch in the Quintons' sitting-room before two amazed and anxious people, he said to them, 'I think if she hasn't fully recovered by tomorrow morning you should call in the doctor.'

When William Quinton asked, 'What on earth happened? Look at her clothes!' Bernard said, 'Come outside for a moment.'

In the hall William was given the details as far as Bernard knew them, but they were enough for him to say, 'God Almighty! That woman will cause murder one of these days.' Then apologising, he said, 'I'm sorry: I forget she's a relative of yours, Bernard.'

170

'Well, I can tell you this much, William, I'm sorry that she can claim that distinction, even if it's only as half-brother. Anyway, I'm leaving in the morning.'

'I thought you were here for the rest of the holidays?'

'No. The atmosphere's too strong for me.'

'The old gentleman'll miss you.'

'Oh, I don't think he cares very much one way or the other whom he sees these days.'

'Will you go home?'

Bernard laughed gently.

'No, William. My father's third wife is expecting the first addition. What relation that will make me to it, I don't know. Still a half something or other. No, I think I'll return to Oxford. I have a number of friends there and I'll get down to work again.' He paused for a moment, then said, 'Are you happy in this job, William?'

'Yes. Yes, most of the time; but I know I wouldn't have it if it wasn't for the old man and his association with my grand-dad and my father. Anyway, being the runt of the litter of ten, I'm glad to have any post at all.'

'I've always thought you were worth something better than this. Yet still, if you're happy. But' – he looked towards the door – 'that poor child in there. I doubt you won't be able to keep her.'

'No; I can see that.'

'She's very beautiful. I don't think I've seen anyone so beautiful. She certainly caused a stir up there tonight. My! you should have seen the faces: the resentment, the bitterness. Odd, isn't it, how people hate beauty. She stood out like a princess on a dung heap.'

'Well, it's odd: she mightn't have come from a dung heap, but she lives pretty near it, for her guardian's an old rag woman.'

'Never!'

171

'Oh yes. An enormously fat old thing, a bundle of rags herself. She's got the famous taggerine place, such as they call it, on the outskirts of The Courts, beyond the market. She's well known in the town. She's got a nickname, "Raggy Aggie". For years she used to push a barrow, and that child with her, I understand. Now they've risen to a horse and cart. There's a warped fellow comes for her on her days off and brings her back. I say warped . . . well, he's only about five feet tall, but if his legs had been longer he would have been a massive individual, and good-looking into the bargain. But he, too, from what I can gather, was picked up and looked after by the old rag woman.'

'Amazing. But she seems . . . well, educated. Yes, that's the word; she doesn't talk like the rest of them.'

'Oh, she's been educated in bits and pieces; she was under the nuns for one period, and later attended a pay school; and believe it or not, she asked to attend school with my tribe. In fact, she did a little manoeuvring. It was either she went to school or she left, and the children are crazy about her. Oh' – he put his hand to his head now – 'I don't know what's going to happen there: they've never been so good in their lives before; she can handle them and they love her. Dear! dear! Why had this to happen? By the way' – his voice dropped – 'do you think she was . . . ?' He shook his head, and Bernard answered, 'I don't know. I just don't know. I heard her screaming. Apparently, Yarrow, one of the maids, was told off to tell the girls to go along to the study and she had sense enough to tell Winters, and he told Raymond. I happened to be there. There you have it. Well, I'll have one more look at her, then I'll go.'

And that's what Millie remembered for a long time afterwards: the kind face above her, saying again, 'You'll be all right.'

172

9

Three days later William Quinton drove Millie home in his trap. It was a Friday and the yard was quiet. Ben was dealing with a man who had brought in some scrap iron, and Aggie was in the barn watching two women sort through a pile of oddments and making sure that they didn't stuff any up their coats. She had lost a few good pieces of late and she felt she knew where they had gone, and one of the two customers was under suspicion. But when, glancing out of the door, she saw a well-dressed man helping Millie down from a trap she almost sprang across the yard, as did Ben. And they both called out together, 'What's up? What's the matter?'

'Oh! Mrs Aggie.' Millie put out one hand towards Aggie and the other towards Ben and muttered weakly, 'I'm home. I'm home for good.' Then turning to the well-dressed man, she said, 'This is Mr Quinton. He's been so kind, like Mrs Quinton. I . . . I must sit down. I'm still a bit dizzy.'

In amazement, one on each side of her, they helped her into the house, and William Quinton followed, his eyes growing wider as he passed through a room filled with odd furniture and into another which, he observed straightaway, was used as a kitchen-cum-dining-room-cum-sitting-room. And there

173

the enormous woman turned to him and said, 'What is this all about? Is she ill? What's been done to her?'

'She . . . she had a fall and slight concussion, but she is all right. I can assure you, she's all right. And more so, I can assure you she is so glad to be home with you. But her return is my loss and that of my wife and children, because, I may say, she brought order and a cheerfulness and happiness into my home. The children loved her and my wife found her a very great help.'

'Yes, I'll bet she would.' Aggie was nodding at him, not sure how to take him, when Ben turned from bending over Millie and, looking at Mr Quinton, he said, 'Will you be seated, sir? And could we get you a drink of something?'

'No. No, thank you. I . . . I must return as quickly as possible.' He smiled at the shorter man, adding, 'I have a job to do. As you know, I'm bailiff to Mr Crane-Boulder.' He gave this last piece of information in turning towards Aggie; and, still addressing her, he said, 'I would consider it a favour if I could call now and again and bring one or two of my children to see Millie. They would love that.'

With a forearm Aggie now heaved up her sagging breasts and glanced at Ben, and whatever expression she saw on his countenance, tempered what she now said to the visitor: 'Well, if that's your wish, sir, you'll be welcome. And . . . and thank you for bringing her back home.'

He now walked over to Millie and, taking her hand, he said, 'I'll come and see you soon, and bring the girls and Patrick. If I promise them such a treat it might keep them tolerably quiet for a time.' He pulled a small face at her, and she said, 'Thank you, Mr Quinton. I would like that. Yes, I would like to see the children again. Will you give them my love?' And she smiled faintly now as she ended, 'And tell Paddy to keep playing his pipe.'

174

'I will. I will.' He straightened up, then turned and looked from Ben to Aggie, saying, 'Goodbye, then.' And as Aggie answered, 'Goodbye, sir,' Ben said, 'I will see you out.'

In the yard Ben demanded, 'What's all this about, sir?' And after taking in a deep breath, William Quinton gave him a brief outline, finishing by saying, 'That's as much as I know, and from what Bernard . . . Mr Thompson told me, he didn't think she had . . . well, been touched. You know what I mean?'

Ben's answer was a growl. 'Yes, I know what you mean. My God! You're telling me that the son of the house tried to . . . Good God in heaven!'

'They were very drunk, the young men, and I'm afraid their mother was the instigator of the whole incident. Unfortunately, her drinking is habitual, and nobody is more sorry than my wife and I that all this has happened, because we became very fond of Millie. And my children, well, they adored her. She was like a child with them, yet she could control them.' He nodded his head now while adding, 'In a strange way the other side of her seemed very adult. Well, I hope to see you again, Mister . . . I'm sorry I don't know your actual name. Millie has spoken of you, and often, but by your Christian name.'

'Me name's Smith.'

'Oh, Smith. Well, I think I prefer Ben.'

Did Ben detect a little slackening of class, a slight condescension? Whatever it was he retorted quickly, 'Me name's Smith.'

William Quinton's expression changed, and stiffly now he said, 'Well, good day, Mr Smith;' then he mounted the trap and left the yard.

Ben re-entered the house; but he did not immediately go into the far room, he stood with his hand gripping the back of an old couch and his head bowed to his chest for some

175

minutes before he pushed the door open, there to see Millie with a cup of tea in her hand.

She looked at him as if she had been waiting for him, and as he approached her, she said, 'Oh, Ben. Oh, I'm so pleased to see you again. I've . . . I've said to Mrs Aggie that . . . that I never want to leave home, leave either of you ever, ever again.'

'Well, that'll suit us both down to the ground. But . . . but how you feelin', really?'

'Not too bad; but I have a headache most of the time. The doctor said it would go if I rested for a week, say.' Then her head drooping and her voice low, she said, 'My dress is ruined, Mrs Aggie,' which brought no harsh retort from Aggie; instead, she put her arm around the thin shoulders and pressed her into her side as she said, 'Who cares about a frock? There'll be another where that came from. If that's all that's worryin' you, you can stop. But can you give us the rights of what happened? I mean . . .'

Millie raised her head and looked from Aggie to Ben, who was on his hunkers before her, and hesitantly she said, 'I . . . I shouldn't have gone dressed like that, but . . . but they said it was a party. Yet every one of them was in uniform.'

'Is that a fact?'

Ben poked his head towards her. 'All in uniform at a party?'

'Yes. Except' – she nipped at her lip now before adding – 'the mistress, of course. And . . . and I seemed to stick out. And then Mr Thompson, him whose birthday party it had been on the Monday, you know. He was twenty-one. He asked me to dance and we did the polka. He was . . . he was very nice; and yet' – again she bit on her lip – 'he is the half-brother of the mistress, they say. But . . . but he's not a bit like her. Then . . . then they had a quadrille and the master asked me to dance.'

'The master asked you . . . ?' Aggie's expression was one of disbelief and she drew her head back into her thick shoulders, repeating, 'The master asked you?'

'Yes. Well, he didn't ask me, he sort of took me into the dance, and . . . and he swung me round. And I didn't know my petticoat and stockings were showing, but Jane said they were. You know, I've told you about Jane. She has all the dirty jobs, and she was so excited about the party. She told me yesterday when she came to see me that the mistress had been watching from the doorway, and it was after that that she sent for her and me to go along to the study.'

With a quick movement she thrust her head into the back of the couch and opened her mouth wide, and Ben said, 'It's all right. It's all right. You needn't go on if you don't want to. It's all right.'

But she went on haltingly, and told them as much as she could remember, and when she had finished they were both gaping at her. Presently, Aggie said, 'This Mr Thompson carried you from the house?'

'Yes; and I understand Mr Winters, the valet, helped him, and they brought me home . . . well, I mean, to the Quintons'. And Mr Thompson came the next day to see how I was. He was leaving the house. And Annie said there was a lot of talk about that because he had come for the holidays.'

She raised her head again and said quietly, 'Oh, you've got no idea how wonderful it is to be home. But do you think, Mrs Aggie, I could go and lie down for a time?'

'Lie down, me dear? You're goin' to bed and you're goin' to stay there for the next few days, as that doctor said. And what's more, I'll have old Partridge come and see you.'

'Oh, I don't need a doctor, Mrs Aggie.'

'Leave it to me, girl, to know what you need. Anyway, old Partridge has been wantin' to get his foot in this door again for years. The last bill I paid him was sixteen years

177

ago when me father died. Two shillings a visit he charged. Daylight robbery. And I told him that.' She smiled softly and, holding her hands out to Millie, she drew her gently up from the couch, saying, 'Come away. Come away.' . . .

It was the same evening. The yard gates were closed. They'd had their evening meal. Millie was asleep upstairs and Aggie and Ben sat facing each other, Ben with a mug of beer to his side on the settle and Aggie with a glass of gin resting on a shelf to her hand. They had been sitting in silence for some time.

When Aggie spoke her voice was quiet. 'I know what you're thinkin',' she said. 'It's such as my own thoughts. We did what we thought was best: we sent her away to save her being picked up and from the outcome of what that would mean; yet she walks straight into it; and all arranged by that bitch of a woman. Have you thought what would have happened to her if the men of the house hadn't come in at that moment?'

'Aye, I've thought what would have happened to her. And aye, me thoughts have just been similar to your own. Well, here she is and here she stays. And she won't get out of me sight if I can help it.'

'Huh! And how long d'you think you can keep your eyes on her? She's growing fast. The solution for her is to be married, that's the only safeguard . . . '

She hadn't finished the last word before he sprang to his feet, crying, 'Married? She's only thirteen, woman!'

She stared at him for a moment and, her voice deceptively quiet now, she said, 'She's near fourteen and she's an old fourteen.'

'Aye, all right, she's near fourteen, but you're marryin' her off.'

'I'm not marryin' her off now, but in two years' time she'll be ready for it, aye, if not before.'

178

'What's come over you, woman? You want rid of her?'

Aggie now heaved herself up and on to the edge of the sofa, and her words were ground out: 'Yes, I want rid of her because she's brought into me life the only happiness that I've ever had. Of course I want rid of her: I want rid of her because I love her; I want rid of her because I won't know a minute's peace until I see her safely married. Yes, I want rid of her.'

Ben was standing, his feet apart, his arms away from his side, his stance giving the suggestion that he was about to spring; but bending his thick body forward, he said, 'And where do you propose to find her a husband? Someone from The Courts? Or are you thinkin' someone from that big house will come riding down and offer to take her off your hands? Say, this Mr Thompson who carried her from the house? You were asking her about him, weren't you? Well, which is it to be?'

Aggie wriggled herself back on to the couch, and in a subdued tone now, she said, 'I wasn't thinkin' of anyone from The Courts or a big house, but somebody in between, like one of those teachers you learn from at night.'

'Oh. Oh, you've had your spies out, have you?'

'No, I haven't had me spies out. I don't have to; in my business I just keep me ears open, and I hear everything. Rosie Dillon, she's an old customer, her brother apparently is caretaker for that, what do they call it? national school, and for the rooms that are used at night. She said, "I hear your Ben's goin' to school again." You would have told me sometime, I know. Anyway I have it in me mind that one thing she'll be wantin' is to take some kind of learnin' again and that it would be safe for her to go to the night class along of you. And you never know who she might meet there, not among the learners, oh no, but one of the teachers, perhaps. And, you know, with her head on her shoulders she could become a teacher herself.'

'It hasn't taken you long to get it all worked out.'

'Well, there's a sayin' about desperate needs need desperate measures. And—' She paused, reached out, lifted up her glass, took a sip of the gin, then placed the glass back on the shelf before ending, 'I want to see her settled before I take me last journey, because where would she be then? Any day now I'm likely to hear you're goin' to go off and marry your Annie.'

'What did you say?'

'You heard what I said right enough. And I'll add this: it's not before time, the years you've been hangin' on.'

Walking over to the couch and bending over her, Ben said with emphasis but quietly, 'Get this into your head, Aggie. I'm not gonna marry Annie, sooner or later. She knows that. Right from the beginning she's known that. I can't get it into your head that she's a friend. She's good company, she's good chat. She took notice of me when nobody else did . . . I mean, as a lass might. How old was I when I first came to your dad? Eight? And she was then sixteen. She seemed grown up to me, but she was kind and she was lonely and lost, like I was. Behind all me chatter there wasn't anybody more lonely an' lost than me. I'd known her for more than a year before I came into the yard here, and what you don't know and what I've never said is that she gave me shelter many a night when I would have frozen to death otherwise. She had only one room. Her mother was in bed in the corner, had been for years, her body like a balloon. She lay there all day by herself while Annie was at the mill. Each night Annie would dose her with laudanum to keep the pain down, and when she went to sleep she'd let me in and I'd lie on the mat in front of the banked-down fire till early next mornin'. For two winters she did that. An' then her mother died and she let me carry on, sleeping there on the mat, until your dad offered me the room above the stable. And for the first time in me life I had a place of me own.'

180

When Aggie's head began to wag and she was about to speak, he held up his hand to silence her, and went on, 'Now that I've started I'll give you the whole story. There were times when, lonely, we comforted each other. And I was still a lad, mind; but I told her that I'd never marry anybody and she understood that. She's still nothin' to look at, just skin and bone, mostly; but I had noticed over the last few years that she had started to titivate herself up a bit, and then when she got the chance of moving from The Courts to one of the New Buildings, she took it. It was then I found out the reason. A man she's worked alongside for years in the mill, he's a widower and much older, but he must think something of her for he comes a-courtin', you might say. And I'm happy for her.'

'My! My! My! But tell me, if that's the case, why you still go along there.'

'For the simple reason, Aggie, as I've tried to pump into you before, we're friends. We can play cards, we can chatter, we can discuss the gossip of the day. And she's got a lot to gossip about because, as you know, her cousin's the best-known whore on the street. And sometimes she pays a call on her and we have a laugh at her tales.' He paused. 'Not always, though, because there's some things that happen down on the street that turns even Nancy Pratt's stomach. And, I can tell you, that takes some doing. So there you have it, Aggie, and you've no need to pry any more. But to go back to your . . . what the teacher would call, demise, and what would happen to Millie should that come about. There'll always be me here until my demise, which, not knowin' the Lord's intention, could be, I must admit, any time; but given a fair deal I'll have a few years ahead of me yet, being but twenty-three.'

Once more Aggie pulled herself to the edge of the couch and, thrusting her face close to his, she almost spat her next words at him: 'And you expect her to grow up an' to go on livin' here under your . . . what? your guardianship? A girl like her, growin' into a woman that'll bring men round her like flies? Oh, be your age, Ben Smith. And let me tell you somethin'.' She now thrust her doubled fist into her chest. 'I'm willin' to let her go, and by God! I'm goin' to see that you do the same, because, where she's concerned, your head's not recognizing your short legs. I know what's in the back of your mind. I know what all this education business is for. I know what the new overcoat and the high hat is for. Well, all the high hats in the world won't put inches on you, nor smart overcoats see you any other than you are. So, get that into your head, Mr Ben Smith.'

He couldn't speak for a moment; his Adam's apple was jerking up and down in his throat; when he did, his voice was quiet: 'Aggie,' he said, 'I'll never be out of your debt, for I know I owe you what I am today, and never for one minute in all the years I've known you have I ever wished you any harm. Just the opposite. Oh, just the opposite. But in this minute I could take me fist and land it between your eyes, not because you've tried to read me mind with regard to Millie, but because you've made me feel less than a man.'

They stared at each other as they had never done in all their acquaintance; then he turned and went from her.

PART THREE

The Cook

1

From the day Mr Quinton had returned her home and she had entered the kitchen, Millie knew that, although she never wanted to be separated from these two people again, her outlook was changed with regard to her surroundings.

As the days passed and she filled her time with cooking and cleaning, she knew there was a want in her. Even though she now accompanied Ben to his class on three evenings a week, there was always the nagging question: what was really to become of her? How could she earn a living? At first, she had thought it could be through cooking, only to reject this immediately. Her experience at The Grange had left her with no desire, and a real fear, of ever finding herself in service again.

Yet, she was faced with the fact that cooking was the only thing at which she was any good. When she had put this to Aggie, Aggie had added, 'And talking. Why don't you think of learning to teach children, like?' to which her answer had been, 'You have to have a special education.' Yet at times, she felt she knew more than Mrs Sponge, who took one of the classes, but then not anything near what her husband, Mr Sponge, knew. He was a clever man, Mr Sponge, not only with dates and history but about things that went on in the mind. It was he who had said there was a solution to every problem; you only had to sit down and spread your problem out before you, as it were, like cards on a table, then look to see if there was an outlet through any part of the pack that would present a solution to your problem.

Well, she had thought about it, and she had spread her cards on the table, and most of them pointed out to her that she could make good meat pies, scones, and currant buns. She could also make a very good nourishing stew. Another card pointed out to her that she had a craft at her hands that would enable anyone to start a cook shop. But at the idea of a shop she turned the card face down, as it were. Almost immediately another card pointed out that she already lived in a shop. That yard outside was a shop; well, a kind of one dealing with the residue of many trades.

And the card seemed to jump from the table and confront her with a picture of an absolutely clean yard and, at the open gates, a long wooden bench on which were arrayed her pies, scones, and currant buns. And at the end of the bench, a big kale pot full of hot stew, with herself standing at the other side of the table, dealing with customers.

But what about customers? Why! the mill workers: most of those who worked at Freeman's passed the gates to reach their particular Court. At six o'clock every night there was a stream of them. And then, too, during the day, all types of people were passing up and down the road; although she had to admit they were mostly the ragged, filthy children and those adults emitting the stench of gin and filth, that made the smell rising from the yard seem like that from a herb garden.

But it was an idea, and who knew, it might in the end lead to something. Although she never wanted to leave either Aggie or Ben, she knew that Aggie, at least, would die

186

sometime, and Ben would likely marry Annie; and although she liked Annie as . . . a nice little creature, she could not imagine Ben living with her. But then, on further thought, she could not imagine Ben marrying her. What would they talk about? Annie had no conversation. She had noted she could listen, but she didn't talk or discuss anything . . . well, not when she was present anyway.

It was one evening when they were sitting round the kitchen table and enjoying Millie's new dish, a rabbit pie, not stewed in the old way, with potatoes round it, but baked in the oven in a thick gravy, dotted with sliced apple and covered with a pie-crust. She had seen the recipe in the *Sunday* magazine. It was a nice paper and had lively stories in it, more so than *The Band Of Hope* and *The Good Words Magazine*, both of which Mrs Sponge kindly passed on to her every week.

The pie had caused much pleasant comment. It was after the dishes had been cleared away, and they were sitting round the fire that she dropped her bombshell. And a bombshell it was.

When Aggie got over her surprise, the first words she said were, 'Are you thinkin' of pushin' me out?'

'Don't be silly, Mrs Aggie. But, you know, you say yourself you're tired of doing the rounds, and Laddie is twice as old as you thought he was when you bought him.'

Then she had asked Ben: 'Well, what do you think? Don't just sit there staring; tell me what you think.'

'I think it's a fine idea. You're a cook. No matter what else you'll be in your life, you'll always be a cook. And aye, I can see the yard bein' cleaned up, and a bench at the front gate. But, I'll say, like Aggie, what's goin' to happen to me? Where do I come in this? Are you willing to pay me eight shillings a week?'

187

'I won't pay you anything; it will be Mrs Aggie who will pay you.' She inclined her head towards Aggie. 'And likely twice as much because, you know that shop we pass on the way to the school, well, the pies in there are tuppence ha'penny each.'

'Aye well, be that as it may. But again I ask you, what's to become of me in this new business venture? What am I to do?'

'Well, you don't think I can do it all on my own, do you? It'll take me all my time cooking with Mrs Aggie here, and somebody will have to look after—' she laughed now as she said, 'the shop.'

'Oh, I can't see meself servin' in a shop. Never!' He wrinkled his nose.

'Well, all right then, I would do the cooking at night; well, in the evening, and I would stand at the table the next day.'

Aggie and Ben looked across at her now, and Aggie said to him, 'She's got it all worked out. My God! I can't believe it. This place has been a taggerine yard for as long as I can remember, but now she proposes to make it dainty with pies and buns, and such like. But would you tell me, miss' – she had turned now to Millie – 'how many pies et cetera, et cetera, do you think you can cook in that at once?' She was now thumbing towards the round oven.

'Twenty-one, twelve on the top shelf and nine on the bottom. And if the meat's cooked beforehand they'll take only about half an hour. And at the least I could do four lots in the evening. Of course I'd want someone to stoke up the fire and someone to go for the stores' – she glanced from one to the other now – 'because I'd need a lot of fat, and flour, and meat, and currants, and things like that. And I had thought of peas. There's a place in the market that sells mashed peas. You pointed it out to me once.'

188

There was a rumbling sound from Ben; then he was doubled forward on the settle, his laughter filling the room. And Aggie, looking at him, endeavoured to keep her face straight, too, as she said, 'He's findin' it funny.' And Millie, gazing at the old woman, asked quietly, 'Aren't you?'

For answer Aggie said softly, 'Aw! love; I can't see it happenin'. It would take an earthquake to move that lot in the yard. And then, look at the weather. How about that? You couldn't have a table out there in the wind or rain.'

'Yes, I've thought about that. It could come under the arch, or the barn could be cleared. Quite easily the barn could be cleared.'

Aggie said nothing to this, but she looked to where Ben was lying back against the settle, his hand now held tightly against his side. His face was wet with his laughing until Aggie, looking at Millie, said, 'Lass, have you ever thought that you won't be in this place for ever. Sixteen, comin' up. And who knows? you could be married.'

They both gave a start as Ben sprang to his feet, all laughter and fun now gone from his face as he cried, 'Don't start putting things into her head. You would damn well think, the way you talk, that sixteen was the limit for any lass marrying. She'll marry when she's ready, and she'll know when she's ready. And who she wants to marry an' all. So you get that into your head, woman.' And on that, he turned about and marched from the room, leaving Millie greatly perturbed; but not so Aggie.

'Gets worked up, doesn't he?' she said. 'But you know, me dear, what I say is true. Come sixteen, if not afore, that's the way your thoughts'll be goin'. By the way, how long is it since that Mr Thompson called?'

'Three months.'

'Yes; yes, it'll be that. And I thought you would remember. That was the third time he's looked in, wasn't it?'

189

Millie was on her feet looking down into the wide, sagging face, and her voice was just above a whisper as she said, 'No, Mrs Aggie. No, never; he's . . . he's just a kind man. He's a gentleman and, what's more, don't you remember who he's related to? That . . . that awful woman.'

'She's just a half-sister, so you said.'

'Mrs Aggie, please, don't ever think such a thing. I . . . I wouldn't be able to look at him or speak to him ordinarily if I thought he'd imagine that I . . . Well, it's as Ben said, sixteen is no age and I've never thought about being married. Well, not really. I'll not marry for years and years. And then it would have to be someone I was at ease with, never anyone like Mr Thompson. Anyway' – her voice was louder now – 'I wouldn't like the way they live, and they certainly wouldn't tolerate anybody . . . well, like me, coming into the family. I know that. Oh, yes, yes, I know that. You've just got to listen to Mr Sponge at the school. He was speaking the truth, and that's why they stopped him teaching. But he just pointed out the gulf there is between them and us, I mean, the middle classes and the working class. And not only just . . . well, like the people around here, but the artisans . . . you know, those men with trades whom the middle class still think of as scum. Do you know what? They won't allow working men on to the station when the gentry's there because the sight of them might offend their eyes, not until the train is about to go, when they can scramble into the third class, and have to stand up most of the way. Oh! Mrs Aggie. And you think that Mr Thompson . . . ?'

It was she who now turned about and hurried from the room, leaving Aggie sitting quietly nodding to herself. Then as if she were speaking to someone, she said aloud, 'Well, we'll see what we shall see. I hope I live long enough.'

2

It took nine months for Millie's suggestion to bear fruit in the form of pies at tuppence and fourpence each. Plain scones at a ha'penny each, currant ones at a penny each, or three for tuppence; mutton soup at a penny a ladleful, the implement being of a generous size; peas to be served as required, a ha'penny or a penny a scoop, with the Saturday being the currant teacakes and light pastry squares day, both at a penny each, yet the latter thick enough to be split and hold some form of preserve or a slice of meat.

But the business had brought with it a disappointment, at least for Millie: there was no chance now of her attending the night school; and although there had been no pressure on Ben to give up his free time, he had done so. One thing, however, he would not do was to accompany her into the adult Sunday School in the Methodist Hall. No; they weren't going to get him among the ranters, he said.

Millie was happy; at least she appeared so most of the time. And Aggie was happy, very happy, particularly on a Friday and Saturday night when she reckoned up the takings. But always Millie had to remind her that the cost of the ingredients, and of Ben's eight shillings and her own wage of five shillings, had to be taken into account before she could say what amount was profit.

'Well, Miss Smarty,' said Aggie, 'what d'you make of it tonight?'

'If you give me a few minutes I'll tell you, but it won't be as much as you think.'

'Well, there's seven pounds, four shillings here. How much have we made?'

'You, my dear Mrs Aggie, have made one pound, seventeen shillings and two pence.'

'Well, I suppose I can pay meself, say ten shillin's, takin' all in all, so that leaves a profit of one pound, seven shillin's and tuppence. Well, that isn't bad. And what we've made durin' the rest of the week, how does that answer?'

Millie started to scribble on the slate on which she had worked out the accounts, and then after a few minutes she said, 'Well, altogether the profit for the week looks to have been four pounds, eighteen and sixpence.'

'Not bad, not bad. I would have had to travel the town for nearly three weeks before I touched on that. A little gold mine this, isn't it? But' – she now put her hand out and touched Millie's – 'you can't keep it up, lass. You're at it from early mornin' till late at night, except like tonight, when we've sold out. And it's no use talkin' about gettin' a two-oven grate in, 'cos you've only got one pair of hands, no matter how Ben an' me help. You've got to make the stuff, and you're gettin' as thin as a rake where you should be filling out. You're as flat as a pancake.'

'I'm not.'

'Well, if you're not you've got it well hidden, both up your front and in your rear. No, dear, I can't see you goin' on like this. In a fortnight's time you'll be sixteen; and a great age will have come upon you; and I'm not bein' funny now either, because then you'll be really enterin' womanhood.'

192

When a bell clanged she turned round impatiently towards the door, saying, 'Can't they see that we are closed? Why he had to go and stick a bell outside, God alone knows.'

'Because,' Millie put in, laughing now, 'you complained about them walking practically into the kitchen here after we were closed. That's why he put the bell outside, Mrs Aggie. Anyway, I'll go and see who it is.'

'You'll do nothin' of the sort. You'll sit there. You've never been off your feet since first thing. An' the more you sit the more chance there'll be for you to grow a little bit of shape. Look at me.' She went out laughing at the joke against herself. And Millie sat back in her chair and closed her eyes for a moment. It was true; she did feel tired. It was also true that in a fortnight's time she would be sixteen, when Aggie had suggested she would enter into womanhood. But hadn't she entered that area some time ago? At what stage did one become a woman . . . ? When one lay thinking in the night how wonderful it would be if . . . if . . . if, yet had sense enough, when daylight came, to deny every night thought, with such terms as, 'Keep your head on your shoulders,' or 'Have sense.'

As if she had been suddenly transported back into the night she saw with a gape of surprise the man who had been in her thoughts. There he was in the flesh, standing by Aggie's side and smiling at her.

When she sprang to her feet, she toppled the chair over, and he came rapidly forward and straightened it, saying, 'I'm so sorry. Were you dozing?'

Before she could answer, Aggie put in, 'She's tired, sir. She's never off her feet. This business was her idea, but it's wearin' her out.'

'Oh, be quiet, Mrs Aggie, and don't talk nonsense.' Millie now put her hand out and indicated the settle, saying, 'Won't you sit down?'

193

'Yes. Yes, for a moment or so, but I won't stay, as I'm putting you out.'

'You're not. You're not at all, sir,' Aggie put in. 'Can I offer you a drink?'

'No, thank you. I . . . I had a meal a short while ago, and it was washed down. You understand?'

Aggie's head was bobbing now and she was smiling widely as she said, 'Oh, yes, sir, I understand that all right. It's a habit of me own. Mine's called cream of the valley. Eeh!' She swept her arm towards Millie, saying, 'Look at us both! Saturday evening and not changed out of our old duds. Well, if I can't offer you a drink I won't offer you my conversation, 'cos it wouldn't be what you would call edifying. But I'll away and change meself into something better. If you'll excuse me; I won't be all that long.'

Millie made a sign of protest with a half-open mouth and a gesture as if to halt Aggie's departure; but Aggie was not to be stopped; she was already disappearing through the door leading to the hall.

As Millie stood staring at him he rose to his feet, saying with a smile, 'I can't sit while you stand.'

'Oh.' As if coming out of the night dream, she turned and lowered herself slowly down on to the couch, and he resumed his seat on the settle.

'How are you? You look tired. As Mrs Winkowski says, you're working too hard.'

'It's natural. One is always tired towards the end of the day and Saturday is an especially busy day.'

'Yes. Yes. Is the business still going well?'

'Very well indeed.'

'Have . . . have you ever thought of taking a shop?'

She looked to the side before she said, 'Yes. Yes, I have, but that would mean leaving here and Mrs Aggie and Ben.'

He did not reply saying, Yes, I understand, but sat staring at her, all the while wondering how she could tolerate these surroundings after having, for a time at least, lived in the more refined, even though boisterous, atmosphere of the Quintons'. This room for instance: it was really dreadful. Of course, it was a working room, but it was taken up mostly with the couch on which she was sitting and the two tables, one under the window on which was laid out the various flours and substances for her cooking; the other, at which, he imagined, they would have to eat, was also used by her for writing, for on it were sheets of paper and a pencil, besides a slate. And that room which he had just come through; it smelt; not a bad smell, but a stale smell as one would get from old people. And here she was, this beautiful lily-like creature who, besides looking so beautiful, had also a mind, which had been so apparent in the short conversations they'd had previously. God! If only things were different. If only . . . if only. How often, over the past months, had he said that to himself, whenever the picture of her had sprung like a vision unheralded before his eyes, that picture which had brought him here tonight. How long could he go on and what would she say? 'You have a birthday soon,' he said now; 'I remember you telling me it was in September.'

'Yes. In a fortnight's time.'

'And then you will be sixteen. Do you feel grown up?'

She did not answer him immediately, but she was looking him straight in the face across the narrow space when she said, 'In a way, I can't remember not feeling grown up. Yet, in another way, I resent the feeling and want to remain, if not a child, then young.'

He laughed gently, saying, 'But you are young; and you're the type of—' he stopped here, not knowing whether to say lady, or woman, but tactfully substituting, 'personality that will always retain a youthful freshness right until you are

195

a very old lady like my Aunt Chrissie. Yet—' He waved his hand now before his face, saying, 'that was a bad comparison, because although, at sixty-five, she still has that girlish vitality, unfortunately she has become a little troubled in her mind. She lives not so very far away from here in a sweet little house, with an old retainer. I would dearly like you to come and meet her some day.' To this he added playfully, 'When you are sixteen and allowed to go out.'

'I'm allowed to go out now, Mr Thompson; no-one stops me.'

'But I've never been allowed to take you out, have I?'

She stiffened slightly as she replied, 'As yet you have never extended the invitation.'

He had a nice laugh; what she called a clean laugh.

'This conversation,' he said, 'could be taking place in a drawing-room with tasselled mantelborders there' – he pointed to the bare wooden mantelpiece, bare except for a pair of brass candlesticks and two ornamental jugs – 'and the windows almost obliterated with heavy brocade drapes, the table with an ivory marquetry top. Oh, and that one' – he laughingly now pointed to the table under the window – 'oh, that one is carved Indian style. And over there' – he indicated the far door – 'is a piano, but you can't see the top of it because it's covered with a huge Spanish shawl. And the walls are thick with paintings, all by great painters. Oh yes. And the floor? Well, nothing less than a Brussels carpet for the floor. And under my feet here' – he now tapped his feet on the home-made mat – 'is a bearskin rug, an actual bearskin rug that once kept the poor old bear warm somewhere out in the snows. And you know' – he now leant towards her – 'your reply just suited that room.'

'I don't know whether to take all that as a compliment or the reverse.'

196

Her answer evidently surprised him, and he was definitely nonplussed when she said, 'Well, you've described the drawing-room you are used to, so how do you find this in comparison?'

She watched him blink two or three times, wet his lips and then say softly, 'I don't draw comparisons. It was a picture to match your voice at that moment; although, I may add,' his tone dropped still further, 'that you would fit admirably into my description.'

He rose from the seat as if about to come towards her, but at that moment the door opened and Ben entered, to pause, then slowly walk towards the kitchen table.

'Hello, there.' Bernard Thompson's voice was light. 'I . . . I was just passing and popped in to' – he inclined his head towards Millie – 'to see how our young friend was getting on.'

'Oh, aye. Were you makin' for The Courts?'

'The Courts?' It was a puzzled question.

'Aye, the only destination past our gate is to The Courts; you know, Nelson Court and the like.'

'Ben!' Millie's voice was quiet. 'Mr Thompson called in to see me as he has done before; he knows what The Courts are like.'

'Huh! I doubt it. Have you ever been along there . . . sir?' The word seemed to come as an afterthought.

'No, I haven't been along there, but the stench proclaims the condition of the houses.' Bernard Thompson's expression was stiff now, as was his tone. 'And although you might not believe it, I'm well aware of the disparity between one end of this town and the other. In fact, I could say that, in a way, I'm as much concerned as Mr Engels is. And now that I'm part-owner of a mill I shall do my utmost to alleviate the situation wherever possible.'

197

He now turned and looked at Millie – his face was flushed – and by way of explanation he said, 'Mr Crane-Boulder senior, my godfather, died recently and in his will was kind enough to leave me co-owner with his son. So' – he now jerked his head towards Ben – 'whereas before I was somewhat restricted in my efforts, not having anything to do with the mill, I hope now to make some favourable changes, at least where I can within the law.'

There was silence for a moment before Ben spoke, and the sarcasm in his tone was evident as he said, 'Aye, of course, within the law. Well, I hope when you count the young 'uns who die between five and ten in your mill that you'll pop up to London and have a word with Mr Disraeli, or Gladstone, or one of 'em. Of course, they're all in deep mournin', aren't they? up there and all over, because since Prince Albert died, everybody is in black. Even *I've* read about the piano legs changing their stockin's to black. One fella dies and, after all, he was just a human bein' like the rest of us, only he, of course, was brought up with some form of sanitation. But who mourns for those who are thrown into paupers' graves by the dozen, aye, by the dozen? Or them, too sick to work at nine years old, pushed up the hill to the workhouse from where they can view the stinkin' river? And . . . '

'Are you quite finished?'

'No, I could go on; but of course I can't explain as well as Mr Sponge. Now he's a teacher along at the Methodist Hall and he's been educated as much as you, or more, and he's had first-hand knowledge of both sides of the line. He was born over your side, so he tells us, but that didn't stop him living in The Courts for a while just to taste their bit of comfort, you know.'

'Ben!'

'Aye, Millie?' He raised his eyebrows towards her in mock enquiry. 'You want to stop me tongue? Well, you should

198

know better than that by now. You know, as Mr Sponge has told us, once you start thinkin' there's no more rest for you. It's like a blackbeetle in a walnut shell; you know, tied on a bairn's belly to make it cry in order to get sympathy. It nags at you, scratches.'

'Perhaps your instructor, Mr Smith, has not yet come by the axiom that a little learning can be a dangerous thing. Now I will bid you good evening.'

After inclining his head towards Ben, he now turned to Millie, saying in a most stilted and polite manner, 'Will you do me the kindness to walk with me to the gate?'

Millie did not answer, but she rose from the couch and, as she passed Ben, she turned her head and levelled at him a look that held disdain; then, walking forward, she opened the door and led the way through the other room and into the yard; and it wasn't until they reached the locked gate and she stood staring through the rusty bars that she said, 'I'm sorry. I . . . I must apologise.'

'There's no need. And do you know? I understand how the—' He was about to say, 'the fellow', but went on, 'How he feels in more ways than one, believe me. Well now, look at me.'

She turned slowly and looked into his face, and again it was brought to her notice that he wasn't all that tall and that her eyes were almost on a level with his; and in his eyes was a look that was bringing into her throat that tight restriction which she could describe as having risen from some place behind her breast bone. It was like a pain.

'I'm sorry I won't be here to wish you a happy birthday; I'm due in London over the next two or three weeks. There is so much business to be attended to. At another time I might have enjoyed the free hours, after dealing with the business side of my visit, but as our friend' – he turned his head now and looked back across the yard towards the house door – 'so

199

aggressively put it, London is in mourning and is likely to be for some time, as the Queen is so distressed. However, as soon as I return I'm going to come and ask leave of Mrs Winkowski to drive you out to Aunt Chrissie's little house. I feel sure you will like her, as dithery in all ways as she is. And also, you may be taken with the house. If permission were granted would you be agreeable?'

The answer was simple: 'Yes,' she said; 'yes, I'd be agreeable.' And immediately he was comparing it with the reception his proposal would have received had it been offered to any other female of his acquaintance. There would have been a little simpering, a little hesitation and the answer would have been coy, implying, how adventurous, if not even naughty it was. But this girl's answer had been straightforward. There was nothing false about her, nothing frivolous, yet there emanated from her something that was really indescribable, like joy. The only thing he knew was, he longed to hold her, and had done, he thought, since the time he had carried her to William's house. William, too, had sensed the quality in her.

Thinking of William, he recalled their last conversation, in which he had told him that Raymond had asked if he had heard anything further of the fair child, and had probed him as to where she lived. And William had answered that she used to live in one of The Courts, the unsavoury Courts, but that she had since moved, and he didn't know where. William was wise. Oh, yes, William was wise. As had been his godfather in leaving the Little Manor to William, together with an acre of freehold land: he had known that once he was gone Raymond would have got rid of him, because there was no love lost between them, for William could never be subservient.

She had opened the gates, and he was now holding out his hand to her; and when she placed hers in it he held it tightly, saying, 'When we next meet you will have come of age, at least a certain age. Goodbye, my dear.' The last words were soft and deep with feeling. But she didn't reply to them, she just stood and watched him walking away, a gentleman in a fine grey suit, high hat and carrying a silver-mounted walking stick. And he had said he was coming back when she became of age.

Not until he was out of sight did she leave the gate. Then she almost marched across the yard and into the kitchen, where she found that Mrs Aggie, too, was present. But as if Mrs Aggie weren't there, she went straight for Ben, crying, 'If it wasn't that we live almost in the same house, I would never speak to you again. Your behaviour was simply dreadful, atrocious! Spouting your theories. He knows more about them than you do, and he can do more for the people than you can ever do.'

'Finished?'

'Yes. But I could go on.'

'Well, why don't you? I'm all ears. But I'm not finished, because I'll tell you this much: he's no good; none of his type are; in their own class, yes, but not when they come from yon side of the track to this side and smile at a young lass, and talk fancy to her, and fill her head with ideas, and her knowing nothing about life' – his voice was rising – 'but what she's learned in this muck-hole. Because that's how he saw it, isn't it? A muck-hole.'

As Aggie went to say something, he rounded on her, crying, 'Shut up! I'm goin' to have me say and I can start with you.' He stabbed his finger at her. 'You've got big ideas for her, haven't you? You think that bloke's on the square. You think he's goin' to come and say: "Mrs Winkowski" – his voice had altered now – "May I ask you for the hand of your ward . . . in marriage, that is, Mrs Winkowski, and not just leading her up the path with ideas of takin' her behind the bushes?" Oh no.'

201

Aggie's voice was almost a scream now as she, too, yelled, 'Ben Smith, shut your mouth! And get yourself outside before I level something at you. You'll be sorry for this night. Yes, you will. Oh, yes, you will.'

Ben put up his hand and pulled his bootlace tie tight under his collar. Then it appeared as if he had now to force himself to speak, for his jaws clamped two or three times before he brought out, 'Aye, I might be; but there's two people that'll be sorrier. That's a prophecy, and you'll live to see it.' And on that, he did not hurry or march from the room but turned slowly about and as slowly walked out, closing the door behind him.

Blindly now, Millie stumbled towards Aggie and threw herself into her arms; and as she sobbed, Aggie stroked her hair, saying, 'There now. There now. What does he know about it? He's an ignorant pig, that's all, an ignorant pig.' Then after a moment she gently pressed Millie from her and, looking into her streaming face, she said, 'Did he say anything to you . . . well, you know?'

Millie shook her head, and then stammered, 'He's . . . he's not like that. I mean, Ben's impression, it's all wrong. Mr Thompson's a gentleman, kind and . . . '

'D'you like him? I mean, a bit more than like him?'

Millie bowed her head before she muttered, 'Yes. Yes, I do, Mrs Aggie. I . . . I more than like him.'

'Well, me dear, if that's the case, we'll take it from there an' see what happens. But look, you haven't got to hold it against him; I mean, Ben, 'cos he can't help it. He's jealous.'

Millie was drying her eyes on the end of her white apron, and when she stopped, her face screwed up and she said, 'Jealous? Ben, jealous?'

'Aye, lass. He's a man. His legs might be short but he's all man. You take it from me.'

'But . . . but well, he's practically brought me up and . . . and been like a brother.'

Aggie gave a short laugh as she said, 'Get it into your head, lass, that no man will ever look on himself as a brother to you. The mirror in our bedroom is cracked; I think I'd better look out for a bit of decent glass so you can see yourself.'

'Oh, Mrs Aggie. Life is not easy, is it?'

'No, lass; life's not easy. And you've been very lucky so far, you know, because you're late in learnin' that. With the majority, especially around here, it comes soon after they can crawl.' And this elicited no further remark or question from Millie; instead she walked slowly to the couch and sat down, the while thinking, she's saying the same thing as Ben said, only she's not bawling it. She had said Ben was jealous. How silly! How silly! Ben jealous of another man? Then he must think . . . She almost sprang up from the couch, saying, 'I'm going to change my frock,' and went hastily from the room. And Aggie, taking the gin bottle from the shelf, poured herself out a generous measure and sat down to the side of the fire, looked down into the mug and sipped at the liquor, then said to herself, 'Aye, change your frock, my beautiful dear. Change your frock.'

3

The hostility between Ben and Millie came to an abrupt end three days later, and the bond that had existed between them before became stronger. It was brought about by the arrival of a stranger.

Being a Tuesday, the inhabitants of The Courts were short of money for all commodities, so there were only half a dozen people standing on the far side of the long table. And two of these were small children, each pushing a thin plate across the table for a ha'porth of peas. And after Millie had put a generous ladleful on each plate, the dirty and ragged mites did not immediately pick them up and run, but stared at her, until she smiled and, moving along the table, took up a square of pastry and, breaking it in half, dropped the two pieces beside the peas, whereupon the urchins grinned at her, grabbed up their meal, but without a 'ta', and ran off.

The next customer was a woman who said, 'Lucky, those 'uns. It's a scandal. She's got five workin', but the most of it goes in the gin shop, an' two of them with her, an' they just ten. I ask you.'

'What can I serve you with, Mrs Bright?'

'Four pies, lass.'

'The fourpenny's?'

'Oh, no. No; not on a Tuesday' – the woman laughed – 'he's lucky to get the tuppeny's. An' I'll have a scoop of the broth. It sticks to your ribs, that does. I can say this, I've never tasted better, 'specially when you find a nice lump of fat mutton in it.'

Millie took the hint and saw that there was a piece of mutton in the ladleful of stew she poured into the woman's basin. But as the woman moved away and made room for the next customer, Millie became aware of the man standing across the narrow roadway. She had never seen him before, and she knew a great many inhabitants now by sight, because it was a close quarter and very few strangers made their way here, at least to pass the gates and towards the main Courts, unless they were unfortunate enough to have just come to live there.

Yet there could be a man, or many men, who lived in The Courts whom she hadn't seen. This man, however, appeared different: he was dressed differently from any of those round about. He was wearing a black suit and a white collar; at least, it looked a lighter shirt from this distance, and he had a high hat on his head.

By the time she had served another four customers there was no-one in sight but the man; and now he was approaching the table.

As he came closer, she saw that he was tall, almost six foot, and he was very thin and his suit appeared baggy.

When he reached the other side of the table he stared fixedly at her and when he spoke his voice, too, was strange: it did not hold the rough and loud hoarseness that she was used to among the working class. Yet it wasn't the voice of a gentleman of whatever station.

'Millicent Forester. That's your name, isn't it?'

'Yes, that's my name.'

205

'Well, my name's Forester an' all. Reginald Forester. I'm your father.'

The ladle slipped from her hand on to the wooden table. Then she took two steps backwards, saying, 'No; my . . . my father's dead.'

'Well, she would tell you that, wouldn't she? But . . . but I'm your father all right. I didn't expect to find you so soon: the parson's wife said she had last heard of you here; but then you could have been anywhere by now. I recognised you as soon as I saw you, you're the spitting image of your mother.'

Again she said, 'No, no,' because instinctively she didn't want this man to be her father. She didn't like his face. There was a thin scar running down one side of it. The top of it was lost in the shadow of the hat brim, although she could see where it ended at his chin. She turned swiftly and ran across the yard, and as she did so Ben came out of the barn.

Seeing him, she turned and rushed towards him and, clinging to his arms, she whimpered, 'There's . . . there's a man at the gate, Ben. He . . . he says, he's . . . he's my father. He . . . '

'What?' He looked across the yard to the figure standing beyond the table, then said, 'He what?'

'He . . . he said he is my father. I . . . I thought he was dead. Will you come and see?'

'Stay where you are.' Ben now walked slowly towards the gates and the man who was standing there, and demanded, 'What's your game?'

'Who are you?'

'I'll tell you when I know who you are. You say you're her father. Well, to her knowledge an' my knowledge, he's dead.'

The man placed his two hands on the edge of the table as if for support, and his head drooped as he said, 'That's

206

what she would want her to know, her mother. I've been away for a time.'

It was some moments before Ben said, 'Aye, and I can guess where you've been an' all.'

The head came up sharply. The voice, too, was sharp: 'Well, if you can, then you'll know why I haven't come for her sooner,' he said.

'Come for her? You've got no claim on her. She's Aggie's, I mean Mrs Winkowski's.'

Ben turned his head as he heard Aggie's voice in the yard, and he called, 'Come here a minute, will you?'

When Aggie shambled up to them, Ben said, 'Here's a do that'll have to be tackled. This fella says he's her father and he's come for her. What d'you make of that?'

Aggie stared at the man, and she seemed to see somewhere in the thin face a resemblance, and it was as if she had been waiting for this moment for years. She said quietly, 'Let him in.' Then she turned away and, hurrying as fast as she could towards the house, she caught hold of Millie who was standing under the porch, her eyes seeming to be staring out of her head, and she said, 'Come away in. Don't worry; we'll get this sorted out.'

'But he said, Mrs Aggie, he . . . he said . . . '

'Yes, and likely he is. Yes, likely he is your father, so calm yourself down.'

A minute later, the man was standing in the kitchen looking about him in as much amazement as Bernard Thompson had done, and when Aggie turned to him and said, 'Well, get off your legs,' he sat on the settle. Then, looking towards Millie, who was standing to the side of the window as if to keep her distance between them, he said, 'I . . . I knew it would come as a bit of a shock but . . . it isn't my fault that the truth's been kept from you for years. It was hers: she should have put you in the picture from the beginning. I heard yesterday that she did herself in. Well, I'm not surprised . . . nervy.' He was nodding at Aggie now. 'Her mother was always nervy. She'd had it too soft, you know. Well' – he laughed now – 'we both had it too soft at one time.' He passed his lips one over the other, before saying, 'D'you think I could ask you for a drink of something?'

'Is it in the way of tea or beer you would like?'

'Oh, beer, please. Oh yes, a beer.'

Aggie nodded towards Ben, and he went to the cupboard and brought out a bottle of beer and a mug and placed them none too gently on the settle by the side of the man, who looked up at this odd-shaped fellow and said, 'Ta. Thanks.'

They watched him fill up the mug with beer, which he then swallowed, almost it seemed in one draught, then take out a handkerchief from his pocket and wipe his mouth. It was an odd gesture from someone of his appearance; it would have been more natural had he wiped his mouth with the side of his hand.

He now placed the mug and the empty bottle on the hearth and, looking towards Millie, he said, 'Come here. I'm not goin' to eat you. I think it's about time we got to know each other, don't you?'

Millie made no move to comply; and what she said now altered the man's expression, for she spoke sharply: 'I don't know. I've always understood you were dead; so why has it taken you so long to claim the relationship? That's what I'd like to know.'

'Oh well, you see, that's got to be explained. I was away.'

'He was in gaol,' Aggie said flatly.

The man half rose from the settle; then sank back, saying, 'Yes. Yes, I was in gaol; but it wasn't my fault. It was self-defence. I was nearly killed. Look at this! I've got the mark of it.' He was pointing to the scar on his face. 'It was

208

to save her, your mother. I could have swung for it, only they brought it in as self-defence.'

'The man died then?'

He turned to Aggie, saying, 'Aye. Aye, he died some time after . . . well, a week or so; and I nearly did an' all. But still, they gave me twelve years. My God!' They watched him grind his teeth now and droop his head and look to the side, and his eyes moved over the floor as if he were watching something crawling. Then, his head snapping up, he said, 'They cut me time a bit for good behaviour, and I couldn't wait to get out to see you.' He nodded towards Millie. 'But it's not much of a welcome I'm gettin', is it?'

'What d'you expect?' Aggie was standing in front of him.

'Well . . . well I could say that at least she could give me a civil word and let me explain to her how all this happened. Let me tell you, missis, I wasn't always like this.' He drew his hand down from his shoulder to his knee. 'I was in a good position once, and she was brought up well until the trouble. But anyway, as we're talkin' plainly, because there already seems to have been a lot of plain speaking—' he glanced now at Ben, then went on, 'I've got a claim on her: she's mine and . . .'

'My God! mister,' Aggie interrupted him, 'you've got to get your ideas straightened out, and I'd better do it right away for you. You've got no claim on her. I signed a paper years ago. She's what you'd call my ward, and it was done by a legal man, and a friend, who is now a police sergeant, was a witness.'

'Oh my God!' The man was on his feet now. 'Don't tell me I've stepped from one gaol to another. Bloody police!' He was shaking his head in frustration. 'What d'you think it's like to see nothin' but bloody warders an' jump to their bloody orders. Look—' He now gripped at his throat, as if to help himself to breathe; then presently, he turned to Millie and in a

209

somewhat calmer tone said, 'All I want, lass, is to . . . well, to talk with you. We can get into who claims who after. After all, you are my daughter. I . . . I brought you up until you were five years old. I worked for you to give you the best.' Quite suddenly now he dropped down back on to the settle, and his hand again going to his throat, he pulled on his breath, which brought Aggie to her feet and saying to him, 'Are you all right? Are you ailin' something?'

'It's nothing, just a bit of a chest cold.' His arms were now limp by his side, his head drooping; and after surveying him for a moment, Aggie turned towards Millie, beckoning her towards her.

Slowly Millie went forward; but when again Aggie signalled her to sit beside the man, she shook her head; instead, she stood to the side of him, and she looked into his face as she said, 'I'm . . . I'm sorry, but . . . but it's all a great shock, and I have to have time to get used to it. You understand?'

This brought a smile to the man, and he said, 'Yes. Yes, I understand. Perhaps I should have broken it in some other way, but I couldn't see how to do it. And you know, prison doesn't encourage you to develop the niceties of life.'

The words were those that Bernard himself would have spoken, only the tone was different, which made her tell herself that he must have been a nice man once and, in a way, educated; it was prison that had coarsened him. But . . . but if he only looked different. It was his face that repulsed her, and something about his manner.

'It'll work out. We . . . we'll get to know each other; and not afore time. But of course that's my opinion. I . . . I must look for work.'

'What was your work?'

He turned towards Ben; then he sighed before he said, 'I . . . I was a butler in a large household. It was a position of prestige. My wife was lady's maid, and we married. But we left there. Later I was manager in an—' He drew in his breath before he said, 'an emporium. It . . . it was there the trouble started. You see, my wife was as beautiful as her daughter, so perhaps you can understand me wanting to protect her.'

For a moment, Millie's feelings against him were overcome by a wave of pity. Of a sudden she wanted to take his hand and say, It's going to be all right. Mrs Aggie will let you live here, and I'll look after you. But her thoughts were checked by his addressing Aggie now, saying, 'Can you put me up for a few nights until I get settled?'

'No. No, I'm sorry I can't do that. We're stuck for room.'

Millie's mouth fell open: there were two other bedrooms upstairs. Mrs Aggie definitely didn't want him to stay. But then, she knew that she herself was relieved. She watched the man stare at Aggie, then at Ben, before pulling himself to his feet and saying, 'Well, if that's the case, I'll have to look about, won't I, for some place to lay my head?'

The last words were spoken almost in a whine, and they weren't lost on Millie, nor yet on the other two. And so no-one was surprised when he said, 'Since I came out last week I haven't been able to pull myself together – you can probably understand that – and . . . and the bit that I had is . . . is gone. I wonder if you could loan me a few shillings until . . . ?'

Before his voice trailed off Aggie had gone to the sideboard, and there, lifting the lid of the tin cash-box, she took out a florin, which she handed to him, saying, 'That should see you berthed for a couple of nights.'

He looked at the coin in the palm of his hand and the sound he made was like a huh! or a slight laugh; then he picked up his high hat from a chair, put it on, pulling the brim slightly to the side of his face where the scar was. His eyes now on Millie, he said, 'Be seein' you, daughter. I'll be poppin' in, naturally, 'cos we've got to talk, haven't we? Settle things, like.'

On this he went out, followed by Ben; but Millie and Aggie remained where they were. When the door was closed Millie almost threw herself on to the couch and, thumping the seat with her fist, she said, 'I . . . I've dreamed of what he was like for years, and years, and years, Mrs Aggie, I've dreamed of what he was like. He had a lovely face, his manner was kind. He . . . he, in a way, was a gentleman. The only resemblance left is that man's height.'

'Girl! . . . Listen. You've got to face up to it, he's not that man; he is your father, as he said. And, you know, there's one thing: we can't pick our parents. Oh, I wish to God we could. What different lives we'd lead. Now, there's none of you in him; rather, I should say, there's none of him in you. You're on your mother's side.'

On this Millie sprang straight up and, thrusting her face out and up towards Aggie, she hissed, 'And she was a street woman! Sister Mary said that; she was a street woman. I didn't know what it meant then, but I know now. I've known for a long time. I've a prostitute for a mother and a murderer for a father. Oh, Mrs Aggie. Mrs Aggie.' The tears were spurting from her eyes.

Taking her by the shoulders, Aggie shook her, the while crying at her, 'Your ma was no prostitute! She was a young woman who was reduced to doin' the only thing she could do to keep you alive. But she found she couldn't stand it. So don't you ever despise her. Whatever you come to think about him, leave your mother out of it . . . '

Aggie suddenly found her arms pulled away from Millie's shoulders, with Ben yelling at her, 'What d'you think you're up to? Knockin' her brains out! That's all she needs is some rough handling after seeing that individual.'

'She was goin' into hysterics.'

212

'Well, it's not to be wondered at.' He sat down on the settle beside Millie and, putting his arms about her, he brought her head to rest on his shoulder, saying, 'Stop it now. Come on. It's goin' to be all right. You won't have to go near him again if you don't want to.'

'Oh, that's marvellous advice you're givin' her. Marvellous! Now, you get it into your head, Mister clever bugger, the man's her father. He'll have a right to see her. You won't be able to do anything about that. And I should imagine he's here for some time unless he gets up to something and goes along the line again. And that really wouldn't surprise me.'

Millie drew herself from Ben's hold and, looking from one to the other, she said, 'It's awful. It's awful for me to say this, but . . . but I don't want to see him. Yet, he is my father, I know he is, so why should I be repulsed by him? But . . . but I can't help it. I . . . I can't see me ever getting to like him.'

'Oh my God! there's that bell again. But don't you worry, lass, I'll go and see to it. Just sit there and calm yourself down.'

As Aggie left the room Ben stood for a moment and looked at Millie; then, turning swiftly, he went out and caught up with Aggie as she was entering the yard, and, ignoring the customer standing waiting to be served, he said, 'Look here; how long is it since you saw your friend . . . the sergeant?'

'Oh, I don't know; weeks. Why?'

'Well, I think I would take a toddle down and have a word with him, because, you know, I don't believe that bloke's story, him gettin' twelve years for protectin' his wife. No; there's something slimy, sly, about that bloke. Now, people like your sergeant should have ways and means of connectin' with . . . where was it? Durham, and he could likely get the ins and outs of the real story. I think it would pay you to take that little walk. What d'you say?'

213

'Aye, well, there might be something in it. And if he can help, I know he will. But I can't see it'll make much difference what he got the twelve years for . . .

'Funny—' She now looked around her while nodding to herself as she said, 'I've never gone more than a few miles from this yard in me life, yet troubles walk in from different quarters of the country; and, when you come to think of it, none of it concerning me. Life's funny. It is that. All right. All right!' she yelled towards the impatient customer. Then giving Ben her last words, she said, 'It was a mistake, you know, startin' this game. You're at people's beck and call from Monday mornin' till Saturday night, and it's not me . . . not my way.'

214

4

The man did not put in an appearance the next day; nor the day following; and they began to question the probable reason. It was not until the Sunday, and then just as Millie was about to leave the house, and escorted by Ben, to attend the Methodists Adult Sunday School, that he came.

When he confronted them in the kitchen he looked different altogether from on his first appearance there: he was wearing a new suit which fitted him; his boots, also, showed a newness; and one could say his manner, too, was new; it was alert and cheery.

'Hello, there,' he said, addressing Millie. 'Off some place?'

'I'm . . . I'm going to Sunday School.'

'Sunday School?' The words came from high in his throat as if in surprise. Then he said, 'Oh, well then, this will give me an opportunity to walk with you. It will be like old days. I used to take you out on a Sunday, you know: we would go along by the river at Durham. Ah yes.' He nodded, as if recalling those happy times. Then looking from Ben to Aggie, he said, 'I hope I find you well?'

'Well enough, thank you.' And she added, 'You seem to have fallen on your feet since your first visit.'

'Well, I said then I was lookin' for work, and I've found it. Anyone can find work if they want to. I knew that years ago, and it still seems to be so.' And the manner of his speaking was another surprise for Millie.

Aggie was saying, 'Well, what's this marvellous job you've got that's provided you with a new rig-out?'

'Oh, it's a kind of hotel, eatin' house. By the way' – he turned quickly to Millie again – 'there's a concert in one of the main halls in the town. I see it's well advertised. Up-to-date singers and entertainers, it says. My knowledge of them, of course, is now naturally scanty; but I used to like a concert. How about comin' along?'

However, before Millie could answer, Aggie put in, 'As you've just been told, she's ready to go to Sunday School; so I shouldn't imagine one of them concerts would hardly fit in. And anyway, she doesn't go out at night.'

The man's whole manner and tone altered as he confronted Aggie again, saying, 'Well, from what I understand she hardly goes out any time, and she's going on sixteen years old. You cannot keep her tied up here for life. She is my daughter, and to my mind she should be outside away from here seein' and being seen.'

An odd quietness followed on this statement: it was as if they were preparing themselves for a verbal attack. Ben was the first in, crying, 'See an' be seen! What the hell d'you mean by that? And where, may I ask, did you get your information about tying her up. The only tyin' up she's had is protection from the likes of—' He swallowed deeply, and instead of adding, 'you', he said, 'scum. And they're not all to be found among this quarter, let me tell you. See an' be seen? As for being her father, you, mister, have waived any right to that title. What's more, you have no jurisdiction over her. It's Mrs Winkowski, there, whose word goes with regards to her.'

Ben had used the word jurisdiction. Amid her confused and mixed feelings that were not without fear, Millie felt a certain pride at what he had achieved from his reading and his learning. Then it was as if she were aiming to show her learning, too, when she said, 'Listen to me, all of you, and particularly you, sir.' She could never call this man 'father'. 'I don't wish to go out to see or be seen, and I haven't been restricted by these kind people. I may say I have been lucky to have been brought up in this house and under the protection of Mrs Winkowski. You, sir, were irresponsible enough to do something that caused you to be imprisoned. I can't see that you could have been concerned about your wife and child, although you tell us it was because of my mother you committed the deed. I remember my mother, very clearly. She was a loving person and a gentle creature, and she would not have wished you to go to such lengths in her defence.'

She felt that last bit to be silly because her mother would not have had an opinion on what her husband should do in her defence.

'Well! Well! Well! I'm bein' put in me place. I can see that. My God! After all the years I sat in that stinkin' cell just countin' the days when I'd be free and be able to pick up me life again, a family life. Yes, I thought of it as a family life, and this is what it comes to.' He now pointed his finger accusingly towards Millie. 'You've never given me one kind word or shown me one scrap of sympathy for what I've been through. Well, I can tell you now, you're not a bit like your mother inside. Oh no. To my mind you're a hard young bugger.'

'We'll have none of that language, not in my house,' said Aggie. 'And now I'll ask you to get on your way. And when you decide to call again, see that you're sober. But then I'll be pleased if I'm not to see your face again.'

'Oh, missis, you'll see me face again all right. I'm goin' to take up the case. I might as well tell you I haven't let the

217

grass grow under me feet this past week. I've had a word with a man who knows about this kind of thing. He told me to take the matter to court and she'd be mine until she's twenty-one.'

'Out!' Ben's threatening stance in front of him made the man back two paces; even so, he sneered down at Ben, saying, 'And what would you do?'

'Have you flat on your back before you know where you are; and that would only be the beginnin'. Take your choice.'

The man turned towards Millie and in a thick voice he said, 'You know, I used to sit thinkin' of the reception I'd get when we met; but never did it strike me it would be like this. This fella here' – he thumbed disdainfully towards Ben – 'has just said "Take your choice". That's what the bobbies used to imply in Durham, only they used to say, "Which way d'you want it? Quietly or otherwise?" Well, good day, daughter. We'll be meetin' again, and shortly,' at which he turned from them and walked out; and as if of one mind, Aggie and Millie dropped down on to the settle.

Aggie was breathing heavily, and she had her hand pressed tight against her side. 'That man upsets me,' she said. 'I've never known anyone get under me skin so much, and—' She reached out and patted Millie's arm. 'Don't worry, me dear,' she said; 'you'll not have to see him if you don't want to. And you don't want to, do you?'

'Oh no, Mrs Aggie. I . . . I'd be happy if I never saw him again. Yet . . . yet he is my father.' She now looked towards Ben, adding, 'I can't believe that, you know. I keep telling myself he can't possibly be, yet all the time I know he is, and I feel—' she paused, then shrugged her body as if throwing something off as she ended, 'well, ashamed.'

'You've nothin' to be ashamed of. Anyway, if you don't want to miss half the class we'd better be gettin' along.'

'I don't feel like going, Ben.'

'Now, we're goin' to have none of that.' Aggie was pushing her from the settle. 'It's the only break you have in the week and you enjoy it. So, go on, get yourself off and away. And once Ben sees you safely inside, he'll take his usual dander round the town, forgettin' to mind his own business and pokin' his nose in here and there.' She accompanied these last words with a tight smile as she looked towards Ben. 'So go on; let me see the back of you both. I want a little peace, because, you know, I don't get much of either in the week.'

'I'm very sorry for you.' Ben took his cap off the knob of a chair, pulled it on his head, and buttoned up his coat; then with an effort at lightness he grinned at Aggie, saying, 'Instead of puttin' your big fat legs up, what about giving them a little exercise and you comin' along to the Sunday School? It's for adults, and you're an adult all right. And you would learn something; and they would an' all, wouldn't they?'

Aggie's answer took the form of her hand snatching up a tin plate from a shelf to the side of the fireplace and, with an adroit swing, letting it fly at him. But just as adroitly, Ben lifted his hand and caught it, saying, 'You never could see straight;' then threw it on the table before pushing Millie towards the door.

As they walked side by side the disparity in their heights was hardly noticeable, for Millie was a little taller than him; but he was wearing a long overcoat that touched his calves and which made him appear to be just a normal smallish man.

They had walked some distance before either spoke; and then it was Millie who asked quietly, 'What's going to happen, Ben? What's going to be the outcome?'

'I'd be a relation of God's if I knew that, Millie. But there's one thing I can assure you of: nothin' I can prevent is goin' to happen to you. As for him, your so-called father, leave him to me. If he tries any of his tricks, he'll find himself back in one of them cells.'

'Oh, Ben, don't say that. It must have been terrible.'

'Aye, it must be terrible for some men if they're innocent. But I have no pity for them who set out to murder a bloke. And that's what he must have done. And we haven't really got the rights of the case; just his version. But, you know, Aggie saw her dear friend.' He turned towards her, grinning now, and interposed what he was going to say with, 'I don't dislike the bloke, it's just what he stands for, I suppose . . . Anyway, he'll do some investigation. An' then, I hope one day we'll come by the truth.' . . .

When they reached the hall, she said, 'Won't you come in? It's just like the night class, except that they sing a couple of hymns.'

'That would be the finishin' touch to the meetin' because, you know, I've got a voice like a corncrake. No, you go on. I'll do me usual dander and I'll be back in ample time to pick you up. Enjoy it, and if you get the chance to ask any questions, put it to them that you'd like to know what happened to the rest of the apples in the Garden of Eden. I hate to think of them all goin' rotten.'

She pushed him as she laughed, then turned from him and went into the hall. He then made his way purposefully towards the centre of the old town.

It was about five o'clock when he brought Millie back into the house. Aggie had prepared a high tea, and after they had eaten and cleared away, they sat round the fire and talked, as they had done over the years. Prior to the baking business, they might have discussed what was happening in the rag and scrap-iron world; or if Ben and Aggie should be on their own, the discussion would be mostly about Millie and her learning

220

and, of course, her future life. But it had become a sort of rule that Ben would never leave them on a Sunday night. He would go to his classes during the week or visit Annie, which visits were becoming rarer, but Sunday night was always for the house, so, naturally, Aggie showed a little surprise when, about half-past seven, he rose from his chair, saying, 'I'll be leavin' you for a little while. I'm goin' to take a dander. I want some fresh air; that's if I can find any roundabouts.'

'Where are you going?' asked Millie.

'Nowhere in particular; just as I said, a dander. Want to come with me?'

'No.' She laughed.

What surprise Aggie felt she kept to herself. She didn't even ask him where he was going, but she knew he'd be going somewhere, and not just taking a dander. She had learned that Ben Smith, Jones, or Robinson never did anything without it had some meaning, some purpose. So, after Ben had left the house she chatted for a while with Millie until nine o'clock, when Millie went up to bed, and she promised to follow her in a very short while.

She didn't. She sat waiting, for she knew when he returned he wouldn't make for his rooms above the barn but would come to her.

It was ten o'clock when he knocked on the door and she shambled quickly through the room to let him in.

Seated opposite to her, he said, 'Is there any beer left in that jug? I'm as dry as a fish.' And when she answered, 'No, I'm sorry; but there's a drop of gin there,' he said, 'Well, you know what I think about gin; but nevertheless, let me have it.'

She waited until he had drunk the gin; then she said, 'Well, out with it!'

'I know where that fella's workin' ... Reilly's Meat House.'

221

'*Reilly's?* You mean . . . ?'

'Aye, Reilly's, Slim Boswell's place, where he feeds all his pimps and harlots, and his faggots; all the ladies and gents of the street. They say Big Joe's got shares in it an' all. Well, he would, wouldn't he? 'Cos his lot must have some place to eat.'

'How did you find out?'

'Well, on me dander round, you know, this afternoon I got talkin' to one and another. Fred Miller, you know, in the fish market, an' Randy Croft, he deals with the vegetables. They're two decent blokes, and I described the fella to them and asked if he had been round there for work. Fred couldn't place him but Randy did straightaway. He said, "I think he's workin' at Reilly's, 'cos he came through here yesterday with one of their suits on. Boswell, give him his due, always dresses his crew decent, male or female." He laughed; so I laughed with him. But it's a fact, he is workin' there . . .'

'You didn't go in that place? They would have set their bullies on you.'

'I didn't need to' – he laughed – 'there's a big glass window and you can see the bar through it, but not the eatin' place. They tell me it's very plush behind there. Anyway, one of the *ladies* came out of the door an' spies this handsome fella, not over-tall, but standing glancin' through the window, and she comes up to him and says, "Good evening, sir. This is a good meat house, an' would you . . . ?"' Ben stopped and chuckled deeply before going on, 'Then I turned to her and said, "Not at the present moment, Nellie, but I wouldn't mind some other time." And she pushed me an' said, "Oh! Ben, Ben Smith, Jones, or Robinson . . . " Aye she did, she gave me me full title. Then she asked what I was doin' there, and so I asked her if she knew of a new fella, a waiter, in there called Forester.'

' "Oh aye," she said. She knew him all right and who he was. And then, to use her own words, Aggie, she said, "He says he's father of Raggie Aggie's darlin' fair nymph over in the woods." She said he was somethin' of a big-mouth an' he liked his duckie and the more he drank the more his mouth opened. And something else she said.' Ben paused here, nodding his head. 'And Aggie, this sets the seal on him for me, because he'd told them he hasn't turned up before because he's been to sea and was stranded with some shipmates on some foreign coast. Can you believe it? Well, apparently they do, they've swallowed it, at least some of them; but not Nellie. You know what she said? "He may be her father but I think the faraway foreign coast where he was stranded was some clink or other. The first time I saw him," she said, "I noticed he had a pallor on him that spoke of the clink, an' you don't get that unless you're stranded on that particular shore for a long time." And then she asked me what I thought. I said I thought along of her. And then she asked me to walk along with her because, as she said, laughing, in her business they don't stand about. Lie, aye, but not stand. She's a good 'un really, you know.' He now grinned at Aggie. 'Then you know what? She walked as far as Bale Street, Aggie. They're not small houses, an' that street's on the fringe of respectability. Anyway, the first three, she said, belonged to Boswell; in fact, the end one was where she and the lasses are apparently housed. There are six of his specials. But the other two . . . well, by then it was getting dark and I couldn't see her face when she was speakin'. There was enough in her voice, though, to tell me that she wasn't quite in favour of what they were used for. She said they were kept for special customers. Known as guests, relations or visitors. As she laughingly said, nature had to have its way, and one way or other it did: rich men havin' strange pastimes had to be provided for.'

223

He drained his glass of the gin, then said, 'I was daft enough to ask her why she stayed on the game, for, after all, she's been picked up by the coppers more times than I've got fingers an' toes. And, from what I've heard, there's no gentle examination by the police doctors. You know, Aggie, she can't be thirty . . . well, she might just be that. But the answer she gave me dried up me mouth: "I started young, Ben," she said, "even before I was made into a woman. You understand what I mean? So, after twenty years in the business, you haven't any time to learn anythin' else." And Aggie, I knew she wasn't laughing then.'

Aggie made no comment for some time; and then she asked practically, 'Did you give her anything?'

'Yes. Yes, I did. I . . . I slipped her half-a-dollar.'

'Oh, half-a-dollar! That was generous. Enough for two and a half tries.'

'You've a mucky mind, Aggie. But anyway, I know this, an' we can both be grateful for it, it's good to know somebody workin' on the inside of that lot.'

'Huh! Don't bank on it, lad. They don't give their own away; they know if they did, they would wake up in a gully somewhere. Look at the young lad who stood as witness against Big Joe. He was supposed to've hung himself. Well, if he did, it was because he decided he was for it in any case an' he might as well do it himself. So don't bank on any help from Nellie Pratt, or go soft in the head 'cos she relates her life story to you. I've got little time for any of them; an' less for them that live off them. But I don't like what you tell me about that fella workin' in Reilly's, although it does fit in with him somehow.' She now pulled herself up from the couch, saying, 'Well, here's one off to her bed. I'll let you out. I hate Sundays. There's something about Sundays; they're weary days. I'll be glad when the mornin' comes.' She paused as she was opening the back door and, turning and looking at him in the dim light

224

from the candle lantern hanging from a nail in the wide wall, she said, 'But can you understand him breedin' her?'

'No, Aggie. No, I can't. But it's been known afore that a pip from a rotten apple can start a good tree. Good-night to you.'

'Good-night, lad.'

She bolted the door top and bottom, then took the lantern from the nail; and went back into the kitchen, where she turned down the wick of the oil lamp. As she pulled herself wearily up the stairs with the aid of the banister, she thought, She must get married. She must get married. We've got to get her married; and he's there ready and waitin'.

5

Millie's birthday came and passed without much fuss. Aggie gave her an envelope in which there were two sovereigns: enough, she said, to get her a new coat and bonnet; only to feel outdone in her generosity when, after breakfast, Ben went back to his room and returned with a box, a fancy box with stripes on the lid and tied with a brown cord; and Millie, in some excitement, opened it to reveal a really beautiful large, pale-blue, silk shawl with motifs of flowers worked in each corner and edged with a deep fringe, and she held it up, saying in genuine amazement, 'Oh, Ben. It's beautiful. I've never seen anything so beautiful.'

'Well, it's for a bonny lass.'

'Look, Mrs Aggie, look.'

'Aye, I'm lookin'.' Aggie now turned to Ben, saying, 'You must have travelled a bit up to the top end to come across that.'

'And ... and it must have cost ... oh ... oh ...'
Millie shook her head, then impulsively rushed at Ben and placed her lips against his. It was the first time she had ever kissed him. She had, on occasions, hugged him, and on occasions he had held her when aiming to soothe

her crying, but never before had she touched even his cheek in a kiss.

His arms hanging limply by his sides, he made no attempt to return the embrace; but when she drew herself back from him, saying, 'I'll treasure it all my life; and when I'm very old I'll still wear it,' he managed to gain a little of his composure and say, 'Well, it'll likely be in shreds by then.'

After the excitement of the shawl the day was to pass as any other: there was baking to be done, the customers to be seen to, then more baking to be done; and then the short sit round the fire, and so to bed . . .

It should happen on a Saturday and into the fourth week of her seventeenth year that they should have three male visitors, and none had come to buy any pies or pastries.

The first was Sergeant Fenwick. He'd had to ring the bell because the gates were never opened now until half past eleven of a morning, and after the long table had been set out.

It was Ben who answered the ring and greeted the sergeant with a joke, saying, 'I know nothin' about the diamonds, the pearls, or the tiara;' and assuming a very stiff countenance, the sergeant kept it up by saying, 'Well, my man, if you don't, then nobody does. So, until you get your memory back I think you'd better come along with me, because we must find that tiara.'

For the first time in their acquaintance they exchanged a laugh. And now Sergeant Fenwick said, 'Where is she?' and Ben answered, with a jerk of his thumb, 'She's over in the barn there.'

'Is Millie with her?'

'No. She's indoors, cookin' as usual.'

'Well, from all accounts I hear she's good at that.' They were walking towards the barn door now and as they entered, the sergeant said, 'Pity she hasn't a shop. She'd do well in a shop.'

'Who'd do well in a shop?'

'Your ward, Mrs Winkowski, your ward. With the proper help and the proper settin' she'd make a go of it.'

'She has the proper help. What's the matter with us two?'

The sergeant looked from one to the other: 'Oh, I wouldn't know where to start on that question,' he answered; and he shivered, saying, 'It's freezin' in here.'

'Yes, I know it is,' responded Aggie; 'and that's what you call an asset to the business because it keeps the food fresh . . . Well, have you come to tell us anything?'

'Yes. Yes, quite a bit, Aggie, quite a bit. But I can only give you the bare details. Part of what that fellow said was true; he was a butler and his wife was a lady's maid. But she wasn't his wife at the time the jewellery went missin'.' He turned now and cast a laughing glance at Ben, saying, 'I think it must have been that tiara you seem to know about.'

'What's that? What tiara are you talkin' about?'

'It's a joke, Aggie. It's a joke. Your assistant here has a sense of humour. I've always known that, but I haven't experienced much of it until this mornin'. Anyway, there was this jewellery missin'. The fella denied takin' it and the family didn't bring a case against him; it seems he was the son of an old retainer who had recently died. But the lady's maid believed in the fella's innocence, and so she left with him and they got married. But not havin' a reference, it was difficult for him to find work. Eventually he must have succeeded, because he became a shopwalker. He also became enamoured of one of the women on the staff; and apparently she wasn't the first. Her husband, so it appears, was on a boat trading between the Tyne and London. It was a rough passage and could take anything from two weeks to two months, all depending on the weather and the blockages in the river. Anyway, the crux of the matter is he must have returned one day and found the two of them together, and he sets about him with the definite intention of killing him, as the scar on his face shows. But our man must have been stronger for he managed to relieve the outraged husband of the knife and stab him in several places. The fella eventually died. At the trial, the woman in question stated that our fella had followed her home and had assaulted her and it was then that the husband had found them. Well' – he smiled – 'as my informant wrote to me, if you told that tale to the cat it would scratch your eyes out. Anyway, the court didn't believe her either, and it's as well for him that it didn't. It was proved the affair had been going on for many months. So it was brought in as self-defence, which saved him from the rope and he got twelve years. Well, what have you got to say, Aggie?'

'That I'm not surprised; in fact, I never believed his version of it. But all I can say is that that lady's maid was a damn fool. Yet, I've got to look at it in another way. If she hadn't been, I wouldn't have had Millie's company for the last nine years and I would have been the poorer for it.'

'Yes, Aggie, I think you would, because she's a bonny lass, and a good lass into the bargain.'

'But what's goin' to be done about him? Can we stop him comin' here?'

The sergeant turned to Ben and, shaking his head, said, 'I can't see how that can be done, he's her father. He's done nothing, at least so far, that can bring him under the law. Now if he were to threaten . . . '

'Well, he's done as much as that. He says he's seen somebody. It sounds like a solicitor man, and he's under the impression he can get control of her until she's twenty-one.'

'Well, he'll have to fight that out in the court, and with his record I doubt but that he'll come off second best. I shouldn't worry. Well, I must be off,' and he added, 'before

I freeze to death in here. It's warmer outside. How does it keep so cold?'

Aggie smiled. 'It's likely the draughts comin' through the cracks of the old timbers,' she added. 'Even years ago when it was stacked with hay, as I remember, it still remained cold. Anyway, will you come in and have a hot drink?'

'No. No, thanks, Aggie. I must be on me way. But I thought you'd like to know the facts about that fella.'

'Yes. Yes, I wanted to know the facts. Somehow, though, they don't surprise me. Nevertheless, thank you very much, sergeant. And if at any time there's anything I can do . . . '

He turned to her, laughing now and saying, 'What can you do for me, Mrs Winkowski, unless you get that cart out and get on the road again? I bet you don't hear much gossip over that pea and pie table.'

'Oh, you'd be surprised. Oh, you would indeed.'

'Would I now?'

'Yes, you would.'

'Well, would you like to surprise me?'

'Not at the moment, not at the moment.' She, too, was laughing now, loudly. 'But pop in again, any time, when you're stuck an' you want something solved, you know.'

He left with a wave of his hand and his broad smile and when, at the gate, he turned to Ben, saying, 'She doesn't change,' Ben answered, 'No, she doesn't; and it's a good thing . . . Thanks for comin'.'

The sergeant turned a look on him, and he said quietly, 'You're a good fella, Ben. Take care of her. Take care of them both.' And with that he walked away. And Ben, crossing the yard towards Aggie, who was about to enter the house, said to himself, he's one of the decent ones, as she says; but they're few and far between, I'd say.

*

The Saturday rush was over. Again they had sold out, and it was not yet two o'clock. They were in the kitchen now and Aggie was answering Millie: 'Well, if you had help could you bake twice as many?' And Millie came back impatiently, saying, 'No; I've told you, it's the oven. It isn't so much the making of the stuff, it's the cooking of it. The oven won't be hurried.'

'What she's sayin',' put in Ben, 'is that you need a new kind of fireplace. I've said it before and I'll say it again, you should spend out and get in a new range.'

'Would you like to go to hell and mind your own business?'

'I wouldn't mind; it would be warmer than here. Anyway, I've been under the impression for some time that this was part of my business.'

'Be quiet, both of you, will you?' There was a weary note in Millie's voice, and they both turned and looked at her, and Ben, glancing at Aggie, said, 'She's tired.'

'Tell me something I don't know,' Aggie said; 'And anyway, who gave their blessing to her becoming a cook? I didn't want it; I was happy enough with me yard as it was.'

'Look, both of you, I say again, be quiet,' said Millie. 'I'm not tired, and I'm happy enough with the yard as it is now. We can talk this thing out quietly.'

'Can we? Listen to that!' Ben thumbed towards the door. 'The bell again.'

'Well, go and tell them to get the hell out of it. There's a sign out there says "closed" and if they can't read they still know what it means.'

As Ben left the room muttering to himself, Aggie turned back to where Millie was sitting on the settle, her head leaning back into the corner of it, and she said softly, 'Look, I'm not goin' to ask you to take to drink, but when you're feelin' like that, just a little nip of gin does you the world of good. Now will you have it?'

'No, thank you, Mrs Aggie. You know I've said so many times I don't like gin or beer. And I'm not tired, I'm just a little weary.'

Yes, that was the word. She was weary. She was weary of the daily routine. She was weary of the house as it was now, for she couldn't keep it as spruce as she used to. She was weary of that lonely feeling inside her, that longing feeling, that wanting feeling.

Suddenly as if touched by a magic wind, all such feelings were swept away, for there, coming through the door behind a stiff-looking Ben, was Mr Thompson ... Mr Bernard Thompson ... Bernard.

She rose from the settle, her hands pressing down her ruffled apron before going to her hair. But he wasn't looking at her, he was addressing Aggie, saying, 'How are you, Mrs Winkowski? It seems such a long time since I saw you.'

'As you see me, sir, as you see me. No better, nor worse. Take a seat, will you?' She pointed to the settle.

Now he did look at Millie, saying, 'And you, Miss Millie, how do I find you?'

She managed to keep her reply cool as she said, 'I suppose I could answer the same as Mrs Aggie; no better, no worse.'

'She's tired. She's overworked and it's all her own fault.' Aggie's voice was louder now. Then speaking to Bernard again, she said, 'Have you just come back from the city, sir ... London?'

'Yes. Unfortunately, I was kept down there longer than I anticipated, although I wasn't in London all the time. It's very dismal there now. But I had to drive into Sussex to visit some friends. It was to be only a short visit, a matter of two or three days, but it stretched into a week or more. You know how things are when people get talking and' – he shrugged his shoulders – 'and arranging everyone's life but their own.'

'Can I offer you a drink, sir?'

232

'No, thank you, no. But there is something you can do for me, Mrs Winkowski; I have come with a request.'

'Me, sir? Now you tell me what *I can do for you.*'

'Well—' He inclined his head towards her, then towards the stiff countenance of Ben, before looking at Millie and saying, 'You could grant me permission to take your ward on a little journey to inspect my new abode. I have a house . . . well, it's really a cottage, on the outskirts, you know. It's a very small affair and presided over by an aunt of mine. She would be delighted to entertain Miss Millie to tea.'

Aggie was standing next to Ben, and whatever movement he made she checked with the pressure of her elbow; then, her head wobbling on her fat shoulders, she said, 'Well, now, sir, put like that, could I refuse your request? I ask you. But it's up to the *lady* in question. Don't you think so?'

'Yes. Yes, of course.'

Millie warned herself to remain cool and to keep looking at this wonderful man and not to take any notice of the look on Ben's face, and to resist jumping forward and throwing her arms about Mrs Aggie, who recognised the direction in which her heart was now pointing and had been for some time.

'That would be very nice. I shall be pleased to take tea with your aunt, Mr Thompson.'

She took no notice when Ben swung round and left the room; but went on to say, 'I shall have to change. Would you mind waiting?'

'Not at all. Not at all. I'm sure I shall be amply entertained by Mrs Winkowski here during your absence.'

She inclined her head slightly towards him, then walked from the room, forcing herself not to run. She didn't, until she reached the stairs, and then she bounded up these and into the bedroom. And there, once the door was closed, she leant back against it and cupped her face in both hands. Her lips were pressed tightly together for a moment until they

233

sprang apart and, her mouth opening wide, she drew in a long gasping breath before flying now to the wardrobe.

Pulling open the doors, she gazed at the clothes hanging there. Then she almost snatched a dark green skirt and short coat from a hanger; grabbed up a pair of brown buttoned boots from the bottom of the wardrobe, and these she dropped on to the floor before throwing the suit on to the bed. Finally from the top drawer of the old chest she took a white blouse. Then she almost jumped out of her working clothes.

She now tipped some cold water from a ewer into a basin and washed her face and hands; then, telling herself she wouldn't have time to undo her plaits, she arranged them on the top of her head. Anyway, her bonnet would hide most of her hair, and so she simply and hastily combed down a tiny fringe of hair on to her brow and two curling strands on to her cheeks.

When she was dressed, complete with a brown velour coat covering her suit, she took from one of the two drawers to the side of the dressing table's cracked mirror, a handkerchief, and, from the second drawer, a pair of gloves. Lastly, she picked up a bead bag, and, bending, she surveyed herself bit by bit in the upper half of the mirror.

She did not pass any opinion on her reflection, yet when she was about to open the door she stopped and her eyes travelled down the green suit that was showing between her open coat. And she asked herself if she had chosen rightly. But it didn't matter. It didn't matter.

She made herself walk down the stairs, across the hall and into the kitchen, where Bernard immediately rose to his feet. And he gazed at her for a moment before he said, 'I'm . . . I'm glad you've dressed warmly; there's a bitter wind blowing. I hope you don't mind walking as far as the ostler's where I've left the horse and trap?'

'Not at all. I like walking.'

'And what time may I expect you to bring her back?' Aggie was asking now.

As he paused before answering her, there came the sound of the bell ringing again, but neither Aggie nor Millie took any notice of it. They were looking at Bernard who, taking out his watch, said, 'It is now just on two o'clock. It is a good half hour's drive to the cottage as it's beyond the outskirts. Let us say I will return her to you just after six o'clock. How does that suit you?'

'Well, it'll be dark soon after then but she'll be safe with you, I trust.' Aggie was stepping towards Millie now, her hands outstretched as she added, 'We'll button that coat up,' when the door opened and Ben entered, followed by Millie's father. And if Ben had brought in a bucket of iced water and thrown it over them both the effect could not have been more deadening.

The sight of the man caused a groan inside Aggie which said, Oh, God! No! Just when things were goin' well for her.

As for Millie, she wanted to close her eyes to shut out the sight of him. The only thing she could be thankful for at this moment was that he didn't seem to be in any stage of drunkenness.

She was asking herself what she could say. Could she say to Bernard, 'This is my father'? But the man forestalled her, having to do so by introducing himself.

He had taken in immediately that she was dressed for the road, as was the gentleman, and although the words 'Aye, aye' jumped to mind, he didn't express them. What he said was, 'Well! Well! daughter. I see you're ready for out. And is this gentleman your escort?'

Bernard looked from the man to Millie, and back to the man again, and he said, 'Yes, I'm about to have that pleasure.'

'Well! well! And where are you takin' her?'

'That's none of your business.' Aggie was stepping forward now. 'Get out of the road; they're about to leave.'

She now turned to Bernard, saying, 'I'd like to point out, sir, that this man isn't welcome here. And . . . ' Before she could say anything further, George Forester exclaimed loudly, 'I have business here. As long as my daughter's here nobody can stop me seein' her. I made that plain to you before, missis. And since I've come to give her a birthday present, I'm givin' it to her.' And with this, he put his hand inside his breast pocket and pulled out a small box. It was unwrapped but it was unmistakably a ring box. And pushing past Aggie, he thrust the box out towards Millie.

Sick at heart now, Millie glanced from Aggie to Bernard, and then to Ben, whose expression, even if she had been asked, she couldn't have described.

Slowly she took the box from the extended hand, saying, 'Thank you.'

'Well, open it.'

And still slowly, she lifted the lid and looked down on the gold ring with the three stones set at an angle across it: the middle one was red, the other two looked like pieces of pale glass.

'Put it on.'

'I . . . I will some other time.'

'No, now. I want to see it on you.'

She looked helplessly from one face to the other, but no-one moved. And so she took the ring from the box, then hesitated on which finger to put it. When she tried it on the first finger of her left hand it slipped off, but when she put it on the middle finger of her right hand it stayed. Grabbing her hand, he said, 'Now, look at that! And that's no cheap ket, I'm tellin' you. And always remember that I gave it to you.' He now turned and looked at the others, saying, 'Seein' I'm not wanted, I'll make me way out the way I came in; but I'll be back;' then turning back to Millie, he addressed his last words to her: 'Did you hear that? I'll be back. And by the way' – he pointed to the ring – 'that's only the beginning. You take my word for it.' Then hunching his coat over his shoulders, he pushed past Aggie and Bernard to the door, already being held open by Ben, who then followed him out.

'I'm sorry, sir, you've had to put up with him. I'm very . . .'

'Oh, please, don't worry. But—' He was looking at Millie now as he said, 'I understood your father was dead?'

Her head slightly bowed as she answered, 'Yes, I thought so, too. We all thought so. But he's very much alive and it's awful of me to say, unfortunately. But . . . but that's how I feel about him.' And she tried to pull the ring from her finger, but it stuck against her knuckle. 'I'll have to get some soap to ease it off,' she said to Aggie.

'Don't. Don't do that; let me have a look at it.' Bernard Thompson lifted her hand and looked at the ring; then moved it gently around her finger and back again. And he stared at it for some time before he said, 'It's a beautiful ring.'

'It'll be an imitation, sir. That's all he could afford.'

'Oh, I don't think it's an imitation. I'm no authority on jewellery, but this one looks genuine. I should leave it on. And it enhances your hand. Anyway, shall we go?'

Instead of answering him directly, she walked over to Aggie and, bending, she kissed her on the cheek. And they stared at each other for a moment before, straightening up, Millie walked towards the door, whilst he, taking Aggie's none too clean outstretched hand, said softly, 'It will be good for her to have a change, don't you think?'

'I do indeed, sir. I do indeed,' she said in a conspiratorial whisper.

237

Why, Millie wondered, had she to stop half-way across the yard when she met up with Ben and say, 'I won't be all that long.' It was something in his face that drew the words from her.

Ben merely looked at her hard for a moment before he turned and walked towards the barn.

'He's . . . he's very protective of you.'

'Yes. Yes, he is; he always has been.'

They were outside the gate now, picking their way along the ridges of dried mud. He had his hand on her elbow, guiding her, not only because of the roughness of the road but in order to avoid the numerous unsightly children who were milling about. When a small boy, one of a crowd of about a dozen, cried, 'Hello, Millie,' and the others took it up, almost in a chant, crying, 'Hello, Millie,' she forced herself to smile at them and lift her hand in a wave.

'You are well known.'

'I should be; they're among my best customers,' she said and curtly, for she felt his words to be unnecessary.

When he laughed softly she turned and looked at him. He was smiling at her and she smiled back, thinking, he understands, he really does. He doesn't look down on them or on Mrs Aggie, or Ben.

Ten minutes later, seated in the trap, he jerked the horse into a trot, and she said, 'It's a very smart outfit.'

'You like it?'

'Yes. I like horses. We had one called Laddie. The name was misleading: I think he must have been in his late twenties when Mrs Aggie bought him because we found him dead on his bed one morning. She said it was because she had overfed him. But she was as distressed by his going as I was.'

'Did you drive the horse?'

'Yes; but he wasn't a horse, he was really a pony.'

'Well, you can drive this outfit whenever you like.'

She did not respond to his suggestion, for some reason feeling that the offer suggested more than the words implied.

They were going through a district that was new to her. It wasn't as poor as The Courts but it was certainly full of low-class dwellings interspersed between mills, and she said, 'I have never been this way before. Mrs Aggie had certain routes she kept to but she was never as far out as this.'

'This is The Hulme district,' he said. 'But don't worry, we'll soon be out of it.'

'Oh, it doesn't worry me.' She turned her head now and looked along the warren of streets going off this main one. Two up, two down, the backyards leading into narrow alleys, piled high here and there with rubbish. She imagined the insides of the houses to be really no different from The Courts, except that they were terraced instead of going upwards.

They crossed a main road, one that was thick with traffic of all types of vehicles from barrows and handcarts, through the cheap straw-floored hired cabs, to carriages and chaises.

'Now it will get better,' he said; 'we are approaching the residences.'

The first residences were still terraced houses, but all neatly curtained and brass-knobbed. These led to the detached houses, each set in a small patch of garden, and gave way to larger ones still, each with two entrances, one double-gated, the other single and holding a board which read 'Tradesmen' in large painted letters. Beyond these residences was open country with here and there a stretch of woodland; and, passing one, she exclaimed, 'That puts me in mind of the Quintons. Do you ever hear of them?'

'Not much; I very rarely go that way. I sometimes see William, that is, Mr Quinton, in the town, and he gives me news of the children. And he always asks after you.' He inclined his head downwards. 'They missed you very much, you know; and the children were quite unmanageable after you left.'

Recalling why she left she did not go on to further the conversation in that direction, or to say Mr Quinton had said he would bring the children to see her, but that he never did. What she said was, 'Your house is quite a way from the town?'

'We're almost there, another few minutes;' and it seemed almost instantly he was saying, 'Here we are.'

He drew the horse to a stop, jumped down from the trap and opened two small iron gates; then he mounted the trap again, turned the horse and trotted it up a short drive and round a curve. And there she saw his house. Or was it a cottage? Or was it a palace? As she sat staring at it, he held out his arm towards her, saying, 'The outside is pretty but the inside is much prettier.'

She stood on the gravel drive looking at the leaded windows gleaming in the sunshine, and the thick root of the creeper climbing up the wall by the side of the porch. When he took her hand as if to run her into the house, the appearance of a young man round the corner stopped him, and he called to him, 'See to him, Geoff. I'll want him again about half past five.'

And now he was pulling her through the doorway and into a hall, and he was actually untying her bonnet; but when he went to unloosen the buttons of her coat she smacked his hand gently, laughing and saying, 'Please!' which made him stand back from her, his teeth nipping his lower lip. And then he said, 'I'm sorry, I'm sorry, but I'm so excited. You're here at last. I've always imagined you being here . . . well, since I got the place.'

Her coat and bonnet off, she stood gazing about her. It was a small hall, about the same size as the one in the Quintons' house, not more than fifteen feet wide and perhaps twenty feet long, but it was beautifully furnished. At the moment she couldn't distinguish one colour from another, only that there was a maze of rose and gold from the floor coverings and the draped curtains at the small arched windows. The staircase rose from the end of the hall, and she could see that this, too, shone with colour. And now he was leading her towards a door, and when he pushed it open Millie saw a tiny doll-like woman rise from a blue-satin upholstered chair, and she was crying, 'Oh! my dear. My dear. I didn't hear the carriage. Oh! how nice to see you. My dear boy. Is this the young lady?'

'Yes, Aunt Chrissie, this is the young lady.'

Millie found her hands taken between two tiny white ones, which were so soft she felt they would melt within her firm grasp. They hardly seemed real, not quite human. Nothing about this little person seemed real; certainly not her voice, which was like a high thin musical note and sang as she said, 'Tea's all ready. It's been ready this hour. I love my tea. Don't you like tea, Miss . . . Miss . . . ?'

'Millie, Aunt Chrissie.'

'Millie. Oh that is a sweet name. Of course, Millie. But, as I said, don't you like tea?'

'Yes. Yes, I enjoy tea very much.'

'Shall I ring for Fanny?'

'Aunt Chrissie, sit yourself down and behave yourself and stop your chattering or you'll frighten Millie away.'

'Oh' – the tone of her voice sank – 'I wouldn't frighten you away, would I?'

'No, I'm sure you wouldn't, ma'am.'

'She called me ma'am.' Her laughter made a tinkling sound. 'I am not a ma'am or a missis, I am merely Miss Christine Lavor. But dear Bernard here has always called me Aunt Chrissie. The others—' She turned now and looked up into Bernard's face as she added, 'You remember, Bernard, the

241

others always called me Lavy. I never liked that. That was, of course, with the exception of your dear mama, not Berenice's mother, no, your mother . . . '

'Aunt Chrissie, you will be entirely confusing Millie. She is not acquainted as yet with the family history. Now will you hold your tongue and let us be seated?'

'Oh my!' The slight figure now tripped up the room, saying, 'I was playing patience; I must move the cards. I don't want to disarrange them, it was a good hand. I've had it out twice today. Do you play patience, Miss Millie?'

'I haven't done so yet—' She paused before saying, 'Miss Christine,' which she noted brought an appreciative smile from Bernard, but passed as though unnoticed by Miss Lavor, who was now carefully moving the tray on which her patience cards were set out.

Bernard now led Millie to another blue brocade chair, and when she was seated he put his hand out and pulled on a bell-pull to the side of the open fireplace. And Millie noticed that here again, even in the bell-pull, the pattern of rose and gold was carried through, because on a long strip of rose velvet was placed another of gold braid, ending in a gold and rose tassel.

She looked about the room. It seemed that everything that was made of material had been chosen to fit in with its partner: the carpet with the curtains; the curtains with the upholstery on the chair; the voluminous ladies' dresses in the two paintings, one at each side of the fireplace wall. The whole had really taken her breath away. She felt that she would like to be alone in this room just to savour the colours and finger the material and pass her hand over the patina on the furniture. It wasn't a large room, not much bigger, she thought, than the kitchen back in that place she had just left; and the thought led her to ask herself if that was her home, a place that she had loved and in a way still loved. But this

242

was different. This was like stepping into a fairy-tale world. One could live a different life altogether in a room like this, in a house like this . . . and with people like this. Yes, even with this dainty little chattering lady. Bernard might be related to those in The Grange, but those people lived a different kind of life from that which was led in this house. It could even be better than her experience at the Quintons' house. Oh, yes; because there she had just been a servant . . . and here she would be . . .

'You are far away.' Bernard's hands were resting, one on each side of her chair; his face was hanging above hers: 'What were you thinking?' he asked.

She looked back into his eyes, her own soft and unable to hide her feelings, and she said, 'I was thinking that this is a beautiful room and that I have, for this afternoon, stepped into fairyland.'

The smile went from his face, and his voice came deep from within his throat as he said, 'You could live in fairyland, my dear, if you so wish.'

'Oh, here's Fanny with the tea. Have you rolled the bread and butter, Fanny? I always like it rolled.'

'Yes, Miss Chrissie, I've rolled it.'

The woman who was speaking and who was now placing a heavily laden tray on a side table, straightened her back and looked towards Millie; and in a quite cheery voice, she said, 'Afternoon, miss.'

'Good afternoon.'

'Will you get me that table, Mr Bernard, the one near the window with the pull-out leaf?'

'Yes, Fanny. Yes.' As if he were a small boy, Bernard hurried towards where the spindle-legged table stood and brought it to the maid. And Millie told herself that this woman was a maid and she had spoken like that to Bernard as a mother might have done. Oh, the atmosphere in this house!

243

And the woman herself, she was far from young. She must be well into her fifties and she looked so cheery, so bright.

The tea was set out, the rolled brown bread passed round, followed by minute scones filled with a fruit preserve, and the whole covered with the chatter from this little lady. And if Millie hadn't liked her from the moment she saw her, she endeared herself now when, laughing her tinkling laugh, but rather ruefully, she said, 'I talk too much. I chatter too much. Everyone says I do. But then, you see, I haven't always had people to talk to, and when the opportunity arises I make up for lost time. But since I have found dear Bernard, or Bernard has found me, I can talk to my heart's content. And it's so nice to find someone who remembers the books that I once read and we can discuss them. But I can't always remember them . . . Do you want this last piece of brown bread, Miss Millie?'

'No, thank you. I've had a wonderful tea.'

'Then you won't object to my having it?'

For answer, Millie merely smiled, then glanced at Bernard; and he smiled back at her. It was an appreciative smile as if he were thanking her for something.

The tea over, he now got to his feet and, standing before Millie, he said, 'Inspection time. I want to show you the house. It won't take very long because, compared to the usual residence, it is but a doll's house. But I would like you to see it and tell me what you think about my choice.'

'Shall I come along, or shall I stay here?'

'You stay here, Aunt Chrissie, and finish that game of patience, and see if you can beat yourself. You've never worked out three games in a row yet, have you?'

'No; just two. But I will one day, I will.'

They were in the hall now, where he not only took her elbow but her arm, and, drawing her to a halt, he said, 'That's Aunt Chrissie. What do you think?'

244

'I . . . I think she's sweet, most unusual.'

'Yes. Yes.' But there was no smile on his face as he said further, 'Yes, she's most unusual. I'll tell you all about her later, when we're upstairs. But now come and see Fanny's kitchen. By the way, Fanny has been her maid for forty-two years. She has never left her, no matter where she's been. She's devoted to her.'

'She seems a very nice person, very warm.'

'She is, and a very understanding woman.'

He pushed open an oak door, and then they were in the kitchen. It was a long room with whitewashed walls, and at the far end was a large window, not lead-lined or mullioned, but with three long clear panes; on a side wall was a fireplace with an open grate and with an oven to each side of it; on the opposite wall was a delfrack holding what she saw at a glance must be a complete dinner service. To the side of this was a glass-fronted cupboard full of tea china.

Her heart swelled and she could see herself in this kitchen, at this table, which had a white scrubbed top but mahogany legs; she could see herself baking here morning after morning, and afterwards sitting in that easy basket-chair to the side of that oven and putting her feet on that brass and steel fender. Of course, that would be when Bernard wasn't here, because then she would be in the drawing-room.

'You have that faraway look in your eyes again. Were you looking at them out there?' He pointed to the window through which could be seen the maid talking to the man whom Bernard had called Geoff, and he said, 'They get on well together. As Fanny has been Aunt Chrissie's woman, Geoff has been my man for years. He'll turn his hand to anything.'

She hadn't noticed them; she had been taken up with the kitchen; and her comment was: 'You're both very lucky.'

245

'Yes.' He nodded. 'I've always been lucky. Sometimes, I'm rather fearful that my luck might turn; it seems too good to be true. My most recent experience of it was when my godfather left me a half-share in the mill. You couldn't know what that did for me. And then, of course, he also left me quite a sum of money, which enabled me to buy this house. Anyway, we'll go into more details as time goes on. But there's another room here downstairs, in fact, two.'

One room turned out to be a small book-lined study, the other was unfurnished, and about this he said in an aside, 'Could be a ladies' toilet room.'

Then they were upstairs. There were four bedrooms on the first floor, and a steep staircase that led from the landing to two attics. These, he later informed her, were Fanny's domain. Geoff had a room above the stables. And, he had added, all very comfortable.

When he opened the door of the first bedroom she just glanced in, and he said, 'That is a guest room.' Of the second one, he again just opened the door and said, 'We won't disturb Aunt Chrissie's privacy; but you can see it is like a doll's house. She loves dolls and stuffed animals. But I insisted that they don't wander all over the house, and she's very good in that way.'

The third bedroom was a single room, and this time he just partly opened the door and said, 'So far, this is my abode.' But he pushed open wide the door of the fourth room, saying, 'This is the best bedroom. I . . . I keep it select.'

When she stood in the doorway hesitating, he said, 'It's all right, my dear. I . . . I just want to see if you appreciate it as much as you do the drawing-room.'

'It's a beautiful room.' Her voice was low. She did not mean to pretend any demureness, but she found that she couldn't raise her eyes to his until, taking her hand, he said, 'Come and sit by the window; I want to tell you about Aunt

246

Chrissie.' The words were so matter of fact, the tone too, that she allowed him to lead her to the window seat.

When she sat down at one end, he did not sit close to her but left a space of perhaps three feet between them; and what he said was, 'People can be very cruel. You wouldn't think, just because that little creature downstairs chatters as she does, and merely it would seem because of her manner and inconsistencies and the lack of a good memory, that her relatives would put her away for years.'

'They put her away? In a . . . ?'

'Yes. Yes, in a form of asylum. She was lucky, I suppose, for, together, they were able to send her to a private place; just so that they wouldn't have to put up with her. She hadn't previously been badly used; no, she had just been ignored, left. My mother used to take her for a few months every year, until she became ill, when, of course, my father wouldn't put up with her; he wouldn't allow her even to visit my mother.'

He paused and sighed here; then went on, 'Well, after I came into the money and part of the mill, a plan began to form in my mind.' He paused and looked away from her for a moment, then back again, and he said, 'It seemed to be not quite complete; and then I suddenly felt Aunt Chrissie could be the key to it. And she's so grateful for a home, and she understands the situation. She's had a tragic life, really. My mother told me that until she was seventeen or eighteen she was perfectly normal; in fact, she was shy; and then she fell in love with a neighbour's son and he with her, but his father would have none of it. You see, Aunt Chrissie was tiny, small; she didn't look as if she would be a good *breeder*' – he had stressed the word as if with bitterness – 'so he whipped his son away. Following this she developed a nervous illness: where she had been so quiet before, she now chatted about anything

247

and everything. She's much better now than she was, at least in that way. And you know, given the opportunity, she would likely, as well as anyone, have bred a fine family. She still has two sisters, you know. They're both married, and they're both unhappy, although no outsider would guess it. Their marriages were arranged, made in the cradle, so to speak. It's still happening.'

He turned to look outside again; then with a sudden jerk he lifted himself over the space between them, caught her hands and, pressing them tightly and his voice coming as if being dragged from some depth within him, he said, 'Millie, I love you. Oh God, how I love you! You know that, don't you? You know I love you.'

She had to bend her head forward, her brow almost touching his, before she could swallow and mutter, 'Yes, I do, and . . . and I love you.'

'You do? Really, really love me?'

'Oh yes, and . . . and have for a long time. Perhaps from when you carried me home; I mean, to the Quintons', that night. I don't know. I don't remember ever not loving you.'

'*That*—' He was pressing her hands against his shoulder now and saying, 'That night was the night, too, for me; I knew it then. But you were just a child, a girl; I knew I'd have to wait, and it's been hard waiting, Millie.' His lips were near hers, and their gaze was linked with longing; then they were enfolded, their lips pressed close.

How long they remained like that she didn't know; she was aware only that she really had entered a sort of fairyland and life was stretching away before her in the blue and gold haze of this house.

When he pulled her to her feet she swayed, and he had to steady her. His face was bright with laughter. 'Millie! Millie! I'm the happiest man alive. You have no

248

idea. But come along; let's get out of this, at least for the time being.' He drew her towards the door and on to the landing. 'We must have a little decorum, mustn't we?'

She, too, laughed, but aloud now, saying, 'Oh, yes, sir. Yes; we must have a little decorum.'

'I'm going to take you home now,' he said; 'it will be safer for you.'

'Oh Bernard. Bernard.' She leant against him. 'I'll always feel safe with you, always.'

'My dear, dear, Millie. You've always looked like a golden angel. That's why I had the drapes done in gold. Besides that, you are an angel, so understanding. Come, come; there's a lot to be talked about. And I must talk with your dear Mrs Aggie. She understands the situation already. She knew how I felt.'

'And she knew how I felt, too.'

'You think so?'

'Oh, yes. I might as well confess I've had the miseries for the past month because I didn't see you.'

'*Millie! Millie!*' he stood in the hallway cupping her face. 'Look,' he said, 'I don't want you to go, and I want to see you tomorrow and the next day, and the next day and the next day, but ... oh dear!' – he now closed his eyes and tossed his head from one side to the other – 'I've got to be away into Cheshire tomorrow, and I'll likely be kept there for a week. I'm not looking forward to it.'

'You have business there?'

'I suppose you could call it business. For the rest of my life you could call it business ... Oh, let me get you away from this house, because if I don't, I won't let you go at all.'

'I must say goodbye to Miss Chrissie.'

'Well, make it quick. I'll tell Geoff we're ready.'

He went out the front door and she went into the drawing-room and approached the table where the little woman was playing patience, and she said, 'I'm leaving now, Miss Chrissie.'

'Oh, you are, dear? You are? What a pity! I thought you were staying.'

'No, no.' She laughed. 'Not yet, anyway.'

'But you will, won't you?'

'Yes. Yes, I will.'

'And soon?'

'Yes' – she paused – 'and soon. Oh yes' – her head was bobbing now – 'yes, and soon.'

'I'm so glad. It'll be wonderful to have you here. You are a very lucky girl, you know, to get a man like Bernard. He's very exceptional is Bernard. And he arranged all this, and so kind.'

'Yes, he's very kind.'

'You'll be very happy, dear.'

'I'm sure I shall. Goodbye for the present, Miss Chrissie.'

'Goodbye, my dear . . . You may kiss me if you like.' She held up her tiny cheek, and when Millie bent down and touched it with her lips, she felt as if she were kissing a large china doll.

Outside, the trap was waiting. Bernard lifted her bodily into the seat, then took his place and, with a 'Gee up! there,' they were off on the return journey . . .

It was almost half an hour later, as they were nearing the livery stable, when she exclaimed, 'Oh, dear me. I've talked as much as your aunt. Wouldn't it be dreadful if you had to live with two of us like that?'

'Dreadful?' he said. 'It would be wonderful. And it will be wonderful. Oh yes, it will.' He passed the reins to one hand and, reaching out, he gripped hers. 'As long as I live

250

I'll remember this day, and this drive, for never before have I held reins in my hand and felt like this.'

It was as he was leading her out of the livery stable yard that a man stepped forward, saying, 'Hello, there.'

'Oh! Ben, Ben; what's the matter? Anything wrong with Mrs Aggie?'

'No, no. Nothing's wrong, but I got to thinking that your escort' – he glanced towards Bernard – 'Well, after he had set you home he'd have to walk back on his own. And I doubt if anybody dressed like he is—' He did not say, 'as you are, sir,' but, 'he is, would get out of that quarter without being stripped, an' not only of his wallet. So I thought I'd relieve you' – he was looking straight at Bernard now – 'of the trouble, and take her home.'

'I think that was very unnecessary.' Bernard's voice was cool. 'I'm quite able to take care of myself. And this walking stick' – he lifted up the walking stick that he had taken from the back of the trap – 'is not only part of one's dress, it's a weapon.'

'Aye, it might be, if you're face on, but not if the blows come from behind, or a dozen or so kids trip you up first. Well, you can walk back if you like, but that's up to you.'

Millie now turned to Bernard, saying, 'He's . . . he's right, Bernard, he is. It is dangerous in that part at night. Please don't be offended; he . . . he means well.'

'I don't mean well, I'm bein' practical.' Ben had snapped the words out.

A short silence followed before Bernard said, 'Goodbye, dear. I'll write.'

'Yes. Yes, do. Goodbye, and . . . and thank you for a wonderful day.'

'I thank you, too.'

It was all so formal, so stiff an ending to a beautiful fairy-like day, and all through Ben. Oh, Ben! At times he

251

got on her nerves. At times she wanted to strike out at him; at other times she felt so deeply for him.

They had gone about a dozen steps when she said, bitterly, 'You do spoil things for me, don't you? You set out to do it.'

He didn't answer her until they had taken another dozen steps or so, and then he said, 'Well, far better spoil the night for you than spoil his face for him, 'cos you wouldn't have liked to see him with it bashed in, would you? You know what happens down that lane, especially on a Saturday night.'

Yes, she knew what happened in the lane, and not only on Saturday nights; and the mobs of children and young boys seemed to smell a stranger. Oh, she wished she was miles away, miles away in that lovely house. And she would be soon. Yes, she would be. And she couldn't get in quickly enough to tell Mrs Aggie.

Once inside the gates, she ran across the yard and into the house. Aggie was sitting in her usual place and she greeted her with, 'Well, you've got back then.'

'Yes. Yes, I've got back. Did you know that Ben was meeting me?'

'Aye, yes; he said he would. And I thought it was sensible.'

'Oh, Mrs Aggie, he makes me mad. He . . . he's practically spoilt my day. But . . . but no, he couldn't.' She now threw off her bonnet and her coat, then flopped down beside Aggie and, gripping her hand, said, 'I'm so happy; I feel I could burst, explode . . . go into fragments.'

'Well, what's made you so happy?'

'You know.'

'He's spoken?'

'Yes.'

'Ah, lass, lass. I'm glad for you. Oh, I am glad for you. Did he give you a ring?'

252

'Ring?' She lifted her hand and looked at the ring her father had put on her finger, and she said, 'Oh, no, no. It . . . it was all of a sudden, just before we came away. We seemed to . . . not to be able to hold our feelings any longer. And he said he's coming to see you. Oh, Mrs Aggie, you should see that little house. It's a palace, it's paradise, it's beautiful. And he's had it all done out with me in mind, he said.' She turned her head away now. 'Oh, I can't believe it, I can't believe it. He's done it out in rose and gold because . . . because of my hair and . . . well . . . Oh, Mrs Aggie, he's wonderful. And . . . and you know, Mrs Aggie, he didn't seem to really mind about him . . . I mean, my father. He just mentioned him when we left the house, and . . . and I couldn't tell him the truth. I will sometime, but I know it wouldn't matter to him.'

'What is the aunt like?'

'Oh . . . the aunt. Oh, Mrs Aggie, imagine a large china doll who prattles all the time. She is really sweet, so dear. Slightly, I should say, what you would call eccentric. Poor thing, she was crossed in love when she was eighteen; then she had a nervous illness and, from being a shy girl, she started to talk and chatter. He says the family couldn't put up with her and they put her away privately for years. But he's brought her out and to this house; and she's got a maid, and she, too, is such a dear, so kind.'

'How many servants have they?'

'Oh, only the maid and Bernard's man, who, as he says, is a jack of all trades. And it's only a small house. There's a drawing-room downstairs and two small rooms and a kitchen, and four bedrooms and a couple of attics. It's just a small house, but it's beautiful, exquisite.'

'Well, when's he comin' to have a talk with me?'

'I don't suppose it will be until next . . . perhaps a week today. I don't know. He's going to write. We couldn't say

253

much to each other, could we now?' – she thrust her chin out towards Aggie — 'with Ben standing over us like a bear. Oh—' She jumped up from the couch and, standing on the old mat, she spread her arms wide as she said, 'Oh, I wish we had some music, Mrs Aggie, a piano, anything; I want to dance.'

With the sound of the far door opening, Aggie said, 'Go on now, dance yourself upstairs and change your togs. Then come down an' we'll have something to eat. Did you have anything to eat there?'

'Yes, tea, with rolled bread and butter.'

She ran from the room now, chanting, 'Rolled bread and butter. Rolled bread and butter.'

Ben came in and, taking his usual seat, he looked across at Aggie and said, 'Well?'

'It's done, lad. They're goin' to be married.' She watched him now gazing into the fire; then, when he rose to his feet and made for the door again, she said, 'You've got to face it. Where're you goin'?'

'Where d'you think?'

'Now, don't you go off and get sozzled.'

He turned and looked at her. 'I wouldn't waste me money,' he said.

'Well, where're you off to on a Saturday night?'

'Believe it or not, I'm goin' to school.'

'Like hell you are!'

'Aye, like hell I am, Aggie. You've had one surprise tonight, you're not ready for another. I'll wait a day or two. But, by the way, do you know that if a fella in his class took a lass out without her having what is called a chaperone, the lass would lose her good name; in fact, from what I hear an' read, any bloke who had respect for a lass wouldn't risk it . . . Think on that, Aggie. Aye, think on it.'

254

She stared at the closed door for a moment; then she put her hand to her brow as if to support her heavy head, and she said aloud, 'Oh God! why didn't You give him decent legs? At bottom, he's worth a streetful of gents.'

6

'He's like a fly in the ointment.'

'Aye, lass, a fly in the ointment. There's always a fly in the ointment in everybody's life. But you've got to understand why he's actin' like he does.'

'Oh, Mrs Aggie, I can't take that in. He's had Annie for years.'

'Well, from what he tells me, Annie wasn't what we think she was to him, at least hasn't been for a long, long time. Anyway, lass, you haven't got to let him spoil your happiness. No, this is a chance of a lifetime, because nothing like it will ever come your way again. He's a fine man, and once you're married to him you'll go up in the world.'

'It seems too good to be true at times because you can't imagine it ever happening before, can you, not with a gentleman and someone like me and . . . ?'

'Oh' – Aggie flapped her hand, thrusting the suggestion widely aside – 'don't you believe it. There's those titled Johnnies up in London, an' just recently it was in the news-sheet, one of 'em married one of them actresses, not real actresses, just one of those dancing girls, an' now she's a Lady something or other. And don't you remember . . . well, you'd be old enough, it was the talk of the town, when one of the Broadhurst family took up with a mill lass?'

'Yes, but he didn't marry her.'

'No, he didn't; but Mr Abel Rundell did in the same situation.'

'Who was he?'

'He was afore your time. No, he wasn't; it was just about when you came on the scene. It was said he was from a ship-ownin' family, and he married this girl who worked in Mullens, you know, the milliners yon side of the market. Oh, you're not the first, an' you won't be the last, my dear, to be lifted out of the lower end.'

'But . . . but what's going to happen to you? I mean, the business will go. How are you going to manage?'

'Look, that's the least of your worries. I've wanted this business to go for a long time now, although I must say it's been very profitable, an' that's been through your efforts. But once you're gone I'll get back into me old seam.'

'You'll not; you'll never be able to go out with a cart again.'

'Oh, I have no intention of doing that, but the gates will be open and they can bring what stuff they like. And if there's any writing out to do Ben'll see to that. He'll stick by me, come rain, hail, or shine.'

'While I leave you.'

'Oh, lass, you're a different kettle of fish altogether.'

Millie now asked thoughtfully, 'Where do you think Ben's going at night all dressed up if he's not going to Annie's? And he didn't dress up to go to visit her.'

'I don't know, lass. The only thing I know is he's not comin' home drunk. And what's more, he's taken to smokin' a pipe.'

'Smoking a pipe?'

'Yes. Of course, there's nothing strange about a man smokin' a pipe, but I've never known him bein' at it. I smelt the waft of it coming down the stairs. And when he was out ... well, I made me way to his abode an' there it was. An' not a clay one either, oh no; it was a wooden one. And I recognized the type, too, a meerschaum. My dad used to smoke one of those, an' they don't come cheap. You can get two clay ones for a penny, but you'll not get one of those under a bob. And you know, lass, I've got it in me mind he's up to something. If you're puzzled as to where he goes off to at night, I'm more puzzled, I can tell you. He's never sat down with us one night this week, and here's Thursday.'

Millie's thoughts were not on Ben now, but on how near Thursday was to Saturday and Bernard. Oh, she couldn't wait for Saturday. She was literally ticking the hours off. She hadn't had a full night's sleep this week: she had lain in bed imagining she was in another bed, in that lovely bedroom set in that wonderful house which would soon be hers. Could she believe it? *Could she believe it?*

Yes, she could, because, as Mrs Aggie said, there were men such as Bernard who, through love, stooped and lifted people like herself out of the mire; although, she must give credit where it was due: she had never considered this house and the company of Mrs Aggie and Ben such as would come under the name of mire, even if it was set in a district amid the dregs of society, working dregs maybe, but, nevertheless, dregs.

She was brought from her musing by Aggie having a bout of coughing which seemed to rack her broad chest; and it caused her to say with concern, 'I've told you, you should be in bed.'

The bout over, Aggie sat gasping for a moment or so before she could bring out the words, 'Bed? I've never taken to bed yet with a cold an' it'll have to step itself up before it gets me there now. Look; pour that bottle of beer into a pan and warm it, and put a spoonful of ginger in it. That'll do the trick.'

258

'It hasn't so far this week, has it? You must be burnt up with ginger inside you.'

'Well, I'm dilutin' it now, miss, havin' it in the hot ale. So, get on with it.'

Millie now hurried into the scullery and returned with a pan, and, as she was about to pour the beer into it, the door opened and Ben entered.

In the ordinary way, after glancing at him, she would have carried on with the job in hand; but now she straightened her back, as did Aggie. Why, neither of them could have explained, only that he looked different. It wasn't his face. Perhaps it was the new top hat he was sporting or the good second-hand coat that had a bit of astrakhan on the collar. But no; not even the coat and hat made the difference.

'What you lookin' at?'

'You, of course,' said Aggie. 'Who else is there to look at?'

'Well, why look so surprised; you've seen me before.'

'Aye, I have, more times than I want to, I can tell you. But what have you done with yourself?'

'Oh, you've noticed. Is it me new coat?'

'No. No, not quite, it isn't your new coat, it's . . . '

'Oh! Oh!' He looked down at his feet now. 'It's me boots. They're new, you see.'

Both Aggie and Millie looked at his boots. They were new.

'I had them specially made.'

'*You had them specially made?*'

'Aye, Aggie, that's what I said: I had them specially made. An' the difference you're findin' in me is . . . well, me legs are still the same length, but I've gone a little taller, a good inch and a half. Oh yes, a good inch and a half, which makes a difference.'

Aggie's voice was low as she asked, 'How did you manage that?'

259

'Oh, it's somethin' I should have thought about long before now if I'd had any sense. But of course, you've got to have the boots made, an' they don't come cheap. An' they haven't got to be heavy, so as you can't lift your feet. And the uppers have got to look as if they come down within a sole distance of the floor; they've got to look natural like. And you'll notice, if I turn round,' which he did now, 'there's a good bit of heel on the back. And, you know, the best part about it is they're not even as heavy as me workin' boots. Fred Pasternack is a real good snob. He'd have to be, wouldn't he, to make ridin' boots for the gentry. And what's more, he's a very understandin' man, and he likes a challenge.'

'*Well! Well!* We're certainly goin' up in the world, so to speak, aren't we?' Millie had mouthed the words without making any sound; but, as if he had heard them, he said, 'Yes, you're goin' up in the world an' into a new position, Millie; I'm goin' teachin'.'

'*Teachin'? You?*'

The bark he now gave startled both Aggie and Millie: 'Aye, teaching. Me!' he said. 'I haven't wasted me time all these years, Mrs Winkowski: me body's lived in this warren but me head's been somewhere else. You mightn't, but other people have noticed it. Aye, they've got their wits about them, they see beyond the clothes, an' the height, not forgettin' the voice that knew nowt at one time about speakin' properly. It's some years now, Aggie, since I learned that a noun is a name of anything.'

Aggie didn't come back at him with a protest louder than his; instead, her answer was, 'Well, now that you've got that off your chest, you can tell us how all this has come about.'

After a moment of hesitation, he said, 'Well, in the first place it was Mrs Sponge.' He was looking at Millie now. 'She asked me if I'd like to take the little 'uns. Of course, I laughed at her and said I wasn't fit. But she

260

said I was fit enough to learn them their ABC. And . . . well, I found I liked it. I got interested.' He now glanced towards Aggie, saying, 'They wanted to know if I would take the morning class, but I explained I had a job to do. So they decided I could go there at nights, an' suggested that I could rake in a few youngsters from this end.'

'Huh!' The sound came from Aggie, and she added, 'That'll take some doin'. You'd have to have a pocket full of coppers to bribe them.'

'You'd be surprised, Aggie, you'd be surprised. I've got four, I'll bet, waitin' for me outside the gate now. Of course, it could be the mug of cocoa they get at the end; but they've been regular over the past few months.'

'You've been doin' this for months?'

'Oh, aye, for months. But—' He now looked down towards his new boots and his voice was just above a mutter as he said, 'But the learnin' of the bairns only proves one thing, I've got a lot to learn meself. But I'll get there . . . They wanted to send me away, you know, to learn proper; there's schools for such as me; but I said, no.' His chin was up now and he was staring at Millie. 'You'll see, I'll get there. And on me own, with a little help, of course. I might even become another Terrence Sponge and stand on a box in the park on a Sunday. Anyway,' he ended, on a short laugh, 'that's me life all set ahead. Now we all know where we're goin', don't we? And I hope it turns out as we intended. We'll just have to work at it, won't we, Millie?'

She didn't answer, but her mind was crying, Oh, Ben. Oh, Ben. He was so bitter and so sad. The sadness was in his eyes and behind the bitterness in his voice. If only . . . What was she talking about? As he said, their lives were set out before them.

'Good-night, Aggie. By the way, I'd go to bed early if I were you, with that cold. You can lock up 'cos I won't be callin' in later. But I'll see to the back gate.' . . .

After he had gone the room seemed strangely empty, and neither of them made any comment for some time until Millie said, 'He's right, you know: you should go to bed, Mrs Aggie.'

'Oh, shut up, girl. Don't turn the conversation. But there's only one thing I'm glad about concerning him: he's workin' it out of himself. An' because of it I shouldn't wonder he'll make something of himself in the end.' Then, her voice lightening, she said, 'But he did look taller, didn't he? Couldn't tell what it was at first, but it's made a difference. It's a wonder he never thought of it before. Amazing what an inch or two will do. But when you think of it, I bet you a shillin' there's not a man over five foot six in all The Courts. Aye, but now—' Her voice changing, she muttered, 'But what a difference six inches would make to any man.'

7

'I shouldn't be going.'

'Look, we've had this out, haven't we? And you're all dressed up.'

'Well, let him come in just for a moment. I think he wants to speak to you. He said he did.'

'Lass, I can hardly get me breath. An' the place stinks of camphorated oil, besides other things. And it's like a hovel, because you can't be in three places at once: at your cooking, at the gate, and here lookin' after this big fat hulk. Now, just tell him I'm under the weather and I'll see him next week, or when he would care to come, once I've got over this bout. Anyway, lass, it's you he wants to do the talkin' to. And look, I want to see you come back with a ring on your finger . . . on your other hand. Why' – she pointed – 'why have you put that one on again?'

Millie looked at the ring on her middle finger, saying, 'I don't really know, but it's very pretty. I only wish it hadn't come from where it has, but—' She pulled at it now, trying to get it over her knuckle, saying, 'It's odd how it will go on but I can't get it off again without using soap.'

The door opened, and Ben, standing there, said, 'Your escort's arrived. I haven't opened the gate; you can do that for him.'

Millie turned to Aggie and bent over her with the intention of kissing her cheek, but Aggie pushed her away, saying, 'You don't want to carry this cold, do you?' Then she added, 'Well, mind, be back at five or before that, because Ben there, as he's told you, wants to be gone by half-past five. Although I don't know why he's stated a time; it must be something special.' She now heaved at her breath, then called to Ben, 'Is it? Is it something special?'

'Yes, you could say it is, at least, it's special to me.'

As Millie attempted to pass him at the door, he didn't move out of the way – she had to press herself against the stanchion – but even so their bodies touched and their glances held, and when she was past him, she turned and said quietly, 'I hope your new friends have manners and you learn from them.'

He made no rejoinder, and she marched through the outer room and into the cool air, then hurried across the yard towards the gates. And as she unlocked them she was apologizing through the bars: 'I'm sorry. I'm sorry. He should have let you in.'

'Is something wrong?'

'No, not wrong, but Mrs Aggie has a dreadful cold;' and she added tactfully, 'As she says, colds are infectious and she wouldn't like you to . . . well, have gone away harbouring a cold like hers.'

'I've never suffered from a cold in my life. Anyway, how are you?'

'I am very well, thank you.' Then glancing at him, she said, 'Except that I have been lonely and . . . and longing for today to come.'

264

He had taken her arm, and now he pressed it to his side, saying, 'Not more than I have been, my dear. It has been a long, long, tedious week.'

When three scantily dressed boys ran in front of them and began jumping backwards, calling, 'Got a copper, sir? Got a copper, sir?' he took his crop and waved it, saying, 'Get yourself away. Off with you! Off with you!' And they scattered. But one of them stopped and shouted to the others, ' 'Tis Millie.' And a voice answered him, ' 'T'isn't.'

' 'Tis, I tell you . . . Millie! Millie!'

She did not turn round or wave her hand as she would normally do, but allowed Bernard to hurry her on; and as they emerged from the lane, he said stiffly, 'Oh, how glad I am I'm going to take you out of this, my dear.'

At the ostler's stable, he apologised as he again lifted her up to the seat of the trap: 'This is no vehicle for this time of year,' he said; 'I must see about a carriage. It's all right for me trotting backwards and forwards into the town, but you need protection.'

She laughed. 'My looks belie me,' she said; 'I'm very hardy; in fact, I'm tough.'

The 'Gee-up! there,' came out on a deep laugh. 'Hardy and tough. Oh yes, madam, you give off the impression of both qualities.' He slanted his glance at her. 'Pull that rug well around you. It's surprisingly cold today,'

Arrive home. Arrive home. Each turn of the wheel sang the words: Arrive home. Arrive home.

As they drove through the lower part of the town, he said, 'I've never seen so many people about; but then, it's the new factory law, I suppose. The Saturday half-day starting at one o'clock makes all the difference; although it also gives more time for the gin shops.'

'Did you get all your business finished in Cheshire?'

265

'Business?' His head jerked towards her, then away again. 'Oh, it wasn't business in that sense; more, family conferences: one can never really untie those strings that tie you to a family. But I did have another journey to make, to visit a friend's house. I'll . . . I'll explain all when I get inside.' . . .

It was as if it were but yesterday and not a week since she was in the house and had met Miss Christine Lavor, for there she was in the hall, her arms outstretched, saying, 'Oh! how nice to see you. I've been thinking of you. Are you ready for tea? Fanny has rolled some extra brown bread. I've been watching her in the kitchen: she has made some tarts and filled them with a lovely conserve. Oh, do take your things off. Let me have them.'

Bernard laughed, because he had already taken Millie's coat and bonnet and her bag and gloves and laid them on a chair; and so, turning to his aunt, he said, 'Now you run into the kitchen, dear, and tell Fanny we are here and we want tea right away, because . . . because we are both hungry and cold.'

'Oh, yes, yes, of course, Bernard.'

After she had trotted away, Bernard took Millie's hand and drew her towards the drawing-room. And after hastily closing the door behind them, he put his arms about her and looked into her face for a moment before placing his lips on hers, but in no mild fashion: it was a hard and hungry kiss, and when it was over she laid her head on his shoulder, gasping as if at the end of a long run. As for him, he let out a deep sigh as he held her tightly to his body and muttered, 'I've been longing for that all week, more and more.' Then pressing her from him and gripping her shoulders, he said, 'Have you any idea of the depths of my feelings for you, Millie Forester?'

'No, sir; but I hope to find out, during which time I express mine for you.'

266

'Oh, Millie' – he was walking her up the room now – 'just to hear you talk. It is this, not only your appearance, your beautiful, beautiful, beautiful, beautiful face, and that marvellous hair' – he gently flicked the fringe on her brow – 'but it's the way you deport yourself and how you speak ... and coming from that place! Oh, I'm sorry, I'm sorry. I shouldn't denigrate it, but ... but how, I've asked myself, and keep asking myself, how have you remained so beautiful, so pure, so good, amidst all that mire?'

Her voice was quiet now as she answered, 'I had Mrs Aggie and Ben to guide me and protect me. I can't say that too often, Bernard. I owe them everything. I certainly owe them what I am and how I am today, for without their care I don't know what might have happened to me. Something ... something terrible. I must tell you about it sometime. But enough it is that you take me as I am.'

'Oh, Millie, yes, yes, I take you as you are, and always shall ... Oh dear! Here we go!' The door had opened and Miss Chrissie entered, followed by Fanny with the laden tray. And again Millie's thoughts were that it was as if she had never moved from this room, that everything was the same as it had been last Saturday.

And Miss Chrissie chattered as before, remarking, early, 'I like the colour of your attire, Miss Millie. I've always liked green. I suppose it is because I used to play in the green fields when I was a child and I used to make long, long daisy chains. Do you know how to make a daisy chain?'

'No,' Millie answered; 'I'm afraid I don't.'

'Oh, then I will show you. There are lots of fields behind the house. I've never been out in them yet, but we will walk in them and I shall show you how to make a daisy chain. I used to put them round my dolls, but there were always one or two that didn't like them. I said to them, you can't

267

please everyone. Do you agree with me, Bernard, that you can't please everyone?'

'Oh, yes, Aunt Chrissie, I do agree with you there.'

'There won't be any daisies for some time, it being autumn; but that will soon pass, because you'll be staying with us from now on.'

Millie laughed and said, 'Well, not from now on, Miss Chrissie; and today I must be home on time because Ben — he is,' she paused, 'a friend of mine — he has an appointment for early evening, and you see, my guardian, Mrs Winkowski, she has a cold, and it wouldn't be nice to leave her alone with a cold, would it?'

She was talking to the little woman as if she were a child, and as a child Miss Lavor answered, 'Oh, no, no, it wouldn't. You mustn't leave anyone alone if they've got a cold or are sick. But I thought you would be staying tonight. Still, perhaps next week.'

Millie smiled kindly and said, 'Yes, perhaps next week.' . . .

A short while later she was a little surprised when Bernard drew the little woman to her feet, the while saying to her, 'Run into the kitchen, Aunt Chrissie, and tell Fanny to come and clear. And I want you to help her because I've got a lot to say to Millie. You understand?'

'Oh, yes, dear boy. Oh yes, I understand. Of course, of course, I will help Fanny. Of course, she will not let me dry up the teacups because I'm apt to drop them.' She giggled as she went tripping down the room.

Bernard now sat down beside Millie, saying, 'Oh, I wish I could have had a word with your Mrs Aggie. I did want you to stay tonight.'

She looked at him, puzzled for a moment; then she said, 'There'll be other nights.'

'Of course, of course, I know, but . . . but I'm so impatient. And it is ridiculous that I can see you for only

268

a few hours a week. But all this will soon change, won't it?'

She smiled up at him as she answered softly, 'I hope so, Bernard. I hope so.'

The tea things were quickly gathered up, the pleasant-faced Fanny beaming all the while. And after lifting the heavy tray, she turned about, her arms still outstretched, and she bobbed her head towards Millie, as if saying, there now, I couldn't have been quicker. And Millie felt inclined to say, thank you, but she knew it wasn't her place: she wasn't the mistress of the house yet.

Bernard now pushed the two single chairs back and, pulling the small lounge sofa forward towards the fire, he said, 'Come, dear.' And after seating her on it, he put his arm about her and again he kissed her, pressing her to him so hard that a button on her costume made itself felt through the bottom of his cravat and fine undershirt. Laughing, he took hold of it and twisted it, saying, 'You are stabbing me through the heart, do you know?' Then he added, 'Wasn't it funny about Aunt Chrissie and the daisies and the colour of your costume?'

'Well, it showed she liked it.'

He pulled a face, as he responded, 'She may have but, my dear, I shall dress you so differently, and in gold colours to match your skin.'

She pressed herself from him and her indignation was slightly mocking as she said, 'You do not like my attire, sir?'

'Oh, madam, it would be all right on another person; very smart, but on you, it does nothing to enhance, not that you need enhancing at all. Your beauty wants to be matched, and I shall see that it's matched. We shall go to London one day – there are some splendid, splendid shops there – and I shall sit in a satin chair and you will parade before me' – he swept his hand back and forth – 'in the gowns that have taken your fancy.'

Why she should feel slightly perturbed she didn't know, except that perhaps her costume was not of the smartest; but it was good thick homespun cloth and of a nice shape.

'Have you ever thought of going to Paris?'

'To France? No, never. I think I should like to see the sea, though.'

'You have never seen the sea?'

'Never.'

'Oh, my dear, dear, Millie. Oh, what pleasures there are in store for you. But there are places and places from which to view the sea. Especially so are there places across the channel, in France and Italy and Venice. But you have to go on the sea in a ship to go to France.'

Her face was straight now as she said, 'You have been to all these places?'

'Yes; I spent some time abroad, from when I was seventeen to almost nineteen. I had family connections in Holland.'

'In Holland?' Her head was nodding now.

'Yes, in Holland. Then last year I did a short tour of about six months in . . . Oh, but Millie' – he was holding her again – 'imagine if we could travel those places together for six months.' He looked over her shoulder now, away down the room, and his voice lost its high excited note when he said, 'But what am I saying? Our visits now would indeed have to be on occasions. But what will that matter?' He was again holding her at arm's length, and he leaned towards her as he said, 'We have this, this great, great mansion, this seven-roomed castle, this secret cave, to which I can escape from the world and to you and as often as I can. Oh, yes, as often as I can, Millie. Believe that every minute I can I shall spend with you. Oh! my dear' – he was now stroking her face – 'if only things were different and we could be married. But

270

you understand the situation. We have the next best thing though, a freer thing without . . . What is the matter? What is the matter?'

She had edged from him and was pressing her back against the wooden arm of the couch; then, slowly and as if sliding from something that she was afraid might spring upon her, she rose to her feet, and she looked at him, where he still remained seated, a puzzled expression on his face, and again he said, 'What is it?'

Her voice wouldn't come. She tried to get words through her throat, but they just stuck there. Her brain seemed to have stopped working; yet no, its thoughts were flying, dashing themselves against each other.

She watched him get to his feet and put his hand to his brow, then say, 'Oh, no, no. You must have understood. Mrs Aggie understood. Of course she understood. She's not a fool; neither are you. Millie! Millie! please, have sense. See the situation. And . . . and there would be no scandal, none whatever. I've worked it all out. That's why I took the house and brought Aunt Chrissie here. You are to be known as her nurse. No-one would know any different. Please! Please, Millie; don't look at me like that. And don't move away from me; stay where you are. Look! Listen to me!' His voice was loud, hoarse. 'I love you. Every word comes from my heart. I love you, and . . . and I'd marry you tomorrow if it were possible. But . . . but I've been promised for years; I told you. Last week we talked about the breeding business and families and how things are arranged. When I was eighteen I made a mistake of promising myself to someone. All I can say is, it had been arranged in the cradle. We were brought up together, a neighbour's daughter. I . . . I've got to go through with it. It's not only the families, it's to do with business and my godfather who left me the money and the shares in the mill. It's all bound up together. It's . . . it's his niece . . . *Millie!*'

He had taken two steps towards her before she found her voice, and it didn't tremble: it wasn't a whine and it made a statement that even surprised herself, for what she said was, 'I've been what Ben would call a bloody fool. I should have known there was no such man as I thought you to be. Mrs Aggie said there were men here and there who married beneath them, gave the name of Lady to dancing girls, but she did indicate they were few and far between.'

'Millie. My darling Millie, believe me when I say, if I'd had the slightest inkling that you didn't understand the situation I . . . I would have never gone ahead. Believe me in this. I thought, coming from that' – he swallowed – 'quarter, there would be nothing you would be unaware of in such matters. That you were pure, oh, yes, yes, I never doubted that for a moment, but I thought you would gauge the situation in its true context, if you know what I mean.'

'Yes. Yes, I know what you mean: I was to be your mistress; I would be here for you to use at odd times. You have seen my father. To my mind he's a man of low character, and he has only come into my life these last few months. But my mother died when I was seven. She died by her own hand; she hanged herself because she was used. You didn't know that; that was what I meant to tell you later on when we married. Oh my God! You have a right to be astounded at my ignorance, at my stupidity, but let me tell you this, no matter how life deals with me I shall never become any man's mistress. Never. *Never!*' The last words came out as a shout. 'Now, Mr Thompson, I shall take my leave. But one last word I will give you. Do you know who you remind me of at this moment? The son of your half-sister.'

He had been standing with his head lowered, but now he jerked it upwards as he cried at her, 'Don't you dare say that

272

to me, Millie! I'm no better nor worse than most men, but in character I'm not in any way connected with my half-sister's offspring or her husband.'

She now walked behind the chairs in order to avoid him, but when she reached the door he was there before her, his hand on the knob: 'Please, Millie,' he said. 'Please try to understand. And I'll say again, I love you. I do.'

'And can you describe the feelings you have for your future wife?'

'Yes. Yes, I can. They are, in a way, loving, bred on liking and kindliness, but in no way can they reach the passion that I have for you, nor would our association ever permit of that, I am sure.'

'Well, you have plenty of time to find out. Will you please let me pass?'

Slowly he opened the door for her, and in the hall she dragged on her coat and bonnet, but when he was about to call to his man to get the trap, she said, 'You need not bother with your conveyance, I am used to walking.'

'Don't be silly!' His voice was harsh now. 'It will soon be getting dark. You could never make your way back home.'

'I am used to walking among the poor, as you have already experienced; so the journey holds no fear for me.'

'Wait a moment.' He went to grab her arm, but she brought her other hand down on to his wrist, saying, 'Don't touch me!' That it had been a hard slap was evident by the way he gripped his wrist; then grabbing up her handbag and gloves, she was out of the door and running across the gravel front and then down the drive.

As she reached the road she could hear him calling loudly, 'Millie! Millie!' It was then she lifted up her skirt and fled.

The light was going and she knew it would take all of twenty minutes to reach the built-up area, through which

273

she would have to pass before reaching the main streets and the district that she knew.

When she could no longer hear his voice calling her, she drew in her run to a stumbling trot, then into a walk.

Between trotting and walking she covered about a mile before twilight really settled in. Her breath coming in gasps, she was hurrying along a stretch of open road which she could still make out had fields on both sides when she saw, in the distance coming towards her a vehicle of some kind with its carriage lights already on. Then hearing the sound of a trotting horse behind her, she turned, thinking that he had brought out the trap after all.

In order to pass on the narrow road, the drivers had brought the horses to a walk. The oncoming vehicle passed her first; the other she recognized now was a cab . . . and cabs were for hire.

Its driver was still walking his horse, and she stood on the verge and called up to him. 'Are you for hire, please?'

When the man drew the horse to a stop and bent forward, she could make out that he was a big man, and he said, 'What's that you say, miss?' And she called back, 'Are you for hire?'

'Huh! Am I for hire? Well, well, well. I've already got a passenger, miss. I'll have to hear what he says about it.'

The passenger was looking out of the window and he couldn't believe his eyes. He must be dreaming, he told himself. But he believed in luck, and this was his lucky day: he had just made a very nice deal with a gentleman who lived away back along this road, a regular customer.

He opened the door of the cab and stepped down, and, his tone assuming what he imagined to be that of a gentleman, he said, 'At your service, miss . . . or madam. Do you wish to be taken into town?'

'Yes, if you please.'

'It is very late for a young lady to be out on her own and on this lonely road.'

'I . . . I missed my friends.'

'Where do you wish to go, miss?' The man on the box was now speaking, and she said, 'If . . . if you would just drop me near the market place; I can find my way quite well then, thank you.'

It was as she went to pass the passenger that his face showed clear in the light of the carriage lamp and her body stiffened; then, and for the second time on this day, she walked backwards, and, gasping now, muttered, 'No. No, thank you. I will walk.'

'As you wish. As you wish.' The man did not seem at all put out by the answer, but said, 'It is a very lonely road, you know, and we are coming into a rough district. So, if it will be any help to you, you can walk by the side of the cab, and the driver will walk his horse and you can take protection that way. And may I add, you have nothing to fear from me;' and much to her surprise, he got back into the cab; then putting his head out of the window, he called up to the cabbie, 'You can take the short cut through Caxton, cabbie.'

'Yes, sir. Yes, sir. As you say.'

The cab had moved forwards some yards before Millie could force herself to follow it.

She was sure that was the man with the thin face who had been after her all those years ago. She would never forget his face. And yet he seemed changed, different altogether.

Walking as it were in the tracks of the cab, she realised that long before they reached the built-up area some mishap could easily have befallen her: there was a ditch running along each side of the road, and she could tumble into one or other.

By this time, she was actually holding on to the leaf springs, as much for support as for guidance, because she was so tired. But more so she was miserable, and heart-broken.

275

And as on that occasion when she was brought back from the Quintons, and she had promised herself that once inside the yard and that house with those two people she would never leave them again, never! so she was doing now, and with equal fervour.

They were now in a district where lights were hanging outside the taverns and shop windows. She thought she recognised the street, but then again, at night, everything looked the same. When they entered a narrow road with people coming and going, she would have slipped quietly away, but here and there were groups of men and youths whom she could see and hear were the worse for drink.

Outside one tavern, a number of men seemed to be arguing, and when one pushed another, causing him to stumble, he landed against the side of the cab and gripped her in order to save himself from falling. And then, peering into her face, he said, 'Hello, lovey.'

'Leave go of me! Go away!'

But her cry brought another two men shambling forward, one of them crying, 'What've we here? Oh my! My! A nice piece all dressed up, an' left on her own, an' hangin' on to the back of a cab. Eeh my! Where've you dropped from, love?'

The cab continued moving, and neither the driver nor the passenger seemed to take any notice; but when she screamed, 'Leave me alone!' and kicked out at one of her would-be molesters, and he came out with a string of oaths and, lurching towards her, missed her and fell heavily against the side of the cab, it was stopped and its passenger hurriedly alighted. Pressing herself tightly against the wheel, Millie watched him lay about the men with a walking stick. It would be a pliable stick, because she could hear the swishing of it. When others, drawn from the bar by the narration, would have assailed them too, he grabbed her arm, saying, 'Get in! Get in! Quick!' And he followed her, banging the door shut.

276

The driver yelled, 'Up there! Up there!' and the horses were off into a trot. Even so, some of the men continued to beat on the back and side of the cab.

She lay gasping against the back of the seat and staring before her.

'I'll have to send you a bill in for a new hat,' the man said, pointing to his bare head.

'I'm . . . I'm very sorry.'

'Oh, you needn't be, Damsel in distress. Anyway, tell me, why were you on that road alone?'

'I . . . I had gone to visit someone. They . . . they weren't at home.'

'Am I to believe you?'

'Doesn't matter if you do or not. Will you please ask the cabbie to drop me off at the market?'

'He knows where he's going.'

She sat in silence. Sometimes she could see his face when they were passing a well-lit shop or an inn, otherwise they were sitting in semi-darkness, for the coach lamps sent merely a mist of light into the cab.

She knew now that the cab was going over a cobbled area and she voiced this by saying, 'We're in the market now, I think.'

'No, not quite. You'll know time enough where you are when we get there.'

It was shortly after this that the man put his head out of the window and called up to the cabbie, 'Go straight round the back and into the yard, Will.'

'*What? What yard?* Please! I want to get out.'

'You'll get out in a minute.'

She heard the horses being drawn back to a walk and she felt the cab turn at an angle, turn again, then stop. Immediately, the man got out quickly; then held out his hand to her. And when she stepped on to the ground and

277

saw they were in a walled yard, she opened her mouth; but the scream never had voice because he was behind her and his hand came tight over her mouth; at the same time, his knee was pushed in the middle of her back with such force that her arms sprang out. And the man she had imagined to be the cabbie had hold of them in an odd way: he had his back to her, and he gave a heave, and the next instant she was thrust up practically on to his shoulders. Her mouth was free now but she couldn't cry out for she was frozen with terror. Her head was bobbing, her eyes, staring wide, were blinded for the moment by a bright light shining from a room. Then they passed through a dark passage and into another room, which she was surprised to recognise was a kitchen. Two women were in it. And when, with an expert swing, she was brought from the man's back and into a high-backed wooden chair, she could not utter a word; all she could do was stare and listen.

The thin man was talking to the women, saying, 'I tell you it's unbelievable. There she was on the road alone. Talk about luck. Anyway, Nell, you come and see to her. There's things to be done. And Rosie, you go along to the bar. Tell Peter to go to Firman's club and ask to see Mr B.'

'Mr B?' the woman said.

'Aye, just say that. Peter'll know. But tell him to change his togs, go very decent like. He knows how to go about it.'

'But what message has he got to give him?'

'Oh, the usual. There's a parcel for him. Well, let's get going.'

'You don't want a cup of tea?'

'No, Rosie; I don't want a cup of tea. Go on.'

The woman laughed now and said, 'All right, you don't want a cup of tea, but I'll say this: by the look of her, you'll have to give her somethin', else she'll be dead of fright before

278

he gets here.' Then in a laughing tone, 'And that would upset you, wouldn't it, dearie?'

He made a playful rush at her, saying, 'Go on; off you go!' Then turning to the woman he had called Nell, he said, 'Bring her up,' and made for the door, saying as he passed the supposed cabbie, 'Quick thinkin', cabbie. Yes; nice piece of acting. You can stable him now; I won't need that any more tonight.'

'Aye, boss,' said the man.

Millie did not resist the woman's hands on her as they followed the man from the room; they were firm but not rough, not even when she was pulled to a stop at what appeared to be a double door. The man opened it, to reveal, not a room, but what seemed to be a blank wall. But he twisted something and the wall opened.

They were now in another hall and she had the momentary impression of the house from which she had recently escaped: everywhere in this place was pink . . . no, red, deep red: the carpet, the heavy hangings, the upholstery of chairs.

They were crossing this area when, to one side, she noticed another door. Life seeming to flow back into her, she swung round from the woman and dashed to it, tugging at it and yelling now. But then the futility of her efforts came to her, not at the size of the two heavy bolts and the large lock without a key, but with the realisation that her two captors had not moved: there were no restraining hands on her.

She swung round and pleaded with the man: 'Let me go! Please, let me go!'

'Why should I? You walked into this; I didn't ask you to stop my carriage. Anyway—' His voice dropped, and he moved slowly towards her: 'I've been waiting to meet you for a long time – you remember me, don't you? – from when you first saw me. But that was a long time ago. You've grown. Oh my! you've nearly grown past being any use to me. Do you understand that, dearie?'

When his face came close to hers, instinctively her hand came out in the form of a fist and she banged it into his face. Then, bringing up her knee, she caught him in the groin, causing him to step back for a moment; but the sounds he was making were outdone by those of the woman, because she was crying, 'Oh! my. Oh! my.' And it wasn't evident whether the words were emitted in laughter or in amazement.

The man straightened and thrust up an arm, but the woman's voice checked its coming down as she cried, 'You don't want to mark her, do you, not with him comin'? That can wait.'

Reluctantly, he stepped back; then, fingering her cheek, he turned to the woman, saying, 'Am I bleeding?'

'It's only a scratch,' she said. 'She must have a ring on.'

Millie's arm was jerked almost out of the socket, and he was looking down on her hand now; and then he came out with a string of oaths, and, thrusting Millie's hand towards the woman, he cried, '*Look at that!* Do you see what I'm seeing? I can't believe it. Look at it!'

He began to pull the ring off her finger, and when she cried out, he took no notice. Then the ring was in his hand and he was twisting it from side to side as if to examine the light of the stones.

'You sure?'

'Am I sure? Bugger me! I know me own. Twenty years I had it . . . Who gave you this?'

He was now gripping her shoulder and he repeated, 'Who gave it to you?'

'My . . . my . . . it was a present.'

'*Who . . . gave . . . it . . . to . . . you?*'

'My . . . my father.'

280

After a long moment the hand left her shoulder and he turned to the woman and in another explosive fit of exasperation, he cried again, 'Bugger me!' and, following another string of oaths, he said, 'Her father, she says. He was the one: he nicked the lot, and the rest. My God! I thought I was too old a fox to be hoodwinked by a rabbit. And he was going to sell her to me, remember? He had it all set up in his own mind. He was taking her for a walk, a fake fight and that would be that. He'd have his thirty quid and I'd have someone I'd been wanting to get my hands on for years, because her mother owed me a lot. My God! Yes, she did.'

He now turned to Millie. 'Do you know, my rag nymph, you're just the spit of your mother? She double-crossed me, she did, using a rope, just before she was due to sail. My God! I could have hung her meself when I had to give that money back. Things weren't as flush then as they are now. But I'll get it back with interest, on you! Come here!' Gripping her again, he hauled her forward and pushed her towards the stairs. And as he did so she screamed; but his only answer to this was, 'You can scream your head off, dear; nobody will hear you in this quarter because this nice house was made especially for little girls like you; although you're a little girl no longer, more's the pity. Still, he's had his eye on you for a long time and he'll pay good money. Oh aye, he will, before I let him set his eyes on you. He couldn't get you on his own and I didn't seem to be able to oblige him . . . get up there!' She had gripped the banister, and he had to push her over the top stair.

When she fell on her knees, the woman helped her to her feet, saying quietly, 'Come along; it's no use.'

The landing, too, was all red. They had passed three doors on one side, and the woman said, 'You'll want number eight?'

'Where else?'

She opened the fourth door, then said, 'Stay there, ducks, until I turn the lights up.'

After attending to the two oil lamps the woman returned and pulled Millie into the room, leaving the man standing in the doorway, and he said, 'Strip her ready. If he's at his club, he could be here any time.' And with this he turned away, closing the door behind him and leaving Millie and the woman looking at each other. Millie began to whimper. Her voice like that of a child's, she pleaded, 'Please! Please, let me out. Please! Mrs Aggie has money; she will pay you. Please!'

'It's no use, lass. Come on, get your things off.'

When the hands came on her, she slapped them away, still as a child might, saying, 'No! No, don't touch me. I won't take my clothes off. I won't!' Then again she was pleading, 'Please, miss. I have never done anything like . . . I mean, I know nothing.'

'I know what you mean, love. I know well what you mean. But you're a big lass and it's got to happen sometime. And you could have worse ones than you'll have tonight. Oh aye, I can tell you that. He's all right. In fact, nothin' might happen at all with him. You never know. He's just that kind: he wants to play a bit. Come on, let me have your coat.'

'No!'

'I'll have to get rough then, because you've got to get your things off. And look, I'm tellin' you' – her voice changed – 'there's worse things than what you're in for. By God! yes. And you should be thankful for small mercies. Now come on.'

With an expert twist, Millie was swung round; her coat ripped off her; her bonnet, which was already hanging by its strings down her back, was thrown aside.

By the time the woman reached the last petticoat Millie had no fight left in her. When she was stripped naked and

282

sitting on the side of the bed, crouched forward, the woman gathered up her clothes, took them to the door and threw them outside; then came back and, opening a cupboard, took out what looked like a small shift. It was a flimsy thing of very fine lawn, and when it was slipped over her head, reaching only to her knees, Millie crouched further forward and began to moan.

The woman placed her hand under her chin and lifted her white terrified face towards her, and she whispered, 'I know who you are. You are Ben's lass, aren't you? Listen. I'll try to get word to him. It won't be tonight. I'm on duty tonight, but if I can, I'll slip him the wink tomorrow, somehow. I don't know what he can do. He'll likely want to go for the polis, but that'll be fatal. You could disappear altogether if that happened. Anyway, I'll try.'

Millie was unable to make any response; she was shivering from head to foot; and the woman, throwing back the silk coverlet to expose fine sheets and lace-edged pillow cases, said, 'Jump in, lass, and keep yourself warm. I'll make up the fire.' She nodded towards the end of the room, and Millie followed her gaze, so frozen with fear she hadn't noticed there was a fireplace in the room. She hadn't noticed anything about it, but she was to have plenty of time to take in every little detail of it during the next hours, the coming night, and its following day.

8

It was seven o'clock and Millie hadn't returned. Ben stood by the couch and looked down on Aggie and she said, 'Well, she would keep her promise, I know that. They could have been held up on the road. Anything could have happened; more so, they could have been set upon gettin' here from the stables where his trap's left. But you say the trap isn't there?'

'What am I tellin' you, woman? Have you gone soft in the head? I was there on time to meet her, as I was before, because when you come to think about it she's got as much knowledge of life outside these gates as he has of life in this quarter.'

'And you're blamin' me for that?'

'No, I'm not. If there's any blame it goes to both of us. But we did it for the best; she had to be protected.'

'Well, I didn't think I could give her any better protection than the man she's with now. He's a decent fella, Ben. Look around you; look where she's been brought up; and yet he's so taken with her he's goin' to marry her. It seems to have been his intention from when he first saw her, by what she tells me. And he's been waitin' until she was sixteen. So, I think that's very honourable.'

'I have me doubts.'

284

'What d'you mean, doubts? What could you doubt in a fella like that? He's been open and straightforward.'

'Aye, apparently. But it's all been too nice and too straightforward. These things don't happen, Aggie. Let's face it, the sleeping beauties are only in fairy tales by the Brothers Grimm.'

'Who? What brothers?'

'Oh, it doesn't matter.'

'No, it doesn't matter, but what matters is, I'm worried, Ben.'

'Well, you're not the only one.'

'And here's me stuck in this bloody kitchen, with me chest burnin' when I should be out lookin'.'

'Where you goin' to look? We'll just have to sit and wait.'

'How long d'you propose to sit and wait?'

'Another hour. And then if she's not back then, well . . . '

'Well what? What d'you intend to do then?'

'Well, I intend to hire a cab and go to this wonderful house he took her to, and likely where she still is and bein' persuaded to stay the night.'

'Oh! you are a bitter pill, Ben. You would think the worst, wouldn't you? I'm surprised at you, even when I know that this is the best thing that has happened to her, or could happen to her.'

'Aye, perhaps you're right; but time will tell . . . Will I heat you some beer?'

'Aye, you could. Put extra ginger into it. Oh God!' She lay back. 'I wish I had me life over again. I would never have got to this stage, eatin', eatin', eatin'. I was big to begin with, but I could have controlled it if I'd had any sense or will power. But no, I had to comfort meself in food.'

'It could have been worse. It could have been the gin, whole hog.'

'Aye, you're right there, it could have been the gin . . . Ben?'

'Aye, Aggie?' He turned from where he was putting the pan of beer on the fire.

'I'm worried. In a number of ways, I'm worried; and it hasn't been made better by the dream I had last night, because I saw her—' She heaved twice now before she finished, 'She was floatin' down the canal.'

The beer splashed over into the fire causing a great hiss. And after Ben had plonked the half-empty pan on to the hob and turned to her, it was as if his voice, too, hissed as he said, 'For God's sake, woman! You would say things like that, wouldn't you?'

'Look; don't take that manner with me. In any case, let me finish: she wasn't dead, she was sort of clingin' to a plank and I tried to reach her. I couldn't, and she went on past me.'

He turned from her and poured what was left of the beer into a mug and handed it to her, saying, 'Now, I'm not waiting. If they're not there I'm getting a cab. It'll take me an hour and a half to two hours, so you can lie there worryin' yourself; but don't go to sleep and have any more of your damned dreams. 'I'll take one of the keys with me and lock it from the outside.'

Ben found no-one at the ostler's stable. The cabs were all out; there wasn't even a trap for hire. All that was left was a small flat cart and a work-worn pony. He was more used to this kind of conveyance anyway. But the pony turned out to be not so old as it looked; it was spritely on the road.

Just before leaving the built-up area of the town, he stopped at a public house, and ordered two pints of ale, one of which he himself drank, the other he took outside and gave to the pony, who made short work of it, and then thanked him by trotting briskly for the rest of the journey. Laddie, too, used to love his ale, and he guessed that all his breed were alike and that they worked better on it.

He found difficulty in locating the house. He had to take the lantern from the cart and investigate the number of each one. Then, there it was, number 7.

The low gates were open and he walked the pony between them and up the drive and on to the gravel. There were lights in the ground-floor rooms of the house, and when he knocked on the front door, it was opened almost immediately by a maid, who stared at the short man holding a lantern head-high and saying, 'Is Miss Forester here?'

'Oh, come in, come in. Please, come in.' Fanny pulled open the door, and immediately Ben realised the effect that this place would have had on Millie, because it really was bonny. Aye, very bonny.

As he was looking about him a door opened and there appeared a woman whose height would make him look tall and whose voice brought his mouth into a slight gape as she said, 'You've brought her back? You've brought Millie back?'

'No . . . no, ma'am. I thought she was here. She hasn't come home. I . . . I've come for her.'

'Oh, dear me, dear me. She's a naughty girl, and so silly. Don't you think so, Fanny? She was so silly. Everything was arranged.'

The maid broke in now, saying, 'It's a great pity. It's a great pity.'

'What is a great pity, miss?'

'Oh. Well, that all arrangements have been . . . ' But her voice was cut off by the little creature chirping in, 'That's why I came, you see. That's why I came. Dear Bernard had it all arranged. There would have been no scandal, no scandal. He explained it all to me and I understood the situation.

287

Yes, I did. And she should have; he made it plain. Oh, yes, he made it plain. How could she imagine otherwise? He couldn't marry her, now could he? He couldn't marry her. But she was to come as my nurse, and it would have been all very discreet.'

Ben's mouth had grown into a much larger gape, and his head had dropped forward, his chin pulled into his neck. He had been right. He had been right. Dear God! And she had thought he meant marriage. And Aggie? Oh, Aggie had been sure of it. And all he wanted was a mistress. He wouldn't take a whore for a mistress. Oh no; it would have to be someone untouched, like his Millie. Where was the fella? If he were here he would throttle him. Oh yes, without the slightest compunction, he would throttle him. The thought struck him that he had used the word compunction. He was learning, wasn't he? Oh, yes, he was learning all right, but more things than English and a better way of speaking. Oh, yes, he was learning; and yet it was something that he had known all along.

The little creature was still chirping: 'Bernard was so distressed. He ran after her, right down the road, and he was without his hat or coat, and even his walking stick, but she was gone. Then he met Mr Tyler's carriage. Mr Tyler lives in the next house, you know, and he said he had passed a hired cab; in fact, he was annoyed that his carriage had had to go practically into the hedge to let the cab pass. And he remembered seeing Millie hurrying along the road. At least, he didn't know it was Millie, now did he? he just knew it was a young lady. But his footman, who was also with his coachman, said he happened to turn round because he thought it was surprising to see a young lady hurrying along the road in the dark. He naturally thought she had stopped and hired the cab.'

288

She had hired a cab. She should have been home by now. Which cab?

'Where is he?' he asked the little woman.

'Bernard?'

'Yes, Bernard.'

'Oh, Geoff packed his night bag and they went off together. Geoff was taking him to the train. Would you like to wait and talk to Geoff?'

He did not reply either yes or no, but with a withering glance he turned from her and, addressing the maid, said, 'When he comes back, tell him I'm goin' to call and see him, will you? And tell him something else. Remember this: tell him to be ready for me.'

'Yes. Yes, I'll do that.' Fanny's face was without a smile for once. And as he went out of the door the bell-like voice from the little woman came at him, saying, 'You are a very rude young man. I couldn't be fond of you.'

And he thought, My God! And that was part of the plan for Millie, to look after that one.

It took him until ten o'clock to visit the various ostlers, the hostelries, and the plain stables along the way, but not one could remember any of their men bringing back a young lass. In fact, as one proprietor said on a laugh, 'When the cabs come back, they're empty, lad. The customers don't live here.'

When Ben arrived back, Aggie was up and pacing the floor, every step bringing a wheeze from her chest, and the first words she said were, 'My God! Where've you been? I thought you were lost an' all.'

'Sit down.'

'I've sat down long enough. Tell me.'

'Sit down, will you? 'Cos I'll have to.'

She dropped back on to the couch, and he sat in his usual place on the settle, and bending forward, he leant his

289

forearms on his knees and said, 'She's gone. Get it into your head straightaway; it's no use beatin' about the bush, she's gone. How she's gone and where she's gone, I don't know, but she's gone.'

'Ben, look; tell me and quietly, tell me what you know.'

'I'll put it briefly, Aggie. She found out that your dear friend Mr Thompson didn't want to marry her; he wanted her for a mistress. He had it all planned out with a barmy little woman there whom Millie was to be nurse to as a cover-up. Apparently, from the beginning he'd had no intention of marryin' her. He bought that house and planned it all, your dear Mr Bernard Thompson.'

Aggie did not say a word, but she heaved herself up on the couch, lifted one leg after the other on to it, then lay back. It seemed a long time before she said, 'And she's gone off with him?'

He sprang up from the couch, saying, 'Bloody hell, no! We'd know where she was if she'd gone off with him. She ran away from him, apparently. An' from what I can gather, she hired a passing cab of some sort.'

A cab . . . of some sort. She turned her head towards him now, saying, 'Well, cabs have to be housed. Have you . . . ?'

'I've been around about here where she might have got off. Nobody's had a cab that brought any young lass back; nor do they remember picking one up. And as I've worked it out, whatever cab came into the town from that district would be nearly sure to come through the market. And she would know where she was then, and would have got out if she could. Aye, if she could.'

Looking at the mountain of flesh heaving on the couch, Ben wanted to cry out, 'Oh, Aggie! Don't cry. For God's sake, don't cry.' He had never seen her cry, not during all the long years he had been with her. Her lips trembled, aye, but never a tear. But wasn't that what he wanted to do himself?

He wanted to lie on the mat there and beat his head on the ground and cry. Oh aye, cry out with love and his loss, the loss that had happened before tonight. For weeks and months now he had been striving to better himself in his mind so that he would come up to her, or even surpass her so that she would be able to learn from him; and if it should never come to anything else, they'd be able to sit and talk . . . or walk and talk. And that was as far as the dream went, because his mind was sensible enough to know that he couldn't finish it, even to himself, and lie in bed and talk.

What were they going to do? What were they going to do without her? Of course, if there had been marriage in the air they would have had to do without her. But marriage and what she might be going through now was a different thing . . . What she might be going through now.

He sprang up from his seat and went over to the couch, and kneeling down by the side of it, he took Aggie's hand in his and said brokenly, 'Come on. Come on.'

She took a none-too-clean piece of rag from the pocket of her apron and rubbed her face with it, and, her voice breaking, she said, 'From somewhere in the Bible, I once heard it read out that the things you fear come upon you. An' God Himself knows that I've feared her bein' picked up all these years. Whoever's hands she's fallen into, God help her this night. But I pray to Him that it's not Slim Boswell's.' She now looked at him pityingly as she said, 'Is there anything more you can do, lad?'

'Well, as I've said, I've raked most of the town where she might have landed if she'd been in a hired cab, so I think it was likely a private carriage that picked her up. A lot of the moneyed blokes have ordinary-looking cabs; they use them for business. But there's still that one quarter I haven't been to yet. Anyway, it's half past ten now and it

291

would be near on eleven when I got there. And what's more, the place would likely be swarming with drunks; and with only those street lasses hanging around who had been told off to clean out the pockets of them lying in the gutters, probably tripped up by their pimps. I can't see us doin' anything till mornin', Aggie, anyway. Then I'll make for the polis station.'

Neither of them said, 'If she doesn't turn up before then,' for they both knew it to be a fruitless hope.

After a moment Aggie said, 'If you could see the sergeant.'

'Aye, if he's anywhere about I'll talk to him. But no matter which one of them I talk to, I know the answer will be the same: What do I think they can do? There's bairns bein' picked up every day. They all know it, but they do little or nowt about it. Look; are you goin' to manage the stairs?'

'No, lad, no, I couldn't. I feel I must stay down here tonight. You go on up to your bed; you'll need it.'

'No. I feel the same as you, so I'll bring a chair in from next door, and I'll keep the fire goin'.'

She put out her hand and gripped his, saying, 'What I did, Ben, I did for the best, in lettin' her go with him. Before me and God I never thought . . . '

'It'll be all right. It'll be all right. Somehow, it sort of had to happen; she was fated right from the first. That's why we tried to protect her. She was like her mother.' He stopped here, for the thought had entered his head that, rather than go through with it, she might take the same way out as her mother had.

On this he swung about and hurried into the other room, and lifted up an old armchair as if it were only a featherweight and returned with it to the kitchen. Then, with the raker, he drew some pieces of coal from the back of the grate and on to the fire. He then dusted his hands,

292

sat back in the chair, put his feet on the fender, and closed his eyes, telling himself that if he pretended sleep she would soon go off, too. In any case, it was going to be a long night, and one in which he knew his imagination would run riot.

9

It was still dark when he went into the police station. The constable on duty blinked at him, yawned, and said, 'Aye, well, what's your trouble?'

'I . . . I want to report a missing person.'

'Oh. Well, give me details.' He pulled a book towards him, wet the end of a pencil in his mouth, then said, 'Go ahead.'

'She is sixteen years old; she is Mrs Winkowski's ward.' The constable looked up now, and the tiredness seeming to go from his face for a moment, he said, 'Oh, her? When was this?'

'Last night. She had been to a friend's house. She was walkin' back. Somebody saw her gettin' into what they thought was a paid cab. That was the last that was heard of her. I was waitin' for her – she was to be back at five o'clock. I went round all the ostlers; but nobody's seen hilt nor hair of her.'

'That's the fair lass, isn't it?'

'Yes. Yes, she is, she is very fair.'

'Oh. And you say she stays with Mrs Winkowski, better known as . . . ?'

'Aye, I know what she's better known as, but her name is Mrs Winkowski.'

The tone brought the constable's chin up. 'Very well then,' he conceded, 'she's the daughter of . . .'

'No. The ward.'

'The ward. All right; she is the ward of Mrs Winkowski.' He took a long time to write the name, his lips spelling out what he thought the letters might be; then he said, 'She could have gone to friends or anything; I mean, that's after she left the house where she had been visitin'? What was the name of the house, sir? And where was it situated?'

Ben looked at the hand holding the pencil; then he looked up into the man's face. It was expressing enquiry. 'It was a house on the outskirts of the town: Elm Road, number seven,' he said.

So the constable repeated, 'On the outskirts, Elm Road, number seven. And it was from there she was leaving when she was last seen. Is that what you mean, sir?'

'That's what I mean.' They exchanged a hard look.

Ben now asked, 'When will Sergeant Fenwick be in?'

'About nine o'clock, I would say.'

'Well, would you mind telling him about this case and that I'll be back to see him?'

'I will do that. Certainly, I will do that. As soon as he comes through that door I will inform him.'

'There's nothin' funny about this.'

The constable's manner quickly changed, and he said, 'I'm aware there's nothin' funny about this. And I would warn you to keep a civil tongue in your head. I don't like your attitude.'

'Nor me yours. And when I see the sergeant I will relate to him the substance of our conversation, and ask him if it is usual for his officers to use a mocking manner to members of the public reporting serious cases.' For a moment, Ben had taken on the manner and voice of Mr Sponge; in fact, he had imagined himself to be Mr Sponge.

Following this, he inclined his head towards the astonished man, then abruptly left.

He began to walk the streets: first in the vicinity of Reilly's Meat House; but everyone could have been dead, for there was no movement, not even of a cleaner. He then went as far as Bale Street, and as he passed Slim Boswell's place he could not help but question whether she would be there. But no; he couldn't see Slim Boswell riding in a carriage or even a cab in that area where Mr Bernard Thompson resided.

At the end of the street he turned into the short lane which led into a back lane. This, too, was broad, unusually so, and showed that there were gates to most of the houses on both sides of the lane. And the place was clean, with no excrement or litter lying about.

Seeing the hatches in the walls, he realised these were the newer innovation of dry closets. They would be half-filled with ash, and the scavengers would come and clean them out once a week. What a pity, he thought, they didn't put them in The Courts. But, of course, it would require twenty or so in one of the square yards.

He emerged from the alleyway, feeling desperate. There seemed to be no way he could plan ahead, but just go on aimlessly searching.

At twelve o'clock he returned home. Aggie was up. Her chest, she said, was a little easier. She had put on a pan of broth and heated some pies left over from the previous day. When she set it before him, he said, 'I'm sorry, Aggie, it would choke me, I can't get a bite down. I'll have a drink of beer.'

'What have you done?' she asked him.

'I've travelled the town,' he said; 'but there's hardly anybody out this mornin'. Bein' Sunday, I suppose. I've been up and down the workin' street, but it's too early for the lasses

296

to come out. In fact, there's not many make an appearance till dark on a Sunday . . . any Sunday. Odd that.'

'Well, what d'you intend to do now?'

'I think I'll hire the cart again and drive out an' see if that fella's man has come back, and hear what he's got to say.'

'Don't do anything that's goin' to cause more trouble. If he can only help to get her back I'll forgive him everything. Ben' – her voice was low – 'I've had some rough times in me life. You could say that all me life has been rough. There were times, when I was a young lass, that I ached physically almost daily from what work I had to do, but the hardest was to accept the inside bit and what I looked like. But all the years of pain combined couldn't come up to what I've gone through since six o'clock yesterday. And you an' all. Oh yes, you an' all. Our lives will never be the same again, lad. D'you know that?'

He took his coat from where it was lying over the back of the settle, put it on, and picking up his cap from the seat, he pulled it tight on his head, before saying, 'I'm off. Look after yourself. I'll lock the gate.'

After the door closed on him she looked at the table. She couldn't be bothered clearing it, so she returned to the couch and lay down.

Closing her eyes and joining her hands together, she began to mutter prayers.

It would have been about two o'clock when she heard the gate bell ring, and she turned her head towards the door, saying aloud, 'Get on with it! Get on with it!' But when the ringing went on continually for almost ten minutes, she pulled herself up, saying, 'Oh! my God, they never let up.' They could keep ringing; she wasn't fit to go out there. If she crossed that yard the cold would kill her.

How long after it was when she was almost startled out of her wits by somebody knocking on the kitchen window,

297

she didn't know. The back of the couch faced the window and she pulled herself up and peered towards it. There was someone out there beckoning to her, a woman.

She lumbered to her feet, walked round the couch and, stopping, she looked at the face that was close to the pane and the hand that was beckoning to her. It was Annie Blackett. What did she want? How had she got in?

She shambled down the room and into the scullery and to the side door that led into what had once been the garden. And when Annie came running towards her, she called to her, 'What's the matter? How did you get in?'

'I . . . Oh, Agg . . . I mean, Mrs Winkowski, I've been ringin' the bell but couldn't make you hear, an' so I came round the back here. I had to climb over the wall.'

'You climbed over the wall? Come in. What is it? What's the matter?'

'Ben mustn't be in else he would have opened the gate, wouldn't he? Well, I've . . . I've got news, I . . . I mean . . . er . . . can I sit down?'

'Aye, yes, of course.' Aggie led the way back into the kitchen, and there she pointed to the settle, inviting Annie Blackett to sit down.

Nervously, Annie did so, but at the end of the seat, for she felt she had really bearded the lion in its den; it was the first time she had stepped foot in this house and she didn't know what to make of it. It was a muddle and it wasn't clean. But she must tell her what she had come about. She said, 'It's . . . it's about Millie.'

'What about her? You know something?'

'Well, it's like this, Mrs Winkowski. You know my cousin . . . I mean, I've got a cousin. She's Nellie Pratt, an' I'm not proud of her, but she's not a bad sort. Sometimes she looks in on me when she can. It isn't very often 'cos . . . 'cos they are kept down to that quarter, you know. Well . . . well, she came in like a devil in a gale of wind not half an hour gone, and she wasn't there two minutes; I tell you, she wasn't there two minutes, an' she was gabblin'. An' what she said was, tell Ben that Millie is in the middle house in Bale Street, upstairs in the end room. But he can't get in that way; he would have to come in through number one. She said, being Sunday, there won't be many kickin' about, but Slim will be there in number one. That's where he lives. Number two's the middle house and it's been proofed against noise. An' she went on and on and I didn't get half of it. She said she'd be there till half-past six; then she would have to leave. But if Ben came in the end one' – she now put her hand to her head – 'I don't know whether she meant the first one or the third one; I don't know, but she said, the end one, and got over the wall, she'd try to leave the kitchen door open. But what she seemed so firm about was not to go to the polis, 'cos they've got ways and means of scarperin'. There's a hidden cellar there. Take him unawares, she said, if he's there. That's the only way. She was in a state, 'cos they'd murder her if they found out. She said to tell Ben the quicker the better, 'cos there was a client comin'. That's what she said. Where is he? I mean, Ben?' She now got to her feet and walked across to Aggie who was supporting herself by leaning against the table, and she asked, tentatively, 'Are you all right?'

Aggie turned and looked at this woman whose name had irritated her for years, but it was many a long year, too, since she had seen her. She had considered her plain with nothing about her, but the face she was now looking into was quite homely, and she was clean and tidy, and she said, 'Yes, lass, I'm all right, but I'll be more all right when he gets back. He's gone lookin' for her, taken a cart and horse out into the country, where she was yesterday when she was picked up. But the minute he comes in I'll tell him. Oh aye, I'll tell him. If only I had the use of me limbs, like once upon a time,

I'd be down there meself. And Annie' – she said the name gently – 'thank you, lass. And if you see your cousin you can carry me thanks to her an' all. I don't know what may have happened to my lass, but whichever way it goes I'll always thank you for your help. And be she what she may, that goes for your cousin an' all. An' you can't go climbin' back over that wall. My goodness! I don't know how you made it.'

'There's a couple of stones juttin' out at yon side, but there's no help this side.' She smiled weakly, and Aggie said, 'There's a little back gate to the side there, but you'll have to go round by the barn. I'll get you the key. It'll be a bit rusty 'cos it's never been opened for years.'

She rummaged in the scullery cupboard now and brought out a large iron key; then, dipping the end in a bowl of fat that was standing on the wooden bench, she handed it to Annie, saying, 'That'll help.'

At the door, Annie said, 'I hope he gets back soon, 'cos the way Nell was talkin'—' She looked down to where her long coat was resting on the top of her boots, and she moved one foot after the other as if scraping them on a piece of flagstone that formed the step. Then she asked, 'What'll I do with the key?' and Aggie replied, 'Just throw it over the wall.'

After closing the door, Aggie turned to the kitchen; but she did not sit down, she walked the length of the room from the door to the couch and back again. And she did so over and over again until, almost collapsing, she dropped down on the couch and, her hands clasped, she actually prayed aloud, saying, 'Oh, God, bring him back soon.'

It was six o'clock the same evening. Slim Boswell's guest had just arrived by the same means that had brought Millie to the house the night before. And now Boswell was leading him through the first house and into the hall of the second, which was brilliantly lit.

300

Smiling, Boswell said, 'We sent to your club last night, but you weren't there, but, knowing of your keen interest, I took the liberty of sending my man to you with a message; also of arranging for you to be picked up by my conveyance, because it wouldn't have done for you to come from your home in your own conveyance, now would it, sir?'

'No, not at all. Not at all. And thank you, thank you very much. You will be compensated for your trouble, I can assure you . . . Is she all right?'

'Well, she is a little nervous, naturally.'

'And you say she has been here since yesterday?'

'Yes.'

'What a pity! What a lot of wasted time.' He smiled.

'Indeed, sir, indeed. I don't know whether you're aware that she had been visiting a Bernard Thompson, whom you know, I believe. Oh, yes, he's had a keen interest in her. I learned this from . . . well, her father.'

'I understood she had no parents.'

'Her father turned up, sir. He had been doing a long stretch. He told me this young gentleman was in the habit of taking her to his house.'

'I can't believe it.'

'Oh, you can, sir, you can.'

'And she has a father?'

'Oh, you needn't worry about him, sir. He's been dealt with. Oh, yes, yes; he's been dealt with. A wily piece, if ever there was one.'

There was an almost ecstatic look on the man's face as he said to Boswell, 'I never imagined this would come about – you know how interested I was some years ago.'

'Yes, sir; yes, I do. But then I had to wonder if your interest still held, because she is no longer a little girl; in fact, you'll be surprised, but she's very attractive. Oh, yes, very pleasing. But I took the chance of sending for you, sir, because, you

301

see, unless arrangements are made she won't be able to stay here permanently. If you aren't interested it would benefit me to send her on to . . . '

'Oh, don't you worry, Boswell. Don't you worry. I'm interested, and for her future, too, if she'll be amenable.'

'You may find her a little quiet and perhaps unresponsive, because this morning we had to give her a slight dose, although Nell tells me it's mostly worn off. You know the way, sir. I leave the rest to you.'

10

The terror in Millie that had frozen her into silence for a time disappeared with the morning, and frantically she examined the room, only to find it was windowless. The curtains were covering not a window but a bricked-up window space. She'd heard tell of this kind of thing having happened a long time ago to avoid a window tax. Nor could she find an implement that she could use. There were no vases or candlesticks on the narrow mantelpiece. The only article on the wash-hand stand was a large china bowl with a jug standing in it, and to the side, a small dish holding soap. The bedstead was brass, although it was draped in the same material as the bedspread. At each end of the bed and looped over a knob was a piece of rope about half an inch thick and all of three feet long, the ends frayed like a tassel. There was a chamber pot under the bed, and against the wall was what looked like a mahogany seat with a loose lid, which she lifted and saw contained a china pail. There was nothing in the wardrobe except two other shifts similar to the one she was wearing.

She had been too terrified to sleep, although she must eventually have cried herself to sleep, because she woke up to hear a key turning in the door and see the woman who had spoken kindly to her last night enter. She was carrying a tray on which was a cup of tea and a plate holding a slice of bacon and a fried egg, and, beside it, a small plate of bread and butter. The woman smiled at her and said, 'Did you sleep, dearie?'

She couldn't answer her, but she pulled herself upwards when the tray was placed on her knees, and the woman said, 'Eat that up; you'll need it. Then I'd have a wash, and use the slop pail.'

It was now that Millie pleaded, 'Can't . . . can't you do anything for me, please? Please get me out of here. I'll go mad, I will. Do you know that my mother committed suicide because of that man? And I'll do the same before anybody touches me . . . I'll do the same.'

'You'd better not say that, lass, or he'll have you tied up. Now that's a good warnin'. Anyway, you'd have a job to commit suicide in here.'

With an impatient movement Millie pushed the tray away from her, saying, 'I don't want that. I'm not going to eat.'

'Well, that's up to you. You'll eat it before it eats you, and you might find you'll be glad to in the end. Now, what I'm sayin' to you is for your own good. It's got to happen, an' the sooner you get it over with the better.'

'What . . . what are they going to do to me?'

'Oh' – the woman smiled now – 'it won't be they; it will be just one fella. And I happen to know who it is, and it'll be all right. As I told you last night, nothing at all might happen, not at first, but you've got to co-operate, like.'

As she was speaking, the door opened again and Boswell entered, and on the sight of him Millie pulled herself back against the pillows.

And she watched his approach until he was standing close to her at the side of the bed and pointing to the breakfast she had pushed aside and saying, 'Aren't you going to eat?'

'No, I'm not; and you'll get into trouble when they find out. You'll get into a *great deal* of trouble.'

'Well, I'm used to trouble. I can always handle it, especially when I get trouble from little girls like you.' He now bent forward, picked up the tray and pushed it on to her knee, and instinctively she picked up the plate and levelled it into his face. There was a scream, but it was from the woman, and then she was standing between the bed and the man, saying, 'Don't . . . don't mark her. You'll . . . you'll be sorry. He'll be comin' today. Don't mark her. Don't mark her. Look, give her a dose to quieten her down. Bring it up and I'll get her to take it.'

'Take it!' He ground out the words between his teeth. 'I'll take the skin off her. If we don't get him today I'll take the skin off her, and then she'll be for the boat, and before long she'll wish to God she was dead.'

Trembling so much now that she had to grip a handful of the bedclothes, Millie watched the man walk to the end of the bed and grip the rope that was hanging from the post, then swing it backwards and forwards for a moment. Then he left the room.

'That was a bloody silly thing to do, girl. It was the worst thing you could do. I'm tellin' you—' The woman bent forward, her face close to Millie's now, and said, 'He's a devil when he's roused. There's nobody worse. You should never have done that. My God! it was the worst thing you could have done. Look, when the client comes, now I'm givin' you good advice here, and listen. When your client comes . . . '

'I have no client. I have no client. I don't care; I won't be handled.'

'*Shut up, girl!* Shut up! Listen to me! For God's sake and your own, be nice, and co-operate. That'll mean he'll come back and back again and Slim won't be able to touch you. At least he'll be well paid to keep his hands off you. Now that's

305

all I can say to you. That's all the help I can give you.'

She now bent down and picked the plate and the bacon from the floor; but when she came to the egg and its broken yolk, she muttered, 'I'll have to go and get a flannel for that.'

She locked the door behind her.

When she returned with a pan and brush and a wet cloth, she was also carrying a small mug, which she laid on the dressing table. After cleaning the floor, she picked up the mug, went to the bed, and said, 'Here, drink this.'

'No. No, I won't!'

'Look, lass; I don't want to force you. Drink it.'

'It's got something in it?'

'Yes, it's got something in it, but it won't make you sleepy, it'll just make you feel better.'

When her hand came out to knock the cup away, the woman yelled at her, 'Don't do that! I don't want another spill. And I tell you I won't be able to stop him goin' for you again if you do that.'

Something in her voice checked Millie's hand, and she again gripped the bedclothes. But with a quick, practised movement, the woman nipped her nose, jerked her head back, and so forced her to swallow the contents of the mug, and Millie coughed and spluttered and sent a small spray flying on to the counterplane.

The woman now gathered up the pan, brush, flannel and mug and left the room; and again the key was turned in the lock.

Millie lay back on her pillows, and for the next few hours she knew a feeling of contentment, which was strange and not unpleasant. And when the woman brought her a meal at dinner time, although the feeling was wearing off, she ate it, and the woman said, 'That's more like it. Now you'll feel better. I'd have a doze if I were you.' And she did. She didn't know how long she dozed and because of the bricked-up window she didn't know what time of day it was, or even if it was day; what illumination there was came from two lamps.

But as the hours wore on, the feeling of calmness disappeared, and she was once again herself and stiff with fear. At about this time the woman appeared with a scuttleful of coal, and as she was leaving, she said, 'It shouldn't be too long. And you mightn't have me the morrow, so I'd advise you to behave yourself. D'you understand me?'

Millie didn't answer, but after the door had been closed and locked she began pacing up and down the room.

She was still pacing when she heard the key being turned in the lock, and she stood rigid, her hands clenched by her sides. When the door opened slowly and she saw the man whom all the Quintons had called 'master', her jaw dropped, her eyes widened and a strange creeping feeling spread over her scalp as if the hairs were rising from it. She could feel his arms about her in the dance, and him lifting her from the ground, and she could hear Jane say her dress had come up so far that she was exposing her white stockings. And then, after she had lain for those three days on the Quintons' couch downstairs, he had come and stroked her hair, and she had wished he wouldn't. Raymond Crane-Boulder . . . !

'Oh, Millie.'

At the sound of her name coming from his lips in that strange way, she screamed. It was a high scream, and she turned and ran to the other side of the bed. But he remained where he was and his voice was soft and soothing as he said, 'I'm not going to harm you, dear. I would never, never harm you. Do you know, from the first moment I saw you I loved you? Oh, yes, yes, I loved you; and you were just a child then, but how you have grown. You are more beautiful now. But come, let us sit down and talk, eh? Trust me, dear. Trust me.

307

I wouldn't harm you for the world. We could have wonderful times together.'

He was now sidling along by the bottom of the bed; and with a spring she jumped on to it and off the other side and, in a rush, she made for the door. But he was there before her. And now he was holding her by the trembling shoulders, saying, 'That would be no good. He is downstairs. There is only one way out, dear. I must be brutal by telling you that. But . . . but I could take you out, I could take you away. Oh, yes, let us talk. Come, let us talk.' He was drawing her towards the bed, and with a swift movement, he thrust an arm under her knees and lifted her up and laid her on it. Then he sat on the edge of it, holding her hands in his, patting them together as he would a child's, saying, 'Millie. Millie. You're not afraid of me, are you? You mustn't be, because we're going to spend quite a lot of time together. You wouldn't want to stay in this room for ever, would you? Or, as he could do, be sent away by Slim? He's not a nice man, you know, Millie, not at all. But I'll see to you if you'll only love me a little. That's all I want, just for you to love me a little.'

A faintness was coming over her: she couldn't protest, she couldn't scream; she felt she was going to pass out. She mustn't. She mustn't pass out. Mrs Aggie. Mrs Aggie. Ben. Oh, Ben, Ben, Ben. Ben.

Ben had arrived home at five o'clock to Aggie's greeting of, 'Where've you been, man? For God's sake! where've you been? I know where she is. I know where she is. Look, Annie said you hadn't to get the polis, but I think you'd better go to the station; you can't do it on your own.'

He had to take her by the shoulders and push her back on to the couch and yell at her: 'Steady! Steady! Now give it to me word for word.' And so, doing her best, she repeated Annie's words.

Before she had finished he had left her, at least he had got as far as the outer room when he sprang back again and said, 'That old knife, like a cutlass, the one you used to have in the case, where is it?'

'No, no; don't take that. There'll be murder.'

'Yes, and it could be me. Yes, it could be murder. Where is it?'

'It's in that drawer, there.' She pointed to the sideboard. 'At the back of it.'

He pulled open the drawer so quickly the whole lot spilled on to the floor with a crash, but it revealed a brown leather case with a curved end and an ornamental handle sticking out of the top. And when he pulled on the handle it revealed a dagger. He ran his finger along the curved blade. It was as sharp as on the day, many years ago, when Aggie had picked it out from a load of rubbish that was being thrown out of a house. He had wanted it then but she wouldn't give it to him. But now it was in his hand, and he thrust it in his broad leather belt, leaving the shaft supported by the strap of his braces.

'Take care and don't use that unless you have to. It's like a razor.'

He did not seem to hear her, for he had started to run, and he ran until he came to Bale Street; and there he slowed up, panting, when he saw the lights of a cab approaching the end house. When it turned into the lane, he hurried silently up by the black wall and was in time to see a figure getting out of the cab, and another at the house doorway. Then he could see by the carriage lights the horse being manoeuvred in order to get it out and into the lane again, and he guessed it must be a sizeable yard for the cabbie to be able to do that; likely the three back yards had been knocked into one.

He pressed himself against the wall as the cab came into the lane, and remained so until it disappeared from his view.

He had the urge now to rush up the yard and into the house, but he warned himself to take it easy; he didn't know how many he'd have to contend with. On the way, he had paid a flying visit to Annie, and she had said that Nell had indicated it was quiet there on a Sunday night, but that Boswell was likely to be about. Well, he hoped he met up with Boswell. By God! he did.

He waited a few minutes; but then the thought struck him that the back door might have been locked or, worse still, somebody might come out and close those gates. He now shot across the lane in the direction of the yard. The only guide he now had in the gathered darkness was a glimmer of light coming from a window. He guessed that the door would be near there. Hugging the wall, he soon came to a doorway; but it was far from the window, and when he tried the handle it did not move. He continued towards the window and when he neared it he could just make out where the wall ended and another door began. His heart was thumping against his ribs and he was holding his breath as he gripped the handle and slowly and quietly turned it. And his breath seemed to become still when the door gave way to his touch.

He was in a dark passageway now, but there, at the end of it, was a light showing beneath another door.

He moved silently along the passage to the door, and listened. He could hear no sound. He gripped the handle and turned it quietly, but then pushed the door swiftly open; and there, smothering a gasp, was Nell.

She had been doing something at a table; she did not, however, cry out, but turned her head quickly away and, thrusting out her arm, pointed towards a door as though she were speaking to someone just across the table, and she muttered, 'Careful in the hallway.'

Within seconds he had opened this door and was in another passage; but this was illuminated by a light coming from a half-open door at the far end. And what he saw through it was a movement as if someone were crossing the room.

As he thrust the door fully open, so the figure swung round; and now they were staring at each other, with neither uttering a word.

Ben was prepared for an attack – his heavy upper body was bent forward – but he wasn't quite prepared for the leap that Boswell gave, for it was like that of a wild animal, and it gave him no time to withdraw the knife from the sheath under his belt.

He was wrestling with a man who seemed to have as many arms as an octopus and who was groping for his throat. He, too, was groping for a throat, and as his fingers clawed the thin neck, Boswell's foot came out and kicked at his shins; then his knee found Ben's groin. It was then, as automatically his hand should have gone to his pain-racked lower stomach that it went to his trouser belt. The next minute the knife was free from its sheath and he was striving to bring it home into Boswell's narrow chest.

Amid groans and gasps, the struggling brought them on to the floor and, unfortunately for Boswell, he was the first to hit it, and when Ben's heavy weight struck him it forced him to relax his hold. And it was in that instant that Ben brought the knife down into the man's neck, and the gush of blood from his action almost blinded him, and he rolled off the contorted figure.

He lay gasping, but only for a second, before he managed to get to his knees, then drag himself up and stumble towards the far door, then into darkness again, except for a gleam at the end of what seemed to be a passage.

This led into another hall; and there were the stairs. As if galvanised by new life, he was up them and across the landing, making directly towards the fourth door. Thrusting it open, he saw a tall man leaning over the bed, his hands on the stiff, still, white figure. And he let out a guttural cry as he sprang towards him with almost the same agility as had the man downstairs, minutes earlier. But whereas Boswell had been silent and not much taller than himself, this man, though slight, was head and shoulders above him. The knife was still in his hand, but he was unable to use it, for the man was aiming to batter his face. However, his own stature and a natural instinct to duck, enabled him to avoid the blows, and automatically he bent his body forward and, as if it were a battering ram, he thrust his head into Crane-Boulder's stomach, causing him to fall back gasping against the end of the bed; and to save himself from falling, he clutched at the end rail, and as he did so, his hand came into contact with the rope looped around it. In a split second, it was off the knob and he was whirling it.

When the tasselled end splayed across Ben's face, it blinded him for a moment; and then he gave a great gasp as the rope came round his neck. Having to use his two hands in a struggle to release himself from its grip, he was borne to the floor.

Kneeling on Ben, and his face like the devil's, his mouth wide, his teeth clenched, his eyes seeming to stare from his head, Crane-Boulder pulled the crossed rope tight . . .

On the first sight of Ben, the paralysing faintness brought on by fear left Millie and she had crawled from the bed and stood transfixed, watching the struggle. But now it seemed that all the fight had gone out of Ben and that he was on the point of dying. Looking wildly about her for some implement she might use, she could see nothing, apart from the hand-basin on the wash-hand stand. It was a large basin. It held no water, and the jug wasn't in it. As she grabbed it up, she was instantly aware that Crane-Boulder had taken off the rope and had picked up the knife that had dropped from Ben's hand, and she screamed as she saw him raise it above Ben's head. It was as he brought the knife down, his aim just missing Ben's own neck but striking his shoulder, that she crashed the basin on to his head.

It stunned him, but at the same time her action would have toppled her had she not fallen against his back. When he made an effort to straighten up and shake her off, she pulled herself away and, lifting the basin again and using all her strength, she brought it down once more on his head. This time the action not only split the basin in two but also brought the blood flowing through his hair.

The pieces had dropped from her hands, and now she was staggering back, watching him toppling to the side. He seemed to go slowly, or perhaps she was imagining it; but she wasn't imagining that Ben had now raised his head and was gasping for breath.

She rushed to his side, crying, 'Oh, Ben, Ben.'

'Mill . . . Millie.'

He turned his head to look at his left arm where his coat and shirt were ripped from the shoulder to the elbow, and at the blood still running freely and flowing over his wrist on to his hands.

She helped him to his feet, but he stood swaying for a moment before he could gasp: 'The knife.'

She picked it up from where it lay near the prostrate form.

For a matter of seconds Ben stood staring at the man: then, clutching at her arm, he muttered, 'Come on.'

On the landing, she had to steady him before they made their way to the stair-head.

When they reached the bottom, she murmured fearfully, 'There'll be others about, Ben. There'll be others about.'

'No . . . there won't. There won't. Come on. Come on.'

He pushed open the door into the first hall, to see Nell standing some way from the grotesque and blood-covered body of the man who had been her master for years, and as Ben staggered towards her, holding Millie with one arm, she said, 'My God! Ben, you did it thoroughly. Eeh! my God!'

Then she added sharply, 'Come on! Get out of this before they murder you.'

'What . . . what about you?'

'I can take care of meself. I'll have a tale ready.' And she did sound in control of herself.

They were passing through the kitchen when she looked at the scantily clad young girl, and she said, 'You can't go out like that. Wait a minute.'

She pulled what looked like an antimacassar from the back of the big chair set in the corner of the room, and she was putting it round Millie's shoulders when her head went up and she said, 'Oh God above!' Then without another word, she gripped them both and pushed them towards a door while hissing at them. 'Don't make a move. Stay still! Still! I'm telling you.'

Millie knew they were in some kind of a cupboard as her foot came in contact with what she recognized as a broom. She had her arms around Ben and he had his uninjured arm around her shoulders holding her tight against him as they now listened to Nell's voice, saying, 'Oh! am I glad to see you, Rosie. There's been hell to pay here. They've got her.'

'The lass?'

'Aye. Four or five of them. I think it was five. I'm not sure. They scared me to death. An' . . . an' they've done Slim in.'

'Wh . . . at!'

'Yes; dead as a door-nail. Now don't start an' say you're sorry; don't be a hypocrite. But I don't know what's happened to the one upstairs; likely he's gone an' all. They were a terrible lot.'

'Eeh! What does it mean, Nell? The polis?'

314

'Don't be a bloody fool, Rosie. Get the polis in here an' you know what would happen; they'd close us up. An' where will you go? 'cos your legs won't take you back on the street again.'

'Was it Big Joe's lot?'

'I . . . I don't know. But listen, listen carefully. Get yourself back to Reilly's. They'll all be in the back, but don't make any fuss, 'cos the quieter this is kept the better for you, an' me. Yes, an' all of us. Get Ted's eye, get him alone; an' remember, it'll be him in charge from now on. Tell him to bring Mike and Sonny. Tell him . . . well, just say that Nell said there's trouble, an' for them to come on their own; there's things to be done. He'll understand. Now get yourself away. An' stop shakin'. Everything'll be all right. There's only one thing: he can't be found here; it'll have to be like an outside job. As for the other one up there, I don't know. It'll likely be the same with him. Now go on. Go on.'

It was a full minute later when the door opened and she pulled them into the kitchen, saying now, 'For God's sake! get yourselves away from here. Take the long way round. Oh, lass, you need something on your feet. Here!' She rushed to the end of the room, picked up a pair of old slippers and helped Millie to put them on, saying, 'They're a bit big but better than nothin'. Now go on. For God's sake! go on. If you were found they'd do for me straight off, 'cos nobody gets in here except through me.'

She took them to the back door and thrust them into the yard, saying, 'Keep to the side ways, else that blood'll give you away or bring a polis on you, that's if the sight of her doesn't.'

After the brightness of the kitchen, and in spite of the indifferent light from the window, outside in the yard seemed very dark, and Ben muttered, 'Hang on to my coat,' and thrust his arm out towards the wall and guided them to

315

the gateway and so into the lane. When they reached the road the light from the few lamps made it appear almost like twilight. And now he began to stumble more quickly forward, while she shuffled beside him, trying to keep the slippers on her feet.

It was fortunate it was a Sunday and that there were few people in the streets; even the side road and alleys were clear, apart from urchins gathered in doorways; and these presented no danger to them, for at that moment they must have looked like two individuals no better off than themselves.

When he fell against her she had to gather all her strength to support him, and she muttered, 'Oh, Ben, Ben, don't fall,' and she half dragged him towards a wall, and he leant against it, his head drooping as he endeavoured to recover himself; and when she begged, 'Try, Ben. Try; it isn't far now,' he muttered something and dragged himself away from the wall, and they went stumbling on.

It was Millie who had to push open the gates, and as they made their way across the yard towards the light of the open door, Aggie came stumbling towards them, crying, 'Thanks be to God! Thanks be to God! Oh, lad, what's happened to you? What's happened?'

'Let's in. Let's in, Aggie.'

It was only by the light of the kitchen lamp that the sight and plight of them both became evident. Her mouth wide and her head shaking, Aggie muttered, 'God in heaven! God in heaven!' because by now Millie had stepped out of the slippers and dropped her covering on to the floor, so exposing the slight figure in the flimsy shift. And when she threw herself into Aggie's embrace, the old woman hugged her and rocked her, crying, 'Aw! child. Aw! child. Aw! me poor child. God strike them down dead, every one of them.' And Millie, her face streaming with tears, whimpered

316

through them, 'If it hadn't been for Ben, Mrs Aggie. If it hadn't been for Ben . . . '

Ben had dropped on to the settle and Aggie, standing over him, looked in horror at the ripped sleeve and the blood still oozing, and she exclaimed, 'Oh, dear God! Let's have your coat off, lad, and see the damage.'

Being relieved of his coat brought no sound from Ben, but when Aggie went to take his shirt off, the frayed ends of which were sticking here and there to the torn flesh, he groaned aloud. And when the extent of the damage was exposed, he turned his head to look at it.

Millie and Aggie were looking at the arm with amazement that was tinged with fear, both aghast, and it was Millie who said, 'He should have the doctor. It'll have to be sewn.' What Aggie muttered, was, 'Another inch higher, lad, and it would have started at your gullet, an' that would have been that. My God! Look at the length of it.'

'Well, it was me own knife. It had worked well on Boswell.'

'Did Boswell do that?'

'No, no; the knife had put the finishing touches to him before I went upstairs and met the gentleman . . . Oh, what did you do with the knife, Millie?'

'I stuck it in your pocket. Look, it's still there.' She pointed.

'The gentleman, you said? Who?'

Ben glanced wearily at Millie and she, bowing her head, said, 'Mr Crane.'

'*You mean Boulder-Crane?* Where you went to the party?'

Millie made no reply; but her head drooped further and Aggie exclaimed, '*Oh, my God! lass.* My God! And when did this happen? When did he get at you?'

'Mrs Aggie, *please.*' Millie was covering her face with her hands as she rocked herself from side to side. 'I'll . . . I'll tell

317

you all about it later, but . . . ' She became still and, aiming to be calm, she exclaimed, 'We must see to Ben's arm, it needs bandaging. Will . . . will I get a sheet?'

'Aye, lass, aye. Can you make the stairs? Are you all right? An' put something on.'

As Millie ran from the room, Aggie thrust the kettle into the heart of the fire, saying, 'That'll have to be cleaned out before any bandage goes on it. Aw, lad, it seems a miracle that you're alive an' that she's back here again.'

'You never said a truer word, Aggie.' His voice was weary. 'Never a truer word . . . Give me a drop of something, will you?'

'Oh, yes, lad, yes. I don't know where I am. I've been out of me mind.'

She went to the corner shelf on which the gin bottle was kept and poured a generous measure into a glass. And when he threw it off without even a shudder, she said, 'I'll get some whisky in, lad. I'll get some whisky in for you. An' look; you can't sit like that. Come over to the couch and lie down.'

He didn't need a second bidding and stumbled towards the couch, but as he was about to lie down Aggie said, 'Put your head towards the foot, lad; it'll be better to get at your arm. I'll pack you up with pillows at that end.'

He lay down as Aggie had bidden, his arm over the edge of the couch; but the blood began to drip from his fingers on to the floor, and Aggie pulled a towel from the rail and wrapped it roughly round his hand.

When Millie came back into the room she was wearing a dress, a short woollen jacket, and a pair of her own slippers on her bare feet. While she tore up the sheet, Aggie gently washed the gash that started at Ben's shoulder and went down to the front of his elbow. But the bathing with hot water, which made him grind his teeth, brought the blood flowing more quickly from different parts of the gash; and

318

when Millie said, 'I think we'd better tie it up tight,' Aggie agreed: 'Aye, lass, aye, we'd better,' she said.

It was as they were finishing the bandaging that there came a knock on the outer door. They all looked at each other for a moment, and when the fear leapt back into Millie's face Ben said heavily, 'I know who that'll be. It'll be Annie.'

A minute later, Aggie opened the door, to see Annie standing in the light of a lamp held by a man; and Annie said to her: 'I just wondered, Mrs Winkowski, if . . . if he had got back. Mr Burton, here, was kind enough to bring me round.'

'Come in. Come in both of you.'

As she closed the door on them, Aggie said, 'Aye, he's here, what's left of him. Go in and see for yourself.'

When Annie stood by the couch looking down at this man who was her friend but whom she held in her heart as something more, she said simply, 'It was bad, then, Ben?'

'Aye, it was pretty bad, Annie. But thanks to you and Nell, she's here.' He lifted his eyes towards where Millie was standing near the table and ended, 'She's back.'

Annie looked at the thin, but beautiful, white-faced girl who, since she was a child, had captivated the heart of her friend, the girl who had changed him from a lover into a friend, and she looked back at Ben and said under her breath, 'I hope you were in time.'

'I hope so, too, Annie. Aye, I hope so, too.'

'Is your arm very bad?'

'He did a good job on it.'

Annie now turned to Aggie, saying, 'Mr Burton, here, looks after accidents in the factory, things that don't need the doctor. Perhaps he could help. You would, wouldn't you, Alfred?'

Alfred nodded, saying, 'Aye, only too pleased to.'

319

'Well, we've bandaged it up now,' said Aggie; 'thanks all the same; but by the look of it I think it'll have to be stitched.'

'Well, if it's a bad gash, missis, it should be done as soon as possible.'

'Aye, perhaps; but I can't see old Wheatley comin' out tonight even for the Queen, 'cos as it's said, and truthfully, he's tight most of the day, but paralytic after six.'

'He's got a new assistant now,' said Alfred Burton, 'and he's a good fella. He comes round The Courts and he doesn't ask for his tanner before enterin' a house. And 'tis said, if they can't pay he'll come back, not like old Wheatley. This one, he would come out all right.'

Ben's voice broke in on them now, saying, 'Leave it. Leave it. Tomorrow will be soon enough. All I want to do now—' he paused, then ended, 'is sleep.' Then as he closed his eyes he said, 'Thanks, Annie. I'll owe you till the day I die.'

Annie turned quickly away, and as she passed Millie she stopped and said quietly, 'I'm glad you've got back, lass.' And Millie said softly, 'I say with Ben, I'll . . . I'll owe you, too, till the day I die. Yes; yes, I will.'

Without further words, Annie turned to go, and her companion nodded to Millie, saying, 'Good night, lass,' and she answered, 'Good night, Mr Burton.' Then they went out of the room, followed by Aggie.

Left with Ben, Millie went and knelt by the couch again, and, gently touching the hand that was protruding from the rough bandages and lying across his waist, she said, 'Oh, Ben; I daren't think, I just daren't think what would have happened if she hadn't come to tell you.'

Ben still had his eyes closed when he said, 'Or what would have happened, lass, if Nell hadn't gone to her first and given her the message to bring to me. We must never forget Nell. D'you hear?' His voice trailed away;

'Never forget Nell. Now go to bed. Be a good lass, go to bed.'

On his last words Aggie came back into the room, and she repeated them, saying, 'He's right, lass, get yourself upstairs to bed and we'll talk the morrow.'

Millie walked over and stood before the old woman and asked softly, 'Will you come up soon?'

'Aye, lass; I'll be up soon, but I'll stay a while with—' and she indicated Ben's slumped figure, but the next moment she almost overbalanced as Millie threw herself once more into her arms, whimpering now, 'I'm still afraid. Don't ever let me leave you and Ben again. Will you promise me, promise you'll not ever let me leave you? I . . . I don't want to move out of this house, ever, ever.'

'Stop it! Now stop it. It's all over. You need fear no more. Go on, get yourself upstairs. Nobody can touch you up there. Nobody can get past me.'

Millie reached up and kissed the flabby cheek, then went to the couch and looked down on Ben who lay with his eyes closed. She bent down and stroked his cheek gently with her fingers before going slowly from the room.

The door had hardly closed on her before Ben said, 'They'd get past you all right, Aggie, if they knew it was me who killed their boss, and that delicate lookin' lass just gone and done for their rich client. It's been a night. Odd, when you come to think of it, isn't it? but we could both swing for killin' two pieces of vermin, because that's all they were, vermin. When I jumped on him I wasn't seeing a man, not in either case, just a big sewer rat, a big sewer rat . . .'

'Go to sleep, lad. Go to sleep. 'Tis over. Things'll be different now.'

11

Aggie was worried, Ben was feverish, and they were waiting for the doctor. When the gate-bell rang Aggie went through the other room and glanced out of the window facing the yard before going out, because she was still taking no chances of seeing a stranger there. But when she glimpsed the uniform of Sergeant Fenwick she rushed as quickly as she could back into the kitchen, saying to Millie, 'Cover his arm up. Tuck the blanket under his chin; it's the sergeant. I can say he's got a cold because there's nobody quicker than him for putting two and two together, and, as good as he is, he's still the law.'

She went out again, shambled across the frozen yard, opened the gate and said, 'Well! well! you're early. What have I done now?'

'Nothing that I am aware of yet, Aggie. How are you?'

'Oh, just gettin' over a bout of cold, and I've passed it on to Ben, I think. He's in a low state with it.' She was slithering back over the yard now as she said, 'What brings you here this morning'?'

'I have a bit of news for you. I don't know whether you'll think it's sad or otherwise.'

'Well, come on in and let me have it.' She stood aside until he was in the room, then closed the door, while he waited for her to precede him into the kitchen; and there, he looked from Ben, lying covered up to the chin, to Millie, at the fire poking it into a blaze, and it was to her he spoke first: 'Ah, you've got back then?' he said; then, turning to Ben, he apologised, 'I'm sorry about your message. I didn't get it until this morning. It was my day off yesterday and he should have told you. I had a word with him, a strong word. He should have put somebody else on it. Anyway, where did you get to?'

Before Millie could answer Aggie said, 'She got lost on the road after visiting a friend, but she happened to come across one of her teachers, you know, in the night schools. An' she took her in an' let her stay there for the night, but there was no way she could let us know. She got the length of me tongue when she came in, I can tell you, puttin' everybody to so much trouble.'

The sergeant was looking hard at Millie now and he said, 'By! it looks as though she did go for you, Millie; you're looking very peaked. You got a cold an' all?'

'I suppose so. It . . . It's catching.'

He kept his eyes hard on her for a moment before he said, 'Well, I've come with some news. It concerns you mostly, I should say, and I don't know how you're going to receive it.'

As she put her hand to her throat Ben stirred on the couch and made to turn on his side, but Aggie, tucking the clothes tight under his chin, said, 'Now you lie quiet. Whatever it is, you lie quiet.'

'Your father's dead.'

Millie's hand moved slowly from her throat and now fell on to the edge of the table, which she gripped as if to steady herself, and the sergeant said, 'Well, I didn't think there was much love lost between you, but you never know in these cases; blood is thicker than water.'

'How . . . how did he go?' It was Aggie asking the question, and he answered her: 'Not very nicely, I'm afraid. He was found in the canal. We think he must have been attacked; it didn't seem to be robbery, because he still had a few shillings in his pocket and one or two other things that you might want to collect, such as a couple of brooches.' He paused here, then said, 'He hadn't been long in the water . . . well I mean, not a matter of days; hours I would say. One of my men recognised him by the scar on his face, otherwise there was nothing on him in writing to prove who he was. And I went down and verified that he was the same man who had said he was your father.'

Millie had dropped on to a chair, and Ben had turned slowly on to his back again: but then immediately stiffened slightly as the sergeant added, 'And he wasn't the only one that had to be identified. Slim Boswell was murdered last night, and that was a straightforward murder: he had his throat slit. Of course, a lot of people have been wishing that should have happened sooner. What d'you say, Ben? You never liked Boswell, did you?'

Ben pulled a breath up from his chest before he muttered, 'Tell me who did.'

'Oh, you're right there. Then there was another body found, not . . . not quite dead, but he's in hospital. He is a well-known mill owner, the Mr Crane-Boulder, and no other. He'd had his head split open just when he must have been coming out of his club because he was found in the back alley next to it, and that appeared to be a plain, straightforward robbery because he was stripped of everything except his suit. They even took his boots. Strange how these things happen, and all about the same time. Three bodies found in a matter of as many hours, or nearly so. It was funny about Boswell, and Mr Crane-Boulder though, because between you and me and a number of other people in the town Mr Crane-Boulder was

324

not unknown to visit Mr Slim Boswell and his establishment, and, too, that of another gentleman who goes under the name of Big Joe. But then if we were to run in all the well-known men of the town who take their amusement in diverse ways, our gaols would be full. What d'you say, Aggie?'

'Well, you seem to know best, sergeant, you seem to know best – it's your business – but I'm no hypocrite an' all I can say is, Boswell's got his due at last. As for the other one, well, strikes me that those that visit them places are all tarred with the same brush.'

'Yes, you're right, you're right. But if he manages to come round, he'll be able to give us some explanation, at least, as to how he was brained. That's if, of course, he saw his assailant.'

'Oh, my goodness!' The exclamation came from Millie, who had lowered her head on to her outstretched arms on the table, and as the sergeant watched Aggie put an arm around the girl's shoulder, urging her: 'Come on, love, go on upstairs for a while and lie down,' he said, 'I'm sorry, it's all my talk about murders and such, and young people have weak stomachs. And she wasn't looking very well to begin with. Anyway, I'll be on my way before I cause any more damage, but I'll be looking in again. I'll likely want her' – he was nodding to Millie now – 'to receive his belongings, at least' – he paused – 'what we think might belong to him.' He now glanced towards Ben, saying, 'I hope you'll soon be on your feet, Ben. Colds are nasty things. I'll let myself out, Aggie. Don't worry.'

As he made for the door they all heard the gate-bell ring again and he, smiling at her, remarked, 'It's visitors' morning.'

'It'll be the doctor.'

'The doctor?' He widened his eyes at her.

'Aye, for Ben.'

325

'For a cold? My! my! you do look after your stray lambs, Aggie. Well, I hope he soon gets over it. If it's old Partridge he'll have him out of there in no time.'

When she opened the door and looked across the yard, she said, 'Well, 'tisn't old Partridge; this must be the new one. Stevens they call him. They say he's good.'

'Yes. Yes, I've heard something about him, the new type they're breeding now. Works for nothin' at times, so I hear. Well, he won't get fat on that. He'll learn. Like us all, Aggie, eh? he'll learn.'

'You've taken a long time.'

He said nothing, only smiled at her, and when they reached the gate, it was he who greeted the doctor, saying, 'Good mornin', doctor.' Then laughing, he added, 'You've got a very sick man awaiting you in there; he's got a cold.'

'Is that so, sergeant? Well, then I'll have to see what I can do for him.'

'And while you're there I would have a look at the youngster, too, because I think she's sickenin' for something; probably picked it up when she went missing. Goodbye, Aggie. As I said, I'll be callin' in in a day or two to see Millie. I hope she's a lot better by then. You'll have to stop her getting lost.'

Aggie said nothing, but her mind was galloping: he's got wind of something, he has, he has. She closed the gate on him, then turned to Doctor Stevens, saying, 'I'm sorry to have had to trouble you, doctor, but it isn't just a cold. Anyway, step inside 'cos it'll freeze you out here.'

As she was leading him through the first room, he said, 'Well, if my coming patient hasn't got a cold I think you have, and you really shouldn't be outside in this weather.'

'Oh, I've never died of winter yet, doctor,' she countered, at the same time gently patting his arm and indicating he should stop; then, lowering her voice, she explained, 'The young man in there hasn't got much of a cold, but I think he's got a fever, and it's from a wound he's received. You know what the polis is' – she thumbed now towards the yard and the now-departed sergeant – 'the least they know the less trouble they can cause. Although he's a good one, they're few and far between. Now, about Ben, that's the young man you're goin' to see, Ben Smith. I've looked after him since he was a lad. Now he's got into a little trouble, but it's the kind of trouble that has to be kept under your hat, so I hope, doctor, I can trust you not to say anythin' about what's happened to him. I know it's a large order, because we've never met before, but what I hear of you is all to the good. So, that's why I feel I can ask you to keep your mouth shut.'

'Well, Mrs . . . '

'Winkowski's the name. It's a mouthful.'

'Well, Mrs Winkowski, like priests, we're used to keeping our mouths shut unless we're offending the law, and even then we do stretch the limit at times. And if you've heard about me, I've also heard about you, and not only about the boy you mothered but also the girl, who, you say, or I mean . . . er, the sergeant says, went missing.'

'Aye. Aye, she did. It's a complicated story and some day, when we know each other better, I'll tell you the ins and outs of it. But at the moment, I'd like you to have a look at his arm. I'm not happy about it. So, will you come this way?'

In the kitchen, the young doctor looked first at the man on the couch, then at the girl sitting at the table, and his eyes remained on her for a time before he looked again at his new patient. Then, putting his black bag on the table, he went to the couch and said, 'Hello, there. Now what's the trouble?'

Ben was sweating and his face was flushed and his return greeting was brief: 'Hello,' he said.

Aggie pushed a chair forward, and the doctor sat down; then, pulling the cover from under Ben's chin to disclose the blood-stained bandaged arm, he said, 'Oh, I see. Well, now, we'll have to have that off, won't we; I mean, the bandage.' He gave a short laugh now and Ben answered, 'I hope you're right.'

When the arm was bared, the young doctor looked at the long jagged gash, then muttered, 'My! my!' before turning to Aggie and saying, 'Could I have some boiled water, please? I want it boiled.'

'In a jiffy, doctor, in a jiffy; the kettle's on.'

Turning to Millie, he said, 'Have we any more clean sheeting?'

Without answering, she went straight to the sideboard drawer and brought out a number of strips. Taking one from her, the young man folded it into a pad, lifted out a bottle from his bag and, again addressing Millie, said, 'A clean basin, please.'

When she returned from the scullery Aggie was already standing by him with the kettle of boiling water. After pouring some liquid from the bottle into the basin, he half-filled it with the boiling water and put in the pad of linen. Then, his fingers moving quickly against the heat, he squeezed this and, looking down on Ben, said, 'This might sting a bit here and there, but we've got to have this wound cleaned. And don't worry if it starts to bleed again. When did it happen?'

'Last night.'

'Oh, last night. Then you should have sent for me sooner. Why didn't you?'

Before Ben could answer Aggie put in, 'Well, it bein' Sunday, doctor, and I knew old Doctor Wheatley wouldn't thank me for rousin' him on a Sunday night.'

When the doctor again muttered something which Aggie interpreted as 'or at any other time', she made no comment, for she might have been mistaken.

328

'I'll have to sew this, you know.'

'I expected that.'

'It's some length and it's not goin' to be pleasant.'

'I didn't think it would.'

'You should really have gone to the hospital.'

Ben said nothing.

The cleaning of the wound over, the doctor went to his bag again and, taking out a small case, he extracted from it a needle and a length of what looked like thickish thread. Then, addressing Aggie, he said, 'Have you any spirits about?'

'I've only got gin, but I mean to get some whisky in. I do, 'cos he's not partial to gin.'

'Well, gin will have to do.'

After Ben had drunk half a mug of gin, the business of sewing up his wound began. It was a long process; but he made no sound during it. And when the doctor at last cut off the thread from the end of the wound, he said, 'Well, you've stood that all right, and it certainly wasn't a straightforward business. Doubtless the gin helped. Now I'm going to bandage it, but lightly. Don't worry if some blood oozes through; that will be caused by the cleansing. But this business certainly hasn't done you any good; you've got a fever on you, so what I want you to do until I pop in again, which could be later this evening, is to lie as still as you can in order to rest that arm. And I can see you've got two good nurses here. Now don't baulk at being spoon-fed for the next day or two, because I don't want you to exert yourself. You understand?'

He smiled down on Ben, but received no comment on his statement, for Ben was feeling as he had never done in his life before: there was a weakness on him as if he had been trying to shift a heavy load, and an excruciating pain was spreading from his arm through his whole body. At this present moment he wouldn't have minded if he died.

329

On his way out, the doctor said to Aggie, 'You're going to have a sick man on your hands for the next few days . . . Was he in a fight?'

'You could say that, doctor, you could say that.'

As he shook his head and made to step out of the door, he turned to her again and said, 'The young girl? She looks ill. Has she been ill?'

'No, not really, doctor.'

'What do you mean, not really? Does she have the consumption?'

'*Oh, no, no,* nothin' like that. She had a bit of a shock. She heard this mornin' from the sergeant who just went out that her father was found in the canal.'

'Good gracious! Good gracious! And I hear there was a murder and an attempted murder last night, and over the week-end I signed a death certificate for five children, and there'll likely be more today. Are you a praying woman?'

'No, I'm not, doctor.'

'I thought you wouldn't be. Well, as a matter of fact, I'm not a praying man either, especially when I look at the churches and the chapels and all these supposed good folk hurrying into them to have words with their God, asking Him to keep them living comfortably, never mind about those being turned out of their hovels for not paying their rent because they let themselves live in stench and among vermin, having brought it on themselves through gin.' He grinned at her now as he repeated, 'Yes, gin. But they don't say why they drink, what drives them to gin, do they, Mrs Winkowski?'

He now poked his face towards her, still grinning, and she replied, 'No, they don't, doctor, an' I'll not take your remarks to meself, either. I'll only say I'll be pleased to see you any time, even when I don't need your ministrations and have to pay you for poisoning me with your pills.'

He laughed openly now, saying, 'Get back indoors, else my next visit *will* be to see you and to sound that chest of yours. And that wouldn't be a bad idea at any time.'

She watched him stride across the yard, a young virile man, and ironically she thought, God's good, before turning indoors again.

It was two days later. The young doctor had paid three visits and had said that, although the arm was doing nicely and showing no signs of gangrene or undue inflammation, Ben had lost a great deal of blood, and, consequently, couldn't expect to recover straightaway. But being the kind of man he was, Aggie felt he was just trying to allay their fears.

She had sat up the previous night with Ben and she'd been on her feet all day. Millie had insisted that she should go to bed and that tonight she would sit in the basket chair by the side of the couch.

She had bathed Ben's forehead and his chest. His body was bare to the waist, for it was impossible to get a shirt on to him. He had been dozing, but now his eyes were open wide and, looking at her, he muttered, 'Millie.'

'Yes, Ben? Yes, I'm here. What is it?'

'I . . . I feel rotten.'

'I know you do, Ben, I know you do. But you'll soon be better. It's the fever; it will soon go.'

'Fevers don't often go . . . Millie, unless they take you with them.'

'Please, please, Ben.' Her face was twisted up now with grief at the thought of what his words portended. 'Don't talk like that. You'll be all right in a couple of days.'

'I . . . I hope so. Sit down.'

She sat down and reached out for his good hand, which she stroked as she said, 'Oh, Ben, Ben, don't ever talk like that, or think like that, because' – she half rose from her seat

331

and leant over him – 'I . . . I couldn't go on without you. I know that now. I've been mad, stupid, and I brought you to near death. Ben, don't . . . don't ever leave me.'

'Millie, do . . . ' He now started to cough. It tore at his chest, and she took a piece of linen and cleaned round his mouth, and he laid his head back and drew in an agonising breath before he spoke again, saying, 'Do you know what you've just said?'

'Yes. Yes, Ben, I know what I said. I . . . I—' She tried to smile now as she added, 'Mrs Sponge would have me say, I know what I've indicated. Oh, Ben, Ben. You'll get well. You must get well, because I need you. I'll always need you; I know that now.'

The sweat was running down his face, and after she had again wiped it away, he lay looking upwards; then with an effort, he said, 'There . . . there are good moments in everybody's life. I think this is mine.' But then, turning his head slowly on the pillow, he murmured, 'But if I was . . . standin' . . . before you . . . as tall as I could in me boots, even then I . . . I'd be a small man . . . what then?'

Her voice was low but firm as she answered him: 'You will never be a small man to me, Ben. I shall always see you as a big man, and the best of all men. I know that you love me, and have for some time, but I didn't know that I loved you, and have for some time, too. I was still in the throes of the Brothers Grimm fairy-tales and I thought a prince had come riding out for me. I was so blind and stupid. I . . . I didn't know the prince was already right here in the kitchen. So, Ben, you . . . you believe me?'

He looked at her for a long moment, before he said, 'I . . . I want to, Millie. Oh, aye, I want to, but . . . let's face facts . . . say I don't . . . make it . . . ?'

'Ben. Please.'

'No; listen. Say that I don't . . . then I want you to get out of this hole. You can make . . . a very . . . good living in bakery. I . . . I've been thinkin' about it . . . for a long time. Pratts . . . the baker in . . . Oswald Road. He's . . . he's selling. He's old. Aggie . . . Aggie's got more . . . than a tiny bit put by . . . I know that. She'll . . . she'll get it for you . . . go with you. Nice place . . . garden and house above. Seen it.'

'Lie quiet, dear. Lie quiet. Here, drink this.' She took a glass from the table and, holding his head up from the pillow, she helped him to drink.

'Now . . . now go to sleep.'

'Millie. Do . . . do what I . . . I say . . . Promise?'

'Yes. Yes, Ben, I promise. But, we'll all go . . . to Mr Pratt's.'

The tears were now running down her face as she sat watching him having to drag at each breath, and just as when lying in that lush bed, she had thought of Sister Cecilia's words, and had even prayed to her, she was again calling to her as if to God, imploring her to keep Ben alive.

What time she fell asleep, she did not know, but she woke to find the lamp almost gutted and the fire low, and she scurried to replenish the light and then to put a blazer to the fire.

When she returned to the couch, Ben seemed to be asleep. But was he? Her heart seemed to jerk: the bedclothes weren't heaving up and down. Almost in panic now, she thrust her hand under the blanket and on to his chest, and when she felt the steady beat she almost fell across him. Then she had to press her hand over her mouth to stop herself gabbling: 'Oh Ben, Ben. Oh, Ben, Ben. You're going to be all right.'

Doctor Stevens said the patient must have passed the crisis during the night and that now he needed only rest and nursing and his bandages renewed; that he wouldn't need a doctor's

333

attention again unless he had a relapse, which he doubted would happen.

When he said goodbye, Ben, looking up at him, said, 'If ever there's anything I can do for you, you've only got to ask,' and the doctor laughingly answered, 'That's a foolish thing to say. The times I've heard people say that and later regret it.' He turned to Millie, adding, 'And now, my young nurse, it'll be you I'll have to come and visit next if you don't get out and put some roses into those cheeks of yours. Alabaster's all right on marble, but it doesn't portend good health.'

Aggie was quick to answer for her, saying, 'She'll be all right now. We'll all be all right now. Thanks to you. How much do I owe you?'

'Well, shall we say, five shillings?'

'Yes, you can.'

She went to the cash box on the sideboard and took out two crowns which she handed to him; and he, looking at them, said, 'Oh, but . . . !'

'If you had said a pound a visit, doctor, I would have doubled it in any case.'

'You are very kind. By' – he poked his head towards her – 'I'd be able to retire at the end of the year if everybody paid up like this, especially in The Courts.'

She laughed now, and even Millie laughed, while Ben smiled.

After seeing the young man out, Aggie returned to the kitchen and she nodded from one to the other, saying, 'Some men are born to make their mark, and there goes one of them.'

It wasn't half an hour later when there came a knock on the outer door.

Up till now, Millie had not once attempted to go and answer a knock, or the gate-bell; and she made no move to do so now. So it was Aggie who shuffled through the

334

room, and she was smiling at something Ben had said; but the smile was wiped off her face by the sight of the man standing there.

Bernard Thompson doffed his hat, then got as far as saying, 'Mrs Winkowski,' when Aggie said, 'And what d'you want here?'

'I . . . I felt that I must . . . well, that I must come and give some sort of . . . explanation and . . . and find out how Millie is faring?'

'Oh, you're interested in how Millie is faring, are you? Well, you'll be pleased to know she's alive, and as far as I can gather she still remains untouched . . . if you know what I mean.'

She watched the colour flood over his face and his head lower before he said, 'I'm . . . I'm terribly sorry. It was a misunderstanding. I . . . I thought . . . '

'Aye, I'm well aware, sir, of what you thought, and of what you thought I thought. Well, you were wrong in both cases, mine and hers. And let me tell you this, sir, there's a lot of scum lives along in these Courts, but they're nothin' compared to your breed. You think you can come down here and take up a lass as beautiful as Millie, and as innocent – aye, as innocent – and use her, like your brother-in-law did.'

His chin went up, his eyes narrowed, and he said, 'What do you mean, my brother-in-law did?'

'Oh, don't tell me that you've known him all these years and not realised what he's been up to? An' what did you think when she ran from you? Where did she run?'

'She took a cab. My neighbour, who was coming from the opposite direction, had to move aside to allow the cab to pass him. And when I stopped and enquired if his coachman had seen her, he said she had stopped the cab. So . . . well, I imagined she would be all right.'

335

'Hell's bells! You imagined she'd be all right. An' you know whose cab it was? She stopped it all right, but when she saw who was in it she ran. But he was wily: he let her run into a load of drunks; and then he was supposed to have rescued her. He rescued her all right, an' took her to his brothel, the dirty whore-master that he is; or was, because, I suppose like everybody else, you'll have heard that he got his throat cut. An' I say whoever did it should have a medal pinned on him.' Now she thrust her face close to his. 'And you know who he pinched her for? Who he kept her for, locked up for almost two days, eh? Your brother-in-law. A special tit-bit for your brother-in-law.'

'You must be mistaken.'

'Mistaken, be buggered! From her own lips I got it. He gave her the choice of having him or being shipped off by Boswell.'

He stepped back from her: 'I still can't believe it. Anyway, my brother-in-law was attacked outside his club.'

'Huh! They can move bodies quickly, that lot. He was attacked all right . . . by a gang that went in to save her. It was a big gang of honest men, but let him come round and open his mouth, and I'm tellin' you this country, for that matter, wouldn't be able to hold him.'

She watched him now close his eyes and droop his head before he said, 'Oh my God!'

'Aye, you can say, oh my God! but it was through you that all this happened. You wanted a mistress, well, why couldn't you go and take one of the lasses off the street? Boswell and Big Joe had a lot to choose from, an' they know the ropes. But no, you wanted somebody clean and innocent. All your family seems to be tainted with one filthy brush.'

He almost shouted at her now as he remonstrated, 'Don't you dare say that! I have no connection with that man. He is my half-sister's husband. I have never liked him, and I've

336

always suspected—' He stopped now and turned his head to the side; then after a moment he was looking at her again, and in a more level tone he said, 'I apologise for all I have done and surmised. I was wrong. So, will you let me see Millie?'

'Yes, I'll let you see Millie, if you knock me down and walk over me. That's about the only way you'll see Millie.'

'I mean no harm by her . . . please! In fact I mean . . . '

'I know what you mean. But if you were seein' Millie this minute, you wouldn't see the lass that ran from your house and you. She's gone, never to return. What she went through with you an' them will last her to her grave. Now, sir, get yourself away from my door an' don't let me see you here again.' And on this she stepped back and banged the door in his face; then stood supporting herself against it for a full minute before she could allow herself to go back into the kitchen.

'Who was that?' Millie laid aside the rolling pin with which she had been pressing the pastry on a floured board.

'Oh.' Aggie had to gather her wits about her now: lying to that one about who had rescued her lass was one thing, but to hoodwink Millie was another. 'It was a fella with some tale about havin' heard that I was thinkin' about sellin' up. He said we had stopped the baking business, an' the taggerine lot, so he wanted to know what I was goin' to do; was I going to sell? He said he would give me a good price.'

'What . . . what does he want it for?' Ben now asked.

'A little factory, I think. You know there was talk of pulling half The Courts down to make houses for the new intake of workers, Irish, Scots, Jews, the lot. Well, he wants to make this into a . . . '

'What does he want to make it into?' Millie was drying her hands now on a damp towel while staring at her.

'Well, as I said, a sort of little factory, and the house to live in; I should imagine, this one.'

337

'Where would he build a factory here?'

'He could turn the stables and outhouses into one, couldn't he? Anyway, what does it matter? I sent him off with a flea in his ear.'

Millie looked at her hard, then turned about and went into the scullery, and there she stood looking out of the small window on to the patch of grass that seemed never to be green. For a moment she had thought she heard his voice, as if he was calling loudly. But the only time she could remember his raising his voice was when he shouted to the horse. For a moment, she had felt sure it was him. What would have happened if it had been and she had opened the door?

Nothing would have brought her any comfort, because she would have told him exactly what she thought: because of him, she had been exposed to a terror that no-one should experience, not a child, nor girl, nor a woman. And because of him, Ben had become a murderer and almost lost his life.

And she? Well, she didn't know yet if she, too, was a murderer; she only knew that it would be a long, long time before she would fall asleep without imagining herself on that satin and silk bed, with the big soft hands playing over her and the sight of his partly naked body; nor would she forget that her mind kept telling her during that experience that as soon as he was gone she would use the rope at the bottom of the bed and go the way her mother had, for only as she lay frozenly staring ahead had she noticed that there was a hook on the door on which to hang a dressing gown. It would hold her weight, she was telling herself just as Ben and his enraged countenance burst into the room.

Would she have told him all that?

Yes, yes; perhaps she would. But she would have told him something else; she would have told him that any feeling

338

she had for him was like a mirage, that it had faded as if it had never been.

And would that have been true?

She took up a pail of water from the floor and emptied some into a bowl before she gave herself the answer: Ben would eventually make it come true.

12

It was a fortnight later when the sergeant paid them a second visit; and his first comment was to Ben, whom he noticed was wearing a coat with an arm in only one sleeve, the other hanging slack on his shoulder.

'Something happened to your arm, Ben?'

'I fell on it and cracked a bone.'

'Oh, I thought it was the result of your cold.'

Both Ben and Aggie refrained from exchanging a look, and now the sergeant turned towards Millie, saying, 'Well, I'm glad to see one of your family looks better. You looked like death on sticks the last time I was here.'

'That must be an old saying, sergeant, death on sticks. I've never heard that one before.'

'Oh, my father used to say that. It's funny where these sayings come from. By the way, speaking of fathers, that's why I'm here.' He lifted the bag he was carrying and put it on the table, saying, 'These were found on your father's person.' Then turning and glancing at Aggie, he said, 'They followed your instructions, I hope, with regard to the burial?'

'Yes, I understand they did that.'

He now emptied the bag on to the table and, having moved the things around with his finger, he pointed to a leather wallet, saying, 'There's a letter in there to a parson's wife in Durham that might interest you. But for the rest, there was this small amount of money' – he moved the coins around – 'but these two brooches and this pair of gold cuff-links and also that little tie pin: do you think they belonged to your father?'

Millie looked at the articles on the table, then at the sergeant, before she said sharply, 'No, except perhaps the wallet and this small amount of money. For the rest, I . . . I suggest he must have stolen them.'

'Well' – he raised his eyebrows – 'you're very plain-speaking. So what d'you propose I do with them, advertise them?'

'I don't care what you do with them, but I don't want them.'

'Well, there's a point here: if we put word out that these have been found, whoever claims them might come under suspicion for doin' him in. What d'you say to that?'

'I've got nothing to say to that, sergeant. I don't know the ins and outs of pickpockets and thieves, nor do I want to. The only thing I'm saying to you is, I don't want these things.'

'Well, I'll return them to the office and let those up above take the matter from there. My! my! the things that have happened lately on my patch.' He was casting his glance between Aggie and Ben now. 'Got a mob war on my hands now since Boswell got his lot, because his crew are blaming Big Joe's. So what have they gone and done just three days ago? Polished one of his men off. They've even got the ladies of the street frightened, 'cos it's bad for business, you know.' He pulled a face now. 'Well, all I can say is, whoever went about the business of finishing Slim Boswell should have done the job properly and put paid to Big Joe an' all. But

341

then—' He shrugged his shoulders as he looked at Aggie now and added, 'The underlings would have stepped up; they're all waitin' for the boss's shoes. It's like every walk in life; there's always somebody wantin' your job.'

As he nodded his head, Aggie said, 'Aye, there's some truth in that. But as far as I can gather, I haven't known anybody be after mine.'

He laughed outright, then countered, 'Well, in a way, I put that down to short-sightedness. Now I must be off.'

But he did not go immediately; he turned to Ben and said, 'Sorry about that arm of yours, Ben. You've seen the doctor, I suppose?'

'Yes; yes, the new one, Doctor Stevens.'

'Oh, that one. He's a good fella, as I said before, quite popular. And what did he say about the break?'

'Oh, that it would mend. Naturally it will take time.'

'Yes, yes. Well, take care of yourself, and of these two here.' He pointed from Aggie to Millie, then said, 'But there's no need for me to tell you anything about that, is there?'

'No; I don't think so, sergeant.'

'Well, I'll be off, Aggie. By the way, I heard that you were thinkin' of makin' a move. Now that would be the day. Is there any truth in it?'

'You never know. You never know, sergeant. There could be. I think it's about time I went up in the world, don't you?'

Again he was laughing loudly, and he pushed Aggie as she walked before him into the other room.

Left alone, Millie looked at Ben, and in a low voice, she said, 'Do . . . do you think he guesses anything?'

'I think he more than guesses, Millie. But what can he do? Even if he wanted to do anything, I don't think he does. I think he's glad to be rid of Boswell. Oh aye. You heard him say it's a pity it wasn't Big Joe an' all.' Then smiling

342

wryly, he added, 'I think it would have taken two of me to tackle Big Joe. What d'you think?'

She went to him and put her hand on his cheek as she said, 'You could tackle Big Joe, Ben, or anyone else who stood in your way.'

He now touched her cheek, saying, 'I'm not going to go into it yet, Millie, because I still can't believe it, and what's more, you might come to your senses.'

'Oh Ben, don't say that, please.'

'You mean, you don't want to come to your senses?' He was smiling at her now.

'I mean I'm in my senses. And, look, tell me, what's this about the baker's shop?'

'Well, you'll see for yourself. We're going there tomorrow. She's been working pretty hard these last few days, in the way of business.'

'But this here . . . she's always lived here, and her father and family.'

'Well, she doesn't want you to live here any longer.'

'But I could be happy here as long as I had you and her.'

'Millie' – he now cupped her chin – 'd'you ever realise how beautiful you are? Don't close your eyes and shake your head like that. You were a beautiful child, you were a beautiful young girl, you're a more beautiful sixteen-year-old, but when you're a woman, I daren't think about that time. But since you were a child you've looked like a lily on a dung heap, set in this place. Yet I'm going to say this, whoever you would have married I would have been jealous of, jealous as hell. I say, if you had married. But to have seen you become someone's mistress, just used as a toy, that would have driven me crazy. I would likely have ended up doing to him what I did to Boswell. And if someone came along tomorrow, some real man, working man or gentleman, and you wanted to marry him, I . . . I'd try to behave meself, and not stand in your way. Of course, it would all depend upon if you wanted to, if you really wanted to. Now, now, now!' – he wagged his hand in front of her face – 'I'm talking sense; so, I'm not going to hold you to anything that you promised me when you thought I was pegging out.' He tried to chuckle, then added, 'And I did, you know. I thought I was pegging out. I didn't like it a bit, but there it was. I remember, though, every word you said . . . every word.'

'Oh, Ben, there's . . . there's nobody like you. There'll never be anybody . . . '

'I know that, the last bit, there'll never be anybody like me again. There's not two of me in this town.'

'Ben, please, please stop playing yourself down, because inside yourself, you know' – now she was wagging her hand at him – 'you are a big head. You think yourself as good as anybody, better than the next. Now don't you?'

Their gentle laughter joined when Aggie came back into the room, and she added, 'Well, what's the joke?'

'I'm telling him he's a big head and that he thinks himself better than the next.'

'Tell me something I don't know; I've had to live with it for years. Well now, are we goin' to get ready and go and see this gold mine, where you're goin' to make your fortune, miss? But don't forget, it's goin' to be no easy job diggin', because I can tell you something for nothing, I'm goin' to sit back and just watch. Retiring, they call it . . . to the ladies' room.'

Ben and Millie began to laugh outright, and Millie said, 'That was in the last story Mrs Sponge would have read to the night class, where the women were always retiring to the ladies' room. And remember the man who asked for an explanation?'

'Well, what's the explanation? Tell me, 'cos I'm as ignorant as a pig. What is the ladies' room? The drawing-room? The boudoir?'

'No, the closet.'

They both exclaimed on the word together, and the kitchen rang with their laughter, which not one of them could remember ever really having happened before, not so light-heartedly, anyway.

They had come by hired cab, and they were now standing on the rough kerb that edged the flags set in front of the two shop windows. They weren't large windows, nor was the door that was set between them, but it was a stout door, black and weather-worn, and what set off the whole front of the shop, too, was the strip of brass along the lower edge of each window: inscribed on one being the word 'Pratts', and on the other 'Confectionery'.

Aggie handed a large key to Millie, saying, 'Well, go on, open it.' And as Millie was inserting the key in the lock Aggie turned to the cabbie, saying, 'You'll wait, won't you?' And he answered, 'As long as you like, missis.'

'Well, in that case I'd throw a cover over that animal, else it'll be stiff before we come out.'

It was almost an hour later when, standing in the sitting-room of the house on the upper floor, Aggie said, 'Well, what d'you think, really, lad?'

'Well, Aggie, if you want to know the truth, it's like the opening of another world. I'm speaking for meself, mind. But what it's like for Millie here, well, I've no words to put into her mouth; she can express her feelings best herself. But I think you know how she feels.' His tone now changing, he said, 'I hope you realise, Mrs Winkowski, that this shop and this street is the last bastion of the "would-bes" of this city, and touching on the fringes of the "we've arrived" class.'

345

'Aye, I'm well aware of that. And as Mr Pratt pointed out with a twinkle in his eye, he had served both camps for many years: the ones that come and buy from the counter, and the ones that send their little maids, or expect it to be delivered by his covered hand-cart.'

'We'll have to deliver?'

'Aye, lass,' Aggie said; 'but that'll be up to trade, of course: if there's a demand for it. Anyway, I've bought his little covered hand-cart. It's only an extra large box on wheels, but light enough for a lad to push. Now look; I'll leave you two up here to see what you're goin' to do about papering an' things. I must make me way downstairs.' As she neared the door she turned and with a mischievous grin on her face said, 'There's an outside closet, modern, he said. Mr Pratt seemed to be as proud of that as he was of his bake shop.'

When the door had closed on her, Millie went to the window again and looked down on to the long narrow garden, and now she said quietly, 'It is wonderful, isn't it, Ben?'

He came and stood by her shoulder and he, too, stared down on to the garden as he said, 'Aye, it is, Millie. It is wonderful.'

She turned and gazed at him. 'What would I have done without her, Ben? If she hadn't picked me up that day, what would have happened to me?' She shuddered visibly as she added, 'The same as almost happened to me the other night. Oh, yes, yes; that's what would have happened to me. I have no illusions.' She bowed her head now, and she murmured, 'Those first days, I thought the world and everybody in it was vile, the high and the low; then I had to remember that Mrs Aggie and you were in it. And Annie was in it. And yes, that woman, Nell, because without her help I'd be there now, or dead. Yes, yes; I'd be dead.'

346

'Come on, come on. Don't think about it any more. It's past, and nothin' like that can ever happen to you again. I'll see to that, or, at least, someone will.'

'Why . . . why do you say that, someone will?'

'I . . . I don't really know, because . . . well, yes, I do, for while I know this house, this business is real and that it will work out, for my own life and yours, I'm still not sure. There's something . . . well, holding me back from hoping. But come; don't look like that, it'll work out. No matter what happens to you, just remember I'll always be there, or here.' He smiled now; then taking her arm, he said, 'Come on. She's bound to have inspected the closet, or the dry midden, or whatever name she's going to give it, by now. Very likely the ladies' room.'

She did not immediately respond to his touch and follow him but stared after him for a moment as if she were puzzled by his behaviour. However, she wasn't to wait long before being enlightened as to why he seemed so reluctant to take her love . . .

'It's hard to believe that this district isn't a mile from The Courts.' And Ben said, 'I don't think it's even three-quarters of a mile, that's as the crow flies.'

'I've never seen a crow for years,' Aggie said, laughing. 'When I was a lass they were always hovering round the barn. Odd that, isn't it?'

They had left the gates open in order that the cabbie could drive straight into the yard, which he now did, only to stop half-way across, because there to the side of the door was a trap, and standing beside it was Bernard Thompson.

As Ben helped Aggie down from the cab, she said, 'He's got a bloody nerve. I told him not to put his face near this yard again. Well, I won't put a tooth in it this time.' But as

347

she started to walk towards him, Millie said quietly, 'Mrs Aggie, please. I'll . . . I'll see to this.'

Ben said nothing, but, gripping Aggie's arm firmly, he led her towards the door, although she would keep her head turned to look at the man who was now moving towards Millie.

Only when the door had closed on them did Millie look fully at Bernard Thompson, and she remained quiet as he began, 'Oh, Millie, I . . . I had to come. I just couldn't keep away. I . . . I had to tell you in person how deeply sorry I am, not only for my stupidity in the proposition I put to you, but for what you have suffered because of me. I . . . I want to have a talk with you, Millie. I have something to say to you.' But before he could go on, she said, 'You have nothing to say to me, Mr Thompson, that I wish to hear.'

'Millie, please, isn't it in your heart to forgive me? I want to make amends, because I . . . I really do care for you, and I know you care for me.'

'I no longer care for you, Mr Thompson. Yes, I may have, at one time, because, as I understand now, there's always a fairy prince in every girl's life. But if we are sensible it is just a figment of the imagination, bred from stories that we read. Youth is a time of fantasies. One grows out of them. But mine were blasted out of me.' Her tone was bitter. 'I don't blame you entirely. It was my stupidity and Mrs Aggie's desire for my happiness and future that made us both so gullible.'

'Millie. Will you listen to me, please? I have something important to say to you, because, believe me, I have your welfare at heart. My proposal to you before was as much to take you away from all this' – he flung his arm wide now – 'as it was to satisfy my own feelings for you. I know you would say that Mrs Winkowski and the man Ben were dear to you, but I felt then that if they really cared for you they would have wanted a better life for you, even such as

348

I offered; but I wouldn't have made it at the time had I not thought that both you and she were aware of my intentions. But now, Millie, knowing how deep my feelings are for you, I am willing to break off my engagement and marry you. That is how deeply I feel for you. Tell me you understand and that you will accept.'

'Please, Mr Thompson, don't say anything more. Even if I hadn't become engaged to be married, and I still held a vestige of feeling for you, I would, at this moment, have scorned your proposal that is evidently being dragged from you, and . . . '

'How can you have become engaged in such a short time? You are just saying this to put me off.'

'No, I am not saying this, Mr Thompson. I am engaged to be married to Ben.'

'*What! To . . . to that man?*'

'Yes, Mr Thompson.' Her voice was loud now. 'To that man, that honourable man who is worth twenty of you and your kin.'

'But you can't, Millie, you can't.'

'I can. And I've got you to thank for being able to say that I will one day be his wife; before this I was blind to my true feelings. So, Mr Thompson, you will have no need to break off your engagement, nor to suffer the humiliation that I undoubtedly would bring among your own circle. Things being as they are, it would eventually come out that you had picked me up from what you consider the mire. Good day to you, Mr Thompson.'

As she turned from him he muttered her name pleadingly, 'Millie. Millie,' and when the door banged closed he stood looking towards it for a moment before he mounted his trap and drove out of the yard. It was over. She had made it final. Yet it was hard to believe she could have refused his offer of marriage – and for that man. Well, there was

349

one consolation: he wouldn't have to face the hurricane of family when he announced his broken engagement to Grace, or the wrath of her brothers.

Once the door was closed behind her, Millie stood, her hands pressed tightly against it for a moment; then she hurried into the kitchen.

Ben was alone. He was standing in front of the fire, his good arm stretched upwards, his hand clutching the rim of the mantelpiece.

At her entry, he turned slowly, and they stood apart for a moment; then, going to him, she put her arms on his shoulders and softly she said, 'Ben Smith, Jones, or Robinson, you have never kissed me.'

She watched him slowly close his eyes, then moisten his lips, and when he looked at her again, he said, 'No, Millie; I never have, have I?'

When he drew her close with his good arm, he still did not immediately kiss her, but gazed into her face; and she was made to ask softly, 'Now are you sure?'

He laid his lips on hers, and when the first long kiss was over he said, 'I'm sure now. Oh, Millie, Millie. Oh, my love. I don't know why, or how you should love me, or could love me, but I know you do, at least a little, for you're still but a girl; but by the time you're a woman you will know just how deep my love is for you, and always has been.'

There was a movement at the scullery door and, hesitantly, Aggie came shuffling in and straight towards them, and, her face abeam, she said, 'Aye, well, that's how it is, an' that's how it should be.' Then, putting an arm around each of them, she muttered, 'You were the only bairns I ever had, or ever wanted.' And when they both leant against her and kissed her, she suddenly pushed them away, saying, 'That's enough slop for one day. But it is an occasion, so pour me out a good drop of me medicine. And there's still some whisky in

350

the bottle. As for you, me lady, it's tea as usual, an' then we'll drink—' She paused now and looked tenderly at them, and, her voice changing, she said softly, 'Aye, I'll drink to you both, Mr and Mrs Smith, Jones, or Robinson.'

And at this they clung together, and their laughter filled that room of many odours.

THE END